ANOTHER Fine MESS

Also by Lindy Ryan

Bless Your Heart

ANOTHER
Fine
MESS

A NOVEL

Lindy Ryan

MINOTAUR BOOKS
NEW YORK

First published in the United States by Minotaur Books, an imprint of St. Martin's Publishing Group

ANOTHER FINE MESS. Copyright © 2025 by Lindy Ryan. All rights reserved. Printed in the United States of America. For information, address St. Martin's Publishing Group, 120 Broadway, New York, NY 10271.

www.minotaurbooks.com

Design by Meryl Sussman Levavi

The Library of Congress Cataloging-in-Publication Data is available upon request.

ISBN 978-1-250-32423-8 (hardcover)
ISBN 978-1-250-32424-5 (ebook)

Our books may be purchased in bulk for promotional, educational, or business use. Please contact your local bookseller or the Macmillan Corporate and Premium Sales Department at 1-800-221-7945, extension 5442, or by email at MacmillanSpecialMarkets@macmillan.com.

First Edition: 2025

1 3 5 7 9 10 8 6 4 2

For the grandmothers

Pie Evans

When the old grandfather clock in the parlor struck midnight, Priscilla Evans celebrated her ninety-third birthday with a box of store-bought vanilla wafers and a bowl of homemade banana pudding—her mother's recipe.

She sat at the small kitchen table with nothing but a blank sheet of paper for company and used the wafers to spoon cold cream straight from the dish while she wrote. From cellophane sack to pudding bowl and down her gullet went the wafers, and when the moon grew bright enough that she could see the space between the trees, and her pencil tip had worn to a nub, Pie pushed up from her seat. She left the letter on the table and covered the leftovers with wax paper.

Pie stuffed the pudding bowl in the icebox and the cookies in the cupboard, and then she put away the supper dishes and tidied her small bedroom in the back of the funeral parlor.

She brushed her teeth.

She wound the clock.

When her chores were finished, Pie braided her long white hair and stripped down to a simple cotton nightgown. She picked up the old Winchester she kept by the back door and slipped a cartridge into her pocket. Pie said goodbye to the pudding and to the cookies, to her small bedroom and to her late mother's grandfather clock in the parlor. To the letter left on the kitchen table.

And then she went out alone into the dark to dig a hole.

Far from the first, she thought, but, Lord willing, this would be the last.

Humid nighttime air tongued Pie's cheek as she made her way to the edge of what remained of her family's property. The shovel stood where she'd left it staked in the ground, right where the moonlight touched grass, where the green grew a little coarser than the rest.

Lightning scratched across a tissue-paper sky and Pie stuck her tongue out to taste the air. This time of year always brought storms through rural southeast Texas. The heat let up enough to breathe and the weather started to change. Nothing turned pretty in late September, and a chill didn't set in until November, but still-simmering temperatures meant rain. All the wet that had blown through earlier softened the summer-dried dirt, but left the stink of ozone hot on its breath. Any minute now, and the sky would open.

But she'd be done digging long before then.

Pie palmed sweat away, wicked the moisture on her dress, and wrenched the shovel free. She could do without the throb in her joints and the aches in her bones, the constant twinge in her bad ankle, but Pie Evans was not the sort of woman to shy away from a little midnight yard work.

She wasn't the kind of woman to shy away from anything, really.

"Never have been," Pie muttered as she traded the gun for the shovel and stabbed metal into earth. "And I reckon tonight ain't the time to start."

Pie spooned soggy dirt from north to south—until brown reached her ankles, then stained the cotton hem of the gown, her calves. When her skirts started to stick to her knees, she tossed the shovel aside and climbed out of the grave.

With the rifle as a crutch at her side, Pie limped back to what used to be Daddy's old farmhouse and settled into her favorite cowhide rocker. She laid the gun across her ruined skirt, and the barrel bumped the other chair, set it rocking. She lit a pinch of rolled tobacco.

And then she stared out into the hot, hungry, crackling dark and waited to die.

Pie had waited a long time for this night to come.

Too damn long, she'd be happy to tell anyone who bothered to ask, not that anyone ever did. Folks around town had given Pie Evans a wide berth for as long as she could remember—but if that had bothered her once, it didn't now. As far as she was concerned, most people didn't have the good sense God gave a goose. With folks like that around, it'd take more than sideways glances and fencepost gossip to get under skin as tough as Pie's. Besides, the way she saw it, all those cold shoulders did her a favor: the less people paid her any mind when they were alive, the less she had to mourn them when they turned up dead.

The less she had to care when she put them back down.

Her braid ticked across her back, a pendulum keeping time, counting down. "Too damn long is right," Pie said to the lightening dark.

Cowhide prickled her thighs under the dirty cotton shift, and Pie raked age-hardened fingernails into the thin cloth. The porch slats creaked under the weight of the rocker, the press of the wood clammy under her bare feet, the first breath of almost-morning fresh on her skin.

In the distance, thunder rolled. Pie licked the taste of the storm from her lips as she chewed at the tobacco pinched between her teeth.

Used to be, when Pie's daddy built the old dogtrot farmhouse for him and Mama and her, before her twin brothers ever came along, a person could sit on this porch and stare out at nothing but pine trees and dirt, far as the eye could see. Back then, most folks who settled on this little knob of swampy prairie between the Neches and the Nothing either raised rice, cattle, or timber, or worked on the river.

But that had been before the derrick struck. Before the black geyser spilled out from the earth, before all hell broke loose.

Before the fire. Pie exhaled the thought in a cloud of bitter smoke and tightened her grip on the bolt-action rifle in her lap, eying the line of dirt trapped beneath her nails. She'd been a girl of twelve when she'd faced her first ghoul right here on her daddy's land. Her bad ankle twinged. A lot had changed between that night and this, but it had all started here, at the Evanses'.

And for Pie, this would be where it ended.

Another flash of lightning clawed the sky open, and dense autumn raindrops splattered against the porch roof. A tug pulled somewhere deep in her gut, and Pie's braid stopped ticking. The long length of white cord slipped over her shoulder as she dug one foot into the wood to halt the rocker.

He'd crossed the property line.

Pie knew this land like she knew the back of her hand. She could feel him move out there in the dark, in the heat, in the wet. The one she'd been waiting for.

At least, she hoped it was.

"Better safe than sorry, I reckon." Pie bolted a round in the Winchester's chamber. She lifted the rifle and peered through its iron sights. "Come on now," she said to the deep smear of shadow that bloomed in the distance, heading her direction. "I'm ready."

The shadow took shape. The dark blur became a figure, became a man, as it stalked through the rain toward Daddy's old farmhouse. Pie's pulse rose and her ankle throbbed, but she held the gun steady. Squinted. Just because her body had stayed strong over the long years didn't mean her eyes didn't give her hell.

And a ghoul at fifty paces was a ghoul at fifty paces.

This time the thunder rolled into a voice, filling the space between raindrops as it wafted over the distance to brush her cheek.

"Happy birthday, Priscilla," it said.

She swatted the noise away and took another drag off the cigarette. Her vision might be shot, but her hearing was still sharp as a tack. She held the smoke in her mouth until her lungs singed, then Pie exhaled through her nose and spit the butt onto the porch to burn itself out.

"Happy birthday, yourself," she grunted back through the gun's sights, then, "and nobody calls me that anymore."

"Sure they don't." The dead man stopped out of the rain's reach, inside the shadows that hung over the edge of the porch. Dark hair, midnight eyes, straight nose, and a jaw that promised dimples. Something flickered across his eyes, maybe the moonlight fighting back the approaching dawn. "You mussed up your dress, Pie," he teased in a low drawl, the corners of his lips quirking up in a way that made him look human. "Course, I haven't seen you so prettied up since you were knee-high to a grasshopper."

Pie stomped, bits of dried mud crumbling on the wood slats at her feet. "Never you mind about my dress, farm boy."

"See you've still got my old gun, too." He stepped up onto the porch, smirking at the single-shot Winchester she kept upright in her arms. "You're not planning to shoot me with it, are you, Priscilla?"

"This old peashooter?" Pie grunted and lowered the gun, then knocked its muzzle on the wood slats at her feet. "Waste of a bullet. Would just make a mess outta you. Besides," she said as she slid the bolt back and removed the round, palming the cartridge. "Evans women are blades women."

"I know."

The dead man settled into the rocker beside Pie's in a cool wind of honey and woodsmoke. Most ghouls smelled like rot and dust, but not him. He smelled exactly the same now as he had the night he'd died. Looked the same, smelled the same.

He's dead, and I'm the one rottin', Pie thought. Figured.

She laid the rifle on the slats between the chairs and flicked her braid back over her shoulder. "There was a time the name Evans meant somethin' in this town. More than a bunch of crazy old biddies who run a funeral parlor," she reminded him. "Back when Daddy farmed this land—before so much of it got sold off, become somewhere to plant the dead instead of crops."

The dead man shook wet drops from his hair, his jacket. "I remember."

"'Course," Pie spat, "that all ended damn near a hundred years ago."

"I haven't kept count."

Pie had. Hadn't had much of a choice, considering. Heat rose in her throat, and she clucked it away. "Nearly one hundred years since I slid headfirst into this world," she said, "and not a single one of them has come easy."

Not a single damn one. Pie studied the round in her hand, the dull shine of metal in the dark.

The dead man gave her a weak smile. "There's your girls."

The girls. Pie had birthed a daughter, and that daughter had birthed a daughter, and her another daughter. Three generations of Evans women had been birthed inside these four walls, had gone off and made their own homes, though all still kept Pie's family business. If anything in this world remained worth dying for, it was those daughters.

And that was exactly what Pie had been waiting for, wasn't it? What she'd written in the letter left on the kitchen table—more or less.

"You'll look after them when I'm gone," she instructed the dead man. "Ducey. Lenore. Grace. The next one, and the next. You watch over my girls just like you've done me."

She made him promise twice, as the sky changed from navy to royal, then, "We'd best be gettin' on. Ducey will be over with the sun," she said. "Girl's always been an early riser. Chaps my hide."

"Can't all be night owls," he said, smiling dimples.

Pie slid the rifle round into her pocket as she pushed herself up. "Do I look like I'm laughin'?" The twinge in her ankle made her stumble, but she swatted the dead man away when he offered a hand to steady her.

His eyebrows furrowed, but the skin between didn't crack. "You sure you're ready to call it a night?" he asked. "You're barely ninety-three."

Pie slipped her arm through his, the clammy press of the ruined nightgown as cool as the dead man's skin against hers.

Too damn long, she thought again.

"You and me both should be nothin' but dust and bones by now, no matter what sort of blood is runnin' through our veins," she told the dead man around the tang of blood in her mouth, the stink of burning oil and smoke in her nostrils. "Now, come on and help an old woman get to bed."

He sighed. "Pie, I don't know if I can—"

"You have to." The words cut her tongue, stung her gums like ant bites, but she got them out. "You saved my life once, now I need you to do it again."

The dead man pulled against her, and his midnight eyes pored over Pie's face, her shoulders, the muddy dress as he turned his head toward her footprints on the wooden porch slats. "We don't know for sure what I did," he whispered, so faint she could barely hear it over the crisp sounds of predawn. "There's still more for me to learn." His free hand clipped her chin. "Give me a few more years, kiddo."

Pie let out one short, sharp bark. "Listen to me," she said, pulling the dead man off the porch, into the grass, toward the shovel. "I've lived my life here and, God willin', I'll die here too—but only *once*."

The dead man stiffened like he might argue. "I'm not a child anymore," she snapped. "Don't you dare treat me like one."

She stopped him at the edge of the hole and looked him square in the eyes. "Now, you do what needs doin'. Take it all," she told him, "and when it's done, make sure I stay put. Make sure I don't claw my way back out of that grave."

The dead man sighed as he watched Pie fish the rifle cartridge from the pocket of her nightgown, watched her slip its length between her teeth.

"You're really not going to tell them," he said, "any of them—about what they are?"

Pie spoke around the metal in her mouth as one of his hands cupped her cheek and the other slid around her back. "I told them enough," she muttered against his cold, unbeating chest, "but some things you take to the grave."

Then she peered up at him, the man who'd died so she could live, the man who had to put her down now so her daughters could go on. "I mean it, Sammy," she said. "Keep an eye on my girls, and make sure I don't come back."

Samael's body tensed, but his words breathed soft against Pie's cheek, and this time she let them rest, warm on her skin. "Anything for my best girl."

"Nothin' to tell them anyway," Pie said as the dead man leaned in.

"My girls know exactly what they are," she said as his fangs touched her throat, pierced her skin, slid under. "They're Evans women."

STILL NO ANSWERS
IN RABID ANIMAL ATTACKS
THAT LEFT SEVEN DEAD, TWO MISSING

Friday, September 24, 1999

Nearly four weeks after the last known attack, the rabid animal that police blame for leaving seven members of the community dead and two missing remains at large.

Among the victims is high school sophomore Alison Haney (15), whose body was discovered behind the Parkdale Mall movie theater. Snow Leger (48), Edwin Boone (55), Clyde Halloran (83), and Grace (38) and Ethel "Ducey" Evans (80) are also among the deceased. Another high school sophomore, Andrew West (16), a paper delivery boy for the *Enterprise*, and Patsy Milner (95), a housebound widow, are missing, and suspected victims of the animal, which authorities believe to be a rabid "ghost wolf," one of the coyote–red wolf hybrids recently spotted along the Gulf Coast.

Sheriff Buchanan "Buck" Johnson (81) was the final victim. In the weeks since the attacks several area pets have been reported missing, but none have been recovered.

"We're doing everything we can to locate and euthanize the infected animal or animals responsible," says Undersheriff Roger Taylor. The attacks began on August 22 at Clyde Halloran's homestead on Farm Road 121 and moved toward town center before ending back where they began. A month later, Animal Control has not located any animal that could have been responsible for the attacks.

If an infected canine remains in the area, it is unlikely to be caught. Chief Medical Examiner Jedediah Quigg says this is "less a question of police efforts than the nature of the infection." According to the Centers for Disease Control and Prevention, infected animals usually expire within seven days of becoming sick.

Which would mean the danger has passed—but has it? Channel Six's Penny Boudreaux isn't so sure.

"Nine community members lost their lives last month, and not a single paw print has been entered into evidence," says Boudreaux.

Quigg told the *Enterprise* that a bite from a rabid animal requires significant treatment, including a round of seven shots followed by three rounds of follow-up immunizations given over the next fourteen days. "You don't want to mess around with wild canine bites, rabid or otherwise," says Quigg, noting that rabies left untreated is typically fatal for both animals and humans.

While the attacks have been officially blamed on a rabid canine, law enforcement continues to pursue other leads. Undersheriff Taylor declined to comment, but Deputy Brandon Hinson promises that no stone will be left unturned as the investigation continues.

Following Sheriff Johnson's passing, Undersheriff Taylor will be confirmed in his placement as sheriff on Tuesday, September 28.

Animal Control will test all expired animals found near FM 121 and advises any community member who feels they might have been exposed to seek immediate medical attention. A research professor from the University of Texas will also be on-site to aid in the search for any ghost wolves spotted in the area.

Forest Park High School will hold an assembly in honor of Alison Haney and Andrew West this upcoming Monday as part of the Homecoming season kickoff. Brett Haney and Katherine Brooks-Haney, parents of Alison, are expected to attend, as well as Tanya West, mother of Andrew. The Homecoming Dance is scheduled for Friday, October 1.

CHAPTER 1

Sissy Broussard

Sissy Broussard disliked a lot of things.

She disliked the kind of rain that came down in sheets, the scratch of a brush through her hair, the chalky pills Mother pushed down her throat every evening. Scents of citrus and mint and pepper. Loud noises. Cold. Sissy especially disliked the necklace Mother gifted her last birthday. She disliked the way it fit, too tight around her throat, how Mother insisted that she wear it, that it looked so pretty on her. She disliked the cool metal clasp that pulled at the hair at the nape of her neck, the glitter the necklace left along the edges of her vision, the silver charm that jangled loud enough to hurt her ears.

But most of all, Sissy disliked cigarettes.

Especially the ones in the green and white package, she thought and sneezed. The acid and peppermint made her nose itch and her lungs burn—which put Sissy in a predicament, because the mint cigarettes were Mother's favorites.

Mother did her best to control the cigarette stink, but she could pump the air inside the house thick with all the Glade she wanted and it would still smell like burning menthol, but with the added fumes of Vanilla Breeze and Rainbow Potpourri. Sissy let the choker squeeze her throat, pull her hair, clink against her chest because Mother said it was important, but the curling acrid smoke that stunk up her beautiful coat and made her sneeze?

That she could not abide.

"Don't you go sneakin' out tonight," Mother reminded her from behind the acidic fog, forever worried about cranky Mr. Gordon, who opened his front door and made sweet sounds whenever Sissy walked by. "Too many gone missing lately," Mother said. "Don't want nobody makin' off with my pretty girl."

Sometimes Sissy listened to Mother's warnings and sometimes she didn't, but the concern that she'd wander too close to the old man's porch was wholly unnecessary.

Offensive, really, Sissy thought. She disliked Mr. Gordon, with his loud catcalls and coffee stink almost as bad as Mother's cigarettes. His frizzy brown hair and frizzy brown eyebrows and frizzy brown beard. She only ever walked on his side of the road to get a better look at the birdbath on his front lawn, and even that she preferred to watch from the comfort of her favorite reading chair.

Aside from a little window shopping, birds were too much trouble for Sissy to bother with.

Too much, really, for Mr. Gordon to bother with. If he wanted to invite birds to his yard, he already had a perfectly good nest perched right on top of his head.

But Sissy disliked involving herself in anyone else's business almost as much as she disliked anyone involving themselves in hers. And so, after a lazy Sunday spent lounging in her favorite reading chair, caught in a beam of warm September sunshine, she nibbled at the dinner her mother served, enjoyed the *clack-clack-clack* of the spinning wheel on her favorite game show, and then, when Mother retired to the back bedroom to smoke herself to sleep, Sissy pushed open the screen door and went out to get some fresh air.

The night's warm breath pushed the cigarette odor out of her nose, tickling along her back as she padded down the center of the quiet residential street.

Daytime strolls were fun but when the sun went down, Mother went to bed, Mr. Gordon shut his door, and all the silly birds that flitted about the ugly concrete eyesore in his front yard hid themselves away for the night.

Everything else woke up.

Sissy knew every house on her street, every pet, every sound, all the way from the small house with the red shutters where she and Mother lived to the two-story at the opposite end of the block where a bratty Pomeranian yipped from behind the window every time Sissy strolled by. Now, from her viewpoint in the middle of the streetlamp-shadowed road, everything lay before her, spread out in every direction—the neat little houses all in a row, with their matching shutters and matching front doormats and closed garages. A few porch lights were on, but all of the windows dark. A tall trash bin punctuated the end of every driveway, lids closed to keep out the sort of nocturnal critters that dined on refuse and rubbish.

That don't have mothers to lay out their meals for them.

Sissy disliked Mother's habits as well as her gifts, but she quite liked her daily servings of cold fish and liver pâté.

Tomorrow morning the big green truck would make its way down the street, snatch up the plastic cans waiting at the end of each driveway, and gobble down their insides, just like they did every Monday morning—just like Sissy did when Mother served treats of chilled cream and crust in a special dish on the kitchen counter.

She listened to the sounds of night as she passed the tall can at the end of her driveway, the abandoned birdbath two doors down on the left, the square tubs the lady across the street always put out one night too early, on green trash night instead of blue recycling night. Sissy crept just outside where the streetlights touched, where the sparkles on her necklace didn't glimmer in her peripheral vision. Her ears quirked at the tiny nicks of squirrel claws on bark, the scuttle of nocturnal critters as they skittered around, the crunch of dry leaves scattered against curb walls.

A possum hissed at her as she passed, but Sissy ignored it.

A squirrel chittered overhead, but she—

A flick of fur caught her eye.

Sissy froze. The stupid silver charm on her neck tinkled at the abrupt stop, then lay quiet against her chest. She stood stock still, the coldest thing in the warm autumn dark, not a wiggle of nose or twist of car. Her eyes locked on the small tuft of what might be a tail, might be a paw, half-hidden behind one of the big green bins at the end of somebody's driveway. She scented the air. Whiffs of moldy food scraps and drying leaves, a trace of Pomeranian scat on the downwind, but nothing that smelled like dinner.

Moonlight deepened the shadows around the trash can, outlining its edges with thick black borders. Even with her night vision, Sissy couldn't make out the fine details of the brush of fur, but she lowered herself onto her haunches and listened.

A twig snapped. A mouse, maybe.

The brush of fur moved, became a ball of dark.

Raccoon, Sissy guessed as the fur swelled around the moon-shadowed edges of the can and she caught the scratch of nails against asphalt. Some little bandit, hoping it could wrench open the tall bin's lid with its tiny humanlike claws, scavenge around in the filth within.

Electricity surged under Sissy's skin. Dinners nibbled out of a tin were easy and cheap, but she'd trade every last puck of tuna and saucer of cream in Mother's kitchen for the feel of a fresh catch between her teeth. A taste of raw meat.

A mouse would make for a delightful midnight snack, even if it would mean extra bathing tomorrow as Mother cleaned the blood from her fur.

Tomorrow Sissy would have all the daylight in the world to bathe, to snooze, to sneeze.

Now in the fresh air and wane of last night's full moon, she'd hunt.

She crouched low enough that her small, lithe form might become nothing but a blur on the pavement, a smear as easy to overlook as an oil stain. As the snarl of dark hair that tried to hide in the can's shadows.

Sissy's ears twitched, her stomach rumbled, when the trash can growled. Definitely not a mouse, then. Not a raccoon, either.

Mr. Gordon?

Sissy's ears flattened against her head. Her whiskers worked, her fur jumping up at the roots when an odor almost as acrid as Mother's stupid cigarettes infiltrated her nostrils. The scent tore the hunger from her instantly, and a new instinct flooded through her. When Sissy pushed her body against the hot top now, it wasn't so she could watch the creature behind the bin.

The ball of dark shifted, stretched, stood on all fours. The mass of fur and teeth atop its shoulders turned toward the street. Sissy stayed still as a statue while gleaming eyes cast out into the night, searching the shadows, scanning the dark—catching the sparkle of Mother's necklace around Sissy's neck.

The cat sprang to her feet and ran.

Another snap, another growl, and the predator behind the trash can gave chase.

The silver bell on Sissy's collar screamed against the sound of the beast's feet as they pounded behind her on the pavement—a *ting, ting, ting,* tracking her every step as she raced away from the thing behind her.

Her paws left asphalt, hit grass, slid over sidewalks, driveways, porches, as she fled, the neat little houses all in a row, their matching shutters and matching doormats and closed garages, all suddenly strange and unfamiliar.

She did not see Mr. Gordon's house, his stupid birdbath.

Didn't see the recycling tubs, set out a day early.

Didn't see Mother's house with its red shutters.

Sissy saw nothing but black. Smelled nothing but fear.

Heard nothing but the sound of her own collar, making it so easy for the monster to close in.

CHAPTER 2

Lenore Evans

Lenore Evans closed the newspaper. She folded it in half, then in quarters, and then she stuffed the flimsy Monday newsprint under a pile of paperwork on the front desk of Evans Funeral Parlor. She patted the clock key in her slacks pocket and did her best to ignore the pinch winding its way up her spine. Even to Lenore, ghost wolves seemed an unlikely patsy for the violent murders that had torn through town the past few weeks. Still, better that the local rag pin last month's attacks on some rabid coyote–red wolf hybrid than on the restless dead. Better that folks calmed down, let the whole horrible mess disappear into the past, where it belonged.

Better that no suspicion fall on the Evans women.

Not that there's many of us left, Lenore thought.

The pinch in her spine settled between her shoulder blades, and she straightened her back, cracking pressure out of her joints. She lifted her chest toward the ceiling and tried to exhale the heaviness from her bones.

Just a month ago, all four generations of Evans women had still been alive and well, keeping to themselves and ensuring the town's dead received the dignity due in their final rest. Now Ducey and Grace lay beneath rosebushes, and Luna, the littlest Evans, had faded into more of a ghost than this critter the *Enterprise* blamed for the seven dead, two missing.

The new Evans matriarch, with her own mother and daughter gone, fingered the spaces between her vertebrae, her collarbone, her ribs.

Lenore checked the schedule on her desktop. She eyed the meeting reminder scribbled in for after lunch.

A lot could change in just a few weeks.

The grandfather clock struck out six notes in the chapel. On the seventh, the desk phone rang. Lenore forced a smile into her voice and picked up the handset. The parlor's regular business hours were eight to five, but death rarely obeyed the clock.

"Evans Funeral Parlor," she said. "Lenore speaking."

Wet staticked across the landline, the old coroner's habit giving him away as he tongued at the receiver. "Morning, Lenore." Jedediah Quigg's voice came across far more cheerful than necessary, and she braced for impact. "I'm afraid you've got more company coming this morning."

A mess of half-finished reports and service flyers covered Lenore's desk. The long, curly phone cord coiled around her as she rummaged through unopened mail. Unfiled documents. A month's worth of daily newspapers, all folded at the obituaries. Lenore's index finger caught inside a phone-cord curl and the pinch between her shoulder blades lit into the back of her skull. She flattened her palm and pulled the cord until her fingertip went white.

Another lick, then, "You get the paperwork I faxed over?" the coroner asked.

Quigg licked over the line, muttered something about newfangled technology, and Lenore covered her delay with a cough, another riffle through the desktop litter.

"It's not right in front of me," she said, about whatever paperwork Jed Quigg called to check on. "When did you send it?"

The old coroner's voice squelched when he spoke. "Oh, sometime late last night."

Lenore spun in her chair, switching the handset to the other side of her head when she spotted the papers resting in the fax-machine tray, the familiar stamp of the coroner's office cover sheet. Without Ducey and Grace at her side, Lenore now had more work than hours. None of the bodies in the parlor's coolers appeared to be restless, but she hadn't got them in the ground yet, either.

Lenore had spent her entire life keeping the restless dead in their graves. She'd never heard tell of a strigoi rising because of a delayed funeral, but she didn't want to play the odds on finding out—not after that Godawful Mess all those years ago, the repeat just last month.

"I've got it right here." She pinched the hard plastic receiver against her shoulder, leaned over so far that the rubber coils straightened across her throat, and collected the pages. Lenore untangled herself from the cord as she scanned the type stamped into the intake form's lines. Mrs. Viola Rose Carroll, age sixty-two.

"Heart attack," she said.

"Happened in the Market Basket dairy aisle." The old night owl suckled each word as it crossed his lips. "Poor thing had a tub of pimento cheese in her hand when she dropped. Busted wide open—the container, I mean, not Mrs. Carroll," he added with another lick. "Her wig caught most of the cheese, by the looks of things, but you might still find some in her hair."

Lenore pulled the phone cord tighter around her wrists. Quigg had a taste for making light of the stranger things he came across in his work, but she had decades of practice brushing off her mother's tasteless jokes.

The pinch in the back of Lenore's skull beat and she resisted the urge to rub at her temples when she squeezed her eyes shut. "We'll take good care of her," she told the coroner.

The silence on the other end of the line meant he'd heard it, too, the plural, the *we*, but even an oral-fixated undertaker had better bedside manner than to comment.

All those decades of practice, and Lenore would give away her soul to hear one more snarky comment from Ducey, retrieve one more butterscotch cellophane from the breakroom carpet. Anything to see her mother, her daughter, alive, just one more time.

But they were gone, and Lenore still had a job to do. She opened her eyes.

"The body will be there soon," Quigg said, voice thick. "We're loading her up now." He recovered, coughing the wet free. "Daniel's the new kid. He'll introduce himself when he gets there."

"I'm glad you finally got yourself some help." A month ago, Lenore would have taken care of the paperwork, the family, and the service details, while Ducey bathed and readied the body. Grace would come behind with her shiny red vanity case, and Lenore would set an appointment with Snow Leger.

Of course, poor Snow's gone now, too. The beautician's death hadn't been the first in the string of attacks, but it'd set off the events that dropped the Evans Funeral Parlor's staff to one.

Quigg's breath fogged against Lenore's ear across the landline. "I hear you'll be getting some help yourself soon," he said.

Lenore summoned her best manners, her brightest tone. Apparently Roger Taylor had shared his recruiting efforts with the coroner, too. "Luna and I are managing things just fine."

The Evans family business—the Evans family *duty*—from one generation to the next, passed from woman to woman. And they'd carried on the work, until the littlest Evans got caught between the women who protected life and the dead that craved it. Luna's mixed blood of human and monster made her special—maybe even the key to understanding why the dead grew restless at all—but ignoring the consequences of the girl's parentage had also exposed gaps in the Evans family knowledge.

Gaps that had cost them dearly.

Cost us everything, almost.

Lenore needed to better understand her granddaughter's nature before dragging Luna into the work, but she was up to her ears without anyone to help at the funeral parlor. If Lenore hired another set of hands, she would bring a woman without Evans blood into their business for the first time.

But if she didn't . . .

Lenore twisted her hands free of the phone cord. She traced the outline of the key in her pocket and stared at the appointment scrawled into her schedule.

A hell of a lot could change in just a few weeks.

Warm scents of roasted hazelnut and vanilla floated down the hall, rolling over Lenore's shoulder from the breakroom coffeepot as she looked through the front windows, watching a sheriff's department cruiser swing into the parking lot. The Crown Vic crawled to a stop at the far end of the pavement beside Ducey's old Rambler, near the white rosebush Lenore had guarded for the past fifteen years. Near the other two seedlings they'd planted the night her mother and daughter died. Already fresh blooms erupted from Ducey's grave like fireworks, but only a mount of matted dirt covered where Grace's body lay.

Leaves gusted under the hood when Roger Taylor cut the engine, but the driver's side door didn't open. Lenore pushed herself to her feet and turned her back to the glass to give the man outside his privacy.

"Well, if you girls need anything . . ." The old coroner let the words drop off. He didn't so much as lick his receiver when the empty air crackled across the phone line.

Lenore would grieve when there was time. Not one second before—and never for Jedediah Quigg to hear.

"I've got to run, Jed." Once she'd gotten Luna off to school with Roger, Lenore would need to get things ready for Mrs. Carroll.

Then, she remembered, she'd have to prepare for that dreadful meeting written on her schedule.

Quigg licked his goodbyes and disconnected the call with a promise the new delivery boy would be by soon with the dead woman's body. Lenore returned the handset to its cradle, pulled a fresh folder from the stack in her desk drawer, and printed the deceased's name on the top tab. She double-checked the contact information for the next of kin printed at the bottom of the page. After she'd finished the intake, she'd need to phone Mr. Wilmer Carroll about his wife's funeral arrangements.

Lenore slipped the fax into the folder as the front door pushed open. Pink from the late-September heat tinged his cheeks, but the dirt stains on Roger Taylor's fingers matched those on the mudpie-brown hat gripped in his hands, the smears on his uniform pants, as he stomped his boots free of fallen leaves on the outdoor mat and stepped inside.

"Morning." Roger stopped short when his gaze landed on the mess on Lenore's desk, the mangled phone cord hanging like a noose down the side. He cleared his throat, fingers twisting at the Timex on his wrist. "She ready?"

The man's voice came husky after his daily pilgrimage to garden at the edge of the building. Usually it worked itself loose by brunch. In all the mornings that the deputy had come 'round to Evans Funeral Parlor, Lenore hadn't figured out whether he did it out of suspicion or helpfulness.

Probably he just came for Grace, like always. The white rosebush bloomed as well as ever, and yellow rhododendrons still dotted the bushes at the edge of the parlor, but the poor man was having a dickens of a time getting something to bloom above her daughter's grave, and he seemed to take it personal. Ducey's bush sprouted rosebud after rosebud, but for all Roger's watering and pruning and fussing, he'd barely managed to coax a few thorny stalks out of the ground. Every day he made a mess out of the dirt over Grace's grave, but not so much as a clod stood out of place by the time he drove away.

When the dead didn't haunt graveyards and cemeteries, sometimes the living did.

The pinch in Lenore's skull twinged behind her nose and her eyes welled up. She thought of Luna, still just a child, kneeling beside her own mother's grave, so near her monstrous father's.

Lenore jerked her head toward the hallway behind the lobby. "She's finishing up in the breakroom," she said.

"I'm right here."

Lenore startled in her chair as her granddaughter slid around the lobby desk. The girl thunked a mug of coffee on top of Mrs. Viola Carroll's intake folder, sending black liquid sloshing out of the mug, racing toward the edge of the wooden desktop. Lenore pinched the cup up by its brim as she ripped sheets of tissue free from the box on her desk. Half the reason she insisted on tile in the rest of the funeral parlor was so nobody could sneak up on her. The other half because carpet was hell to keep clean. But Lenore hadn't heard the soft press of the girl's rubber soles on the linoleum or the tinkle of Belle's collar as the former sheriff's hunting dog, the wounded hound adopted into the Evans family after his death, trailed Luna down the hallway. Now she'd have to clean up the brown drips along with all the chores on her already long to-do list.

Maybe she'd get to that after she spoke to Wilmer Carroll—if she had a spare second before that dreadful appointment.

Lenore ripped another tissue free. "Keep spilling coffee like that and there won't be any Kleenex left for clients." The redbone hound turned soulful eyes to Lenore, and Ducey's voice echoed in her ears. *I don't know why you're bothering with that right now, Len. There's just gonna be a bigger mess.*

"Doesn't mean we should just leave it," Lenore muttered under her breath.

The deputy tittered in the corner. "What's that?"

"I said, 'Isn't that right, Belle?'" Lenore bent toward the dog, who swished her tail across the thin lobby carpet, then padded to the window to whimper against the glass. Lenore tossed the tissue in the trash and looked at her granddaughter, not at the man taking up space in the lobby corner.

Still damp from the morning shower, Luna's wet, dark hair hung over her shoulders the way the sleeves of her late mother's work shirt hung past her wrists. Her backpack flapped against her back, pockmarked with buttons and iron-on patches. The girl wore a scowl severe enough to hollow out the spaces under her black-limned eyes, and she looked so much like her mother that Lenore burned her lips on too-hot coffee to hide the tremble.

But at least Luna had dressed for school.

Lenore tried to exhale the pinch behind her eyes. She pulled her lips into a line, as rigid and straight as when the phone cord had tightened around her neck, then forced the ends up until they cracked into a smile.

"Have a good first day back, honey," she told Luna. "Roger will pick you up and bring you here after school."

Color sparked in Luna's cheeks despite the pale powder she'd patted onto her skin, cheeks flushing from tongue pink to bloodred. Her shoulders squared, and Lenore felt the temperature rise in the room like a body in the parlor's lab—but the girl shifted her backpack from shoulder to shoulder, and her voice came out at a reasonable volume.

"I've been out of school a month already. I don't see what's so bad about missing one more day." Luna dug her toe into the carpet and mumbled, "It's stupid that I have to go back just to sit through a *memorial* for Alison and Andy. Not like I could forget what happened or anything."

Lenore watched Roger's knuckles go white where he clutched at his hat before she looked at her granddaughter again. The man still favored his forearm, last month's wound taking its time to heal, but she'd never thought to ask what became of his old hat, the one he'd used to try to stop the blood pouring from Grace's chest.

"I know you'd rather not attend," Lenore said, "but it's the proper thing to do. The poor dear deserves that much."

"Then *you* go," Luna shot back, midnight eyes so bright with the full moon that Lenore looked away and Roger took a step back, melting into the wainscoting along the lobby wall. "Sorry if I don't want to sit through a memorial for my ex-boyfriend that I accidentally turned into a monster and set loose on the town—on *us*."

Her granddaughter's sentence ended in a sniff, and Lenore rallied, tried to buff the sharp edges from her words. She had meant the girl ripped open on the movie-theater pavement in broad daylight, not the boy that ripped their family apart. Andy had been responsible for the restless deaths blamed on rabid coyote-wolves, but Luna had been responsible for what happened to Andy.

"It's not about him." The pinch in Lenore's skull rattled against her teeth as it joined the saltwater pooling at the back of her throat. At least Roger kept tucked into the woodwork where he belonged and didn't butt into the family business—more than he already had, anyway. "It's about you," she told her granddaughter. "You need to let them go so that you can carry on."

"*Me?*" Luna's eyes went wide. "What about you?"

If it'd just been Andy that had gone into the ground that Godawful night, the youngest Evans might have forgiven herself. But the boy had killed Luna's mother, Lenore's own daughter. Grace Evans had sacrificed herself to save Luna, just as Lenore's mother had done the same to save them all.

Now they both had to live with that.

The girl's body went stiff. Her lips opened, closed, opened, and when they closed again, she rolled her eyes, then staked them directly into Lenore's chest. "You're *really* going to make me go?"

Belle whined against the window, fog blooming across the smooth surface, and pressure bubbled in Lenore's chest. She glanced at Roger Taylor, at his knuckles, white against mudpie brown. As much as Lenore felt the need to keep her granddaughter under constant surveillance, a feat she hadn't quite accomplished while raising her own daughter decades before, she'd feel a lot better about navigating her new parental responsibilities if Roger would stop twisting his damn hat.

"I am," she managed, finally.

The girl spun on her heels, backpack slugging over her shoulders, and reached down to scratch behind the hound dog's ears before she charged out of the double doors of Evans Funeral Parlor without another word.

Roger pried himself out of the woodwork to clamp his palm on the desktop. "She'll come around," he said, as if he had daughters of his own. He tapped his finger against the appointment circled on Lenore's desk calendar. "Give the coffee shop girl a chance. She's been taking classes down at the beauty college," he added. "Could be a big help to you around here."

Lenore pursed her lips. She'd be the judge of that. "There's a big difference between playing dress-up with mannequins and taking care of the deceased," she told him. "Especially in this town."

Roger paled around the edges when Lenore nodded toward the rosebushes planted alongside the parlor's edge. He managed to fit that rumpled mess of a hat back on his head, then hitched up his pants and headed to the glass front doors, Belle on his heels. The dog snuck her snout into the frame, and Roger nudged her aside when he pulled the door open. "Keep Belle indoors, if you can," he said over his shoulder. "We've had a couple reports of pets going missing."

"Must be that coyote hybrid," Lenore said, and they both smiled.

Lenore watched as the man backed his patrol car out of the parking space and aimed its nose toward the street, Luna's profile rigid in the passenger-side glass. The sheriff's department cruiser turned out of the parlor's lot just as a white van with CORONER printed across the hood turned in.

Quigg might take his time making his way through a phone call, but the man was quick at his work. What was his new boy's name again?

When the van disappeared around the side of the building, Lenore plucked Mrs. Carroll's intake folder from the desktop. "Come on, Belle," she called, but the old hound stood, legs stiff and tail ramrod straight, staring out the parlor's front doors at the space where Roger's car had been, at Ducey's blooming grave.

At Grace's freshly tended mount of dirt.

"Belle, come on, honey."

The old hound might be one ear in the grave already, but her training held strong. If she couldn't get outside to hunt down whatever scent she'd picked up, then it seemed lying at the door would have to do.

Lenore left the dog behind with the half-spilled mug of coffee. She passed the breakroom without looking in—without seeing her mama's empty armchair, the dog-eared romance novel Ducey had left on the tray table.

The taste of butterscotch swelled on Lenore's tongue, but Quigg's delivery boy knocked on the back door and the sound chattered against her teeth, filling the space between her bones.

Seven dead, two missing, she thought.

Seven dead, two missing, and the dead didn't stop dying.

CHAPTER 3

Luna Evans

Luna sat in the passenger seat of Roger Taylor's patrol car as the street passed by in a comforting blur. She pressed one ear against the glass and listened to the road noise sweeping against her window—to the jingles that filtered through the in-dash stereo, to the gross gurgles escaping from the deputy's throat. Anything other than the stream of chatter crackling through the center-console police radio, the official voices muttering back and forth about traffic issues, petty disturbances, and whatever else small-town sheriffs paid attention to.

"We've got another 10–91D," a woman's voice hissed through the console speaker, through the receiver pinned to the cop's shoulder, and rattled through Luna's ribs. "This one's missing fur, but it's got a collar on," she said. "Must be somebody's pet."

Luna didn't have a clue what a 10–91D was, but a gurgle bubbled into Roger's throat, and he shifted behind the wheel. In the passenger-side window reflection he reached for the receiver on his shoulder, twisting the volume knob until the chatter popped and went silent. The man cleared his throat. His jaw flapped open and closed like one of those animatronic fish that sang if you plugged four AA batteries into its base.

Roger cleared his throat again and gave up.

Ghost wolves, then.

Nana Lenore tried to keep Luna away from the daily news, but reporters weren't the only ones conned with the whole rabid animal distraction.

The deputy hadn't said a word on the drive, just tossed his hat on the dash and drove from point A to point B like someone made him do it, and not like he showed up at the parlor when nobody asked him to.

Or maybe Nana Lenore had. Easy for her to force Luna back to school when she could stay in the seclusion of the family business.

Luna stifled a groan as Roger swung the cruiser into Forest Park's bus-only lane. She rolled her eyes as he eased his foot off the gas. "You don't have to drive me back and forth to school, you know," she said.

Roger let the cruiser slow to a crawl along the front curb, then came to a full stop behind a row of news station vans.

"Not every day," he said, eyeballing the knot of reporters that lurked around the students gathered outside the school's double doors, their cameras, microphones, and notepads all now turning toward the sheriff's department Crown Vic. "But probably good that I do today."

For the most part, chili cook-offs and community events were the most exciting things to make headlines around town. A string of violent deaths and strange animal sightings worked the bored reporters into a lather. Add an assembly for a couple of dead high school kids at the peak of Homecoming season, and it became hard to distinguish the rabid animals from the media trucking in from Houston. Everyone wanted a bite of the action: a response from the small-town cop supposed to have all the answers, a reaction from the girl who lost two family members and a boyfriend.

A reason why the new sheriff drove the weird Evans girl to school every day.

Because a rabid animal disemboweled the last sheriff and chewed off his face.

She hadn't felt nauseous before, but a Taylor-like gurgle pushed against Luna's lips, and she scanned the mob as he shifted the car into park in the drop-off lane.

Yanking a cameraman along with her, a blonde with a microphone broke away from the student throng and marched toward the car in a gust of purpose and patent-leather pumps. Principal Brevard jumped in behind her, the smug little man's arms outstretched like a mother hen's wings as he tried to corral the rest of the crowd before it surged forward to surround the car, *hungry, hungry—*

Roger's voice rang inside the patrol car. "Ready?"

Students parted, and Luna spotted black leather sleeves within a sea of school-spirit wear and letterman jackets. She swallowed the lump in her throat, curled her mother's shirtsleeves around her fists, and rolled her eyes to meet the deputy's gaze. Roger waited for Luna's nod before he snatched his wrinkled hat from the dash, planted it atop his head, and pushed the driver's side door open.

"Undersheriff Taylor—" Mic in hand, the news lady shunted herself against the car, and a pack of press badges lurched toward Roger. The lunge of questions snapped like rubber bands against Luna's exposed skin, but she kept her head bowed, her backpack firm against her back, and put one foot in front of the other until leather-clad arms wrapped around her.

A familiar voice floated down to brush the top of her head. "There you are, Moon Girl."

Luna buried her face into Crane's trench coat, inhaled patchouli and stale cigarette smoke.

"Miss Evans!" The news lady's voice cut through the crowd, tangling itself in Luna's stomach. When she looked up, a Channel Six microphone hovered so close to her face that Luna could smell other people's breath still on its foam cover.

"Miss Evans, you lost your mother and great-grandmother in last month's rabid animal attacks—"

"Ms. Boudreaux." Principal Brevard's voice slimed over Luna's shoulder as he stretched the syllables of the woman's name. He blocked the microphone with his palm, class ring flashing, and snarled at the reporter. "I'm afraid I can't allow you to interview students without consent from their parents," he said. "Or, uh, their guardians."

The man glared hard at Crane's leather sleeve around Luna's shoulders. Brevard patted down his toupee, quirked his lips even higher, and leaned in so close that Luna could smell Binaca. "But I'd be happy to personally give you an exclusive interview," he oozed.

The bell rang and Luna and Crane left the reporter to peel herself free of the principal's trap as they escaped with the rest of the students.

"As horrible as that woman is, I almost feel sorry for how much

Brevard drools over her." The back of Luna's throat burned and she adjusted the backpack strap on her shoulder. "Not sorry enough to deal with her questions though," she said as they were swept upstream between buildings toward the gymnasium. "Everybody acts like my family are the town pariahs, and now Mom and Ducey are dead and it's breaking news all the way to Houston." Her voice stuck, and Luna forced it free. "I'd rather listen to Brevard read Andy's obituary on a loop."

Crane smirked above her head and his black eyeliner crinkled shadows into the corners of his eyes. "I have a feeling you're about to," he said.

Silver rings pushed against Luna's fingers as Crane cupped his hand around hers so they wouldn't be pulled apart by the herd. Sometime over the last four weeks Crane had started holding Luna's hand— palms together, fingers cuffed, not interlaced. They weren't a couple, but Luna didn't think they were just friends, either. Nobody lived through what they had without bonding for life.

Even if it was all her fault.

Even if she didn't deserve a boy like Crane, not after what she'd done.

Student stink filled Luna's nose. It coated her tongue, rumbled in her belly.

Their fingers still clasped, Crane pulled Luna behind him. He climbed past school-spirit-clad bodies that parted like a sea before them, to the top row of the bleachers, the furthest corner. No one wanted to sit beside the weird girl with the dead mom and the goth boy who reminded everyone of Columbine, but no one was brave enough to tell them off, either.

Luna and Crane wedged into the highest corner they could find. In the center of the room, surrounded by a semicircle of cheerleaders fluttering their pom-poms, Student Council clustered at ground level, ringed by two oversized projection screens. From this height, Luna could spot Dillon's starched collar and Crystal's butterfly hair clips.

Down on the gymnasium floor, the press-badge horde gathered under the basketball hoop, arranging themselves in a perfect angle to capture the podium stationed between the screens, and the three padded vinyl chairs reserved for the parents of the missing and murdered kids. A man in a button-down camo shirt sat in one of the chairs, his hand clamped on his wife's knee, tethering the woman to her chair while she did her best to hide behind a wad of tissue.

Luna nodded to the couple as she shoved her backpack into the empty space at her feet. "Those must be Alison's parents."

Crane cocked his head at the empty chair. "Andy's mom?" he asked.

Luna shrugged. "Weird that she's not here."

"Have you seen her since . . ." Crane let the question drop off. After she'd turned Andy into a monster, he'd fed on Mina Jean Murphy until he drained her life away like cancer, and then he'd started in on his own mother. Tanya had been weak but alive when they put Andy's body in the crematory, but rumor said the dead boy's mom hadn't left her bed since Roger Taylor filed the Missing Person's report.

For the past month, Luna had wondered if Tanya West would become restless the same way Mina Jean Murphy did, but she'd never been brave enough to ask Nana Lenore.

Principal Brevard swanned into center stage and motioned for silence, tapping the mic until everyone got the point. When the chatter subsided, the lights dimmed as the projectors flickered on, then Alison's big doe eyes filled one screen, and Andy's disheveled dirty-blond mop filled the other.

"Alison Haney was not only a Symphony League of Southeast Texas debutante, but as first trumpet in the Forest Park marching band and lead soprano in our choir, she had the gift of music." The principal projected an almost believable amount of affection as he described the girl who'd stolen Luna's boyfriend.

Ex-boyfriend. Petty jealousy aside, Alison had made a much smarter match for Andy than Luna had. She squeezed Crane's hand, enjoying the press of his rings along the edge of her palm. Restless or otherwise, by the time she'd turned him into a monster, Andy West had already been *so* ex-boyfriend.

"Andrew West," Brevard started, and Luna rolled her eyes. Outside of his mother, no one called Andy by his full name. "Andrew was a sportsman who volunteered time to help important community organizations," the principal went on, "like the Symphony League of Southeast Texas, where he and Alison were fast friends."

The principal scanned the bleachers. "The entire Forest Park High community also wants to extend our condolences to Luna Evans, who lost both her mother and great-grandmother in last month's attacks," the principal tacked on before he clapped his hands, smoothed his hair, and shifted the topic to football and tonight's kickoff game.

Luna nestled against Crane's shoulder, breathed in leather and smoke. The congregation's eyes burned in her direction while she bored her own stiff gaze into the rows of colorful buttons pinned down her backpack straps. Rainbow Brite, Tori Amos, Sex Pistols.

Love Kills.

When she first met Crane outside Parkdale Mall, he'd asked to bum a cigarette and told Luna that she'd been named for a moon goddess.

Finally, the bell rang. The projectors went dark, the cheerleaders put away their pom-poms, and Principal Brevard crowed everyone on to second period.

Luna and Crane waited until the rest of the student body cleared out of the bleachers, then caught up with their friends on the lawn between the gym and the school's main building.

"I wonder what happened to Ms. West," Crystal said, adjusting the sparkly butterfly clips in her big brown curls while Dillon sagged under the combined weight of their textbooks. "She was supposed to be here."

Dillon's eyebrows pulled together. "You remember what she looked like when we went over to get pictures for the slide show." He dumped the lion's share of textbooks back into Crystal's grasp and tucked the remainder under his arm. "Sunken eyes, colorless lips—she was *literally* wasting away."

Luna and Crane shared a look while Zen-garden lines raked across the top of Crystal's nose. She crooked the books in one arm and used her free hand to block the sun.

"You should have participated," she told Luna. "The assembly was for you, too."

Luna tugged on her backpack straps and tightened her grip on Crane's hand. It's not like she had anything to say about Andy's "disappearance" or Alison's murder. Sorry wouldn't cut it.

"Everyone expected you to," Crystal pressed.

Crane's hand slipped loose of Luna's, and his leather sleeve wrapped around her shoulders, pressing the buttons' metal pins against her flesh under the thin work shirt. "Sounds like that's their problem," he said.

When silence stretched between the group, Dillon faked a cough and nudged Crystal's ribs.

"Well, at least it's over," she said and sighed. "Now we can get back to preparing for midterms."

"I think you mean Homecoming." Dillon clicked his tongue. "I hear someone with a certain *ladybug* screen name has been seen lurking in AOL chatrooms, trying to snare herself a date to the dance this Friday."

"I definitely mean midterms," Crystal snapped back. "I think *you* mean Homecoming."

"What can I say, I love a man in uniform," Dillon said, then rounded on Luna. "Speaking of men in uniform, Stripper Cop told Kim, who told me, that he thinks Taylor is mishandling the whole ghost-wolf investigation thing." His eyebrow waggle made Luna's stomach churn over the story her grandmother and the soon-to-be sheriff had concocted. "He thinks Deputy—" The boy stopped, tilted his head. "Sheriff Taylor? Anyway, Stripper Cop thinks his new boss is hiding something. That's why Taylor didn't bother to stay for the memorial—he didn't want to take the heat."

Crystal put a palm up. "I think Brandon—"

"Stripper Cop," Dillion corrected, then, "I can't believe my sister is *still* dating him, by the way—I mean, he was a *quarterback*."

Because goth girls like Kim Cole, like Luna Evans, didn't typically date jocks.

Under her backpack straps, Luna felt the buttons' metal pins press into her flesh. At least Kim hadn't turned her boyfriend into a monster.

"Ever since Johnson died, things between Kim and Stripper Cop have been tense." Dillon's voice dropped into a whisper. "I give it two weeks," he said.

"Haven't they been together for like four years?" Luna asked, not that it mattered.

Dillon's face twisted. "Everything has an expiration date, Luna Lou."

Crystal rolled her eyes. "I think *Deputy* Hinson is right—there's more than the police are letting on," she said, and Luna's insides went flat, "but whatever it is, I'm sure *Undersheriff* Taylor is keeping it quiet for a good reason."

"Really?" Dillon's palm swung to his hip and his baby blues rolled over Luna as the fingers of his other hand curled into air quotes. "So Crys thinks there's a 'reason' the police don't want us to know what killed your family last month." His hand peeled off his hip and he crossed his arms over his chest, book still wedged in his armpit. "I don't think it was a rabid animal at all." He whisper-talked into his shoulder. "I think there's a serial killer."

He waited out Crystal's deep sigh, Crane's silence, then blinked his eyes wide. "Maybe *that's* why my sister went all Frenchy Facciano and dropped out of beauty school so she can work at your family's funeral parlor—she could be Stripper Cop's spy!"

Luna's feet slipped, and Crane's arm tightened around her, holding her up. An image of Kim Cole skipping arm in arm through Evans Funeral Parlor with Nana Lenore flicked through her mind, and her gut twisted. She opened her mouth to parrot the party line about some kind of rabid coyote-wolf, but Michelle Bryant's shoulder slapped against her as the cheerleader passed by in a gaggle of pom-pom-bearing groupies, saving Luna from having to lie to her friend.

"Watch out, *Lunie* Evans," the cheerleader spat between her trademark labia-pink lips. Her eyebrows shot up like she might have something to say to Dillon or Crystal, too, but Crane scorched her with a look and the giggling swarm moved on.

"Is it terrible that I kinda wish it'd been her that got eaten behind the movie theater, and not Alison Haney?" Dillon shrugged at Luna. "No offense."

Luna couldn't care less about Michelle Bryant or Alison Haney. It felt ridiculous that she had, just a month ago. Now she had bigger problems.

Much bigger.

Much bigger problems, namely Kim Cole. Just because Deputy Taylor and Crane knew about the Evanses' business now didn't mean they needed *another* outsider in on the secrets they'd guarded for a hundred years.

Nana Lenore must have *really* not wanted Luna's help.

Crane's arm dropped from Luna's shoulders and she felt his body stiffen beside her. "I hate when she calls you that," he said. "Names have power."

"She's called me that since elementary." Luna tried for flippant, then, "Is that why you call me Moon Girl? Because I'm something dark and strange?"

He gave her a smile that warmed her to her bones. "I call you Moon Girl because you're the brightest thing in the night sky."

Dillon's jaw unhinged. He pressed a hand against his chest and Luna felt the heat of her friend's palm in her stomach.

"That's very Edgar Allan Poe of you," she managed around the burn in her cheeks.

Crane slid his long, ringed fingers into his trench coat pockets. He pulled his jacket out so that it fanned around his legs and grinned. "Well, I *am* goth," he said.

Dillon couldn't take any more. "Oh my god, what is going on with you two lately? You're always together, always whispering." His hands curled into little cannonballs and excitement sparkled in his baby blues. "Are you, like, secretly dating?"

"Yeah, that's the real mystery—the private lives of Crane Campbell and Luna Evans." Crystal fumbled her books and rolled her eyes. "We're going to be late if we don't hurry up and get to class."

Luna held her breath until the bell rang, Crystal stomped her feet, and the clump moved toward the main building.

"Do you think your grandma is really going to hire Kim?" Dillon asked.

"She probably wouldn't hire *me* if I applied," Luna grumbled. Not only did Nana Lenore not want her help, she might prefer to bring a spy into the family business than to trust her own flesh and blood.

"I guess we'll find out after school," Dillon said, as Crystal hooked her arm in his and tugged him along.

She shot a look over her shoulder at Luna and Crane. "You guys coming?"

"You know how Mr. Tucker gets," Dillon added, pointing a finger in the air. "'Economicth waith for no one.'"

Luna latched on to Crane's leather sleeve and waved her friends along.

"We need to keep looking for answers," Luna told him the second their friends were out of earshot. "We've already combed through the school library. If there's any information to find locally, it'll be at the main branch downtown."

Sunlight blotted out the boy's face as he looked down at her through his hair. "You want to skip and go now?"

She thought about Mr. Tucker and detention, about the reporters and their microphones. About the 10–91D that had crackled over Taylor's police radio and the way Nana Lenore jumped when Luna snuck up behind her.

She thought about Kim Cole in the Evans house.

Hell yes, she wanted to skip.

Luna forced out a sigh. As watchful as Nana was already, she'd never let Luna out of her sight if she found out she'd skipped on her first day back. "Roger is supposed to pick me up after school, and there are reporters everywhere. If somebody sees us or we don't get back in time, I'm screwed," she said. "And it's still basically the full moon."

Crane's head tilted and he thumbed a dark curtain behind his ear. "Some cultures believe that wishes made under a full moon have a higher chance of coming true. Others use it to explain insane behavior—sleepwalking, fits of violence, werewolves." He squinted at her. "The full moon symbolizes power and intensity, but I'm not sure the lunar cycle makes a difference for strigoi."

Ducey had said stuff like garlic and crucifixes and full moons were nothing but hokum, but even her great-grandmother didn't know everything. "We don't know that it doesn't, either," Luna said.

Crane nodded like that made sense. "Better not to rule anything out yet, I guess."

Luna thought about the small apartment she had shared with her mother over the laundromat, still full of her and Grace's lives. About her grandmother, winding the ancient grandfather clock that she'd dragged into the chapel from the parlor's back rooms with a key she kept in her slacks pocket. Nana Lenore was a haunted house, full of cold ceramic and the ghosts she couldn't let move on. Would Luna end up like that, too, living in her grandmother's home?

"Here." Luna shirked her backpack free of one shoulder, then twisted the sack around her waist to riffle in the pockets for the key ring she hadn't touched since she'd moved in with her grandmother. "Do you think you could go to my apartment and, like, look around?"

Crane's eyebrows crooked. "What am I looking for?"

"I don't know, really." Luna shrugged, still digging. "Journals, books, photos, letters. Mom must've left *something* that would help us figure this all out."

"You've checked everything at the parlor, right?" Crane asked for the millionth time in the past four weeks. "All Ducey's shelves—the lab *and* the breakroom?"

Luna sighed out the same answer she'd given every time and hoisted the kludge of keys from her bag. "I seriously don't get why she loved those smut books so much," she said. "There's nothing in the parlor but medical texts, bodice rippers, and *TV Guide.*"

"Your great-granny certainly had a specific taste in reading material." Crane snorted out a soft laugh. "Wish I'd gotten to know her better."

Luna wished she had, too.

And her mom.

Almost sixteen years, and Luna barely knew much of anything about who Grace Evans had really been.

She found the key to the small apartment over the laundromat, twisted it free of the loop, and pushed the thin gold slab into Crane's palm. "We'll get a ride to the library later," she said, "but until then, this is the best we've got."

Crane's words came out measured. "It's not the *best* we've got," he said. "There's someone else—"

Luna flinched and she pushed her voice as firm as she could make it. "We are not digging up that thing."

"It would make things easier, going straight to the source," Crane pressed.

"He's a *literal* monster, Crane."

"Yes." Crane spoke slowly, like she was a scared animal he'd frighten off if he talked too quickly, too loudly. "But Samael is also your father. He loved your mother," he said. "Do you really think he'd hurt you?"

Love. Luna wasn't so sure about that. Could monsters love? The answer, she decided, wasn't important. It *couldn't* be important.

Her dad was a monster, and so was she.

"Since we're exchanging gifts, I've got something for you, too." Crane's hand slipped into the folds of his black leather coat, emerging with a mass-market paperback. Luna got a look at the mansion shrouded in weeping willows on the curled-up blue cover when Crane thrust the book into her hands. She squinted at the worse-for-wear copy of *Interview with the Vampire*.

"Funny," she said.

Crane's lips twisted into a smile that would have been cruel if he hadn't given her a one-armed hug to go along with it. "Think of it as a memoir about a strigoi finding his way."

"But it's fiction," Luna said.

"According to our research thus far," Crane noted, "so are you."

Fair point. Luna peered up. "You don't think I'm a monster?"

"I like monsters." The boy shrugged. "And you're *my* monster."

Crane's long fingers cupped her cheek, her jaw. He bent toward her.

Luna recoiled, her eyes wide. Hand-holding, she could handle. Holding hands, fingers cupped, not interlaced, meant they were friends, but a kiss—what would that mean?

And if it meant what she thought it would mean, was she ready?

Was she not?

Would she ever be?

A shadow passed through Crane's eyes, but then he laughed and pocketed the key. "Besides," he said, "whatever curse is on this land that makes the dead rise, the Evans women have been stopping it for generations."

"They were," Luna said, "until we started causing it."

Until *she* started causing it, anyway.

Crane shrugged. "If I'm honest, I wouldn't mind hearing more about rabid ghost wolves," he said. "They sound extremely pettable." One palm slipped around hers and the other tousled her hair. "Now, come on, Moon Girl," he said. "Let's see if we can figure out what kind of critter you are."

CHAPTER 4

Undersheriff Roger Taylor

Roger Taylor stood in Jimbo's Java Café, his thumbs in his belt, and stared at the treats lined behind the glass in the pastry case. Muffins big as fists, frosted cakes, cinnamon rolls. Carbs, calories, refined sugar. Saturated fat.

Indigestion flared in his stomach and Roger patted the place where his gut used to jut out. Up until a couple of weeks ago, the sheriff's deputy had led a relatively simple life. Every morning he'd pinned on his badge. Every night, he'd taken it off. No curdle in his coffee then. Just common sense, easy justice, and some quality time every evening with his whittling kit.

A month ago, Roger hadn't had to worry about things like rabid animals, ghost wolves, the restless dead. He'd concentrated on crossing off the days till retirement on his calendar and trying to drop a few pounds. Since the first was a matter of running out the clock, inching shift by shift toward the date circled in red on his calendar, most of his attention had gone to watching his sugars.

Roger's gaze snagged on the second tray in the case, the thin gold slab of flaky, cream-filled French pastry.

Up until a few weeks ago, Roger had still hoped whatever inches he could trim off his waist would help him build up the courage to ask out Grace Evans.

In his wildest dreams, she'd have said yes. They'd have courted for a while, and Grace could have grown to love him as much as he'd always loved her. Roger would have saved every penny he could from his public servant's salary, and when the time was right, he'd have gotten down on one knee. If Grace had said yes, he'd have bought her a nice little house, wherever she wanted it, and together they could count down the days while he spent every one of them trying to be a better husband than he'd ever been a sheriff's deputy.

And Roger had figured if none of that ever happened, there was always *American Woodworker* and dying in his uniform, maybe like Buck Johnson.

Roger pulled at his belt. Hopefully *not* like Buck Johnson.

When Grace died, so had Roger's ambitions of trading in his badge for a pension. As he stood useless to stop the horrors that the Evans family had faced for a hundred years, his own future had dried up before his eyes. All he had now was a mound of grave dirt he fussed over every morning but still couldn't make bloom, a fresh scar on his forearm, and a secret he wasn't sure how to guard—one that, if Roger wanted to keep the peace in his town and preserve Grace's legacy, he'd have to keep buried just as deep as the woman he'd failed.

"Eatin' your feelings again this morning, Taylor?" Jimbo's day manager barreled through the doors from the café's kitchen, her apron hanging from her neck and left untied where it didn't reach around her middle.

Red rimmed the woman's eyes. Either from smoking or crying, Roger figured, and neither were any of his business.

Rhonda hacked out a cough, wiped away a dry layer of frosting that had crusted into the fine lines around her jaw, and tacked a bright pink flyer to the bulletin board behind the counter.

She planted meaty palms on the pastry glass. "Didn't hear ya come in," she said, squaring up for his order. "What'll it be?"

"I'll take a cream-cheese-filled croissant," Roger said, "and a cup of coffee—cream and sugar, if you don't mind."

"Comin' right up." Unlike Kim, who normally worked the mid-morning shift, Rhonda didn't curl her eyebrows at his order, just bent at the waist, yanked out the trays, and plucked the fattest croissant of the bunch.

She rubbed at her knee as she shunted the pastry tray back into the case like a bull into a rodeo shoot. "Figured you'd put on a few pounds by now with all the sweets you been eatin'," Rhonda said as she shook open a pastry sack and dunked the sugary lump in. "But every time I see ya, looks like you're wastin' away. Must be all the stress." The café manager hacked another cough into the crook of her elbow before dropping the sack on the counter in a gust of burned menthol. "This whole rabid animal business getting to ya, Sheriff?"

Roger flinched, his indigestion warming to heartburn. "Undersheriff," he muttered as the woman turned and lumbered to the coffee carafes, poured sludge into a cardboard cup.

Rhonda cracked her neck as she chased the drip with a glug of half-and-half. "What's that?"

"Not sheriff yet." He pulled his wallet from his back pocket and spoke loud enough for the woman to hear over her own wheezing.

Twenty-four hours still waited between Roger and his new title—the black-and-white-checkered flag at the end of the longest lap he'd run since the academy. Putting on the sheriff's badge would be the highlight of Roger's career, but the promotion followed his single greatest dereliction of duty, and came with one he hadn't anticipated.

Didn't want.

"As good as," she said, waving away his dollar fifty. "Half the folks 'round here were waitin' for Johnson to bite the dust. Betcha the other half was hopin' they'd be the one to put his face in the dirt."

Buck's *face*. The burn in Roger's chest spread to his ears. He could still hear the wet, sucking sounds of the body inside Buck Johnson's cruiser—a body without its insides, without its face. Moving when it shouldn't. The Timex on Roger's wrist pulled like an anchor, stretching the leftovers of last month's pain through his arm. By the time he had found Johnson's car parked out at mile-marker seven, all that remained of the man who'd policed this town for the last five decades was a puddle of meat—a sludge of gray and red and purple dripping down from his open head, pooling between busted gums and broken teeth.

"*Tay-lor.*" The ruined Johnson-thing had said Roger's name.

The old sheriff had been a grade-A shit, but nobody deserved to die like he did. If the nightmares weren't responsible for the reduction in Roger's waistline, then the acid reflux certainly was. All those nights, lying awake in his bed, wondering what might have gone different if Roger would have remembered to reload his gun after he'd pumped the man full of lead and gunpowder.

A cream-cheese croissant and hot coffee were the last things Roger wanted now, but he picked them up. If Lenore took his advice and hired Kim out from under Jimbo, he might need to find a new watering hole.

"Here, take these to that young deputy of yours." Rhonda folded a pastry box into submission, then loaded it with plastic-wrapped dough-nuts from behind the counter. "They're day-olds, but still good for dunkin'," she said, and foisted the box over the case. "Help keep you boys in good spirits while you track down that ghost wolf the paper's been talkin' about."

Ghost wolves. Roger's eye twitched and he fought not to look at the bright pink MISSING PET flyer tacked to the café's bulletin board. Nor-mally rabid animals would be Animal Control's problem, but the whole town had gone on red alert over this elusive critter that Lenore con-vinced him to blame for last month's attacks. The station's phone hadn't stopped ringing since.

"That's what they say," he said.

"Well, I hope y'all catch it before . . ." Rhonda's reddened eyes flicked to the bright pink flyer with the collared kitten wearing its silver bell. "Well, before."

It took Roger a minute to swallow the lump in his throat. His eye twitched again, and he hitched up his pants.

"I do, too," he said.

He tried to leave the café without the day-olds, but Rhonda coughed until he stuffed the box under his good arm.

Might as well. Pastries were pretty much all he had left anyhow.

Roger shoveled down one of the day-old doughnuts to clear out the bitter clinging to the back of his throat as he settled back behind the wheel of his patrol car. The radio in his center console sparked to life the second he took a drag from the cardboard coffee cup to wash the dry pastry down.

Dispatch Darla's voice crackled over the small speaker. "Come in, Taylor."

Goose bumps prickled across the wound on Roger's forearm. Blisters still marked his skin from the morning Darla had radioed in a situation at 5445 Garner, just like his tire tread still streaked the parking lot pavement at Jimbo's Java Café.

Roger made sure to swallow his mouthful of coffee along with his déjà vu before radioing back. "Taylor here."

A brush of static, then, "Penny Boudreaux is in the station."

For the love of—Roger set the box on the passenger seat, dug in the sack, and bit off a wad of cream cheese and flaky pastry. He swallowed before his brain could register the sugar, and pushed his head against the headrest. It would have looked better if he'd stayed at the school, paid his respects, he knew that. But Roger's attendance would have put a bull's-eye on his back. If the media didn't chew him down to a stump, the darts shooting from Brett Haney's eyes would have reduced him to ashes by the time the dismissal bell rang.

Haney was busy with a grieving wife to comfort, a daughter to mourn, but the reporter from Houston was a dog with a bone. No wonder she'd tracked him back to the station.

Lord help me. Roger had guessed a woman would be the death of him, but he had zero interest in being eaten alive by one the likes of Penny Boudreaux.

"Better get back quick," Darla crackled. "She's in here with her knickers in a twist, and Hinson is in over his head."

"Tell Hinson to keep his mouth shut." Roger pushed the pastry aside with his tongue as he strapped his seat belt on and tossed his new hat on the dash. "Only one speaks press is me," he managed around the sweet mass in his mouth.

"I'm Dispatch, not a babysitter." Darla's tone cut across the line rougher than the static. "But I'll do what I can to hold her off."

Roger slung the cruiser into drive and stomped the gas, tracing the tread marks his tires had burned into the pavement the day he'd gotten the call about Snow Leger, mutilated in her own living room. Other than a tongue and an index finger, they'd never found the rest of the beautician.

And they won't. Roger had watched Lenore Evans feed Snow's body to the fire in the funeral parlor crematorium. Snow first, then Clyde Halloran and Widow Milner, Andy West. Nobody much cared what became of the town drunk, but it was only a matter of time before Petunia Milner teamed up with Penny Boudreaux and the Haneys, barreled down Roger's throat about what happened to her mother. He'd struggled to stand up to Petunia, after her mother had been the only strigoi he'd managed to stop. Lucky for him, Tanya West was a few screws short of a hardware store, otherwise Roger would have two sets of parents wanting answers.

But there'd been someone else, someone first, hadn't there? Hell. Roger swallowed, thumbing croissant crumbs off his chin. He'd damn near forgotten about Ed Boone.

The Channel Six news van sat parked in the sheriff's department lot when Roger pulled his Crown Vic in. He pushed open the driver's side door just as a muffler rumbled past. Roger held his breath until Brett Haney's rusty Ford turned the corner and disappeared around the bend. Then he let out a deep sigh, reached for his uniform hat and the Jimbo's day-olds. The pain in his arm flared up when he cradled the pastry box, and he marched for the station.

Leaned over the dispatch counter, Deputy Brandon Hinson jumped to attention when Roger dropped the day-olds on Darla's desk. Over the rookie's shoulder, behind the small cluster of desks that waited beyond Dispatch, Penny Boudreaux's teased blond hair gleamed under the fluorescents inside the sheriff's office. Seated in one of the visitor's chairs, the reporter sat with a notepad in her lap, ballpoint pen poised in her fingertips, but with no cameraman over her shoulder this time.

Darla pushed the pastry box away with her pencil. "Says she's finishing up her story on the Forest Park High assembly," she said. "Looking for a sound bite from the new sheriff to cap it off."

"So you stuck her in the sheriff's *office?*" Roger grunted as he hitched up his pants. "Tell her to come back tomorrow."

The younger deputy's eyebrows pulled together, but Roger didn't have time to explain the finer points of the sheriff's department succession procedure while Penny Boudreaux waited to tear him apart in a dead man's office.

Roger stepped out of the frying pan and into the fire. "Ms. Boudreaux," he said.

"Undersheriff Taylor."

The reporter didn't stand when Roger pulled the door shut and slid behind Buck's desk, but she did take her time crossing her legs at the knee.

"Something I can do for you this morning?" he asked, and pressed his own knee against the desk's metal drawer.

Penny leaned forward until her blouse gaped open, but Roger's mama raised him better than to look down a lady's shirt, even—especially—when she wanted him to.

"The next of kin aren't the only ones who have questions, Undersheriff Taylor," she said. "Tanya West missed the memorial assembly this morning at Forest Park."

Sweat beaded under Roger's hat, and he tossed it between them on his desk, using his forearm to blot his wet forehead while the drawer thrummed against his knee. Maybe he shouldn't have closed the door. The silver strands waving from the ceiling corner proved air flowed through the vent, but Roger would put money on it blowing out hot air instead of cold. All these years, and he'd thought it was the old sheriff's temperament that kept him so fired up.

Maybe old Buck Johnson had just been too damn hot.

The reporter tapped her pen against her notepad. If she was looking for a sheriff's note to excuse the boy's mother from attendance, then she was barking up the wrong tree.

"I'm happy to swing by the West residence for a wellness check," Roger said, "but other than that, there's nothing new to tell you, Ms. Boudreaux. The investigation is ongoing, and when the sheriff's department has an update, we'll be sure you're the first to know."

Penny clicked her ballpoint through the canned rebuttal. "People won't sit by without answers forever." She referred to the notes on her pad. "Seven dead, two missing—"

"And as both myself and Chief Medical Examiner Quigg have said on record, all victims of rabid animal attacks." Roger resisted the urge to wipe another line of sweat slipping down the edge of his ear, to open the desk drawer, touch his old hat in its evidence bag. "Sometimes tragedies are just tragedies," he said. "Not conspiracies."

"And that's your official response, Undersheriff Taylor?" She bit the words off one at a time through perfect white teeth.

"Yes, ma'am."

The reporter chewed cherry-red lipstick onto those pearly whites as she scribbled down his quote.

Roger's gaze wandered to the glass pane in the office door. He watched as Dispatch Darla picked up her telephone receiver. Listened for a moment before her face went pale and she motioned to Hinson, then sent the call to his desk. Roger recognized the sickly green pallor that washed over the young deputy's face—the slight bend in his jaw when he returned the phone to its cradle and made eye contact through the glass.

Last time he'd seen the boy that green around the edges was on Snow Leger's back porch.

Roger kept his eyes locked on the rookie. Prayed that Hinson could read the warning in his eyes. *Do not open the door, do not repeat whatever just came across the other end of that phone line.*

But Hinson was already walking toward the sheriff's office.

The reporter's pen didn't stop when the boy pushed the office door open.

"Taylor," he said, "I mean, Sheriff—"

The words sloshed around on Hinson's tongue, and Roger knew he'd eaten his last pastry. Penny Boudreaux caught the look in his eye and didn't turn toward the deputy when he spoke.

"We've got another body."

CHAPTER 5

Lenore Evans

The figure under the white sheet on the metal examination table in the Evans Funeral Parlor laboratory belonged to Mrs. Viola Rose Carroll—or at least it had, until this past Thursday. A retired schoolteacher, Mrs. Carroll had passed half the town's children through her classroom during her tenure at Sallie Howell Elementary. She'd hugged her way through enough temper tantrums, runny noses, and school-board politics to earn her way halfway to sainthood by her retirement party two summers ago, and in all that time Mrs. Carroll had remained loyal to two things: quality public education and good old-fashioned Southern cooking—both of which led to her meeting her end over a tub of pimento cheese in the Market Basket dairy aisle.

"She was shopping for a teacher's bruncheon," Wilmer Carroll had told Lenore when she called to discuss his wife's arrangements, while Quigg's new hire hummed under his breath and struggled to get the woman's gurney out of the van. "I told her all that extra stress and cholesterol was bad for her—doctor kept on her about her heart—but Viola wouldn't hear it. I've won one argument in forty years of marriage," he'd added. "A crying shame it's this one."

In the end, he'd promised to bring over a dress and some other personal effects—Viola's purse and makeup, a fresh wig in her trademark bouffant style.

"But not her wedding ring," Wilmer was clear to say. "I'd like to hold on to that till the service."

Funny what people find important, Lenore thought as she studied the thin sheen of pimento cheese crusted into the wispy silver strands that coiled like smoke rings from the woman's head. Quigg had done a fair job scrubbing most of the stuff out, but the cheddar's high acid content left a telltale stain on aged, porous skin. In the Sallie Howell staff photo clipped to the coroner's paperwork, Mrs. Carroll wore pencil-thin eyebrows and cat-eye liner, half-moon readers, and an appliquéd denim vest patched over with Red Delicious apples and colorful school supplies. Now, under the crisp white linen, it was almost impossible to tell the woman's skin from the stark silver of the examination table.

"She looks so different," Quigg's delivery boy said as Lenore set the dead schoolteacher's head in the headrest. "How do you get her, I mean *them*, to—" Daniel zipped the empty body bag on top of the gurney, then handed the coroner's office clipboard to Lenore, and waved a latex-gloved hand over what used to be Mrs. Carroll. "You know," he said, "look like they did when they were alive?"

His eyes burned into the top of Lenore's head, but she looked at the body, not at the boy. Most of Quigg's assistants were more muscle than small talk, but the new hire's hands tapped out a beat against his thighs while he waited for an answer. Once he'd gotten the gurney's legs free of the van's rear bumper, the boy had done well enough schlepping it from the van to the lab, but he'd started to fidget when it'd come time to transfer Mrs. Carroll's remains from tray to table.

Lenore rolled her shoulders, trying to shake loose the pinch still clinging to her spine. "A little bit of time and a lot of patience," she told the boy, and crooked the clipboard into her arm to sign her name on the designated line. "We want family members to be able to say good-bye to their loved ones, not to someone they don't recognize."

She scratched the date beside her signature, feeling every pen stroke in her joints, and looked at the dead woman's picture. Wilmer Carroll would be by later with a fresh wig and burial clothes, but while Lenore could bathe and dress the woman, there was little chance she'd be able to re-create Mrs. Carroll's signature makeup.

Truth be told, Lenore was much better with paperwork than with the bodies.

The key to the grandfather clock hung heavy against her thigh. *You're much better at paperwork than a lot of things,* she thought.

Lenore forced her lips into a thin smile and thrust the clipboard out for the boy. He traded it for the yellow tag clutched in his fingers, but didn't ask any follow-up questions when the bell to the front door chimed.

Time to get that dreadful interview over with. Even though she had no real intention of hiring Kim Cole, Lenore had to go through the motions. She did need the help, but more than that, she needed to get Roger Taylor off her back. After that first Godawful Mess, old Sheriff Johnson had been content to despise the Evans women from a distance. But at least Buck had left them to their business, stayed out of their hair. If his actions over the past few weeks were any indication, Roger Taylor meant to stay firmly connected to what remained of the Evans family now that history had repeated itself.

Lenore clutched the coroner's tag in her hand. She left Mrs. Carroll's body on the metal exam table as Daniel followed her down the hallway.

In the Evans Funeral Parlor lobby, a young woman squatted just inside the parlor's front doors, her coffin-shaped purse laid to rest on the carpet beside her black combat boots as she scratched Belle behind the ears. The dog's gaze stayed fixed on the other side of the glass, on Ducey's old Rambler, the budding rosebush and the mount of dirt, but her tail twitched when Kim stroked her snout.

"She must remember you," Lenore managed around the ache in her spine.

"I'm glad she does." Kim pushed up on her boots and turned black-rimmed eyes to Lenore, then to Daniel, fingers tapping against the clipboard clamped in his hands. Lipstick almost as dark as her finger-nails stained her mouth purple. Thick with mascara, her lashes brushed against her cheeks under heavy-lidded eyes.

"It's nice to see you again, Ms. Evans," Kim said.

Lenore felt herself go thin. She'd last seen the girl when she and Ducey had brought Belle into the parlor. Kim had found Sheriff Buck Johnson's wounded coonhound bleeding out in an alley, and Ducey had found them both, saw fit to bring them in. Together Ducey and Kim had wrapped the dog in an old bedsheet, and by the time they'd gotten her on the exam table, Belle had already bled halfway out. The Evans women had had to kick Kim out to apply ash salve to the strigoi bite on the dog's hindquarters, but before that the girl had stayed through the blood and the mess and hadn't blinked.

If it hadn't been for that, Lenore would never have agreed to the interview, beauty-school classes and Roger Taylor be damned. Just because the girl's aesthetic suggested she knew her way around a funeral home didn't mean Kim had any idea what went on inside its walls. The Coles were kin to the Hallorans, and Clyde Halloran—or the thing he'd become, anyway—had been the one to tear open Ducey's throat.

Lenore rolled her neck, cracked out a twinge, and Kim shouldered her coffin-purse and pointed toward the parking lot.

"It looks like someone dug up one of your flowerbeds," she drawled. "There's some loose dirt out there by, um . . ."

"Grace," Lenore finished for her. "It's fine," she said, and made a mental note to speak with Roger about cleaning up after himself. She appreciated that the man tended her daughter's grave, but not so much that she'd put up with a bunch of misplaced dirt to deal with on top of everything else. If this weather didn't cool down soon, what was left of the white rosebush might turn to dust. Already half the rhododendron's leaves had begun to curl. "Just had some new flowers planted this morning."

Kim curled her lips under her teeth and said nothing as Daniel quirked a nod at Lenore, then stepped over Belle's long, rust-colored ears. All the way to the bottoms of her feet, Lenore felt the way these two kids exchanged a glance as he made his way through the front doors.

Box-blackened hair brushed the tops of Kim's shoulders when music thumped out of the coroner's van, and she turned to catch Lenore's stare. "We went to school together."

The pinch pulled in Lenore's neck. She didn't have the energy to worry about how the two knew one another. In this town, it'd be more surprising if they didn't.

She began the interview with a quick tour of the lobby. "Hair and makeup isn't exactly a full-time job in the funeral business, not in a small town like ours," Lenore said as she guided the girl through the parlor's administrative areas—the visitor restrooms, the reception room. "There are many other tasks we undertake to care for those who've passed and their family and friends, and everyone helps out where they can."

"That's no problem." Kim trailed Lenore into the chapel. She stopped at the chancel, grunted at the pews, the stained-glass window pouring in midmorning sun. "I mostly worked the front counter at Jimbo's," she said, "but I also had to make sure things stayed stocked and clean, handle vendor orders, that sort of thing."

Lenore pulled the key from her pocket. She wound the grandfather clock against the chapel's back wall until the ache in her fingers made her quit.

"Many decedents make their funeral arrangements ahead of time." Lenore propped one half of the chapel's double doors open behind them as she led the girl into the selection room. She gestured at the shelves of urns, fingers stabbing as she described her way down the line. "For those who choose cremation, we offer options that range from the simple plastic boxes to custom enamel pots, cast bronze vessels," she said. "For more traditional burials, we have a similar range of choices, from pine boxes to caskets—" Lenore's eyes dropped to the purse swinging at Kim's side. "And the occasional coffin."

The girl bit back a purple smile as Lenore guided her to the lobby.

From here, only two pathways remained: to the laboratory, with its full coolers and the body waiting on the table, or to the doors, where Belle still waited in front of the glass, tail straight behind her as she stared ahead in a ray of September sun.

Kim crooked her head. "Does she always lay at the door like that?"

Did she? Hard to say for sure, with how busy Lenore had been since Belle joined the family. She shook the pinch from her head. "Half the time she's under my feet while I work," she said. "But I guess she needed some sunlight today."

Kim bit her lip, chewing at the purple crust in the corners, while Lenore fingered the clock key in her pocket. She'd done what Roger asked—brought the girl in, gave her a chance. She felt no more obligation.

But Ducey had also brought the girl to the parlor, and Ducey didn't bring outsiders around lightly.

"Why did you apply for a job at a funeral parlor?" Lenore hoped her voice came out pleasant and not accusatory. "Surely Jimbo's is a more . . . lively environment."

The girl flushed, pink erupting in her pale cheeks like fireworks. "It was Ducey's idea, sort of."

Lenore's eyebrows pushed against her hairline.

"The day we found Belle," Kim said, "I'd been having a rough time at school, you know? Hard to get teachers to believe that you can make people look their best when they don't approve of your personal style."

Lenore kept her attention on the girl's words and not her all-black garb, her coffin-purse. Cosmetology students practiced on guests willing to take a chance on a student in exchange for a tip, but even the promise of free service might not be enough to convince a West End type to risk coming out dolled up like Elvira.

Poor Snow Leger would roll over in her grave at the thought. Mina Jean Murphy, too.

"Anyway," Kim continued, "Ducey told me that the living aren't the only ones who need to be beautiful, and that maybe I needed a different sort of clientele." A hitch crept into the girl's voice, prickling behind Lenore's eyes. "She said not to let anyone take me away from me, because at the end of the day, that's all I have—just me. Besides—" Kim shrugged. "I don't have much of a sweet tooth."

"I see." Lenore blinked back unexpected tears. Ducey hadn't been one for mushy business, but she'd known how to cut straight to the chase and tell people what they needed to hear. "Well, let's take you to the lab and see what you can do."

Had she inherited some of her mother's recklessness after all? The words were out of Lenore's mouth before she realized she'd spoken them.

Down the hallway, past the breakroom with its quiet television and empty armchair, Lenore pointed to the wide door at the back of the parlor. "That's where bodies are brought in when they're delivered from the coroner's office," she said, then added, "Your friend Daniel."

She gestured toward the lab. "And this is where they're prepared for burial—or cremation, depending on the deceased's wishes."

Kim's eyes swept the room as she stepped in—the shelves, the coolers, the adjoining door into the chapel. "Like embalming and stuff?"

"We do not embalm at Evans Funeral Parlor." The pinch inched down to crawl between Lenore's ribs again. "We respect the dead even in death," she said. "Embalming is a distasteful and unnecessary business."

Kim eyeballed the sterile space. "If you don't embalm," she asked, "how come there's a drain on the floor?"

Lenore pursed her lips. Perhaps she should have stuck to her guns, pushed the girl out the door when she had the chance instead of bringing her back to the lab a second time. Working with her to stop Belle's bleeding was one thing, but watching the strange girl scrutinize the Evanses' most private space tweezed between Lenore's shoulder blades worse than the phantom pinch.

"I assure you," she said, dryly. "Death can be messy."

Kim nodded, then pointed at a long metal spike laid on the lab's bookshelves. "I've seen one of those before," she said. "Ducey kept one in her apron, but hers was smaller, I think."

Lenore padded over to the shelf and picked up the instrument. "This is an adult trocar," she explained, balancing the long metal needle between her fingers. "Ducey carried an infant trocar—easier to fit in her apron pockets, I suppose."

She twisted the tool's pointed awl in Kim's direction, then presented the suction-topped handle at the other end. "The trocar is used to puncture organs and drain fluids through this hollow tube." Lenore mimed the use of the tool above the linen-draped body as she narrated. "Small incisions are made, the trocar inserted, and fluid sucked out," she said. "Embalmers use those same punctures to insert fluid as well."

"But you don't embalm at Evans," Kim said.

Lenore set the trocar back in its place. "Correct."

The girl's black-rimmed eyes stayed on the tool as she bit her lip, and Lenore let her hands fall to the examination table, to the crisp white sheet, the body underneath. She pulled the sheet back to expose the dead woman's head and shoulders. "And this is—"

"Mrs. Carroll," Kim finished for her. "She was my kindergarten teacher. Daniel's, too." The girl fingered the strap of her purse. "She collected little clown figurines."

Something fluttered in Lenore's chest. She'd dismissed the boy's questions without considering that he would have known the deceased, but of course he would, in a town this size. The girl, too, she realized. So focused on finding reasons to tell Roger she'd turned Kim down, Lenore had barely given the girl a chance to prove herself. It took a certain kind to both remember her kindergarten teacher's collectibles and not bat an eye when she saw the woman's corpse laid out on a funeral parlor table.

The kind that should dedicate themselves to caring for the dead.

If Lenore could keep the restless ones at bay.

Her eyes dropped to the body. She'd only taken a cursory look before, but in addition to the ocher stain at the woman's hairline, bruises had bloomed around Mrs. Carroll's nose, under her eyes. Her jaw twisted to the side, leaving her mouth agape, and already her eyeballs had sunk. The poor dear must have hit the floor hard when she fell.

Luckily just the cheese container came open, Lenore thought, then wished she hadn't.

She pulled an instrument tray to the side of the table and snapped latex gloves over her hands. She massaged the dead woman's face, her neck, her shoulders to loosen the rigor. She watched Kim to see if the girl spooked when she inserted caps to shape the dead woman's eyes, or threaded a needle to sew her lips closed.

Kim didn't.

"We do our best to use the least invasive techniques possible as we prepare the deceased for burial," Lenore explained, as she pushed the long, curved needle downward behind the dead woman's bottom teeth, through her chin, and back up the way she'd come. "Wax is the preferred method to keep a decedent's mouth closed." She pulled the jaw up, then pushed the needle through the upper lip, the nostril, the septum. "But sometimes the deceased has an injury or deterioration that requires a little additional support, so we use sutures to keep the mouth closed."

Kim watched, enrapt, as Lenore pulled the jaw shut and tied the string, then used Vaseline to seal the string between the dead woman's lips.

"If the deceased underwent major trauma or sickness that left bruising, wounds, or other deformities, it will require special makeup and other special techniques," Lenore continued, peeling off her gloves to fetch Grace's red vanity case from the counter. "Some are rather unsavory," she added as she set the case in from of Kim.

"Wax, wire, cardboard," the girl listed. "That sort of thing."

Lenore quirked an eyebrow.

"We covered some of that in my desairology class." Kim's voice dropped as she stepped closer to the table. She fingered its metal edge while Lenore wiped down the dead woman's face with a damp cloth. "Working with mortuary cosmetics is different than commercial products meant for living skin," Kim said.

She tucked a swatch of dark hair behind her ear, just like Grace used to do, and this morning's pinch found its way to Lenore's heart when the girl bent at the waist to take a closer look at the dead woman's complexion.

"Thermogenic makeup is for live skin so my usual kit won't be much use," Kim went on, standing to rummage through the red cosmetics case. She lifted out the scissors, her eyebrows scrunching as she studied the tool, then cast it aside. "Body heat breaks thermogenic stuff down, so it applies properly. On dead skin, that makeup crumbles or blots, so it's better to use nonthermogenic makeup." She selected a shade from Grace's kit, held it against Mrs. Carroll's cheek, and looked to Lenore before applying the cream first to a brush, then padding the bristles to the skin.

"Is that jaundice?" Kim asked when she noticed the stain at the woman's forehead.

Lenore shook her head. "Cheese."

Kim bit her lip to one side as she leaned in to study the orangey smear, then reached back into the kit, mixed a few shades together with her fingertips, and concealed the blemish.

The pinch bit into Lenore's shoulder blades for the second time that morning. Sliced in deeper when the girl traced the cheese stain into Mrs. Carroll's hairline.

"Death affects hair, too," Kim said. "Hair is protein, so you need a water-based product to clean and color, if needed." Her fingers lingered on the sharp edge of a pair of sewing scissors before she plucked a comb from Grace's case.

It took every last bit of nerve Lenore had, but she hired Kim Cole on the spot and told her to be there Wednesday morning at ten a.m. sharp.

Belle tried to squeeze herself through the door when Lenore left Mrs. Carroll on the table and saw Kim out, but Lenore lifted a loafer and shepherded the hound back inside the lobby. Together they watched through the glass as Kim's mint-green Buick pulled out of the lot. Belle's eyes stayed locked on the dying rhododendrons outside, rusty snout twitching, while Lenore's caught on the fresh rosebuds on her mother's grave, the mount of dirt over her daughter's.

The trail of dirt on the asphalt that Kim had pointed out alongside Ducey's Rambler.

Lenore would have to talk to Roger Taylor about his gardening.

The grandfather clock in the chapel beat out its afternoon chime, and the clock key hung heavy in her slacks pocket. "Still too much to do and not enough time to do it," she muttered. "Come on, Belle. Let's finish up in the lab."

Just like this morning, the hound didn't budge when Lenore turned. She didn't lift a rust-colored ear as Lenore patted her leg and called again.

"Suit yourself," Lenore said, but Belle's tail stuck straight out behind her stiff legs. She stared out the front door, whimpering as a soft knocking sounded on the funeral parlor's back door.

When the hinges squeaked as the back door pushed open, Lenore craned to see the parking lot on the other side of the front glass.

Roger must have needed to be somewhere else, to drop Luna after school and not come in.

Or come take another pass at Grace's unblooming mount of dirt.

"Luna?" Belle began to whine as Lenore made her way past the chapel doors and down the hallway.

The knocking grew into the shuffle of footsteps, and the short hairs on the back of Lenore's neck raised as she passed the empty selection room, the empty breakroom. "That you, Luna, honey?" she called.

In place of an answer, a knock sounded inside the lab, followed by the sharp clang of metal hitting the linoleum floor. Lenore turned to face the door. "Luna?"

She inched down the hallway, and wrapped her palm around the doorknob to the lab.

Inside, another knock, followed by the raspy sound of a throat that shouldn't work trying to form a name on its lips.

Back in the lobby, Belle began to bark.

CHAPTER 6

Deputy Brandon Hinson

Puke churned in the base of Deputy Brandon Hinson's gut.

Fizzed up his throat.

Pushed against his tongue.

Another whiff of offal, and the muck in Brandon's mouth swelled thick enough to chew, but he forced it back and tried not to look at the animal turned inside out on Farm Road 121.

Don't throw up, Brandon ordered himself. Puking on Snow Leger's back porch a month ago was the last time he planned on emptying his stomach at a crime scene. 'Course, he had hoped that would be the last time he'd sit on a vic's front porch, turning his lungs black with the stench of death, and had prayed he'd forget the sound his boots made on the woman's blood-drenched carpet. They'd found milk burned dry on Snow's stove, a reminder scribbled on the dining table beside her purse, but all they'd ever found of the beautician herself was her tongue, left right there in the middle of the living room floor.

Not the only thing, Brandon remembered. They'd found Snow's manicured finger buried deep inside Alison Haney's intestines.

And they'd found Alison Haney just like Frank McCormack found his prized Angus heifer: split open and spilled out.

Snow's death, like Alison's, had been officially ruled the work of a rabid animal. Maybe one of the ghost wolves spotted along the Gulf. Maybe not. Either way, if a finger turned up inside the remains of the farmer's dead cow, there'd be no blaming this kill on an animal, rabid or otherwise.

Let's see Taylor shake Penny Boudreaux then, Brandon thought, then felt guilty for thinking it. He'd joined the force to protect and serve, and that required him to respect the chain of command, not play politics.

Not to take calls on mutilated livestock and missing pets, either.

Probably, he shouldn't have hung up with McCormack and shot out of the sheriff's department while Penny Boudreaux still had Taylor trapped in what used to be Johnson's office. Probably, former all-star quarterback Brandon "Chuck" Hinson should have called an audible, let Taylor carry the ball as his captain, and gotten here for the pass instead.

But he'd shirked the chain of command and now it was just him, Frank McCormack, and poor, dead Myrtle.

"I've had my fair share of livestock killed off by coyotes, the occasional wolf," the old rancher muttered at Brandon's side. He toed his cowboy boot against the carcass while his fingers fumbled in his breast pocket. "But I ain't never seen one take down a full-grown heifer before."

Frank clenched a strip of jerky from his pocket in his teeth. Ripped it in half.

Brandon forced down a gulp of sour fluid. He may have won the burger-binge challenge at academy graduation, but the thought of ever swallowing another bite of beef filled his mouth with sludge. Still, if he'd been able to pretend the blood spilled out of Alison Haney's body was motor oil, the girl's mangled corpse some haunted-house prop, then he could damn sure hold his liquids over one dead cow.

If it weren't for the smell.

He pulled his notebook from his back pocket, flipped it open, uncapped the pen—with his fingers, not his teeth—and forced himself to look at the carcass at his feet. He held his breath when he spoke. Bad enough he had to smell the death, he didn't want to taste it, too.

"Dispatch says you found her earlier today?" he asked the rancher.

Still gnawing, Frank grunted in the affirmative. "Figure it musta happened in the wee hours."

Brandon's pen bled onto the paper. He sipped in rancid air, swallowed it. "Could you be more specific?"

The old farmer swished his meat cud behind closed lips and mulled

the question over. "Reckon sometime between midnight and dawn."
He choked on a bit of jerky and spit out a wad of brown that landed
too close to the ravaged bovine. "Got a good crop of maggots already.
About ten hours' worth, I'd say."

"Perfect." Wee hours and a population of maggots to measure the
time of death. At least when Taylor fussed about the time Brandon
wrote into his report, he could say he'd quoted the rancher directly.

"Never heard a single sound," Frank said. "Usually there'd be a racket,
ya know. Coyotes screechin', cattle screamin'." He ripped free another
piece of jerky. "Don't know what sort of rabid coyote-wolf-whatever
managed this, but it musta been a big 'un."

Frank spit out a second wad and Brandon closed his eyes before he
could see where it went.

He couldn't block out the sound, though, when the soggy mass hit
gravel.

So long, lunch dates at the Green Frog, he told himself. Not that he'd
had much of an appetite lately. He still saw the poor teenaged girl
turned into so much meat every time he gazed out the diner window.

But those dates were probably a thing of the past regardless—
mostly were already, with the way things had been going, and would be
for certain, if Lenore Evans hired Kim. He'd played along with Kim's
fascination with all things dark and macabre, her horror movie obses-
sion, the dark makeup, but why his girlfriend wanted to quit her job at
the café to go paint faces on dead bodies at the funeral parlor, Brandon
couldn't say. What she found so appealing about the Evans women, a
complete mystery.

Then again, maybe she'd learn something about why Sheriff Buck
Johnson had hated Ducey Evans and her brood so much.

But Ducey was dead now and so was Johnson. Brandon Hinson,
for his part, inhaled the mangled remains of an eight-hundred-pound
cow, and after twenty-two years of dedicated carnivorism, by the time
he exhaled, he'd become a vegetarian.

He spat the taste of dead cow off his lips as Quigg's white coroner
van pulled up, Roger Taylor's patrol car right behind it. No lights, no
sirens.

Quiet, Brandon thought. Just the way Taylor wanted to keep it. Like Johnson had, too.

A woman slid out of the passenger side of Quigg's van. For half a second, Brandon thought the reporter from Houston had finagled herself a ride with the old lip-licker, but then he noticed the woman's athletic build, her messy strawberry ponytail, horn-rimmed glasses. She walked ahead of Quigg and barely looked at Taylor or Brandon.

She only had eyes for Myrtle the Cow.

Brandon had gone steady with Kim for four years, but he stood a little straighter when the pretty redhead arrived at his side before the other men caught up.

Frank's eyes widened, but he swallowed the lump he'd been chewing. "Ma'am."

The woman didn't return the welcome. She pushed her glasses up her nose and squatted by the animal, careful to keep her patent-black Mary Janes out of the fluid ring that stained the gravel. She pulled a handkerchief from her jeans pocket and held it over her nose as she inched closer to poke at the animal with a long metal wand.

Quigg licked out a greeting. "Boys, allow me to introduce you to Professor Corinne Bennick," he said, gesturing to the woman as she put away her wand and murmured into a handheld tape recorder. "She's a biology researcher from the university," Quigg said, "leading expert on wolves."

Taylor pulled off his hat. Maybe Brandon imagined it, but the senior officer looked a bit redder now than he had in the station. It could have been a blush, but probably it was the heat. October would be here by the end of the week, but the temperatures still clung to summer for dear life.

"Need someone to sign off on bringing a civ to a crime scene," Taylor told the coroner, then nodded at the rancher. "Mac."

The rancher tipped his hat. "Roger."

"Crime scene?" the old coroner asked, eyebrow so high it brushed against what remained of his hairline. "This is an animal attack."

Taylor's eye twitched. "Since when does the coroner's office take an interest in animal attacks?" he asked.

Quigg's eyes wandered to the dead animal. When he licked his lips, Brandon couldn't be sure if it was his regular habit, or his interest in the heifer's remains. "I'd say about the same time the sheriff's department did," the coroner said, then jerked his thumb to the professor as she pulled herself away from the cow. "And I called in my own backup for this one."

The professor handed her business card to Taylor and instructed everyone to call her by her first name. Brandon tried not to notice the cute pattern of freckles across her cheeks, how the dots framed the edges of her eyes. "Good thing your dispatcher knows who to alert when something like this comes in," she said. "This is the kind of field-work we don't get a lot of in academia."

Brandon's stomach lurched. The good professor might consider the mess good for science, but it sure wasn't the sort of fieldwork he'd looked forward to when he'd joined the force.

Taylor glared at Corinne, at Quigg, until the old man licked his lips. "Insurance needs a signature for cause of death," the coroner told the soon-to-be sheriff. "Ol' Myrtle's death comes with a dollar amount attached."

"She's worth a pretty penny," Frank added.

Roger grunted. "Fair enough."

"You boys going to come take a look at this, or stand around jabber-jawing all day like a bunch of schoolgirls?" The professor's voice cut through the small distance. She waved them over, and Brandon felt his feet move before he realized he'd accepted the woman's summons. He'd never been one to refuse a pretty girl.

But he could taste the cow.

What the killer had left of her, anyway.

Myrtle's hind legs and tail stretched behind her. Her front legs and head stuck out the other end. Other than a couple of bones, a splash of red, and a few scraps of ligament, nothing connected the heifer's back half to her front.

"The organs are gone," the professor narrated into her tape recorder as she pushed back onto her haunches, pointing at the cow's rib cage, green grass visible through the slats of stark white bone. "The muscle, even a little bit of bone, all the hide." Corinne stood, one hand on a hip and the other raising the recorder up as a makeshift visor to block the sun. "Stomach, too," she said, scanning the area, the blood, the muck, for God knows what. "And its contents."

Taylor beat Brandon to the punch. "That unusual for a wolf kill?" he asked, looking unconvinced.

The professor leaned in for a better look. "Coyotes and wolves don't usually eat the rumen of their kills."

"Canines leave that behind," Quigg licked in. "All the grass that cattle eat don't sit well in their stomachs."

Corinne nodded. "It's actually how hunters tell a wolf kill apart from a bear."

"So maybe a bear got Myrtle, not a wolf," Brandon said. The professor shot him a look, and he held his breath and waved toward the dead cow she stood over. He'd feel better if they could identify the offending animal—and a bear could've carried a teenage boy's body away.

Could have ripped open a teenage girl with one swipe.

And leave behind a human finger?

"No bears around here," the professor said, and that was that, never mind that the supposed red wolf–coyote hybrid hadn't been seen in twenty years, either. The optimism that fluttered briefly in Brandon's chest died on impact.

With the novelty of a pretty girl worn off, Frank gnawed on another strip of jerky. "Still ain't never seen a kill like this," he managed around his mouthful. "Must be one hell of a critter to take down ol' Myrtle."

"The last known red wolves in Southwestern Louisiana and Eastern Texas were captured in 1980 to establish a captive breeding population," Corinne said, lapsing into a teacher's voice that proved she was more than just a pretty face. "The theory is that the genetics were passed down—biologically and geographically—from the wild red wolves that evaded Fish and Wildlife's dragnet in the seventies." She clicked off her tape recorder and stuffed it into her jeans pocket before adjusting her glasses and crossing both arms over her chest. "The wolves brought into the breeding program are descendants of those wolves, bred with local coyotes."

"That what turned 'em rabid?" Frank McCormack barked out around his jerky.

The professor's arms tightened, and her eyes dulled behind her lenses. "The animals bred in captivity carry genetic variants not present in any other North American canid. *That's* why they're called 'ghost' wolves," she explained, making air quotes. "The gene they carry was supposed to be extinct."

Taylor balled his hat between his hands, forcing his voice to stay firm. "Rabid or not, this animal is responsible for nine deaths—" Frank cleared his throat, making Taylor revise his count, gesturing to the cow. "Ten, if you count Myrtle," he said, turning back to the professor.

The woman shrugged. She took another look at the dead heifer and her lips twisted to the side. "Maybe one slipped loose," she said.

Brandon thought of all the missing-pet calls coming across the dispatch desk and remembered the rancher's earlier comment. "Big enough to take down an animal this size, Professor?"

"Corinne, please—and potentially." Corinne's freckles blurred as she shook her head, considering the question. "The hybrids did average slightly larger than either of the individual species. Might be a mutation in the strain."

Brandon's throat clenched. *Mutation* probably wasn't a good word.

"I'm no wolf expert," the coroner said, licking his lips like it was going out of style, "but could be. All the victims—the ones I got to examine, anyway—bore markings consistent with an animal attack." Fluid collected in the corners of his lips.

"Wolves kill by biting the throat, severing nerve tracks and the carotid artery," Corinne said. "Bleeds their prey out quick."

"*Snap, boom.*" Spit accompanied the coroner's sound effects.

Like Edwin Boone, Brandon thought. Taylor had ferried that body to the funeral parlor, but Brandon had read the evidence file.

"Organ meat is the first to be eaten—most all significant muscle." Corinne's finger pointed to various bits of what used to be cow as she explained. "Ribs. Bones."

Quigg must have caught the grimace that crossed Brandon's face, because he added, "These animals kill for food, son. They don't let anything go to waste."

"They will eat a tongue," Corinne said, and Brandon flinched, "but they don't touch teeth." She gestured at the animal's head, then turned to Frank. "Was she already missing any teeth?"

The look on the rancher's face said he didn't pay as much attention to Myrtle's dental hygiene as he did other parts of her, and Corinne pulled her recorder back out to mutter a note about eight sloping incisors removed from the cow's lower jaw.

Brandon gulped down another swallow of bitter fluid, let it simmer in the keg roiling in his gut. Burgers be damned. At this rate, he might not eat again. Ever.

"What about the missing people?" he asked, dodging Taylor's glare. "What you're talking about is consistent with the recovered remains, but what about the ones we didn't find?"

"Wolves left undisturbed to finish their meal won't leave much behind, if anything," Corinne said, "but they are known to hide and cache bits of their kills. It's possible those missing persons are still out there." She shrugged. "Your ghost wolf just doesn't want you to find them."

Frank grunted through his swallow. "All I know is that if I see any kind of wolf, I'm puttin' it down."

The professor whirled on him so fast her horn-rims slid down the bridge of her nose. "The genetic value of these animals alone is immeasurable," she snapped. "They need to be caught, not killed."

Taylor's mouth dropped open, probably to remind the professor that this dangerous animal had shown a taste for human blood, but a Channel Six news van crunched down Frank McCormack's gravel road and the sheriff's jaw snapped shut.

Penny Boudreaux's high-heel shoes touched ground before the van's tires came to a full stop. Impressive work on loose gravel.

"Oh, for crying out loud." Taylor strangled his hat back onto his head and jerked his thumb at Brandon. "Hinson, get her away from here."

The reporter already had her press badge around her neck. If it all turned out that Penny was the man-eater chewing through town, Brandon might not be too surprised. "She'll insist on freedom of the press," he said.

"People believe the threat has passed," Taylor fired back. He jerked a thumb at Quigg. "This one told the paper rabid animals die after a week. That reporter means to cause a frenzy, stir up hunters," he hissed. "The last thing we need is people pulling out their firearms."

Taylor nodded at Quigg and Frank, at Corinne, then he dug his fingers into the sleeve of Brandon's shirt and pulled him aside.

"Do you want to be the one to tell someone's next of kin that some trigger-happy Joe Blow mistook their toddler for a wolf?" he whispered through gritted teeth. "Because I just had to tell a set of parents that something tore their baby girl apart, and I assure you it's not as fun as you might think."

The nausea in Brandon's gut now had nothing to do with the dead cow rotting at his feet. "No, sir," he said.

"Then send her back to Houston." Taylor let go of Brandon's sleeve so hard that he pitched forward, but the look in Taylor's eyes looked more like fear than fury. "That's an order," he said.

But Penny Boudreaux's camera was already rolling.

CHAPTER 7

Luna Evans

That you, Luna, honey?"

Nana Lenore's voice echoed from inside as Luna pulled open the back door to Evans Funeral Parlor. Barking rang out from the lobby, and her grandmother appeared at the other end of the long hallway, one palm flat over her chest, the other pressed against her slacks pocket. Luna caught a glimpse of rusty snout as Belle let loose a long, guttural howl and Nana's head cocked on her shoulders.

She blinked too hard at Luna. Her voice came out too small for her wide eyes.

"Did you just get in?" Nana Lenore asked as the door sucked itself closed behind Luna's back.

"Roger didn't show up." The words pricked Luna's tongue. Bad enough that her grandmother insisted the soon-to-be sheriff chauffeur her back and forth to school. Even worse when her ride left her stranded. "I had to take—"

Belle howled again and Nana's wide eyes ripped away as her head snapped to the side. She put up a palm, cutting Luna's complaint in half. For a second, Luna thought her grandmother was listening for the school-bus brakes releasing in the distance, ready to catch her in a lie, but then the dog's howl tapered off and Luna heard it, too.

Knocking.

Luna locked eyes with her grandmother down the hallway. Any grievances—about being stood up for the ride she didn't want, about the bus full of uncomfortable glares and unfriendly seats, about the shitty first day back at school where people avoided her like the plague—evaporated. Someone else was in the funeral parlor with them.

And if Nana Lenore didn't know who it was, then it could only be one thing.

Belle's howls deepened into bays, and, with her head still turned away, Nana raised an index finger to her lips. She crooked her fingers and beckoned Luna forward.

The rubber soles of her Converses barely made a sound as Luna inched across the linoleum. Belle bayed again, the sound echoing in the blank spaces that the knocking left in Luna's chest as it pounded in time with her heart. Surprise fizzed at the back of Luna's throat as she passed the lab. She counted her steps as she peeked inside the breakroom—at the blank television screen, the stale coffee handle-high in the pot, the empty armchair. Luna let her backpack straps slide down her arms, into her palms, as she slid past the selection room with its closed caskets and empty urns.

She set the bag down against the lobby desk.

"It's in the chapel," Nana whispered under the current of Belle's howls.

Callers and knockers. Ducey had said there were two types of undead: those that called your name, and those that knocked to be let in. Luna resisted the urge to take her grandmother's hand. The past month had seen its fair share of dead bodies, but none had risen since they'd put down the strigoi the night Luna's mother and great-grandmother died.

And no restless dead slipped by Nana Lenore unnoticed.

This time, Belle's bay came long and mournful, and Luna reached down. Her fingertips brushed velvet and the dog quieted. Silence descended on the parlor—the quiet of the grave interrupted by the tick of the old grandfather clock in the chapel and the sound of undead knocking.

"Stay right next to me," Nana instructed as they moved together toward the chapel doors.

A dead woman wandered down the center aisle, her knuckles *knock, knock, knocking* against the edges of the wooden pews as she staggered toward the chancel. One of her ratty blue house slippers lost, her feet left an uneven pattern on the chapel carpet: a stamp of crepe rubber where she'd ambled into the chapel from the lab's adjoining door, a smear of muck where her bare foot circled the chancel. Her pajamas were wrinkled and worn, stained down the back like she'd lived in the two-piece set for days before she'd died—dirt and grime, the vibrant orange of Cheeto dust, the singe of cigarette burns.

With her mess of bed-matted hair, she might have been a sleepwalker, had it not been for the weird bloat in her midsection, the stiffness of her knees, her elbows.

The maggots that, even halfway down the aisle, Luna could see wriggling beneath the dead woman's skin.

A half-smoked butt tumbled from the filthy tangles around the woman's head and shoulders. It dropped to the carpet in a gust of its own ash and Nana Lenore sniffed at the mess.

The dead woman pivoted, knuckles *knock, knock, knocking* against the front pew.

Luna looked at the bloody foam that leaked from the eyes, the corners of the lips, and recognized the dead woman immediately.

"That's Tanya West," Luna told her grandmother. "Andy's mom."

The one he'd fed on. The one he'd drained so low she'd never recovered, and had died after all, then risen again, just like Mina Jean Murphy after Andy had drained her.

Sunken eyes, colorless lips.

Literally wasting away, Dillon had said.

Nana made a sound like sighing. "I'll take care of her."

Milky eyes, still dilated and already sinking into her skull, fixed on Luna, and Tanya's lips peeled back to expose a tongue turned black with death.

"Luna," Tanya said through red-stained teeth, a red-stained jaw, and that slow shuffle began again, slipper, foot, slipper, foot, as the dead woman dragged herself back down the aisle.

Knock, knock, knock.

"Poor dear," Nana Lenore muttered. She eyed the dirt on the carpet, the cigarette ash, and clicked her teeth. "We have a funeral first thing Thursday morning."

Nana Lenore stepped backward. She called Luna's name, but so did Tanya. Luna tried to follow her grandmother, but the soles of her sneakers stuck to the stain-resistant carpet.

A faint scratch of fingernail against forearm, and Luna felt her grandmother's hand fall away as her Converses inched her forward, toward the mother of the boy she'd turned—the boy she'd made into a monster.

Nana's voice behind her. "Luna, this way, honey. They're not as slow as they look."

Black unfurled from Tanya's mouth. Her tongue fell over her lips and her mouth stretched wide, the syllables of Luna's name as mottled and indistinct as the marbling on the dead woman's decaying flesh. Luna watched the lolling tongue as the skin around Tanya's mouth pulled back, exposing those red teeth.

Luna's grandmother spoke behind her, but Tanya's knocking drowned out the words, beating too loud in Luna's chest for her to hear anything else. Electricity thrummed under her skin as the dead woman staggered closer. Each step thrilled Luna, like looking over the edge of a tall building. Each knock of knuckles, like eyes kicking open underwater. The thrum became fire as adrenaline surged, and the edges of her vision blurred.

"Luna, move!"

The words snapped into place in Luna's head. She lunged away as Tanya reached for her, so close now that the red stains on her face were wine, not blood.

"Walk backward, she'll follow you." Nana Lenore's directions pulled Luna, her feet stepping toe to heel. "Come on, now—quickly."

Her name fell out of Tanya West's mouth again, and the surge under Luna's skin thinned into panic as the dead woman pitched forward.

Close, Luna let her get too close.

Andy's mom hadn't liked Luna when she'd been alive. Now her dead eyes glared and her dead lips sneered. Luna tripped over her own feet, her hands sliding over the tops of pews she hadn't realized she'd passed. Her palms hit the wall, then the grandfather clock, and before Luna could think better, she ripped open the pendulum door on the clock's midsection.

"Oh, Luna, not Pie's clock!" Nana Lenore splintered as loud as the wood when Luna wrenched the long wooden rod free.

She held the pendulum like an axe, the brass bob ready to slash downward as the dead woman lunged again, so close now that her fingernails scratched the air in front of Luna's face.

"Aim for her heart!" Her grandmother's words rang out and Luna considered the sharp end opposite the pendulum's bob. Only a few inches, the spire might be too short to penetrate deep enough.

She'd have to push hard.

Luna flipped the wooden stake in her hand, aimed the splintered end at Tanya's heart, and rammed the pendulum into the dead woman's chest until she felt the heat of blood pouring down over her hands.

Luna switched off the bedside table lamp in Nana Lenore's guest room and let her eyes adjust to the dim.

Three showers hadn't been enough to rid her skin of the reek of Tanya West's rotting blood. Luna had washed her hair with her mother's shampoo. She'd pulled on one of Grace's old pajama shirts and tucked herself between the sheets of the same wrought-iron daybed her mother had slept in as a girl. Now Luna let the paperback she'd been reading lie on her chest. She rolled her head into the pillow to inhale the linens, then stared up at the popcorn ceiling.

Had her mom counted those same kernels above her when she'd been a girl?

Had she watched the same stars through the tallow tree branches on the other side of the window?

Maybe that's where she got the idea to name me after a goddess. Maybe one night before she'd given birth and they'd moved into the apartment over the laundromat, Grace had lain pregnant in this bed, stared at the same moon, and chosen her daughter's name.

Luna rolled her head into the pillow. Maybe if she tried hard enough, pulled in enough air, maybe she could catch Grace's scent fused into the sheets.

But the only thing Luna smelled was Tide, and her mother was dead.

And now, thanks to her, so was Andy's. He'd killed her mom, and she'd killed his.

Outside, somewhere in the dark, an animal howled. The sound rolled over Luna, settling into her ears, her heart. She thought of Belle's bays of danger. Of Tanya West's knuckles knocking on the chapel pews.

Of the pendulum shaft that Luna had driven deep into the dead woman's heart.

She dog-eared her page, closed the paperback, and stared at the crackled blue cover. For all the ruminations on his vampiric condition, all the talk about right and wrong and good and evil, all his whining, the titular ghoul in this book had been made, not born.

Still, like Louis de Pointe du Lac, Luna had not wanted what she'd become, or the evil that came along with it.

She slid the novel under the comforter, then thought better and climbed out of bed to tuck the book under a jumble of clothes in the bottom drawer of her mother's childhood dresser.

Her fingers brushed the familiar wound in the wood, the two sets of initials clawed into the inside of the dresser drawer, deep in the back corner where the wood hinged together. Where young Grace had known then that Nana Lenore wouldn't see the mark.

G. E. + S. A.

Luna traced the letters, the misshapen heart that surrounded them. She didn't know her monster father's surname, but she knew her mother's handwriting, even in its crudest form—the way she lengthened the serif on her *G*, swirled the middle bar on her *E*. Without Grace alive to ask, Luna couldn't be sure the *S. A.* etched into the drawer meant her father, or some other nameless love, but she'd doodled her own initials with her crushes' enough times to know what the heart meant.

It meant that whoever those initials belonged to, Grace had loved them for real. To carve their initials into this secret space proved that she'd kept that love private.

And if Grace Evans had loved S. A., and S. A. was indeed the man buried beneath the white rosebush along the side of Evans Funeral Parlor, then maybe Samael had loved her back.

Maybe Crane was right, and Samael could love Luna as his daughter, too.

Maybe I could love him? Luna pulled a sweatshirt over the vampire's interview and shut the drawer. Then she crawled back into bed, threw the covers up over her head, and flicked her flashlight on, cracking open another of the probably useless texts she'd checked out from the school library.

Crane wanted to go back to the past because he thought that's where they'd find all the answers to Luna's future. Find how Old World monsters had shaped new nightmares on the frontier. To see what role the town's history had played in the Evans family legacy.

Luna just wanted to go back, before she and her Nana were the last two leftovers of the Evans family. She listened to the animal howl in the distance while she thought about the moon outside the bedroom window, still almost full, and what Crane had said earlier about moons and wishes.

Maybe Grace hadn't lain in her bed and divined her future daughter's name, but that didn't stop Luna from pushing apart the curtains on her bedroom window. It didn't stop her from peering through the branches of the tallow tree, looking up at the glowing white ball in the sky, and making a wish of her own.

CHAPTER 8

Lenore Evans

She'd hired an outsider.

For the first time in Evans Funeral Parlor's history, a woman outside the family bloodline would work on the dead—would bathe them, dress them, prepare them for bed—and when it came down to it, it had not been Ducey's doing. Not Ducey's recklessness, her impulsivity, her wild hairs.

It'd been Lenore's.

And not five minutes after she'd done it, a dead woman had wandered into the funeral parlor chapel.

"Not just any dead woman, mind you," Lenore told Belle as she wheeled the breakroom TV down the hallway, "but Tanya West." Of course, it had to be that boy's mother. Lenore had hoped the woman would recover, receive a peaceful death when her time came. But those sorts of happy endings were for fairy tales, not for women who found themselves too close to monsters.

She pushed the TV into the lab. "If I had a brain, I'd take it out and play with it," she told the dog.

Belle huffed into the corner of the room. She settled herself under her favorite chair, rust-colored ears splayed out across the tile, and huffed again.

The pinch that had haunted Lenore all day bit between her shoulder blades. She hadn't planned on hiring the Cole girl any more than she'd intended to spend the rest of her afternoon shampooing the lobby carpet after wrestling a dead woman's body into the lab cooler. She'd gotten Luna to the house to prepare for school tomorrow, but by the time Lenore tended her daddy's and her husband's crypts in the mausoleum, and her mother's and daughter's graves in the garden, the sun had already tucked itself in for the night. So much work still left to do before she could follow suit, and already Lenore felt the way she imagined a strigoi did when it first rose—sluggish and brittle, all the joints broken off and reassembled in reverse. She needed to finish preparing Mrs. Viola Carroll for her Thursday morning service.

And she still had to deal with Tanya West.

Lenore eyeballed the pendulum shaft that jutted out of the dead woman's chest. Damn near to the bob, and Lenore didn't even want to think about what she'd need to do to fix the ancient clock in the chapel.

She averted her eyes from the wedding ring still in the soap dish on the counter, the dog-eared romance novels still stacked on the lab bookshelves. Ducey died too soon, but at least she hadn't lived to see what became of her mother's grandfather clock.

Lenore swiveled the TV cart into place, snapped on a pair of latex gloves, and powered on the ten o'clock news. On commercial break, a salesman shouted about the newest deal on lease-to-own vehicles, and in the funeral parlor laboratory, Lenore braced her feet shoulder-width apart and gripped the ruined wooden shaft between her hands.

"After a brief reprieve, tragedy has once more struck a small town by our border with Louisiana," a man's voice boomed out when the car dealership jingle ended. "Our very own Penny Boudreaux was on scene earlier today to report on the newest ghost-wolf tragedy."

Spike in hand, Lenore froze.

Her eyes snapped to the television screen as the image flashed to location footage. Out on Farm Road 121, Penny Boudreaux waved a microphone in Frank McCormack's scowl before brandishing it under Jed Quigg's flapping tongue. A woman in a smart ponytail and glasses stepped into the frame, and the reporter motioned the camera to pan across to where a cow lay in the background, body mostly out of the shot but hooves conveniently in view.

Penny Boudreaux beamed. "With law enforcement's promise that rabid animals expire within seven days of contracting the disease, these locals thought the danger had passed," she said, "but it appears they're not out of the woods yet."

On the tray, Tanya West's mouth sagged. Death had pooled bruises around her eyes, but the raw edges of her nostrils, the broken blood vessels across her cheeks, those had been earned premortem from countless tissues scraped over skin across days and nights of crying. The woman's son had fed on her to stave off his own death, and she'd still died grieving him.

"Professor Corinne Bennick," Penny Boudreaux said from the little TV on wheels, "a biology researcher from University of Texas, says that while there's no reason to believe that the red wolf–coyote crossbreed known as the ghost wolf would attack a human, it's best that people keep safely indoors with their pets tonight."

Luna had let the dead woman get too close before she'd put her down, but the girl had not so much as flinched when she plunged the pendulum through Tanya's heart.

Lenore wrenched the shaft free.

On the television, the reporter flashed a million-watt smile, made a joke about tomorrow night's full moon—which Lenore suspected she never would've done if the latest victim were a person, say, Tanya West instead of Myrtle the Cow—and tossed it to weather.

Tomorrow, Lenore would fire up the crematorium, but tonight she pushed the dead mother's tray into cooler number three. She checked the lock on every single cooler, then left the TV in the lab with Mrs. Carroll and the splintered pendulum shaft on the breakroom table when she closed up.

Lenore's body nearly split at the hips when she folded herself behind the wheel of Ducey's Rambler to make her way back home. By the time she reached her own bedroom, she could not get out of her slacks and into her silk nightgown fast enough.

"Maybe that's why Grandmother Pie lived at the parlor," she told Belle as she pulled the house robe tight around her middle, looped the belt into a knot at her waist. "Easier than driving back and forth across town."

But Pie Evans had been braver than her granddaughter. Than her daughter, too, maybe, since Ducey had refused to take up residence in the parlor and posted up pretty much in Lenore's backyard.

Light slipped through the crack under Luna's door. Lenore stopped at her granddaughter's bedroom, knuckles raised like she might knock, but the crack went dark, and Lenore let her hand fall away.

She fingered the key in the pocket of her robe. "Do you want in there?" she asked the hound at her feet.

Belle's ears brushed along the tile as she sniffed at the door's edge, tail hung between her legs. She huffed and plodded away, leading Lenore to the living room, to her recliner by the floor-to-ceiling window, to her tape of the latest *Wheel of Fortune* episode and a bowl of Blue Bell ice cream.

The dog nestled against the chair at Lenore's feet, stretched herself in front of the long window that faced into the backyard, and slid her snout past the curtains to stare through the glass. Lenore's eyes grazed over the living room clocks as she snatched up the TV remote. The hands on each clock marked a different hour and minute, and none of them were right, not even the one she'd hauled home when she'd moved the grandfather clock from the unused rooms at the back of the parlor to its chapel. She grabbed the VCR remote, too, then queued the cassette in its deck and hit play.

The colorful wheel spun rainbows on the television as, arm in arm, Pat Sajak and Vanna White slid onto the screen, greeting the contestants. Lenore fed herself a spoonful of Fruit Special ice cream and rolled her eyes as the hostess crossed the stage in a haint blue prom gown.

"They've got her dress slit so high it's a wonder you can't see her girdle," Lenore muttered around the cold cream. "Isn't that something, Mama?"

Her hands froze around the bowl. She had to stop doing that.

Lenore finished her dessert while contestants spelled their way through the first puzzle—*Same Name: Baking and Ice Cream Soda*—and introduced themselves. A software engineer, a bathing-suit salesgirl, an overexcited car salesman who'd once worked with alligators.

Lenore blinked, saw Tanya West snap at her granddaughter, then sniffed into her bowl. She rubbed bare feet against Belle's warm fur.

Better a gator than what Lenore had to take care of, any day of the week.

Belle kept her snout pushed through the curtains, pressed against the glass, staring through the window, while Lenore finished her ice cream, and the contestants spelled their way through the next puzzle. When the overexcited car salesman solved *Proper Name: Spanish Explorer Ponce de León* with nothing but two *r*'s, two *s*'s, three *n*'s, Lenore rested her bowl in her lap, then pulled back the curtain to see for herself the little house with the dark lamp in Ducey's bedroom window.

A fireball erupted in the room behind her. Lenore spun back in time to see a robot skull sear across the television. An advertisement for a *Terminator* attraction at Universal Studios, where Pat and Vanna had filmed the episode.

The telephone shrilled on the console table, and Lenore dropped her spoon. Her hand flew to her chest, the curtain swishing against Belle's snout as it fell closed. The spoon missed the bowl and clattered on the living room tile loud enough to wake the dead, but Belle didn't so much as twitch a rust-colored ear.

A pink smear trailed down the house robe. Last time Lenore's phone rang this late at night, it'd been Ducey to tell her they needed to do something about the restless dead.

"Sorry to call at this hour," Roger said when Lenore picked up.

She lowered the volume on the television set, then muted it. Across the line, Roger's voice carried the same quality it had in the mornings when he finished his work at Grace's grave.

"I was just up winding my clocks," she lied.

Roger cleared his throat. "Wanted to check in on Luna. See how she's doing after the assembly today."

This was not what the soon-to-be sheriff called at nearly midnight to discuss, but, "About the same as usual," Lenore said. "Keeping her own confidences."

"She'll come around," he offered. With a stomach full of Fruit Special and Ducey's ghost silent in the darkened window across the way, Lenore wanted to believe him. She touched the clock key in her robe pocket, felt her pulse beat in time with Belle's soft snores at her feet, listened to the sound of silence in a clock-stopped house.

Roger's voice stretched across the line. "How did things go with the coffee shop girl?" He cleared his throat, like he had to force the questions free. "What'd you end up deciding?"

"I hired Kim," Lenore told him flatly. "She starts Wednesday."

"That's good."

Lenore sighed. "We'll see how long she lasts."

She sighed again, filling the space the deputy left empty. "Something I should tell you," she said, as the clock key pushed against her thigh, burned through the fabric of her robe. "A strigoi found its way into the parlor today. It's taken care of," she added, "but Roger, you need to know . . . it was Tanya West."

"For cryin' out loud." The deputy's breath hitched so sharp Lenore felt it rake down her neck. "Where is she now?" he asked.

"In my cooler." Cooler number three, the same one Edwin Boone had woken up in a month ago, the only empty one she'd had left at the moment. "I'll need to cremate her this weekend."

Roger cleared his throat. "Now, wait just a minute, Lenore. We can't just make the woman disappear." His voice stuck and he coughed it free again. "What in the hell am I supposed to say—all of a sudden she disappeared along with her boy?"

"That's exactly what you're going to do," Lenore said. "Luna said Tanya didn't make it to the assembly today, is that right?"

She held her breath until the deputy said he'd told the reporter from Houston he'd follow up with a wellness check, make sure everything was all right. "Use that," Lenore said. "Say you went by and found no sign of her." As a restless dead, she would have forced her way out of the house; surely there'd be signs to support a disappearance. A front door left open, maybe broken window glass. "File a Missing Person's report."

Lenore's pulse beat in her neck while the man growled across the phone line.

"This is my life now?" he grumbled into the receiver.

Welcome to the Evans family.

"Putting Tanya West down means this is over now," Lenore said. "For good."

Roger breathed into the phone for a solid minute before he rallied. "You're not the only one who got a body today," he said at last, voice squeezed at the edges.

Lenore imagined that he had his hat off, clenched between his hands. When she blinked, she saw the bandage on his forearm, red staining the man's fingers as he wrung Grace's blood from the mudpie-brown uniform hat.

"I saw the news," she said.

"One of Mac's cattle out on FM 121 near where—" Roger cleared his throat. "Well, whatever got ahold of this cow didn't leave a whole lot behind," he said, then cleared his throat again as if he heard her open her mouth to interrupt. "I know what you're gonna say, Lenore. But this looks a lot more like what I saw in Johnson's cruiser than any *real* animal attack I've ever seen."

This time when he cleared his throat he didn't quite push the gruff out. "Not sure what we're working with here," he said.

"I've kept a close eye on Luna." Lenore tried to get comfortable in her recliner without bumping the hound at her feet. "No restless dead have passed through the parlor." Not before today, not since Mina Jean, since Edwin Boone. "Tanya West had just woken up, hadn't fed," she added. "Even if she had, a baby strigoi wouldn't have the strength to take down an animal that size. And that's another thing," Lenore went on. "The dead don't attack animals."

She thought of Belle. Judging by Roger's silence, so did he.

"There's something else," he said.

Lenore watched the *Wheel of Fortune* contestants spell their way through the jackpot round and the final puzzle, while Roger explained the oddities of the supposed wolf kill. The cow's missing guts. Missing teeth.

The overexcited car salesman that once wrestled an alligator advanced to the final round. After the usual letter and consonant package, he'd barely needed any of his own letters to finish *Fingertip*.

Lenore had burned Snow's torn finger with the rest of her body.

"Not a wolf, not a bear, not one of the dead," Roger said. "What exactly in the hell are we looking for?"

Whatever got its teeth into Frank McCormack's Angus had managed to take down a half-ton heifer. To leave nothing intact but legs and a skull.

All while collecting a few teeth.

What were they looking for, indeed?

After they hung up, Lenore turned off the television. The key in her robe pocket rubbed down her thigh as she bent over to fetch the spoon. Belle wasn't asleep. The dog still lay wide awake with her snout pushed through the curtains, pressed against the window, eyes trained on the little house in the distance.

And Belle's snores were not snores, but a steady, low growl.

Lenore stroked the length of the animal's back, palmed her ears, and left Belle to grieve, or worry, or watch—whatever it is old hound dogs do—then made her way into the kitchen. Lenore set her dishes on the counter and used a dish towel to blot the pink blemish on her robe. *Have to dredge out the protein before it coagulates,* she thought. Before it left a milky stain, a silver scar—like the one *he'd* left on her daughter's wrist.

Lenore had worried over that cut for days, weeks, months.

Years.

That's when Lenore had started working with the ashes. Ever since she'd come across the old tale about mixing strigoi ashes with water to treat the infected, she'd saved them wherever she could. Scooped in secret from the crematorium, collected from graveside spreading ceremonies.

Reserved for herself.

After Samael tore open Grace's wrist, Lenore had taken action. She mixed ashes with tap water, distilled water, holy water. She applied the salves in secret, mixing the paste in with scar ointment, smearing it into bandages.

In the end, the wound itself had been superficial. A scar marked Grace's wrist, but it had only required three stitches.

The ashes had worked.

They worked for Belle, too. Though she was the only Evans on four legs instead of two, and not exactly the talkative type even by hound dog standards. Lenore had treated the dog's wound with ashes from Edwin Boone. That had healed the wound and Belle had carried on as a normal dog ever since, but only time would tell if Lenore had gotten more than she'd bargained for, using strigoi ashes to save the dog.

And then there was Ducey.

By the time Lenore spit into a vial of what was left of Edwin Boone and rubbed the paste into Ducey's torn-open throat, her mother had already been gone. Of course, pushing a dead man's burnt remains into a ruined neck hadn't been half as hard as what Lenore then had to do to her poor mother's heart.

Lenore rinsed the spoon. Soap suds slid clean off stainless steel. No trace of ice cream.

She'd scrubbed off layers of skin before she'd washed her mama's blood from her hands.

A hint of red still remained in her cuticles.

The ice cream bowl slipped from her grip, but didn't break when it crashed into the sink.

Breathe, Lenore told herself. *Stay calm.*

After she had finished with Ducey, there'd been no ashes left for Grace. First Lenore had failed to save her mother, and then in her own baby girl's last moments, there'd been nothing for her to do but watch.

On the other side of the window over the sink, somewhere not far enough away, a wolf howled.

Lenore froze.

She wished to hell a ghost wolf had gotten Frank McCormack's cow.

That Tanya West's rising had been a loose end, now tied off. Nothing more.

The animal howled again, and the sound ripped out of Lenore's throat—a gunshot, a lunge, a cold stab of steel—and she knew.

Whatever had begun, it was far from over.

CHAPTER 9

Principal Paul Brevard

Principal Paul Brevard took one last look down Forest Park High School's shining, freshly waxed corridors. He surveyed the rows of blue lockers punctuated by quiet classroom doors. The fire extinguishers and fire alarms, all in their snug cabinets and all in working order. He made sure that the memorial easels hung at perfect forty-five-degree angles on either side of the school's bulletproof entrance. Then the principal flicked off the fluorescents on the switches mounted beside the trophy display case, heel-toed his way out the front doors, and locked the school behind him.

Paul let the glow of the football stadium lights roll over him, still ticking down their timers long after the game had finished and the crowds cleared out. He smoothed his hands over his hair to catch any flyaways, careful not to snag his ring, and exhaled.

What a day.

He'd done a remarkable job of the memorial assembly, if he might say so himself. Just the right balance of emotion and instruction, with a hearty serving of sincere aplomb and a dash of helpful optimism. There'd been a record low for tardies when students returned to class after the assembly, and record-high ticket and concession sales at tonight's season kickoff game.

Which they'd won. Confetti still sprinkled down in gusts of buttery popcorn, burnt cotton-candy sugar, sticky soda syrup—all with an undercurrent of sweat and teen spirit.

The one hitch in Paul's giddyup was that he still hadn't bagged himself a date with the hottest new ticket in town—but that morning, he'd swear he had felt sparks between himself and Channel Six's best. As he reached the parking lot, he twirled the bouquet of carnations he'd bought from the Student Council. A class act like Penny Boudreaux deserved roses, but Paul would make up the difference when he drove up and surprised her after she wrapped the late-night news run.

He squared his elbows and leaned into the glow of the stadium lights to check the time on his Casio. Penny's ten o'clock segment should be finishing up about now.

Paul's wingtips popped across the parking lot as he marched to the two-door Dodge Neon in his reserved spot. He flipped his key ring as he walked, enjoying the feel of the world in his hands, the literal keys to thousands of possibilities. The keys to his car, his home, his office— Paul Brevard's chariot, castle, and kingdom.

A candy bar wrapper skittered across his path, through the pleasant tinkle of all he'd accomplished, and Paul chomped down on a grunt. One discarded piece of concession-stand shrapnel meant there'd be another, then more, then too much. If he didn't stamp this out while he could, he'd be up to his ears in empty potato chip bags and Pepsi cans and Famous Amos Chocolate Chip Cookie litter before the Homecoming Dance at end of the week.

And the school board would not look kindly upon Principal Paul Brevard's leadership then.

His soles scratched against the pavement as he jerked to a stop and plucked the wrapper from the ground. The brown and silver foil reflected the stadium glow.

Not on my watch. Paul folded the wrapper into a thin strip and continued on his way. The trash would remind him to get chocolates for Penny when he stopped for gas, and to get after the ground crew tomorrow. Make sure they knew that he wanted clear asphalt, green grass, and zero junk-food garbage on *his* lawn.

When only a handful of quick, confident strides separated him from the Neon, the principal flipped his key ring one more time, and caught the black Dodge fob. He thumbed the lower button, smirking when the coupe's headlights flashed.

Don't worry your pretty, little head, Penny, darlin', he thought. *Paulie B is on his way.*

He stopped at the driver's side window to admire his reflection in the low light that softened the shadows at the edge of the faculty lot. The humid air had licked loose a few strands around his temples, and he smoothed down the hair on one side of his head and then the other. Paul checked his work once, twice, and awarded himself two thumbs up. An A+.

He pressed the fob's button one more time, allowed himself a little extra razzle-dazzle in the flash of the headlights, which sparkled in the gem in his class ring.

Forest Park High School, Class of '80, baby.

He'd walked these halls for four years himself, and by graduation he knew that one day, Paul Brevard would be the man in charge.

If he had a gal like Penny Boudreaux on his arm . . . Well, they'd be two shooting stars, wouldn't they?

He pictured their initials carved into the top of an old desk, and he laughed.

P. B. + P. B.

He smiled at his reflection again. There'd be time for all that. Now he needed to get over to the news station and ask the girl of his dreams to the dance.

He let the fob slip from his fingers and flicked the key ring again, but a noise cut through the quiet.

He scanned the lot for another stray candy wrapper, an empty chip bag or soda can, but nothing fit the sound.

Paul's fist missed the bunch of keys as the noise echoed through the dark.

A howl.

Paul dropped to a crouch. His hand clawed the pavement, each finger a spider's leg reaching for the key ring while he scanned the parking lot, the empty stadium, what he could make out of the vacant bleachers. The lights shined brightest right over the field, glared against the sharp metal seats, but the light thinned as it spread. By the time it reached the edges of the faculty lot, it barely broke through the shadows. Enough for him to primp in the window, but not to see through the dark.

Another howl, and this one came louder, pulsed against the small hairs at the base of Paul's neck.

He held his crouch steady, one hand pressed down, while his other scrambled across the asphalt.

Be cool, the principal told himself. Do not let your mind run away with you. Do not get all spun up over the rabid animal attacks of last month, the ghost wolves sighted this month. The media had worked half his teachers into a frenzy.

But he was the principal.

The one in charge.

A growl beat against Paul's back.

Something stood behind him. Hot breath crowded his knees, a sour, caustic cloud that fused with the heat. The animal's weight pressed at Paul's back, its eyes boring into him, and his body locked into its bent position as tremors rolled up his arms.

Every dream he'd ever had for himself flashed before him. The beautiful wife smiling behind the news anchor desk, the picket fence around the home in the West End side of town, the seat at the mayor's table—

Paul's fingers found the key ring.

He nearly dropped it as he fumbled between the keys—apartment, Mother's house, his office, the bulletproof school entrance, a Master Lock key he'd confiscated from a suspicious student.

No Neon, no Neon, no Neon—

He got it.

Paul clutched the fat rubber top of the car key as he shot to his feet.

The cloud of hot breath rose with him, up his knees to his hips, up his neck. The night pinned him between the breath and the car. A growl swelled, low and guttural, filling the space between, pushing up, up, up, as Paul went limp against the driver's side window.

Stray hair fizzled in the air around his head as behind him, fur and claws and teeth matted together with bramble and shadow, molded into a head and body and limbs.

Paul's entire body trilled, but his mouth refused to open, to scream, as he stared at the beast reflected in the glass. The lights over the football field glowed in its eyes. Gleamed against the beast's claws and teeth.

The door beeped quietly as it automatically locked again.

And then the stadium light's timer went out.

Paul dropped his keys again into the sudden black.

The football field vanished, the empty bleachers, the quiet concession stands. Gone were the scents of food and sweat and celebration.

Now it was just Paul, and the heat, and the stink, and the wolf.

He twisted around, arms raised instinctively to shield his face, his vital organs. He pushed back against the locked door, against the metal and glass that separated him from his only escape.

The beast snarled. Paul splayed his fingers wide enough to see the mass of fur and shadow lick its lips before it lunged.

Blinding pain surged through his shoulder, hot liquid scalded his skin, as the arm blocking his face ripped free of his body.

He saw teeth. Claws.

Then Principal Paul Brevard saw nothing.

CHAPTER 10

Luna Evans

Screams ripped through Luna's head.

Screaming, as Andy drove his claws into Grace. Her mother. Screaming, as his hands plunged into her stomach. The screams hitched as ligaments snapped, as flesh parted, as bone shattered. Blood rushed over skin, pouring across the ground as the scar on Grace's wrist flashed silver in the moonlight and her body crumpled.

Luna reached for her mother. *Mom!* she screamed, *Mom, Mom—*

Only it wasn't Grace's body on the stained grass, not her mother's blood that turned her hands black. It was Tanya West's.

Tanya West, whose mouth stretched open in a yawning, hungry hole. Tanya, who interrupted Luna's own scream to call her name, who stretched its end into a maggot-filled shriek.

Luna's eyes snapped open.

She stared up at the popcorn ceiling over her bed through the thin, gray morning haze, and listened to her own name morph into the living room telephone's *scream, scream, screaming* down the hallway.

The landline took a deep breath between rings, then screamed again.

Luna rolled onto her cheek, groaning into the pillow as one hand flung itself free of the blankets to crawl around the bedside table. Her fingers wrapped around a plastic cube, and she squinted until the thin red scratches on the alarm clock's screen assembled themselves into numbers.

Early. Too early. Her alarm wouldn't go off for another couple of hours still.

The Tuesday morning sun barely peeked over the Texas horizon, but astronauts could probably hear Nana Lenore's phone ringing on Mars.

Fading screams echoed through Luna's head while, outside her bedroom door, her grandmother's house slippers scuffed down the tiled hallway, followed by the quick ticks of Belle's nails. Only one person ever called at dawn, and always about the same thing: Quigg had a new body on its way to the parlor.

What was it Nana Lenore always said—that death rarely obeyed the clock? Apparently it didn't matter if all those pendulums kept time or not. Luna pulled the covers over her head. If only her grandmother had a cordless phone.

That, she thought, *or carpet.*

Another ring and Nana's voice snowballed down the hall. Her grandmother kept her volume low enough to muffle her words, a steady bass beat under the fading current of Grace's scream, of Tanya's, tapping like a drippy faucet in the back of Luna's thoughts.

"What!"

This time the voice that blasted through Luna's brain wasn't her dead mother's, wasn't a dream, and it wasn't the phone. In the living room, Nana shrilled again, and Luna shot upright in her mother's childhood bed. The one-syllable yell meant that probably it was the deputy calling, not the coroner.

And it meant trouble.

"Where was the body found?" The question floated down the hallway from the living room, pausing while someone answered over the line. "What's that mean, what's *missing*?"

Luna exhaled her last hope of falling back asleep and thrust the blankets away, pushing her feet to the edge of the bed as she fought to make sense of the words filtering down the hall. Her ear ticked toward the door as her grandmother punched out more questions, but sleep grog and the still-fading ring in her head ruined her ability to make sense of them.

Probably for the best, she reminded herself. Dead bodies came into the parlor in all sorts of ways—accidents, diseases, old age—but, at least since Alison Haney, none of them had a thing to do with her.

Until Tanya West.

Technically, Andy's mother had been his own victim, not hers. A remainder. Leftovers, like Luna herself, and Nana and Belle.

"Well, it certainly *sounds* like an animal to me," screeched her grandmother from the living room.

A shadow on the other side of the bedroom curtains caught Luna's eye. She stared at the window, at the dark blur that swayed side to side in the morning wind. The shape didn't match the tree branches that Luna knew waited on the other side of the glass. The wind shook the shadow and when it spun around again, Luna saw the points of two ears, like Batman's silhouette.

Luna remembered the baying, the howling that she'd heard last night.

She thought of the rabid ghost wolves Nana and Roger Taylor had blamed for her own monstrous crimes.

And she remembered the wish she'd made on the moon.

Luna's hands shook as she crawled back across her bed and reached for the curtain. She gripped the heavy fabric drapes and yanked them apart.

Like Andy yanked Mom apart, Luna thought.

Then she saw the body hanging in the tree outside her window, and the scream shot back through her head.

A cat dangled upside down from one of the tallow tree's low branches, its tail twisted between twigs. Pink muscle peeked through where calico fur had been shorn away, and one of the legs bent at an unnatural angle, but otherwise the long torso dangled intact—a tail, two back legs connected by a long, lithe underbelly to two front legs, and a head.

No paws, though. And no mandible.

The wind blew. The tree rustled. In the branches, the dead cat twisted. The bell on the pink rhinestone collar tinkled loud enough that Luna could hear it inside her bedroom, as one cloudy amber eye peered at her through the glass.

She leaned close to read the name bedazzled onto the animal's blood-spattered collar.

SISSY.

"What do you mean *claw* marks?" Nana's voice stabbed through the cold morning air again and the thick curtains billowed as Luna let them fall closed. She slipped into a pair of old jeans, tugged a hoodie over her head. None of the dead that had come through the funeral parlor had anything to do with her, but none of the dead animals around town were the work of any rabid coyote-wolf patsy, either.

And, as far as Luna knew, wolves didn't hang kills in trees outside teenage girls' windows. Didn't remove their feet, their jaws, their fur, but leave their collars intact to sparkle in the fresh morning sun.

Wolves didn't.

But monsters might.

Nana Lenore clutched the handset against her ear, lips thinned into a line, when Luna slunk through the living room. Luna dropped her eyes, counting the cool ceramic tiles under her feet as she passed the stopped clocks, the dog in front of the floor-to-ceiling window, the woman seated in the recliner, her fist gripped so tight around the telephone receiver that her fingers might break when she let go.

If she lets go, Luna thought.

The older woman grunted when Luna passed so she looked over her shoulder, clocked the milky smear that stained her grandmother's silk house robe. Luna stepped sockless into her Cons and pushed through the back door. She made sure to avoid the front windows as she slunk around the side of the house, following the crabgrass perimeter to the tree in front of her bedroom window.

To the dead cat in its branches, hung by the tail.

Flies swarmed the carcass, and Luna held her breath as she reached up and tugged the animal free of the twigs. She tried to touch fur, not skin, as she hoisted the cat out of the tallow tree branches, cupping its head in one hand as she laid the poor creature on the coarse autumn grass.

Luna arranged the cat's limbs, tail, incomplete jaw. Along with its paws and mandible, most of the fur along the animal's midsection was gone. Soft black and gold calico still covered its legs and shoulders, but blood stained the white fur around the cat's throat pink, and crusted along its mouth, the backs of its legs, where it had been slit open from neck to gut. The cat's insides had been licked clean. Whatever had killed the animal ate its fill of meat and muscle and bone, but feasted considerately, without mangling the body.

Luna slipped the collar over the animal's ruined head and read the name again.

What kind of monster skinned its prey, took its fur and teeth, but left its collar?

"Luna, honey, are you out here?"

Her grandmother calling from the front door brought her mother's voice from the past. Luna pushed Sissy's corpse into the crabgrass. She stuffed the collar into her pocket and wiped her hands on her jeans just as Nana Lenore appeared at the corner of the house. She was still in her silk robe and slippers, but a cardigan covered her nightclothes and her purse hung off her shoulder. Her auburn hair burned bonfire-hot in the sleepy sunlight.

The key in her hand belonged to a car, and not a clock.

Nana Lenore pointed at Ducey's Ford Rambler. "Get in," she ordered. "Hurry."

Luna put a hand up to shield the red glare of her grandmother's hair. "Where are we going?"

"The parlor," Nana Lenore shot back as she loaded Belle into the backseat, gestured to Luna to slide in the front. "No school today," she said.

"Who was that on the phone?" Luna yanked the seat belt across her chest, but already the car shunted backward down the gravel driveway, swerving onto the street.

Her grandmother chewed her words as she drove, the gas pedal pressed to the car's floor. Luna tried to follow the half-formed sentences streaming out of Nana Lenore's mouth—a body found in the high school parking lot. Missing parts. Ruined flowers. Claw marks.

"I shouldn't have left Viola on the table," she muttered, pushing the accelerator too fast.

Andy's mom rising restless, Luna understood. The sweet old teacher, she did not. The coroner's report said Mrs. Carroll died from a heart attack in the Market Basket dairy aisle.

"Did I lock the coolers?" Nana braked the old sedan too hard at a stop sign, then stomped it back to full speed, sped down another street, swerving onto the town's main roads and then the short two-lane that led to Evans Funeral Parlor.

As Nana pulled the Rambler into the parlor's parking lot, they both saw the dirt tracked in a low brown trail from the rosebushes to the building. Luna watched her grandmother's jaw clench, heard her teeth grind as she jerked the car to a stop at the back door.

She twisted the ignition off.

"Stay in the car," she told Luna, but Luna's door was already open, her Converses already on the dirt-tracked pavement. Luna gawked at the brown footprint stamped beside her shoe. She counted five toes, a sole.

Whatever had tracked dirt across the parking lot, it wasn't some rabid coyote-wolf hybrid.

"Belle!" Nana shouted as the hound dog leaped out of the Rambler's backseat and bolted toward the funeral parlor, barking like mad. "Shit," her grandmother said, and the swear word sounded foreign to Luna's ears, every bit as surprising as the trail of muddy human footprints leading from the garden to the back door, jimmied open in the morning sun.

Luna followed her grandmother into the cool gloom of the unlit building. Footprints caked with diminishing amounts of mud followed a long, safety-orange extension cord that slithered down the hallway from breakroom to lab.

And from under the lab door, the steel guitar twang of a television theme song, the barest filmy glow of the silver screen, and the sound of slurping.

Nana Lenore slipped a dagger from her cardigan. "Get behind me," she whispered.

"No way," Luna whispered back.

Together they crept toward the lab door.

At the threshold, her grandmother lifted the blade. *Do it*, the look she gave Luna said, and Luna pushed open the laboratory door as the dagger's blade gleamed in her peripheral vision.

Draped in a long white gown smeared with grave dirt, skin crusted with grime, white hair gritted brown, a strigoi stood with its back to the door. The body leaned over the metal exam table. Greedy ripples shot through its shoulders, down its back, as the ghoul sucked from the end of a long metal cylinder stabbed into the dead schoolteacher's stomach.

The clang of metal reverberated in Luna's ears as the dagger hit the linoleum.

At the table, the strigoi lifted its head. Dragged the back of its hand across its face. Turned to show one bright green eye, one cloudy one.

Nana Lenore spoke quietly, a dead cat's charm bell chiming in the wind. "Mama?"

"Well, girls," Ducey Evans said as she wiped Mrs. Carroll's blood from her lips, the silver ring swinging on the thin chain around her neck. "Looks like we've got ourselves in another fine mess, don't we?"

CHAPTER 11

Ducey Evans

Lenore stood with her spine fused through her bedclothes to the hinges of the lab door, her palm splayed so heavy across her chest that her fingers might sink through her skin. Beside her, Luna's eyes went as big as saucers. Ducey could hear the thud of the girls' hearts, beating like condor wings inside their rib cages. She could smell them, too. Her daughter, like sanitary citrus and spilled milk. Her great-granddaughter, grass and ink, an undercurrent of menthol.

And on both of them, fear.

Ducey pulled the back of her hand across her mouth and grunted. She'd always been the type to rise with the dawn, but it didn't mean she wanted to wake up when she was supposed to be dead. Only thing worse than that: your own flesh and blood standing around in the doorway like they've turned to stone after you've done the hard work of crawling out of your own grave.

Under a rosebush in the funeral parlor garden, no less.

What did Mother used to say? Ducey couldn't remember. Something about how she planned to be buried on this land, but only once. Maybe Pie Evans was six feet under somewhere on the property, or maybe not, but Ducey herself had badgered her own daughter about always burying family problems in the front damn yard. She'd known Lenore would be too sentimental to cremate her when the time came, figured the girl would shove her into a cement slot in the mausoleum right beside her late husband, Royce, and Jimmy.

But never in a million years would Ducey have thought she'd end up laid to rest near the ghoul who'd brought hell to the Evans family.

Once she'd gotten over being dead, she meant to have a word with Lenore about all that.

"Relax, girls," she said. Belle wound herself between Ducey's leg, little whimpers leaking between her jowls as she begged for pets. Ducey ignored the crack in her hips when she bent to scratch behind the dog's ears. "Whatever I am, it ain't a gorgon." She looked at the dead woman on the tray, wispy silver strands that coiled like snakes from her head, the trocar poking out from where Ducey had plunged it into her stomach.

"I didn't give you a look and turn you both to stone," she said. Ducey licked at the coppery film still stuck to her teeth. Something had to account for the tingle in her taste buds. That red trickle on the white sheet.

"Then what are you?" Luna asked and broke the spell.

What was she, indeed.

Ducey fingered the strip of mottled scar tissue that cragged down the side of her throat, the silver ring on the flimsy necklace, the searing pain between her breasts. Most of her joints didn't want to bend and her limbs seemed to weigh more than they used to, but her chest burned like she'd swallowed an open flame along with that dead woman's blood.

Who knew ghouls could get heartburn—if a ghoul she was.

A damn *ghoul*.

"Hell, I don't know what I am." Ducey patted her bosom to smother the fire, but barely pushed it down to a flicker. "I ain't gonna bite you, though, I know that much."

Lenore's eyebrows shot up. Her house slipper slid out from under her, toeing across the linoleum toward the dagger at her feet. "Strigoi don't talk," she said when her toes tapped metal. "They call. They knock."

Lenore flashed into motion, snatching up the blade, and Ducey put her palms in the air as Lenore angled herself in front of Luna, dagger raised.

Belle growled at Ducey's feet. Rusty velvet fur brushed along her leg, half on fabric, half on skin. The dog bared her teeth at Lenore, but not like her heart was in it.

"Now, Len," Ducey said. "Go on and put that down."

"The dead don't remember who they were." Lenore's brows twisted and her eyes turned to glass, but her breath hitched, and her knuckles went white around the knife's hilt. "They don't come back," she said.

Of all the people the Evanses had buried, all the ghouls they'd put back down, probably none had ever risen that Lenore wanted back so badly as her own kin.

She could understand the shock of seeing her rise from the grave, but to hell with Lenore for waving that dagger in her own mother's face.

Ducey rolled her eyes. She hushed the hound with a muddy foot and wrenched the trocar free of the dead woman on the table, waggling it like a switch at her knife-wielding daughter. "You are pushin' my damn buttons, Lenore Ruth," she said. "Now listen, daughter of mine, and listen good. Last I remember, old Clyde Halloran put his teeth in my neck. Next thing I know, I wake up wrapped in a sheet with my trocar on my chest, my pockets full of candy, ring finger bare, and—" She reached up and yanked the chain from her throat with her free hand. "This ugly thing hung around my neck."

Ducey raised the chain with the silver ring and spun to face the other two women. "This belong to that boyfriend of yours?" she asked Luna. "The one trying to ward off ghouls with sage or somesuch?"

Over Lenore's shoulder, the littlest Evans dared a nod.

Ducey harrumphed, tossing the ring to the girl. "Figured."

"He's just a friend," Luna said, and caught the ring.

The glare of Lenore's dagger under the fluorescents hurt Ducey's eyes, the trocar like an anchor, a dead weight, in her hand, but at least the arthritis hadn't followed her into death.

"Sure, child," she told her great-granddaughter. "And I'm just your guardian angel."

Her throat itched beneath the scar. Thunder rumbled in her stomach, only it wasn't thunder. Belle rubbed against her shin, and Ducey made a valiant effort not to look at the dead woman on the table as the heat in her chest surged, the pain cooking her through. Hard to tell if she was mad or just hungry.

"Oh, hell, Len, you're giving me heartburn," she said, clamping a hand to her chest before it fried her brains, too. "Which is saying somethin' since the darn thing don't beat anymore."

Lenore's eyes locked on Ducey's hand. "I stabbed you," Lenore said, "right there"—she nodded at where Ducey touched her chest, then Lenore's eyes crawled up to the ragged scar on Ducey's throat—"I put ashes into the wound," she said, "then I . . . I pierced your heart, just to be sure."

To be sure that Ducey wouldn't come back, her daughter meant. Oh, Lenore and her ash experiments. Belle seemed all right enough, a little overly attached to Ducey's literal apron strings, maybe. But as with the damn rosebushes, Ducey had warned her daughter not to fool around with things she didn't know enough about.

Lenore's face and her dagger fell before Ducey could punish her with the parental line—not mad, just disappointed.

"If the ashes couldn't save you, heal the wound, I thought they'd at least free you from any taint of strigoi blood. I never expected they'd bring you back," Lenore said. "Oh, Mama." Her bottom lip trembled. "What have I done?"

"We don't know that you've done anything," Ducey said, because it didn't help matters, crying over spilt milk. First she needed to fill in the blanks between the night she'd died and this morning when her eyes reopened. Then they could worry about the rest.

Her stomach growled again, and Ducey set the trocar on the metal instrument tray beside the exam table. She fished a butterscotch from her apron pocket. "Let's get Grace," she said as she twisted the cellophane wrapper loose. "We can all sit down and figure out what to do."

Hard sugar assaulted her in a wave of vanilla and caramel, but Ducey's throat clenched when the candy hit her tongue. She gagged and spat the disc across the linoleum, skittering past the ruined cellophane of her previous attempts. Belle slurped up the candy and slunk with it under her favorite chair on the other side of the room, but when Ducey straightened back up, both Lenore and Luna stared at her with eyes even more soulful than the old hound's.

And those looks had nothing to do with her butterscotches, damn it.

"What are you two not tellin' me?" Ducey braced herself against the exam table, but she knew the answer—knew it the same way she'd known she couldn't go back to store-bought hard candy after slurping down human blood. Still, just like she'd almost choked on her favorite treat, she needed to taste this terrible truth before she could spit it out, too.

"I wasn't the only one to die that night, was I?" she asked.

Luna stared at her sneakers while Lenore blinked too fast.

Ducey's heart burned, but not from the stab wound she'd woken to find there. "Well, hell," she said. "I'm so sorry, girls." She glanced all around the room—at the dog-eared paperbacks, the metal instrument tray, her own glasses still on the lab sink next to her wedding ring in the soap dish—right where she'd left it the night she died. "I never thought . . ."

Never thought she'd outlive one of them, she almost said, but didn't. When Ducey had thrown herself in Clyde's path that night, she'd meant to give her daughters their best chance of beating back the tide of restless dead that had converged on the parlor. Now it didn't seem right that she'd risen, and Grace couldn't.

She looked at her girls, her precious girls.

"How did it happen?" she asked.

Lenore's lips went white. Luna sniffed so hard Ducey felt its pull in her bones.

"Andy," Luna said. "It was Andy." The girl delivered the words to the floor like a confession, the shame in them so dense, so swollen, that Ducey felt their weight try to pull her back into her grave. "He came at me and Mom . . ." Luna's grief sucked the air from the room. "He tore her open, right in front of me."

"But she killed him," Lenore added, and dead or not, Ducey spooked at the sudden sound. "She finished it."

"Where is she now?" Ducey asked.

Lenore's lip quirked. "We buried her next to you, in the garden. Luna planted the rosebushes. Grace's won't grow, but yours . . ." Her words broke off and she pulled her robe tight, buttoning her cardigan over it like armor. "You couldn't sense her there—anything like that?"

Ducey shook her head and said bupkes about the other thing she'd been buried beside.

Her daughter sucked in air, pushed it out. She nodded, then clapped her hands together. "And that's it." Lenore looked at Ducey. "We buried you both one month ago."

A *month*.

Time flew when you were dead.

"What about all those ghouls that night," Ducey said. "What did you do with them?"

Luna perked up. "We cremated them, but Andy's mom—"

"Roger declared Snow and Clyde dead, the result of rabid animal attacks, just like Edwin Boone and the young girl they found behind the theater," Lenore cut in. "There've been sightings of a rare wolf-coyote hybrid along the coast, so Roger made a story out of that." She pulled in her bottom lip as she worked to account for all the dead that descended on the parlor that night. "Widow Milner and the boy were presumed dead."

Ducey counted one name still missing. "What about Buchanan?"

"Got mauled by rabid ghost wolves," Luna answered.

"The sheriff's body was interred right away. No ceremony," Lenore added, and Ducey huffed. "Roger had put six bullets into him, but whoever tore into him first hadn't left much to get up, so we figured that was good enough."

Ducey felt her eyebrow spike hard enough to rattle dirt loose down her forehead. "Oh, you and your granddaughter?"

"No one asked me"—Luna rolled her eyes—"but Deputy Taylor thinks he's part of the family now."

"*Sheriff* Taylor," Lenore corrected. "His promotion is official as of today." A line pulled up the edges of her lips as her eyes went on the move again, this time to the cooler, but it wasn't a happy sort of smile. "Mama," she asked, "any chance you didn't come straight into the parlor after you woke up?"

Ducey squinted at her daughter. Wherever this was going, she already knew she didn't like it. "I came straight in here, Len. You followed my footsteps from the garden, didn't you?"

The look her girls exchanged made Ducey's skin crawl. "What are you not telling me?" she asked.

"A strigoi came into the parlor yesterday—Tanya West, Andy's mom," Lenore said. "The boy had been feeding on her, keeping her alive. She finally succumbed, and after she died, she made her way here."

The restless dead always made their way back to the Evanses', didn't they? Ever since Pie's day.

Lenore nodded at cooler number three. "She's in there. Roger is taking care of that, too."

Ducey took note of how Luna kept on chewing her lip. "What else?"

"We pinned the attacks on a rabid animal, but—" Lenore blinked like she couldn't make her words fit together just right. "But then pets started going missing, and yesterday something tore apart one of Frank McCormack's heifers." She stopped, looking at Ducey. "On Farm Road 121."

"This is the country." Ducey dismissed her daughter with a flick of her wrist. "Lots of things need to eat."

Lenore nodded as she padded across the lab in her slippers. "That's what I told Roger," she said, dropping into the chair over the dozing hound. "But he called again this morning, and Mama, whatever did this, it wasn't a wolf." Ducey's daughter shook her head. "It doesn't sound like one of the restless dead, either," Lenore said.

So that's what brought the girl flying like a bat out of hell to the parlor in her nightclothes. She had a ghoul in the cooler, then a body turned up.

When it rained . . . *hell.*

"Something tore up an eight-hundred-pound cow yesterday, and then a strigoi wandered into our parlor," Lenore said. "Now there's a gutted body at the high school, and you're . . ."

Whatever she was about to say, she thought better and swallowed it.

Ducey retraced her steps until she was certain she could recount every moment from the second she'd glimpsed what was left of the full moon over her head, to the long slog across the parking lot, the fight with the back door. Plunging the trocar into the dead woman she found on the table. Drinking her down. She could trace her timeline, but Ducey knew better than to trust a ghoul, even when the ghoul in question was herself.

Then again, maybe she wasn't the only one who'd risen.

The full moon, she thought, and that damn burn flared back under the scar in her chest.

"There are legends," she told the girls, "about what kind of monsters are born when a person dies holding on to too much anger. That kind of violence," she said, thinking about the dead sheriff buried with his heart plugged full of holes, "it doesn't go quietly."

Lenore shuffled her shoulders like she had a crick in her neck. "What are you saying, Mama?"

Ducey picked up the bloodied trocar. She remembered what dirt tasted like. And she remembered other things. Stories her mother had told her about other legends, other monsters—things that should be hokum, but, all things considered, might not be.

"I'm sayin' there are things worse than ghouls." She held the metal stake in front of her, studying its point. "And I might not be the only one that's crawled its way back."

CHAPTER 12

Sheriff Roger Taylor

On his first official day as sheriff, Roger Taylor had planned to stop by Jimbo's for a coffee and head over to the West house. He'd do his duty—uphold the secret he'd sworn to protect from the town that he'd also sworn to protect—and make it appear that a grieving mother had disappeared for good, become a ghost like her murderous son, so that things could go back to normal and folks could move on. But his radio cracked the yolk on that sunny-side-fried daydream and Dispatch Darla's bad news ran out all over it, so Roger skipped the café and the house. He poured the sludge left in yesterday's pot into his thermos and headed over to the high school and the dead body smeared across its parking lot.

And this time, the body wasn't a cow.

His coffee sat untouched in the console while Roger made his way across town, cooling into tepid bean water by the time he bypassed the bus-only lane and crunched up Forest Park's main drive. Roger's cruiser crept alongside a set of tread marks, leaving distance behind the rookie's car and the coroner's van in case he needed to rush out, and only then realized it wasn't tires that had crusted the parking-lot asphalt.

Mud didn't dry that color brown.

Roger slammed the gearshift into park like he could throw the switch on this whole damn mess, and he stared into the idling van's taillights. *Light it up,* he thought, before he had to see whatever he was about to see, where that drying redbrick road led. Light up the undead, the ghost wolves. Roger closed his eyes. *Light it all.*

He counted faces that he would never see again, all those that he'd helped bury last month, then the new sheriff in town pushed the driver's side door open and threw himself into the midmorning sun. Roger tipped his hat at Quigg's helpers waiting in the van and kept his boots out of the blood trails as he tugged his hat over his head. He nodded to the rookie and the coroner, but his chin stuck and his eyes thinned the moment morning sunlight caught fire on the wolf expert's pretty red hair.

Thought I told Quigg he needed permission to bring a civ. The cow killing he'd let go, but the repeat appearance at a homicide scene made his eye twitch. Probably Roger should pull Quigg aside to set precedent. Make the man get the professor out of here just like he'd tried to make Hinson get the reporter away, out of their town and back to the big-city news stations and the universities where they belonged.

"Mornin', Sheriff," the old man said, and Roger squinted a greeting after a pause just long enough that Hinson wouldn't miss his delay. Last thing he needed was to ruffle things up with the old coroner right when a crop of ravaged bodies started turning up, never mind give the rookie another reason to doubt his commanding officer. Everything to code, Hinson was—i's dotted, t's crossed. By the book.

Just like Roger had taught him.

The professor's eyes stretched too big behind her glasses, freckles pale and arms stiff across her chest, and Roger figured this might be the last time he'd have to worry about finding Professor Corinne Bennick at another crime scene. He hid his frown behind a hanky and pretended the cloth could block the smell.

When Roger had called to tell Lenore about the victim, they'd asked each other if the body might rise. She'd said no, just like he'd expected she would, but ever since his radio first went off, Roger had felt every moment pulse through his neck, his sore arm. Now he studied the glistening, indistinct clumps and drying smears spread across the asphalt, the color bleeding through the thin white cloth laid over the largest lump, and doubted very seriously that, even if they could cobble and scrape everything into the shape of a man, there'd be enough left of Principal Paul Brevard for him to get back up.

Hell, they'd be lucky to fill a casket.

"Anybody find the rest of the body yet?" Roger asked from behind his handkerchief.

"We found a femur under the back tire, most of the extremities, and a patella," Quigg said, ticking off parts of the anatomical drawing on his clipboard as he named them. "But the bulk of the abdominal cavity is gone."

Roger breathed behind the cloth, watching the old man's tongue dart along his lower lip. "English, Jed."

"The man's in bits and pieces, spread from his car here all the way across to the stadium, but most everything is here—enough to make a positive ID." The coroner tapped his pen in the center of his clipboard. "But he's cleaned out just like the cow was. Even missing some ribs."

"And his arm is gone," Hinson chimed in, voice soupy.

"That's not all." Quigg held the page up so Roger could see the areas circled in blue ballpoint, could watch as he stabbed the pen at a series of scribbles attached to various parts of the outlined figure. "Scalp's gone," he said. "Brevard wore a toupee, and that's gone too. The maxilla has been completely separated from the mandible—" Quigg sucked down a glug of saliva, and his pen slit a blue vein down his jowl when his hand jerked to scrawl another note. "Incisors and canines have been removed, too," he said.

"And his *arm is gone*," Hinson repeated, and Roger noticed that the spread of red on the asphalt had washed itself up over the boy's shoes, too. He must have spent time kneeling—blood soaked his trousers all the way up to his knees.

Roger's gaze flicked from the boy's stained uniform to his pale face. His voice came out in a grunt behind the cloth. "You puke again, Hinson?"

Hinson gulped and Roger kept his eyes down and the handkerchief up. He caught a stain on the leg of Corinne's jeans, too, and let out another grumble. Maybe the boy had just been being a gentleman, helping the civ through her first real crime scene, or maybe not. Either way, better to let them think he was being a hard-ass than know that grunt was really him choking back his own vomit.

Quigg slapped his pen against his clipboard. "And his right arm is missing, yes."

First day as sheriff, and Roger's first vic didn't even have all its parts.

He looked to the wolf expert, and the wound in his own forearm thrummed when their eyes made contact. "Wolf probably drug it off," Roger said, and hoped she would agree.

The woman shook her head. She pulled a deep breath, cringed at the taste, freckles bunching up below her glasses, then, "What about Mr. Brevard's teeth?" she said. "Wolves don't take trophies."

Roger stuffed the handkerchief in his pocket. If she could stand around and argue about wolves while breathing in the stink of death, then he could, too, damn it. "Some must have knocked loose when the man tried to fight the animal off," he said. Sticking to the missing limb was easier than addressing the dismembered parts scattered from here to God knew where.

Corinne's eyes returned to their normal size behind their frames. "Perhaps," she said, "but unlikely."

"Good news is, sounds like we'll know it when we find it." Quigg licked. "The arm, I mean."

Roger cocked his head at the coroner, who nodded at the rookie.

"Brevard never took off his class ring," Deputy Hinson said, pushing color back into his dimples, squaring his jaw. "Wore it every day." He managed a shrug that looked like it rolled up from his stomach until it added to the wide set of shoulders, and he tipped his head to the pretty professor. "We used to joke about it in high school," he said, like the rookie thought that kind of humor might appeal to a woman who'd earned a PhD before age thirty.

"You know he was bald, too?" Roger shot back before the boy made a fool out of himself and the department.

Before you have too long to wonder what happened to the principal's ribs, his teeth.

What exactly in the hell did a ghoul need with bones and incisors?

Hinson jerked his chin toward more red lumps on the asphalt. Flower petals, Roger now realized.

"It looks like he was going on a date," Hinson said. "Probably bought the carnations off Student Council at the game."

Roger's chest clenched. If only he'd had the chance to buy Grace carnations. Anything other than roses.

"Anybody report him missing?" Roger asked. "Know who he was planning to meet?"

Silence meant no.

Roger turned back to Quigg. "Are the . . ." What the hell did he call this—a man shredded like a kalua pig slathered in mesquite? "Are the wounds consistent with a wolf attack?"

Quigg gave him a look like he didn't quite know how to describe this, either. "Well, yes and no," he said. "From what we can tell, the marks on the skin and muscle look more like claw than blade, and of course a wolf jaw would be strong enough to snap through bone, but I'll be honest with you, Roger." The old man licked his lips like it might be his last. "I've been with the coroner's office over half my life, and I ain't never seen something the likes of this."

Oh, hell. Not the coroner, too.

Roger pushed up an eyebrow and hoped it was enough.

Quigg's tongue rolled against the inside of his lip. "Take a look at this."

He used the end of his pen to lift the edge of the bloodied sheet, and encouraged Roger to focus in on the row of squares stamped into what might have been a bicep. "These are teeth marks," he said of the rounded indentations ringed with red. "They look like fangs to you?"

Roger shook his head.

"Me neither," Quigg said. "But they do look like bovine."

"Myrtle?" the sheriff asked. How in the hell did the dead cow's teeth get imprinted on the man's skin?

The professor's curiosity overcame her revulsion. She squinted at the page on Quigg's clipboard, then at the red lump under the sheet. She adjusted her horn-rims, pulled on a pair of latex gloves, and dropped into a squat, mumbling into that tape recorder she carried everywhere. A large chunk of maybe thigh bore another row of angry square welts, and the old man held the bloodied sheet up and babbled about the comparative marks of canine versus bovine indentations.

A click followed by the scratching sound of a plastic gear grinding, and Roger's eyes dropped to the disposable camera in the professor's clutches. "What's this?" he asked.

"I'm taking photos to analyze the impression in the bite," she said, and the sheriff raised an eyebrow at the tone in her voice. "If we can match some of the imprints," she said, "we may be able to get a better idea of its lineage, what its genetic makeup is."

"From a teeth imprint?" Fingerprints and DNA samples were the furthest Roger had ever had to go to assemble forensic clues in his small town.

"We can at least verify what kind of animal, or animals, left the prints," Quigg said, still lifting that damn sheet, letting the stink rise up. "Examining animal imprints is similar to identifying human dental records," he said. "We're looking at depth of the bite, but also width and rotation of each tooth, teeth-gap width, distance between teeth."

All things Roger and Lenore hadn't considered when they'd pinned the deaths on rabid animals.

"Otherwise," Quigg said, "there are enough similarities to convince me that it's the same animal responsible." The coroner let the sheet fall and Roger caught the blood on the end of the pen, hoped Quigg would remember to wipe it clean before he stuck the thing in his mouth.

The coroner read the words scribbled on the anatomical drawing aloud. "Brevard's jaw had been snapped in half, just like Myrtle's, to make extraction of the teeth easier. His innards are gone, presumably consumed. His hair, what little he had, is gone—" The pen left a dot of red where he tapped it against his forehead. "And the tears are sharp punctures that slice down," he said, "consistent with claws."

"And there's this," Corinne said, pushing herself to her feet. A red clump dangled from her fingers, matted with God knows what. "Fur."

Roger waited while Quigg called his helpers from the van, his hat held respectfully in his hands while he watched them scoop up the principal's remains and load them into the van. When the professor climbed into the passenger seat, Quigg turned back.

"I reckon you'll want to get this one on over to the Evanses' sooner rather than later," Quigg told Roger, but didn't clarify whether he meant because of the state of the body or the state of the town. Quigg licked his lips. "I'll have the principal sent over as fast as I can so Lenore can get to work."

Roger nodded, feeling the hat's brim curl under his hands. "Sooner rather than later," he confirmed.

"Cause of death is pretty clear," Quigg said. "Man was single, no children. I should have him to the parlor by midnight."

The hour hand of Roger's dinged-up Timex barely brushed ten.

"Fast as you can," he said. Midnight was still over twelve hours away.

Hinson stood at Roger's side while the two watched the coroner's van pull away, turn out of the school parking lot.

"Full moon," Hinson said.

What the hell was that supposed to mean? Roger put his hat on, already turning to his car, steeling himself for the drive to the parlor, the conversation with Lenore. "And?" he said.

"People get weird," the rookie said. "Quigg didn't think an animal could do this to a body." The green edge crept back around Hinson's ears, under his eyes. "We sure we're looking for an animal, Sheriff? What if, what if it's something—*someone*—else? A serial—"

"It's a goddamn wolf, Hinson!" Roger spun on his heel, index finger raised into the boy's face like he could stab the words directly into his brain. "It's a goddamn wolf, and we're going to catch it, and that'll be the end of it."

Roger's hand yanked back, balling into a fist at his side. Blood pounded in his forearm. Last month, Johnson's hand twitched toward his gun when Roger floated a serial killer theory, after Edwin Boone, after Snow Leger. Roger hadn't understood the dark look that had passed across his commanding officer's face then, but he sure as shit did now.

Somehow, and Roger didn't know how, Buck Johnson had known the truth. Maybe not all of it, maybe not about the Evans women, but more than he'd ever let on.

"Get back to the station," he told Hinson. "Call Animal Control."

The boy blinked at him. "Why?"

"All those missing-pets posters plastered all over town?" Roger watched as understanding darkened the rookie's eyes. "Those are your problem now."

In the Crown Vic's driver's seat, Roger didn't look in the rearview at Hinson, still glowering at the end of Brevard's bloody trail across the parking lot, until he pulled out of the school's main entry and turned away. Let the kid be angry with him. Let him be furious and confused and suspicious, but let him keep his nose out of where it didn't belong.

Roger had already buried a sheriff, a beautician, a friend.

A love.

When it came right down to it, he had no interest in burying the rookie, too.

CHAPTER 13

Lenore Evans

Everything is fine.

Lenore pulled two changes of clothes from the stash in the parlor's breakroom—one for herself from the top drawer, one for Ducey from the bottom drawer that she hadn't emptied out. She ran a comb through her ginger bob and pinched color into her cheeks, then she slipped out of her robe and nightgown and into a pair of crisp slacks, a brassiere, a pressed button-down.

The blouse strained over her breasts. One of Grace's, then.

Everything is fine, Lenore thought as she pushed the top button through its hole at her neck, refusing to think of her daughter under the mount of barren dirt in the garden.

Everything is fine.

She smoothed down the edges of her collar and let her fingertips slip over the row of pearls lining the blouse front—*fine, fine, fine, fine*—and then Lenore cricked her spine straight, lifted her chin, and followed Ducey's dirt track to the parlor laboratory and—*Everything is fine*—stepped through the door.

Luna sat cross-legged against the far wall, ankles exposed where she'd forgotten socks. Belle's head rested in her lap. The dog snored, her long rust-colored ears draped like a warm autumn blanket over Luna's legs. The girl snarled as she worked at something in her hands—features twisted, eyes and lips puckering around the wrinkled ridge of her nose—and Lenore flinched.

Everything is fine.

Still in her burial dress, Ducey bent over the stainless-steel sink, sponge-bathing from the faucet like this was perfectly normal. Like she'd just been out gardening, is all. Not digging her way out of the grave, plunging a trocar into poor Viola Carroll's stomach, drinking her up.

Lenore stared at the jagged scar where she'd sealed the wound on her dead mother's throat with strigoi ashes. *Everything is fine.*

"Those for me?" Ducey asked, flashing her good eye at the bundle of clothes in Lenore's arms.

Lenore set the bundle on the counter out of the water's reach and pinned her hands to her hips. "Mama, why are you splashing water all over the lab when we have a perfectly good washroom around the corner?" she asked.

Ducey twisted the water off to rub at her heart, leaving dirt pebbled along the sink's bottom. "That one's for company."

"Not the guest bathroom." Lenore watched her mother riffle through the clean muumuu and fresh undergarments she'd carried in from the breakroom. She rolled her eyes when Ducey tossed the bra away and slipped the flowered dress over her head. "I meant in the back," Lenore said through pursed lips. "Grandmother Pie's old rooms."

The dead woman shrugged. "Don't like messin' with Mother's things."

Ducey knew as well as anyone that, before it had become a parlor, Evans Funeral Home had been the Evans homestead, built plank by plank by Conchobhar Evans himself. After her parents' death, Pie converted the old farmhouse into the parlor, and when she disappeared sixteen years ago, just a year before Luna's birth, Pie's kitchen became the breakroom, and her own rooms were sealed off and soon forgotten. Nearly two decades later, and Ducey went about her business like those little rooms in the back of the house didn't exist any more than her own mother had.

"Wouldn't you prefer a nice shower—"

Ducey twisted the faucet back on and drowned out Lenore's words. More water splashed out of the lab sink as she hoisted one leg up to scrub mud crust from between her toes. Half of it crumbled to the floor where her ankle didn't quite clear the counter.

"Instead of making more of a mess for me to clean up?" Lenore finished.

Ducey wrenched the faucet off. "Nothing wrong with a little whore's bath, Len," she said as she pulled her apron over her head, cinched it around her middle without making eye contact. "Just savin' water."

Lenore doubted that very much, but she dropped her hands off her hips and let her arms dangle at her side. "That's not a nice thing to say, Mama."

"Don't change the fact that it's still true." Ducey mumbled something that sounded like *Miss Priss* and wiped her hands dry on her apron, then reached up to muss the filth from her hair, sprinkling dirt like spilled cinnamon onto the linoleum. "Those women did what they needed to do, and so am I," she said. "Ain't no shame in that."

No shame, just extra time cleaning up grave dirt turned to mud—which Lenore would do, of course, because she always cleaned up everyone else's messes, even her mother's. Her eyes dropped back to the scar on Ducey's throat.

"Let's go talk in the breakroom." At least in there Lenore would be able to concentrate without worrying over the mess waiting for her in the lab.

Ducey snatched her wedding ring from the soap dish on the sink and slid it on her finger, then unhinged her bifocals and pushed them up her nose. She glared at Lenore from behind her frames, one green eye dull and clouded, the other bright and fierce. She set off down the hall, jerking to a stop when she hit the breakroom and noticed the snapped pendulum left on the tabletop. Ducey spun, Belle winding between her feet like the two were tangled together as she rounded on Lenore and Luna.

"What in the hell did you do to Mother's clock?" she asked, good eye sparking venom behind her bifocals.

"It was me," Luna cut in before Lenore could answer. "I broke it off to put down Ms. West."

The dead woman squinted at her great granddaughter. She tightened her lips, then glared at Lenore. "What was the clock doing in here in the first place?" Ducey asked.

"I moved it into the chapel." It'd been the only thing Lenore changed in the parlor after her mother and daughter died. "And that's where it's going to stay."

Ducey's eyes narrowed, her entire face collapsing into a tight line of disapproval. She held the squint so long Lenore thought her mother might pitch a fit, but then Ducey's eyes popped wide like cauldron bubbles, and she clicked her teeth. "Guess you better give Gil Wallace a holler," she said. "He'll know how to fix that ugly old thing back up."

Luna poured grounds into the filter, going through the motions of making coffee while Ducey settled into her recliner. Belle curled into an ottoman under her feet, purring in that way that happy dogs do, and Lenore bent herself into one of the dining chairs. A month ago, Ducey had been the one to put on the pot when they'd told Luna about the family business. Not long after that, Lenore did the same, the night they buried Grace and Ducey.

Everything's fine. At least that time, Lenore didn't have to keep an eye on Ducey, make sure she didn't dredge her coffee with schnapps.

Lenore's gaze snapped back to the scar on her mother's throat, the shadow of dirt still faint in her nailbeds.

She would very much have to keep an eye on Ducey.

"First things first," Lenore said, "we need to establish some . . . rules."

In her recliner, Ducey's eyebrows shot into her hairline. "Rules?" She clucked. "Last time I checked, I was the one in charge around here."

The damn pinch in Lenore's shoulder blade was back. "Last time *I* checked, you were buried under a rosebush in my garden," she shot over the coffeepot's gurgle. "And I reckon we ought to pretend that's still the case while we figure all this out, don't you?"

Ducey's features narrowed again, but she huffed them loose more quickly this time. "And how do you propose we do that?" she asked.

Lenore dropped her eyes to the table and stared hard. *Everything is fine.* "Well, for one, we need to find another way to . . ." She thought of the trocar, stabbed into Viola's chest. "Satisfy your hunger."

Her mother's hand moved instantly to her apron pocket, patted around for butterscotch, clenched around the trocar shaft. Ducey tracked Luna as she poured three cups of coffee, setting two on the table and one beside Ducey's chair. The dead woman's nose curled when she breathed in the steam.

It'd take more than a glug of schnapps to make that sludge appetizing.

She pushed the mug away. "You think I want to chew on dead meat, Len?"

"You might not have to," Lenore said. "Maybe we can mix ashes into . . ." Into what? Soup? Bread? Tea? "We don't know—"

"We don't know a dang thing about those ashes," Ducey finished for her.

Pinch, pinch, pinch, right up into Lenore's skull. "Mama, we can't just have you feeding on cadavers. It's not right."

Luna's hand disappeared into her pocket, fidgeting again. "Everything has to feed," she said.

Ducey nodded like that settled it. "And we happen to have a fresh supply of bodies." She clicked her teeth and winked her good eye. "Cooler to table."

Luna snorted. "Nice."

Everything is fine.

Ducey put a palm up before Lenore could argue. "I know what I am, Len, and I know what that means, even if I don't know why. I know a thing or two about keeping things hidden," she said. "I'll patch up Mrs. Carroll, and be discreet with the rest." Her mouth twisted into a bittersweet smirk and her palm brushed her chest before resting in her lap. "Now go on, I know you're not done."

Feeding on flesh, Lenore had known, was a logic she couldn't avoid, an inevitability she'd have to accept just like her mother had. But the next rule she proposed would not be one her mother would mind willingly.

Lenore swallowed and told herself everything was fine.

"There's the matter of the parlor itself," she started, hunting for words she never thought she'd have to find, avoiding her dead mother's eyes. "Taking care of business on my own, without you and Grace, has been . . . too much." Oh hell, here it came. "I hired help—Kim Cole, the girl who found Belle."

If it hadn't been for the dog under her feet, the sluggish recall of her ancient muscles, Ducey might have flown out of her chair, wrapped her hands around Lenore's throat. "Now why in the hell would you go and do a fool thing like that?" she screeched. "Thought I raised you better than to act like your mama."

"My mama was dead!" The words burst out of Lenore's mouth so hard that tears sprang into her eyes. She'd said it, finally, for the first time. Her mother sat upright in her recliner, an ash scar down her throat and another in her chest right where Lenore had stabbed her, but every bit as dead as a doornail.

The pinch in her back bit Lenore's tears free, sent them spilling down her cheeks. "You were dead," she said, tasting salt, "and I didn't know what to do."

Ducey did push up from her recliner then. She crouched into the chair opposite Lenore.

Everything is fine, Lenore thought when her mother's palm pressed cool, too cool, not warm, not alive, against her slacks.

"Everything is going to be okay, baby girl," Ducey promised. "I'm here now. We'll figure out all the rest in due course."

When Lenore dipped her head to blot her eyes, Ducey returned to her recliner.

"I need you to *stay* here," Lenore said. "Not just here with me, but *here*"—she gestured to include the family homestead—"at the parlor."

Ducey bucked back up, the tender moment past. "Oh, like hell, Lenore Ruth," she spat, and Lenore blinked hard when she saw her mother's teeth snap. "I have a perfectly good house on the other side of town, and I'll be damned if I'm not sleeping in my own bed tonight."

"We can't have anyone noticing lights on at your house, Mama," Lenore said. "Your obituary ran," she added, just in case Ducey got any ideas that Lenore kept the death a secret.

Hell, maybe she should have.

"She could stay with us?" Luna suggested from beside the coffeepot.

Lenore shared a look with her mother. "Pass," they said, together.

"Grandmother Pie lived at the parlor when she was alive," Lenore said when Ducey went on grumbling about how she'd worked good and hard to make a home for herself. "Can't be all that bad," Lenore said.

"We have to keep distance between ourselves and the dead, you know that, Len." Ducey closed her eyes. It was the only lesson she ever shared from the letter Pie left the night she died: *The dead can steal your life, even when you're still living it.* "Spending too much time in this place will mess with your head," Ducey whispered, like just speaking it out loud hurt her ears. "Just like it did Mother's. I heard it all for over sixty years."

Whatever else Pie had written to help that line make sense, Lenore might never know.

"Is that what you meant by 'other monsters'?" Luna asked, sliding into an open chair. She sipped her coffee, then, "The other legends, the things worse than ghouls—did Great-great-grandma Pie tell you about them, too?" She put her mug down and slipped her hand back into her pocket. "Did she tell you why the dead come back?"

Hokum, Ducey had called it before, but now she scoffed, wiggling in her chair. Her palm slid back over her heart, and she clicked her teeth, then tapped her head. "Mother's elevator didn't go all the way to the top at the end," she said. "She had so many stories—'bout the Spindletop fire and the hell that broke loose after, 'bout ghouls and worse. Used to say that the land was cursed, that the Evanses were cursed, that *I'm* cursed." Ducey's words broke into a laugh that ended as a cough. "I bet Buchanan would get a laugh out of that one," she said. "You got a vial of him stashed somewhere, Len?"

Lenore shook her head. "We buried Buck Johnson's body, not his ashes."

Ducey's good eye sparked, but she bit back whatever her first response might have been and sighed instead. "Like I said, by the time she went, Mother wasn't herself," she said, speaking only to Luna now. "She wrote that letter and disappeared one night. I figure she's buried on the property somewhere."

Brakes squealed in the parlor parking lot before Luna could get off another question, and Lenore shot to her feet.

Everything is fine.

She bolted out of the breakroom, out of the back door, putting herself between the new sheriff and the parlor as Roger emerged from his patrol car, mudpie-brown hat already twisted in his fingers.

"Roger—" Lenore barely got the man's name out before his eyes clocked the dirt strewn across the pavement, the muddy prints tracking from the upturned rosebush, the mount of grave dirt, the sagging rhododendrons, to the door at the back of the funeral parlor.

"What the hell," Roger muttered, then pushed past her, his training kicking in as he unholstered his weapon, cocked the revolver's hammer.

"Get behind me, Lenore," he ordered.

You could take the man out of the cop, but not the fool out of the man, apparently. Lenore pushed Roger out of the way, making sure his gun arm aimed toward the cemetery and not at the parlor.

"I'm going to need you to stay calm," she told him. "Put that thing away and follow me."

She waited until he released the hammer before she led him through the back door. Roger tracked the muddy footprints, eyes widening as they made their way down the hallway.

Then he stepped into the breakroom and saw a ghost.

"Well if it ain't Sheriff Big Britches," Ducey said from her recliner.

It's said that for as long as he lived after that night, the man never managed to pull his mouth all the way closed. His eye twitched so hard it might jump out of his head, and he cleared his throat enough times Lenore worried he'd work himself hoarse, but eventually Roger did as she told him and got his gun put away. His jaw flapped a few times, but he managed to fill them in on the scene at the high school.

"Brevard's missing some of his ribs, and an arm," he said and rubbed his chin. "Jaw snapped. His hair is gone, along with his insides." Roger shot Lenore a look she didn't like, a look that said that wasn't all. She had to tell him twice to go on.

"And his incisors have been pulled out, just like with the cow," he finally said.

Lenore knew where Roger was driving, and it wasn't toward the man's missing pieces. A rabid wolf patsy wouldn't stick if the story didn't add up.

Roger looked at Ducey, who snapped her tongue. "Now don't go lookin' at me, Roger Taylor. I just got up," she said, "and I got too many of my own problems to go 'round borrowin' anyone else's."

The man held his head in his hands. "What are we dealing with here?" he asked.

Lenore noticed her mother didn't volunteer any information. She noticed Luna's hands buried in her pockets. Lenore knew when other people were keeping secrets, because she stared at the scar on her mother's throat and kept her own, too.

Everything is fine, she thought, but then she looked Roger dead in the eye and told the man the truth. "I don't know."

CHAPTER 14

Daniel Garland

*T*oday sucked, man.

Daniel lay on the living room sofa he'd dragged up three flights of stairs from the curb and sucked hard on the joint he'd traded a ten for. He adjusted the foam pads against his ears and thumbed up the volume on his Discman. Christina Aguilera's voice ripped through his headphones, and Daniel exhaled a cloud of smoke and closed his eyes. Sure, the singer's self-titled album may not be the manliest CD he'd ever purchased, but he'd slipped the plastic square between discs from Ol' Dirty Bastard and the Offspring on the new-release rack and handed the cashier three hard-earned twenties just the same.

Not that I'm apologizing, Daniel thought and tugged until the hot paper scorched his fingertips.

When his mom died, he'd gone pro in slinging apologies to keep his old man from knocking him one. Now Daniel lay under his own roof, on his own free, trashed sofa, listening to whatever the hell he wanted, however loud he wanted, and stuffing himself full of delivery pizza and twelve-ounce sodas. Apologizing for his eclectic musical tastes was not gonna happen.

Besides, the girl had pipes, he'd give her that. Maybe Christina wasn't quite up to the standard of Daniel's true love, Mariah Carey, but she could hold her own.

He rolled onto his side and plucked the plastic case from the coffee table, eyeballing the photo on the jacket cover as he ashed the joint into a half-empty can of Mountain Dew. The girl wasn't bad to look at, either. Not at all. Daniel took another suck off his joint and puffed out like a dragon as he thumbed the volume another nudge higher and sang along, voice cracking like the shitty ice maker in his shitty rented fridge when he attempted to hit the high notes.

The track clicked over, and Daniel's pager vibrated among the empty pizza box and empty soda cans on the coffee table. He flicked the joint in the ashtray, filled his lungs, and picked up the pager. The coroner's office number flashed on screen, followed by *911*—Quigg's joke that he had another body that needed driving. Ironic, the coroner thought, because the dead were in no hurry.

"Man's got a morbid sense of humor." Daniel grunted himself upright. "But at least he pays well."

Daniel pushed his headphones off, still humming, and snatched the cordless phone. He pulled up the antenna and dialed the number, wrecking the lyrics while he rode out the high and waited for the licky old bastard to pick up. Probably he shouldn't have gone full Cheech on a work night. Daniel agreed to be on call when he took the job at the mortuary, he just hadn't expected his pager to buzz at eleven p.m. was all.

You gotta get a girl, he thought, looking at Christina, pretty on her album cover—and then Quigg picked up.

The man got down to business. "Got a body that needs taking to the parlor," he said.

"Tonight?" Daniel held the phone away from his ear so he didn't have to hear the coroner's tongue dragging across his mouthpiece halfway across town.

"Yessir." Quigg licked, then, "Any chance you caught the evening news?"

Last time Daniel watched the evening news had been the night his mama was killed by a drunk driver on her way home from waitressing at Piccadilly's. His daddy punched a hole through the wall after that ten o'clock broadcast, put another ding in Daniel's left eye to boot. So no, he hadn't seen whatever Quigg was dancing around.

"I have not," he told the coroner.

Another lick, followed by a long sigh, the kind Daniel had gotten too used to hearing.

"Listen," Quigg said, "you'll hear it soon enough, but that wolf—you know, the one that killed all those folks last month?"

Just because Daniel hadn't caught the news didn't mean he'd been living under a rock. "What about it?"

Another lick. "It got the principal."

No shit. "Brevard?" Daniel asked, and Quigg rounded out the particulars—the missing parts, the mutilated remains. Still, "You sure this can't wait till morning?" Daniel asked, though he already had his Jordans on his feet, the laces looped in his fingers.

"Eh, the sheriff is antsy to get the body over to the parlor," Quigg said. "Taylor wants the Evans girls to get the man good and cleaned up the best they can, in case any next of kin needs to come in, that sort of thing."

When they hung up, Daniel took his time tying his sneakers. Maybe it was weird, that the first body he'd driven from the morgue to the funeral parlor belonged to his kindergarten teacher and the second, his high school principal.

Or maybe it was just the weed.

Maybe, if he saw Kim Cole, he'd ask her what she thought. Weird, too, he thought, the two of them bumping into each other.

Or maybe that was the weed talking, too.

Daniel took one last puff, then ran his pinky along the condensation at the bottom of his soda can and let moisture drip onto the cherry of the joint. He kissed the pretty blonde on the album cover and put his headphones on, then started the CD over and scooped up his keys. On his way out, Daniel stuffed his keys in his pocket, snatching up the overflowing trash bag by his front door, and twisted the doorknob lock behind him.

He took the stairs two at a time on his way down, humming along to the music in his headphones, swinging the trash bag at his side.

Daniel glanced at his pickup, then headed over to the dumpster shed at the far end of the parking lot, backed up to the few mom-and-pop shops, the laundromat. Half the town's refuse ended up in his complex, but this close, the air always smelled like detergent—a "Tide" of floral soap that grew stronger the closer her got to the trash bins, like it could perfume the stink of poverty and desperation.

Could be worse, he figured. He could smell the dumpster instead.

The streetlight at the edge of the lot blinked, flickering over the images on the missing-pet posters Scotch-taped to the pole, and Daniel skipped a step when he heard the scratching. This time of night, there was always something digging through the dumpster, especially in an apartment complex populated by poor families, fixed-income seniors, and college kids barely scraping by, willing to live with roaches and ceiling mold so long as they didn't have to cohabitate with their parents.

Like him.

Minus the college.

Daniel's heart panged in his chest. Dad hadn't been the same since the accident took Mom, and neither had he.

He's a genie in a bottle, baby. Just waiting for someone to rub him the right way.

His Discman clicked over to a new track as Daniel neared the shed. The light flickered again, but he ignored it, pulling wide the gate someone had jimmied open, left flapping against its mate.

It wasn't his dad's fist that punched him when Daniel threw the dumpster lid open, but it wasn't Tide floral either. This stank went beyond greasy old fast food, beyond soggy diapers. Something rotten. Something *rotting.* A dead animal, maybe.

He tossed in the garbage sack.

The streetlight flickered again, barely struggling back to life as Daniel turned to go. Behind him, the stink rose.

His Discman clicked over. Christina belted out a new tune about what a girl wants, and Daniel froze.

Probably just a raccoon. Or rats. Feasting on leftover food scraps and baby shit.

Daniel thumbed down the volume on his Discman.

Christina faded and Daniel heard it.

Breathing. Behind him.

Raspy, heavy breathing, like panting around gravel.

Then, a sound worse than breathing. Wet, like his boss on the phone. Like a tongue.

Like *hunger.*

The sound stopped and Daniel turned, scary-movie slow. The streetlight flickered and went dark, because of course it did, that's how things went when you were about to die. Overhead, the moon shone bright enough to still cast some light, enough that Daniel could see fur ruffle in the light nighttime breeze. The shine of moonlight on teeth.

The beast stood on hind legs inside the dumpster, matted and stuck over with garbage.

Daniel watched the creature climb out. The shadows clung to its edges, blurring the lengths of its limbs, the curved back. The shape of the creature's head, the gleam of violent, nocturnal eyes. The thing pitched itself over the lip of the dumpster, mounding into the corner. It shifted like it couldn't gain footing, then growled to its full height.

He froze. Last time Daniel had been this frozen had been the day his mother took her last breath in the hospital ER. *Beep, beep,* then a long, thin, tinny *buzz,* and every cell in Daniel hardened to ice.

He heard that sound again, that flatline at his end, as the beast with him in the dumpster shed stood. Tall enough to stare him down, to size him up.

The streetlight flicked again, shining back to life with perfect timing to illuminate the monstrous thing as it licked its lips. Daniel saw the creature's face—its *human* face.

What the fuck, he had time to think.

And then the creature lunged, Christina shrilled in his ear, and Daniel screamed higher and fuller and louder than any note she'd ever sung.

CHAPTER 15

Kim Cole

Wednesday morning at exactly ten a.m. on the nose, Kim Cole pulled into the parking lot of Evans Funeral Parlor, slung her mint-green Buick into the open space directly beside the old Ford Rambler that used to be Ducey's, and cut the engine. She pulled down the driver's side visor and checked her reflection in the mirror, running her pinky tip along her eye to clean up the edge of her liner.

Kim applied a fresh coat of Revlon Black Cherry and didn't blot her lips. She might leave the parlor smelling like death, but for the first time in forever, she didn't have to worry about clocking out reeking of brittle frosting and burnt sugar, frazzled from bossy customers dissatisfied with the letter work on their baby-shower sheet cakes.

Only thing you have to worry about now is Lenore Evans. Kim's eyes flicked to the rearview mirror and she reached up, twisting the funeral parlor into view. She'd expected Rhonda to give her hell when she'd tendered her resignation at Jimbo's, but the day manager was too preoccupied with her own missing cat to care that she'd need to hire someone to take the morning shift. Brandon, she'd known, would turn his nose up at the idea of her going to work for Lenore Evans, but somehow her boyfriend's bad attitude just made Kim want the job more.

Not that she'd expected to get it. Kim had a feeling that the funeral director's decision had surprised her as much as it had Kim.

The blank look the woman gave her when she stepped through the parlor's front doors at 10:03 a.m., makeup case clutched between her hands like the sole belongings of an orphan fresh off a train, either said Lenore regretted it already, or she'd forgotten about her new hire entirely.

Great.

"You said Wednesday, ten a.m.," Kim said and hoped like hell her new boss just needed an extra cup of coffee—ironic, because if she'd still been at the café, a mug of java to wash away the circles under Lenore's eyes would have been coming right up, no problem.

She could probably get her job at Jimbo's back, right?

Seated behind the large reception desk in the front lobby, Lenore blinked a couple times too many, then held her eyes shut too long before her entire face clicked open. She laid her pencil atop the ledger she'd been writing in.

"That's right, I did," Lenore said, and shut the book.

Her eyes flicked down the hall while Kim dug the toe of her boot through the low-pile carpet, but then her new boss stood, palms firm against her thighs. Lenore's eyes shuttered again. Maybe Kim should have gone easy on her black-on-black ensemble so Lenore Evans wouldn't stand there blinking at her all Dianne Wiest, like Kim had scissors at the ends of her wrists and not a basic cosmetics case.

Which, ironically, was just what Dianne Wiest had held when she sized up Edward Scissorhands.

Ducey Evans had been kooky and raw, the kind of quirky old woman a girl like Kim could've looked up to. But Lenore Evans was something entirely different.

Kim passed the makeup case from hand to hand.

"Well." Lenore's fingertips made little ripples over her thighs while she pattered around like she wasn't enjoying this, either. "Let's get you to work then."

She pivoted on her loafers and marched toward the chapel.

But Kim's first day was Wednesday, not Sunday, and tonight was Mrs. Carroll's visitation. The last time Kim had seen her former kindergarten teacher had been on the metal exam table. "We aren't going to the lab?"

Now Lenore didn't blink at all. "Visitation is held in the chapel." She started toward the double doors, then stopped and turned back so suddenly that Kim nearly bumped into her. "It's best that you stay in the chapel today," Lenore said and forced another bent smile. "I'm still taking care of some things in the lab."

Kim nodded. Brandon had warned her about Brevard, about the state of the body. It seemed a little fast to already have the body at the parlor, but what did she know? Why else would Lenore want to keep her out of the lab?

Lenore swept Kim through into the chapel, waving her toward a metal gurney at the front of the chancel, the rich wooden casket open, its tufted lavender insides empty. A woman's body lay on the gurney. Kim didn't recognize the button-front green silk dress, only the red bouffant wig on the head.

"Viola had a lot of friends, so I expect we'll get a good amount of florals delivered—" Lenore gestured for Kim to set her case down on the front pew, then directed her to the foot of the gurney, putting herself at the head. "You'll need to keep an ear out for that while I'm gone," Lenore said. "Just bring them here and we'll organize them later."

"Wait, you're leaving me here . . . alone?" Dead bodies didn't scare Kim Cole. But ghosts might. If any building was going to be haunted, wouldn't it be a funeral parlor?

"The school is closed today," she said, glossing over the bit about the principal being found chewed to pieces in the parking lot after Monday night's game. "I need to take my granddaughter to the library to catch up on schoolwork." Lenore slid her hands, palms up, under the dead schoolteacher's shoulders. She nodded for Kim to slip her palms under the calves, help from the other end. Once they lifted the body into the casket, Lenore cradled Mrs. Carroll's head on its pillow, then smoothed down her wig.

"If the deceased is married, the ring hand is traditionally placed on top," Lenore said, positioning the woman's right hand atop her left where they rested on her stomach, fingers gently touching. She tapped the bare ring finger of the top hand. "Her widower will bring her wedding band for the service."

She made sure the woman's toes pointed upward, toward the chapel exit, then Lenore left Kim with strict instructions to finish up Mrs.

Carroll, and pushed the gurney back through the partition door into the lab. The doors swung shut, and Kim heard the lock.

"Guess it's just us now," she told Mrs. Carroll.

Mrs. Carroll didn't say *boo* back. Kim looked at the big grandfather clock in the back of the chapel. If it ticked, she didn't hear the pendulum swing inside the wooden cabinet. And where the hell was Belle this morning? The last time Kim visited the parlor, the dog wouldn't budge from the front door. Today the old hound was nowhere to be seen.

Maybe's she in the lab, Kim thought. Along with whatever else Lenore wanted to keep hidden in there.

When the Rambler passed by the chapel's windows, Kim retrieved a brush from her vanity case and approached the casket. She smoothed the dead woman's collar, adjusted the shiny red apple brooch pinned over her breast, then fingered each button down the front of the green dress. She positioned Mrs. Carroll's arms at her sides again and made sure the fabric grain all pointed the same way. The last little round button had come loose over the woman's belly in the shift from gurney to casket, and Kim set the brush aside and pulled the fabric together, hunting for the matching green elastic to bind them. It'd been over a decade since she'd seen her kindergarten teacher, but somehow, Mrs. Carroll looked just the same—

Except for the puncture in her stomach.

Kim's fingertip traced the wound on the dead woman's skin where her camisole had pulled up away from the girdle under her funeral dress. Kim's eyebrows knitted as she raked her fingertip on fresh sutures, twisting free a second button, then a third. Kim parted the fabric, exposing a patch of penny-sized holes, all sewn closed.

What the hell?

Mrs. Carroll had died of a heart attack, right? No need for medical tubes or an autopsy, so why the sutures? And they didn't embalm at Evans Funeral Parlor.

Behind her, the chapel doors swung shut.

Kim jumped. Lenore had left—hadn't she? And Kim still hadn't seen ear nor snout of Belle. She opened her mouth, her lips trying on a series of different options before calling out, "Ms. Evans?"

Quiet.

No, not quiet. A noise, like plastic. Like cellophane.

Kim left Mrs. Carroll at the front of the chancel and tiptoed down the chapel aisle.

She pushed through the doors into the lobby. Empty.

The noise again, louder but slower, like it was scared of being heard. Kim stepped light, careful not to squeal her boots when they hit tile. She checked the breakroom. Empty. The reception room. Empty. The lab's closed door was probably locked, but Kim tried the knob anyway. When it stuck, she turned to the only other room down the long hallway—the selection room.

"Hello?" God, she sounded dumb, like one of those idiots in a horror movie that always called out when the killer lurked near, invited them right over, practically *begged* for it.

Kim snorted. People always blamed the girl, not the bad guy with the knife.

No slashers in the selection room, though. Just a couple of closed caskets and shelves lined with empty urns. She sighed. *Always the red herring,* she thought. Never the final girl.

But then she heard the sound again—the sharp crinkle of a plastic wrapper, down by her feet. Kim looked at the carpet. At the filmy scrap of cellophane under her boot's rubber sole—and another, another, another. She crouched beside a casket and plucked up the wrapper, rocking forward onto her knees to collect the shiny trash.

And then the distinctive sound of another unwrapping.

The faint sound of Kim's knees unhinging as she stood matched the noise the casket lid made as it lifted behind her. Then, she heard a voice.

"Now honey," the voice said. "I'm gonna need you not to panic."

Kim panicked. Of course she panicked. She'd read Ducey Evans's obituary in the *Enterprise* four weeks ago, so that's the feeling that swirled in her stomach, crawled up her throat, clouded out her vision. That was panic.

130 | Lindy Ryan

Until it wasn't. Somehow.

"I thought you were dead," Kim said, far too calmly, even for her.

Ducey shrugged. "Well, child, I reckon I am."

Kim eyed the craggy scar zagging down Ducey's throat, the way one side of her face hung a little too low, how her skin looked a little too mottled, a little too blue, and that cloudy swirl moved through Kim again as she met the woman's remaining good eye.

She swallowed it. "I can fix you," she told the very old and very dead woman.

Forty-five minutes later, Kim watched Ducey study herself in the parlor's bathroom mirrors. The fluorescents gave her skin a yellow tinge like jaundice, but yellow was better than corpse blue.

"Never gave a lot of thought to sticking around after I died," Ducey said. "Think I would've preferred to do it before my knockers hit my knees, but I don't look half bad for a dead woman, do I, child?" Her reflection looked at Kim while her hands inspected her painted neck. "Where'd you learn that trick?"

Kim popped the top back on the can of Rust-Oleum she'd added into her kit this morning, just in case. "*Death Becomes Her.*" Then, "The movie," she added when Ducey shot an eyebrow at her.

The dead woman harrumphed. "Can't say I've heard of it."

"Goldie Hawn and Meryl Streep?" Kim said, but Ducey's eyebrow stayed up. "Anyway, those two, they're sort of frenemies—it starts with a fight over Bruce Willis, but it's really more about them competing with each other." Kim flapped her hands. "Anyway, they both end up taking an immortality potion that's supposed to keep them young and beautiful forever, except they kill each other." Really, the movie explored unrealistic beauty standards and complicated female friendships, but explaining the plot just made the cult classic sound silly.

"Anyway, they stay alive because of the potion," Kim said, "but they're trapped in these decaying bodies that they have to figure out how to take care of."

She waggled the can.

Ducey leaned in close to the mirror and fluffed her hair. She put one side of her profile toward the glass, then the other, to get a good look at the mismatched hues of her cloudy eyes. Makeup couldn't fix her undead pupil, but contacts probably could.

Tricky to get a dead lady a prescription for contacts, though . . . Meryl and Goldie hadn't taught Kim anything about undead vision care. She couldn't even say if Ducey still needed her bifocals.

"Do you, you know . . ." Kim bit her lip when Ducey's bright eye caught on to hers in the glass. "Think you'll live forever now?"

The old woman looked at the balled-up cellophane wrappers Kim had carried into the bathroom with her, and smacked her lips. "Hell," she said. "I hope not."

"How did you die, anyway?" Kim asked as the pair made their way out of the bathroom and down the hall toward the breakroom. Ducey's obituary hadn't mentioned a manner of death, but coming face-to-face with an actual zombie made Kim doubt the credibility of the rabid animal story. "They said it was a coyote-wolf hybrid," she said. "Same one that killed those other people."

"Wasn't no damn wolf." Ducey tapped an arthritic finger along the scar on her throat, pressed her freshly painted palm to her heart, then crossed her arms over her chest. "Clyde Halloran."

Uncle Clyde? Kim's great-uncle's body hadn't been found, but he'd been declared wolf food, too. "I'm sorry?" she said, for her uncle, for the attack, and for anything else she needed to be sorry about.

Ducey held up a finger, her eyes drifting over Kim's shoulder to the windows behind her. "Honey, first thing you got to learn is not to apologize for somethin' that ain't got nothin' to do with you."

One set of tires crunched to a stop on the other side of the parlor's back door, then another. None of this made any damn sense to Kim. "But you said Uncle Clyde—"

"Second thing—" Ducey lifted another digit as the doors opened behind Kim.

Over her shoulder, Lenore's voice came out in a screech. "Mama, we talked about this!" She blew out a breath, eyes shooting between Kim and Ducey, and then she hung her head, defeated. "We can't do this right now. The body is here."

Ducey clicked her teeth and ignored her daughter to clutch Kim's hand. "Second thing you need to learn is that not everything that goes in the ground stays there." She let go and fled down to the selection room, and Kim turned in time to see another gurney push through the back door of the funeral parlor.

She took one look at the mass on the tray and knew who it belonged to.

The question was—if Ducey could come back from the dead, what else might?

CHAPTER 16

Sheriff Roger Taylor

Another day, another body. Sheriff Roger Taylor was two for two. *Three,* he thought, and chiseled another hole in his belt strap with his pocketknife. Roger yawned as he pushed the belt's metal prong through the leather. He did the work with his good arm, but the other still throbbed, holding the belt in place. Roger folded the little two-inch blade into his shirt pocket, secured the buckle, and hitched up his pants. Not two dead bodies, but three, if he counted Tanya West—and Roger figured he better.

Not that the poor woman's body would make its way into evidence, of course. She died in her own bed and then shuffled out her own back door, only to find her way inside a cooler at Evans Funeral Parlor. Once Lenore finished with the body, the dead woman would be fed to the furnace without ceremony, and that would be all she wrote on Tanya West.

Roger slid behind the Crown Vic's steering wheel and smothered another yawn inside his hat, then tossed it onto the dash. Guilty nightmares usually made for light sleep, but a very specific kind of insomnia came after driving over to a grieving woman's house in the middle of the night, making it look like she'd up and disappeared and wasn't waiting in a funeral parlor cooler with a stake through her heart.

He cranked on the engine. On the center console, the police radio crackled awake, and Roger's yawn cut short.

Dispatch Darla's voice staticked over the radio. "Come in, Tay—Sheriff."

Roger pressed the mic on the radio pinned over his badge and spoke into his shoulder. "Taylor here."

Twenty minutes ago, Dispatch Darla's voice had slid smooth across the landline when his phone rang. "We got another one," she'd said, and those four little words had wrenched Roger right out of the thin patch of sleep he'd been able to pull over himself, sent him scurrying out of his bed and back into his uniform. "This one's not as bad as yesterday," she had said before they'd disconnected.

"What's your ETA?" Fizz filled the spaces between the woman's words, and Roger was awake enough now to know that *not as bad* didn't have to mean better.

Hell, he thought as he backed the cruiser out of his gravel drive, aimed his tires toward the other side of town. *Could mean worse.*

"I'm en route," he radioed back.

After he wrapped up with whatever fresh nightmare waited across town, the body would be loaded up and hauled away, probably make the five o'clock evening news. Officially, Tanya West would stay missing, just like her son—the one Roger and Lenore fed to the furnace after Andy had sunk his claws into Grace. That damn reporter Penny Boudreaux could say whatever she wanted, because the only thing Roger hated worse than lying about the dead was watching someone else's loved one get scraped into a body bag.

Which, far as he could tell, was exactly what he was driving toward now.

Roger drove ten-and-two, keeping his boot level on the gas as he passed Jimbo's, then the high school with its collection of orange cones and yellow police tape flapping in the hot morning wind in the faculty parking lot. Any students who hadn't heard what happened after the game knew now that school had been cancelled two days in a row. Now that they'd bagged all the evidence, hauled off all the remains, a cleaning crew would be by to scrub the pavement, make it look like a man hadn't been torn into a dozen pieces right there in the faculty lot, but even the principal's death couldn't stop Texas high school football season.

Roger's throat clenched around the next yawn. Far as he knew, the dead man's arm still hadn't turned up.

He hoped it would, at least before Friday's Homecoming Dance.

If anyone went, anyway. Once news of a second victim turned up, half the town would lock themselves indoors. It was the other half Roger worried about—the half that would pick up their guns, start stocking up on ammo.

Small towns tended to have a lot more firepower than they did brains.

Now if only Roger could remember to keep his own gun loaded.

"Not as bad as yesterday," he mumbled as he turned the cruiser into the apartment complex. He'd been around long enough to know that a mob, scared shitless and hell-bent on revenge, was worse than any monster on its own.

The cruiser cleared the first two-story row building, then another, and when he'd cleared the block, Roger pulled around to the service area in back. When the garbage shed came into view, he braked to a stop behind a utility pole wallpapered in missing-pets flyers.

Roger stared at the pole, not at the dumpster. At the pole, not at the two wooden doors hanging open on their hinges like a pair of broken wings. At the dark stain creeping across the cement, the leg crooked out at an unnatural angle under one side.

He stared at the pole, where papers printed with images of dogs, cats, hell even a guinea pig, flapped in the hot morning breeze like caution tape in a high school parking lot. The wind picked up and a page lifted to reveal bright pink beneath. Its edges already faded, Roger stared at the collared kitten on the same flyer he'd watched Rhonda hang on the bulletin board at Jimbo's.

If Roger didn't know better, he'd think something was going around picking off people's furry family members.

But even with his windows up, he could smell the garbage.

Roger cut the engine, pressed the mic on his radio, and when Dispatch Darla answered, he had her run through the call again as he pushed out of the driver's side door.

"Call came in early," she said, as Roger stuck his hat back onto his head, hitched up his pants, and set off toward the stink. "An elderly couple on the way out to bible study. Went to take out the garbage and found . . ."

Darla's voice dropped off. The woman was a Catholic, and Roger knew she was busy signing the cross over her chest. "Found someone to pray for, by the sound of it," she said.

He was halfway to the smell when the wind picked up, and Roger caught a whiff of detergent riding under the funk of copper and filth. He looked up at the building on the other side of the dumpster shack, at the two little windows on the second floor. He knew those windows, if only from the outside.

Probably just a coincidence that the first kill had been at Luna's high school, the second in a dumpster behind the apartment she'd shared with Grace.

Grace.

In the past few weeks, Roger had seen dead bodies torn open, falling apart. Hell, he'd even heard them speak his name and seen them move. He clutched the gun he'd forgotten to reload while a teenage monster tore into the love of his life. Until yesterday, though, he'd never seen a ghoul claw its way back from the grave after a month of being underground just so it could go straight back to work.

Other than the fact that Ducey Evans couldn't seem to stomach her favorite hard candy anymore, and her eyes didn't match, death hadn't changed much about the old woman. She'd been a handful alive, how Lenore was going to keep her undead mother a secret, he couldn't imagine.

Still, a little voice niggled in the back of Roger's mind as he stared at that second-story window. *Why couldn't it have been Grace?*

If the Evans women didn't stay buried, why did it have to be Ducey who rose, and not Grace?

"Still there, Sheriff?" Darla's voice.

Roger jumped. He barked a sign-off into the radio as a white van pulled into the service lot. Roger's eye threatened to twitch until he only saw one silhouette in the cab.

"Where's your wolf expert this morning?" he asked as the old coroner shuffled over to the shed, clipboard wedged into his armpit.

Quigg wrinkled his nose. "My God, what's that smell?"

They found it on the ground inside the dumpster.

Surrounded by scraps of molding pizza boxes and soda cans slick with backwash and Lord-knew-what dumpster fluid, a dead kid lay in front of the large metal bin. Deep gouges ran the length of the body, with most of its insides—what was left, anyway—splattered along its outsides.

The coroner pulled his clipboard out as he squatted down, close enough to the body that Roger sucked back a gag. "At least the body's in one piece," Quigg said.

And two arms.

Roger grunted. Not as bad as yesterday, his ass.

A Discman rested in pieces next to the mangled remains, the headphones still plugged in, but the cord frayed into nothing and no sign of the actual headphones. The dead kid's head lay at an unnatural angle atop a broken neck, half his face torn off, incisors gone. One of the eyes held wide with shock. The other hung by its optic nerve—a big, brown-pupiled ball, staring up at nothing, from somewhere in the hollow of where the jaw should connect but did not.

Roger smothered another gag under his uniform hat before he tucked it under his good arm. Quigg seemed to study the ruined face of the dead kid. Roger said, "Gonna be hard to get an ID on this one."

He hadn't heard Quigg lick once since he squatted, and now the man's voice came out drier than Roger had ever heard it.

"This is Daniel Garland." Quigg withdrew a pencil from his back pocket, began to scribble onto his paperwork. "My new delivery driver."

"I'm sorry for your loss." The words rushed out automatically, which was fine because Roger didn't know what else to say.

Quigg sighed. "Didn't know him long, but Daniel seemed like a good kid. Lost his mama last year in an accident—drunk driver, if memory serves," he said. "Was looking for a fresh start."

The old coroner rattled off the details of the kid's dead mother in between cataloguing the state of the remains on his clipboard, and

Roger kept his mouth shut. Even a pro like Quigg found it easier to talk about nothing, rather than see what lay right in front of him.

This work hit harder when you knew the victim. Twenty-plus years in law enforcement, and that hard lesson only hit home with Roger one month ago.

He remembered Mrs. Garland's accident, though he would not have been able to recall the name. He kept his head down, eyes on the asphalt, in a show of respect while Quigg worked. Something spotted the ground between his boots. Roger's heart leapt into his throat as he counted five toe blots stamped into the blood drying on the dumpster-shed pavement.

Wolves, rabid or ghost or half-coyote or what, did not walk on five toes.

Roger forced his eyes to the boy's ruined jaw. Strigoi tore bodies open, drank them up. Roger knew this. But neither Lenore nor Ducey ever said anything about the restless dead collecting body parts.

He covered the print with his boot.

"Wounds are more or less consistent with the others—gutted insides, broken jaw, teeth removed, claw and teeth marks," Quigg said, touching the eraser end of his pencil around the kid's remains until the pink rubber turned red. "But then there's this—" He indicated the scratches where the bone around the eye socket had been crushed as something forced it to give up its cargo. "Wolves don't plug out eyes, Roger."

The two men shared a look, and Roger was the first to look away, covering the footprint with his boot when tires squealed on the other side of the dumpster. Hinson's cruiser came to a stop inside the blood pool seeping out under the open doors of the shed, smearing the tread. When the boy pushed out of his cruiser, Roger put his hat back on his head.

"You're late," he told the rookie.

Hinson had the good sense to look embarrassed. "I was following up on a missing pet."

"I bet you were." Roger might be getting up there in years, but he knew the piss-stench of beer when he smelled it.

Hinson froze when he saw the body—then he rushed to the dumpster and threw his head over the edge. Hard to blame him for this one.

When he finished emptying his guts, Roger asked if he knew Daniel, too.

"We were in the same grade in school," Hinson said. "Daniel was in marching band. Some of the band members would hang out with the football team after the game."

Roger hadn't known Hinson played football in high school, but the rookie had the shoulders for it. "When's the last time you spoke to—" He couldn't call the body Daniel. "The deceased?" he asked Quigg.

"Called him in last night to take the principal's body over to the parlor. He never showed." Still on his haunches, the old coroner shook his head. "I'd just assumed he decided he'd rather quit than come in on overtime, and I sent the body with another boy this morning," he said. "Never would have imagined this."

Quigg used a long pair of tweezers to pluck a few hairs out of the red. He put the hairs in a baggie and the baggie in his breast pocket. "We found some fur on Brevard's body. Forensics should have the results in later today," he said, finishing a note on his clipboard. "I'll tell the boys to add this lot into the mix." The coroner started toward his van.

"I'll follow you back to the morgue," Roger said. "Help things get cleared and get the body over to the parlor before you have to call his next of kin."

Quigg licked his approval. Next of kin calls for a man Brevard's age were one thing, but for a kid like this it'd be hell. Drunk driving accidents didn't make for pretty dead, and the father already lost a wife to the crushed metal. He didn't need to see what the animal made of his son, too. Seemed cruel to make a man go through such tragedy twice.

Hinson waited until the coroner was out of sight before turning on Roger. "A wolf didn't do this, Sheriff," he said.

His adrenaline waning, another yawn pushed against the backs of Roger's teeth. Of course a wolf didn't.

"That right?" he asked the rookie, then, "Mind telling me what did, Hinson?"

The boy raked his fingers through his hair. "This is the second victim—the second *male* victim," he said and shuffled his feet.

Roger knew exactly where this was going—hell, it'd been his own theory just last month. "Two *male* victims," he repeated, and when Hinson looked up, Roger nodded. "Two male victims, but different ages, different socioeconomic status. You think this is a serial killer, fine. Serial killers operate on profiles, like a certain regularity in their victims," he told the boy. "Tell me what else our two vics have in common—three," he said, "including Myrtle."

Three dead bodies, if he counted Tanya West.

Hinson shuffled again, but his football shoulders squared. "You told Sheriff Johnson you thought there was a serial killer, before."

"Yeah, well, I was wrong," Roger said, "and Johnson isn't the sheriff anymore."

The boy fumbled, and Roger let him work over all the loose ends that didn't connect. "I know it's hard to swallow, Hinson, believe me I do," he said, exhaustion turning his voice gruff as he forced himself to look at the pile of meat on the pavement—a pile of meat that came from a troubled home, lost his mom to a drunk driver, had just started a new job on his way to a better life.

Not meat, but a boy, a young man with a future, named Daniel.

"But two is a coincidence, not a pattern," Roger said, hating the way the lie tasted on his teeth, in his soul. "Animals kill indiscriminately—they're opportunists, not hunters. Both Brevard and Daniel were in the wrong place at the wrong time."

Those football shoulders squared again. "But you told Johnson—"

"Johnson is dead!" Roger's bark surprised him, and he had to work to keep his boots on the ground, not launching him forward. "He's dead and I'm the sheriff now, and I'm telling you it's a goddamn wolf!" His hip moved on its own, trying to push him closer to the rookie, but he kept his boot firm on top of that five-toed print. "Get back to the station," he said. "You're relieving Dispatch on missing-pets duty until further notice."

He jabbed his thumb toward the rookie's cruiser, parked in the dead kid's blood on the other side of the shed. "And get your tires out of my crime scene—that's an order."

Roger waited until Hinson's car pulled away, until Quigg's helpers had their poor coworker's body loaded up, before he lifted his boot and took in the print he'd hidden from view. He counted the toes, examined the long smear of a sole, then picked up a half-empty soda can and washed the footprint away with flat Mountain Dew.

CHAPTER 17

Luna Evans

Luna slammed a hardcover shut. She coughed when dust puffed in her nose. The public library was an even bigger disappointment than the one at the high school.

And it was their last hope.

"At least Books-A-Million *has* an occult section." She shoved the book across the table until it rammed into a stack of unexplored texts that would probably suck, too. The wooden seat bit into her butt and Luna wriggled herself into a more comfortable position, pushing up her shirtsleeves as she slid another dust-caked volume off the nearest stack. She flipped its cover back, scanned the table of contents, then slammed the book shut with a growl. "How can there be *nothing*?"

Folded into his own hardbacked chair, Crane traced a long, ringed finger down a page. When his nail hit the blank space of the bottom margin, he peered out from under a dark curtain of hair. "Perhaps not nothing, though certainly nothing *useful*," he said, and slid his finger to the other half of the spread to continue scanning. "'Where is the knowledge we have lost in information?'" he quoted, then produced a patient smile. "By which I mean to say," Crane said, "we don't lose anything by being exhaustive in our search."

That's because there isn't anything left to lose. Luna added one more useless text to the stack of throwbacks and put her head face-down on the table.

She gritted her teeth and spoke against the wood. Her breath blew back in her face, coppery and hot from chewing at her lips. The knot in her stomach eased, then clenched at the metallic taste. She should have bought gum.

"I just don't understand how there's *nothing*." Every time Luna said the word, she thought of the strange power in *The NeverEnding Story*, consuming everything in its path, leaving nothing behind. "We've been through every book in town."

Every religious text, Old World monster resource, and gothic novel they could get their hands on, and so far, *nada*. They'd even scavenged through the holiday section. Thanks to a pile of unhelpful Halloween books, they'd come away with some costume ideas and a recipe for something called black velvet cake that might be fun to try, but unless Luna could preserve her family's legacy with black-dyed pastry and half a dozen patterns for her very own vampire cape, she was no closer to figuring out what being the daughter born of a master strigoi and a mortal woman meant.

She was barely even sure what it meant to be a strigoi. Bloodsuckers were thick on the books, but less so their mythological predecessor. If it came before Bram Stoker, it basically didn't exist. And *Dracula*, of course, was fiction.

Probably.

And she could forget anything that might explain how her great-grandmother had pushed herself out of her own grave, or what kind of creature might have left a half-skinned dead cat strung from a tree outside her bedroom window, too.

Luna glanced at her backpack, zipped closed where it hung off the chair beside her. Yesterday morning, she'd found Sissy outside her window. She still hadn't told anyone, not even Crane, what she'd found waiting under the tallow tree for her today.

Luna waved a hand over their meager selection of books. "I guess I shouldn't be surprised we can't find much on Old World monsters in a rural southeast Texas county library," she admitted. "Probably lucky *Carmilla* hasn't seen the other side of a book ban by now."

"Wouldn't want *that* sort of romance to infect the youth," Crane muttered. In addition to having the audacity to precede Bram Stoker's famous novel, Sheridan Le Fanu's vampire expressed romantic desires with her female victim. All due respect to Coppola, Stoker's never did.

Her dead mother's work shirt tickled against Luna's wrist, and she pulled the sleeves over her fingers, stabbing her nails down to pin the hem to her palm. She hadn't told Crane about Tanya West yet, either. Everything had happened so fast. Luna barely remembered pulling Sissy the Cat out of the tree before finding Ducey in the lab. Then this morning. The next thing she knew, she was back in the Rambler on the way to the library.

"Speaking of romance," Crane ventured without looking up from his page. "The Homecoming Dance is Friday."

Luna looked across the table. Thanks to the town's sudden popularity on the regional news, probably everyone from here to Dallas knew the school dance was Friday.

"I know we're buried in ghouls and mystery," Crane said, then closed the volume he'd been scanning, added it to the reject mound on their table, and ran both hands over his face. "But perchance you'd like to be my date?"

Deep in her chest, Luna's heart burned, stabbed just like Ducey's. She fish-gaped her mouth open and closed like stupid Sheriff Taylor.

When she took too long to answer, Crane rippled his ringed fingers on a pile of magazines next to a stack of ratty *Dungeons & Dragons* novels and a Stephen King paperback, all designated for checkout. "*Or,*" he said, "we could stay in and craft." He tapped the shiny gloss cover on top. "All this research has presented some intriguing DIY projects."

Luna managed a smile. "Yes," she said, "to the dance," and Crane blew out a huge breath, like he hadn't been even just a little bit serious about the crafting thing.

He cracked open another hardcover. "And Ducey didn't tell you anything new, right?" he asked for the millionth time since Nana Lenore dropped them off. "I still can't believe she's *back.*"

Luna sighed. They'd had even less luck with zombie literature than they had with vampires—but for all that Ducey had managed *not* to share, there'd been one clue her great-grandma had let spill out. "She mentioned something about 'other monsters,' but she wasn't specific. Just that her mother—my great-great-grandmother—told her about other legends." Luna shrugged. "But everyone says Pie Evans went crazy. Supposedly she just disappeared one night, like, a year before I was born—she wrote a goodbye letter, and no one ever saw her again."

Crane's eyebrow hitched behind a curtain of dark hair. "Your great-great-grandmother's name was Pie?" he asked. "Like the dessert?"

"And yours is Crane," Luna shot back. "Like the bird."

And you're Moon Girl, she kinda sorta hoped he'd say, but, "Other legends?" he asked instead, and the knot in Luna's chest loosened.

She yanked the sleeves of Grace's work shirt over her fists. Everything the Evans women knew had been passed down from generation to generation. Her family had kept one monumental secret from her—much bigger than the secret she had tucked in her backpack—but she couldn't imagine that they'd held anything else back after. Especially now, when there weren't many Evanses left to keep watch over the family skeletons.

Not many alive, anyway.

"Mom said no one knows for sure why the dead get restless in this town," she told Crane, again. "All Ducey said was that the dead have risen here for as long as it's been a town, and our family has always guarded the balance between life and death—starting with Pie."

Luna remembered the key, the possible answers locked over the laundromat. "Did you get a chance to go snoop through my apartment?" she asked.

Crane shook his head. "Not yet, but I will."

"Okay." She thought of the little garage apartment, locked and abandoned. Of Ducey's house, empty and yet full of ghosts, while the dead woman herself haunted the parlor. If coming back as a ghoul didn't help solve the mystery of what made the dead rise, what her family had to do with it, Luna had no idea what would.

Crane pushed back from his chair, raised himself to his full height, and slipped into his coat. Luna quirked an eyebrow at last October's issue of *Southern Living* poking out of the books wedged under Crane's arm. Same season, but the bushel of baby pumpkins and fall leaves on the glossy cover contrasted heavily with its spooky company.

"I'm an avid reader of all things dark and dangerous." The boy shrugged. "Just because I wear eyeliner doesn't mean I'm not a fan of seasonal crafts," he said, then, "Ceremonial magicians need hobbies, too, you know."

Fair enough.

"Let's go talk to the librarian," he said.

"The librarian?" Luna's eyebrows twisted. "Why?"

"Municipal libraries have archives," Crane said, leading her toward the checkout desk. "If we can't dig anything up ourselves—" He shot Luna a look, and she knew he wasn't speaking in metaphors, but about her monstrous father still buried beneath the white rosebush in the funeral parlor's gardens. "Then we can at least dig through the town's records, see if there's anything about your great-great-grandmother's disappearance."

Luna cringed. Her grandmothers would hate it if they knew what she was really looking for at the town library. They'd hate it even more if they knew she planned to go rooting through the Evanses' own history.

But she'd hidden two gifts from a killer in her backpack, and this was the best idea they had.

The pinch-mouthed librarian glared up from her typewriter when Crane asked about studying the town's archives. She pursed her lips and suggested they check the microfiche.

Crane's leather coat deflected the darts from the librarian's eyes. "How far back do the films go?" he asked.

"At least as far back as Spindletop." The librarian spoke low, her words almost inaudible, then remarked that the library would close soon and returned to her typewriter.

"And what's Spindletop, exactly?" Crane whispered as Luna gathered her things and led him to the library's back room, to the row of metal cabinets that housed the microforms.

She rolled her eyes. Everyone knew the story of the great gusher that turned the rural hummock into an oil-boom town. "The Spindletop oil derrick struck a geyser in 1901, but a huge fire burned the whole thing to the ground a year later," she told the boy who'd just relocated from Colorado. "It burned for like a week—it all started over a cigar, apparently."

"Smoking kills," Crane agreed, without even a hint of irony, and Luna crooked a hand on her hip.

Dropped it when the gesture reminded her too much of Nana Lenore.

Come to think of it, she hadn't seen Crane with a cigarette in days, even though smoke scent still clung to his leather coat.

"We can scan through old copies of the *Enterprise*," he said as he opened a metal drawer, plucked out a cartridge, fitted the film into the machine. "Whatever the Evanses do, it's the town your family protects," he whispered, flicking through screens of black-and-white text. "If we can figure out where your family's involvement with the restless dead started, then maybe we can figure out how to end it."

Luna dropped into the seat beside him, clutching her backpack to her chest, and fingered the little metal loop hidden inside the front pocket. Whatever they found, she hoped it would explain the items she kept finding in the tallow tree outside her bedroom window, and she hoped the explanation wouldn't lead back to her.

Again.

Deputy Brandon Hinson

Brandon slumped at his desk, still fuming from Taylor's dismissal. Just because the new sheriff was up to his ears in dead bodies, demanding survivors, and overeager reporters didn't mean he should ignore his junior officers. He shouldn't send them back to the station to chase missing-animal leads when there were two dead humans in the morgue. Sure, chain of command accounted for a lot, but wasn't listening to his junior officers part of the sheriff's job?

After seeing Daniel's body gutted in the apartment complex behind the laundromat, though, Brandon knew, beyond a shadow of a doubt, that whatever was going on around town had nothing to do with rabid animals.

Whatever had happened to Daniel had been a murder. Just because Johnson shot down Taylor's serial killer theory didn't mean it was wrong.

And, like Taylor himself said, Johnson wasn't the sheriff anymore.

Brevard's limbs had been ripped from his body, Daniel's face scratched off his head like a half-used lottery ticket, and, for whatever reason, Taylor was covering it up.

Brandon's eyes blurred over the paperwork on his desk. Landed on Professor Corinne Bennick's business card.

He plucked up the card, studying the burnt orange lettering of the university's logo until sour crawled up his throat and his head started spinning again. The pretty redhead hadn't been at the apartment complex this morning, but that didn't mean she wouldn't want to know what they'd found. He picked up the receiver and made it through the first three numbers—maybe Corinne would be able to convince him that whatever got Daniel and Brevard was a wolf—but then his head swam, and he slammed the phone back into its cradle.

What happened if she said it wasn't?

"It's a goddamn wolf!" His commanding officer had been so insistent, shouting back there in the dumpster shed while he'd stood over Daniel's inside-out body. But what if it wasn't a wolf?

What if it never had been?

"Johnson didn't believe in a killer," Brandon mumbled at Corinne's University of Texas business card. "And now Johnson is dead, too."

More than that, Johnson had seemed to think the Evans women had something to do with it. The local funeral parlor had about as much say about disposing of dead bodies as the coroner's office—more, maybe. Brandon couldn't see how a few old women could be involved with the killings, especially with half of them among the victims—but there's a lot the Evanses could do to cover up a cause of death.

Just like Taylor seems to be doing now, Brandon thought, the hangover banging against the back of his skull. Rumor had it that Taylor had been sweet on Grace Evans, and now as sheriff it made sense that he'd spend a fair amount of time coordinating with the parlor. Why in the hell Kim wanted to work there was beyond him—his girlfriend wasn't involved, too, was she?

Somehow four years together had turned him and Kim into strangers, unfamiliar in each other's lives.

Brandon's head swam. He'd tried to drink it away, but no matter how many beers he put back, the whole thing still gave him the creeps. Then a sound boomed through his fog when on the other side of the front counter, the sheriff's department door swung open so hard the knob banged against the doorstop.

Brett Hancy slammed through the threshold, cheeks red behind the sheen of sweat pouring over his face. "I've been calling all damn morning," the man hollered over the counter at Darla and the sound racked against Brandon's head. "Where in the hell is Taylor?"

Darla gave him a look that burned. "Mr. Haney, I have already told you, the sheriff is—"

"I don't give a good—a good goddamn where *the sheriff* is." Spittle flew from Haney's mouth, pelting angry raindrops on the other side of the desk, and veins popped around the man's nostrils. Brandon wasn't the only one who'd had a rough night.

But Darla was already on her feet, bucking up to the larger man. She might be barely five foot tall on her tiptoes, but a career in law enforcement had turned every inch to stone—and mountains like Darla didn't move for much.

"I'm going to need you to get your greasy fists off my countertop and lower your voice," she snapped at the man. "I already told you, Taylor ain't here. I'll take a message—" Haney scoffed, interrupting her, and Darla's head reared back. "But you're gonna need to walk on out of here," she said, "unless you want me to put you in the back to dry out."

Haney's hands rolled into fists, and Brandon swayed onto his feet and to Darla's side before those hammy fists could pound the counter. Darla's eyes narrowed and her chin lifted. Probably most people didn't have the balls to stumble sloshed into the sheriff's department and harangue the dispatch desk, but by the look of things, Darla wished a fella would.

"Tanya West is missing," Haney slurred, undeterred. "I went by her house this morning to see how she's holding up, and her front door was open, and she was gone."

Darla stood like a cat about to pounce, but her hand went under the counter when Haney leaned over to repeat himself. "No one has reported Ms. West missing," she said.

The man spluttered, "*I'm* reporting it, ain't I?"

He slammed another fist on the countertop and Darla's hand reappeared holding a thin black tube, but Brandon jumped in before she could hose the whole place down with pepper spray.

"Thank you for coming in, Mr. Haney," Brandon said. "We'll follow up and check in on Ms. West."

Darla didn't blink, but Haney's watery gaze ran down Brandon, teeth to toes. When the drunk man scoffed again, Brandon could taste bourbon on his breath.

Haney sneered at the deputy, raising a finger that wilted as soon as it stabbed the air. "I'm damned tired of this, Chuck," he said.

Brandon's breath stuck in his throat. He might be the sheriff's deputy now, but he was still a high school quarterback turned rookie—and everyone around town knew it.

"Mark my words," Haney said, spittle flecking off his words when he balled that finger into the rest. "Either Taylor brings in what killed my baby girl, or I'll take matters into my own hands."

His fist hit the counter, lighter this time, and Haney turned to go.

"Don't do anything stupid, Mr. Haney," Brandon called after him, hand already going for the cuffs on his belt. Last thing he wanted to do was tag the man with a drunk and disorderly, but wants and duty were two different things.

"Like drive!" Darla added when the man stomped toward the parking lot.

Haney threw his hands in the air and swerved toward the sidewalk, and Brandon let his hand drop. Darla adjusted the items his fists had rattled out of place on her desktop. "Damn fool's so drunk he can't even get your name right." The curls on her head bobbed when she shook her head.

Brandon kept his old high school football nickname to himself and returned to his desk.

Today just keeps on getting better, he thought. At least he'd see Kim tonight. Maybe they wouldn't argue this time.

The phone rang and Brandon steeled himself for another missing-pet report. When he picked up the receiver, Forensics was on the line.

Brandon thought of Brett Haney storming back in, of Darla listening in, and put the call on hold. Letting himself into the sheriff's office to take the call might not be entirely appropriate, but then he couldn't let confidential information slip out over the line, either. He transferred the call to Taylor's new office and didn't pick it back up until he'd closed the door behind him and taken up residence behind the sheriff's desk.

"This is Hinson," he told the caller. "You got the results on the DNA sample?"

Brandon rooted around the sheriff's desk for a notepad, for a packet of aspirin, while the forensics tech confirmed the sample. Taylor preferred to keep his desktop neat, but the influx of cases and change of command left the space littered with folders, files, and paperwork.

"We got the initial report back, but we're going to have to run it again," said the forensics guy—Brandon didn't catch his name.

Another one of Corinne's business cards lay amidst the clutter, rumpled and tattered like it'd been wadded up a couple hundred times. Brandon nudged the card aside and found a fresh sheet of legal-pad yellow. "Run it again," he said. "Why?"

The tech made a noise on the other end of the line that Brandon didn't like. "Well, the thing is—" The forensics guy stalled out, and Brandon wished he had a beer. "The sample," he said, "we thought it was fur, but it's not."

Then what the hell is it?

Brandon didn't have time to ask before the voice on the other end of the line told him. "It's hair—human hair."

His pen stopped. His brain banged against his skull. *Human hair.*

"But the victim was bald," Brandon said, feeling every bit like the rookie he was. Sweat beaded along the back of his neck, and he rubbed his hand wet.

"We'll run it through again, but it'll take a couple of days to get the results back," said Forensics. "Unless you can give me an idea of what we're looking for, and we can narrow it down."

Trust me, buddy, Brandon thought. *This would have been over a long time ago if I knew what we were looking for.*

He scanned the sheriff's office like he might find something, half listening to the forensics tech, but no signs in the hot little room spelled out the killer's name in glowing neon.

Then something did flash in Brandon's vision.

Only a sliver, but something gleamed in the open crack of Taylor's bottom desk drawer. The shiny plastic of an evidence bag glinted under the office's fluorescents. Brandon adjusted the receiver in the crook of his neck. He pulled open the drawer a centimeter at a time and hoped like hell his commanding officer didn't walk in.

In the bag, Taylor's hat, the old one he'd said he lost.

Soaked through with blood.

Brandon set the unmarked evidence bag on the desk, stared at it while on the other end of the line Forensics rambled on about the nuances of DNA testing. He rumpled through Taylor's papers again, searching for anything that might tell him whose blood was on the hat, how long the hat had been in the drawer, why Taylor kept a blood-soaked hat hidden in his desk and not filed in the evidence locker like procedure dictated.

A familiar name caught Brandon's eye from the desktop. *Tanya West,* printed in Roger's neat penmanship at the top of an unfiled Missing Person's report.

But Darla had said no one had reported the woman missing, and Darla would know.

What the fuck is happening around here?

The forensics guy was still going on in Brandon's ear. "Does it have to be a hair sample?" the deputy asked, cutting off the babbling. "For the DNA sample, I mean. Does it have to be hair?"

Forensics huffed. He said something about how DNA is the same in hair as it is in saliva, skin tissue, blood, bone, but all Brandon heard was *No.*

"Good." He rummaged around until he found a pair of scissors and an empty evidence bag, then he peeled open the bloody bag and snipped off a piece of cloth from the hat's bloodstained sweat band.

"I've got something for you," he said, stuffing the sample into his pocket. "Let's see what we get."

After his shift, Brandon clocked out and drove directly to Cornwall Lancaster Apartments.

Outside, Kim's building was a lot like Daniel's, right down to the missing-pets flyers taped to the utility poles, bottom edges curling over their crisper counterparts still fresh from the Xerox machine. Inside, Brandon stripped off his uniform and got into the shower before his girlfriend could smell last night's late-night booze still leaking through his pores. Usually he went for a six-pack, but he'd polished off a bottle of Jim Beam after Brevard, and he hadn't even started drinking away Daniel yet.

"Let's rent a movie," Kim said once he'd changed into street clothes.

Brandon wanted to tell her about Daniel but didn't. He wanted to tell her about the unfiled Missing Person's report, and the bloody hat bagged in Taylor's desk drawer.

But he didn't.

After four years of dating, it was suddenly hard to tell his girlfriend anything anymore. When Kim didn't share about her first day at the parlor, he wondered if she felt the same.

Normally they walked the half mile to Blockbuster Video. Tonight, Brandon's gaze swept across the low-rolling fog that hovered over the road as oncoming cool tried to push away summer's heat and suggested they drive instead.

Kim gave him one of those looks that Brandon had grown to dislike, the kind that said she was braver than him. "Too spooky for you, Deputy?" she teased, and when Brandon tried to make a joke about how the full moon brought all the loonies out, she just smirked harder. "Technically the full moon was four nights ago," she said. "Tonight is a waning gibbous."

He'd hoped for an action flick, but as usual, Kim gravitated toward horror. They rented a Jack Nicholson, Michelle Pfeiffer werewolf flick. Back at the apartment, she snuggled a popcorn bowl at the other end of the threadbare sofa and rolled her eyes when Brandon twisted the cap off a beer.

"Just because it's legal doesn't mean you have to," she snapped at him.

"Thanks, Mom," he snapped back.

In the film's opening credits, Jack drove down a snowy New England road. A black wolf ran in front of his car, and when he got out to check the damage the animal did to the grille, the injured wolf bit his hand.

Brandon downed all twelve ounces. "You can become a werewolf just from being bitten by a regular wolf?"

Kim shushed his question away. She shushed him again when he asked how the DNA on Jack's murdered wife could be a wolf's. The movie never made it clear whether Jack's wolf-form killed his estranged wife out of revenge for her cheating on him, or if the unscrupulous protégé, played by James Spader, killed her to frame Jack, but the rising tension between Spader and Nicholson helped Brandon work his way through a six-pack just the same.

"What if," he asked Kim when the credits rolled. "What if what's going on around here isn't a wolf *or* a serial killer—what if it's both?"

Out of arm's reach, Kim rested her head on the back of the sofa and rolled her eyes in Brandon's direction. "Really, Chuck, werewolves?"

He cringed at the nickname. His girlfriend, not a football fan, never used it nicely. "You got a better theory?"

"Yeah." She laughed. "You're drunk."

"I'm not," he lied, but that just made Kim judge him harder. Still, he couldn't shake the sudden thought—what if whatever was killing people just *wanted* people to think it was a wolf?

And what if Taylor had known that all along?

He thought of Jack Nicholson driving down that dark snowy road— what would Brett Haney find if that poor drunk asshole made good on his threat to go out hunting on his own?

CHAPTER 19

Brett Haney

Ever since they'd found his baby girl's body torn open behind that movie theater, Brett Haney had worked hard to man up to his grief. He'd consoled his wife, let the sheriff's department do their jobs and track down the monster that murdered his daughter. He'd played by all the rules, even put on a brave face at the high school memorial for Alison and the boy who'd gone missing, kept an eye on that boy's grieving mother, who didn't have a man's shoulder to cry on. But a month after Brett Haney had buried his daughter, there'd still been no justice.

Now there were two more bodies, Tanya West had gone missing, and Haney was tired of waiting.

"High time I took matters into my own hands," he slurred aloud in the empty cab of his rusted Ford F-150. "Take care of this goddamn wolf once and for all."

Last month when this all began, something had damn near chewed Ed Boone's head right off his neck on his own property. They'd never found hide nor tail of Ed's nearest neighbor, Clyde Halloran. Word was the old drunk had drowned himself in Jim Beam down at Riverfront Park.

Now, as he neared the river, Haney passed the turnoff and kept going.

Not enough coverage down by the water. Too much open space, nowhere to hole up. Haney's old man had fitted him with a rifle the moment he'd been strong enough to lift a gun, taught him how to suss out places that animals liked to hide. Haney had tracked game ever since, and he knew that animals ventured out to hunt their prey, but they always returned to their den, and they always built or dug their dens somewhere not meant to be found.

A mutilated cow had turned up at Frank McCormack's place—two farms down from Ed's. So, guided by the mostly full moon, Haney rumbled over to the edge of town and turned his trusty Ford onto Farm Road 121.

All he had to do was find the animal's hiding place. And then he could kill it.

Waning moonlight filtered through the fog and the truck's windows, and Haney glanced at his shotgun in the passenger seat. Just like he'd thought long and hard about where to begin his hunt, it had taken him some time to decide which gun to bring. He'd considered his .30–30, his .45–70, the .30–06, the 270, even his 10mm—all his best guns for game hunting. In the end, though, Haney wasn't out hunting dinner. He didn't give a good goddamn about ruining the meat. Only thing that mattered was stopping power, and so he'd climbed into his truck with his Mossberg 500 twelve-gauge riding shotgun, no pun intended.

Maybe the gun his father-in-law had given Haney back when he and Katherine got married, two months pregnant with Alison at the time, would bring him extra luck. The pump-action gun held bird shot, buckshot, and slugs—a three-in-one with a single goal: take down the monster that tore apart his daughter and ruined his family.

Besides, if it was good enough for the Marines, Haney figured the 500 was good enough for him.

And he wasn't taking any chances.

Not tonight.

Overhead, the moon shone just bright enough that Haney could see through the dark. He killed his headlights, dropped his speed, and followed the low fog rolling in as the night air pushed down the heat. The stuff pooled on top of the road, so dense that Haney could barely see the gravel under his hood by the time he passed Ed's farm, then Mac's.

Haney cranked up his defrosters and flicked the truck's wipers on low.

He was just about to bite the bullet and turn on his flashers when something ran out in the road ahead of him, a blur on four legs. He stamped the brakes, but the grille guard made impact, and Haney cursed under his breath.

"Better not be no damn wolf." He'd already made Katherine pull down the family portrait hung over the mantel. That's where he'd mount the taxidermized, daughter-killing son of a bitch once he'd shot it, and it'd be a hell of a time getting the wolf stuffed right if he mangled the damn thing with his grille guard.

Haney shifted into park and flicked his headlights back on. He snatched up his gun from the passenger seat and twisted on the flashlight mounted to its barrel before he shoved out of the driver's side. He left the door open and aimed the light at his feet as he walked around the front of the truck.

He'd hit a wolf, all right.

That redheaded girl professor from the university, the one with all the freckles on the news, said that the hybrids were bigger than a standard coyote, but aside from that, Haney didn't have a damn clue what the ghost wolves were supposed to look like. The one bleeding out under his tires seemed larger than the coyotes he'd put down before. A larger, blockier muzzle, shorter and rounder ears, a thicker pelt. Bushier tail.

Haney was no bookworm expert, but he figured he had just hit his ghost wolf, all right. Taylor and his boys had been looking for the damn thing for a month, and Haney managed to hit it with his truck without even trying.

So much for backing the blue.

And so much for my mount, Haney thought as he crept closer to the mangled animal that had torn apart his daughter, left her there to bleed herself dry on the sidewalk. The F-150's grille must have cut it up more than he thought.

The animal's legs twitched, and Haney thrust back. A low howl pushed its way out of the wolf's maw, and Haney squatted inside the headlights to watch with satisfaction as the beast took its last breath.

Good riddance, he thought, then Haney saw the blood on the animal's teeth, the wounds in its pelt where the grille guard couldn't have touched. Shadows made it hard to see, but it looked like the thing had lost an ear. His truck didn't cause that.

Haney pushed up to his feet and followed the blood trail with the rifle's flashlight. A red pool spread beneath the dead ghost wolf under the truck's hood, but the trail went back across the gravel, started all the way back in the tree line at the edge of the road. The damn thing hadn't just run out in front of Haney's truck—it'd been running *from* something.

He swiveled the light back at the dead mass, squinted at the wounds in its gut.

"Hell," Haney muttered into the dark, then left the truck running and headed into the woods.

The farther he walked, the redder the stamps grew, darker and wetter as the track led him deeper into the pine. Haney kept the shotgun's barrel pointed low as he walked, the mounted beam lighting his path, but when his boot squished beneath him, he raised the muzzle up. Probably the thing had gotten into a twist with a deer, gotten itself gored by a buck's antlers, which made it flee directly into Haney's path. Or maybe it'd dragged another calf off Frank McCormack's farm, and the old rancher got a shot off, more than one, hit it in the gut so it had to bleed itself out.

Or maybe Haney would find another body when the tracks ran out. Somebody else's baby girl, spread out on the grass.

He kept walking.

The tracks didn't lead to a body, though.

The tracks led to many.

Even if Haney had been a wolf expert, or a bookworm, he'd have been unlikely to make heads or tails out of the circle of dead animals he found between the pines.

A ring of dead coyotes, dead wolves—hell, dead canine *somethings,* he could tell that much at least—lay butchered in the dark. Shredded and indistinguishable, limbs thrown at odd angles, the beasts' bones broken, pelts torn. Red, so much red. Many of the beasts were missing tails and paws, their bodies pulled apart just like Haney's poor daughter, like the high school principal, guts and intestines flung across the pine needles.

All except the largest.

The biggest of the beasts lay sprawled at the top of its pile, missing only its head.

Haney swiveled as something stirred between the trees. His pulse pushed into his throat, thrummed beneath his skin, as his flashlight beam cut between the narrow pines, tracking each bowed branch, each broken twig—

There.

A shadow, too tall, too thick, rose between twin pines just outside the reach of Haney's light. He caught a whiff of something foul on the breeze, the stench of copper and fur, and when the creature moved, the moon lit up its nocturnal eyes.

Its teeth.

Christ God Almighty, Haney thought, and then he forgot all about the shotgun in his arms, tucked tail, and ran like hell for his truck.

CHAPTER 20

Ducey Evans

Ducey pushed the lab's adjoining door open just wide enough to peek through into the chapel with her good eye. She wedged herself between a metal cabinet and the wall, listening to make sure Lenore had made like a tree and headed over to Eternal Flame Cemetery with the rest of Mrs. Carroll's brunch-time funeral party. When the only sound she heard was Belle's snuffling from her bed in the corner, Ducey brushed her fingers along her empty apron pockets before she rolled her bottom lip under, bit down, and peered beyond the chancel.

Two sacks of hard candy already spit out and wasted on the linoleum, but she'd give her eyeteeth for a butterscotch. Something sweet to suck on while she watched Gil Wallace tinker with the grandfather clock out along the chapel's far wall.

With his back turned to her in the lab, Gil whistled old honkytonks while he worked. Death had ruined Ducey's sense of smell, but the memory of sun-wrinkled skin steeped in the earthy musk of clock oil still flavored the air as the man's bald head gleamed under the lights. The white tips of Gil's mustache stuck out like tusks on either side of his face when he bent at the middle, leaning into the clock's midsection to fondle the pendulum he'd repaired. The facial hair Ducey could live without, but the man used to be a ranch hand once upon a time, and he still wore his shirt tucked into his Wranglers.

Ducey licked her lips and took another gander at Gil's jeans.

Her girdle area thrummed. *Two plump little roasts, brined in decades of sweet sweat and Southern sunshine.*

Along with her lack of scent, Ducey hadn't felt much since she'd died—just that occasional burn in her chest—but her knees turned to jelly when the minute hand ticked forward, and Gil slid the cabinet door shut with a weathered palm.

She clicked her teeth and let the door fall closed as she rubbed over her breast pocket. The heat in her chest now had nothing to do with Lenore's stab wound.

At the lab counter, Kim tittered. "Never would have pegged you for a Peeping Tom, Ducey." She smirked as she arranged a series of eye caps and sutures next to a selection of cosmetics on an instrument tray. "Or in your case, a Peeping *Zom*."

Belle huffed in her sleep and Ducey bent to scratch the old hound behind the ears before she padded to the other side of the lab in her slippers and switched on the television.

Peeping Zom. Hell. Lenore better not get wind of that one.

"Can't decide if I'd rather kiss that man or take a bite out of him," she told Kim over the twang of steel guitar. Lenore wanted the television set back in the breakroom, but if Ducey couldn't enjoy a chicken salad fold-over and a cold can of soda water for lunch, then listening to her programs helped pass the time while she and Kim worked. Besides, the opening notes of *Walker, Texas Ranger* might lure a curious guest to the breakroom, but it'd take a special sort of person to go poking their nose into a funeral parlor lab.

Could always play dead if anyone walked in, Ducey thought. Lenore hated when she said that, but Ducey hated her daughter's incessant badgering on her undead state every bit as much as she hated the house slippers Lenore made her wear to muffle her footsteps on the ceramic tile. Fool things had rabbit ears on the toes, but Lenore insisted the children's slippers were the only ones she could find for sale this time of year.

And Ducey found that spending her lunch hour with Chuck Norris in the lab suited her just fine.

Well, Chuck and the Halloran girl, anyway.

Not that Kim made for bad company.

Ducey ran her fingertips along the wound in her throat. *Better than her drunk old uncle Clyde, anyway.* Maybe that Cole blood had washed out the Halloran muck.

She pushed the door open for one last peek at the tasty meal in the parlor's chapel. Maybe she'd fool around with that stupid old clock, give Gil Wallace a reason to come back out, bend himself over into that pendulum cabinet again. Ducey would need more than daytime soap operas to keep her occupied if Lenore insisted that she spend every second of her undead life trapped in the parlor.

Mother would get a kick out of that, wouldn't she? Ducey thought as Gil packed up his tools. Pie Evans had sworn she'd never leave the land her daddy farmed and her mama and brothers died on, back when everyone around these parts was getting rich on oil and lumber. No one knew what had happened to the grouchy old woman after she'd wandered out into the dark that night almost twenty years ago, but Ducey suspected wherever her mother's body rested, she was probably still mad about nothing, fuming at the dead that dared to get up out of their own graves.

Ducey wriggled her toes beneath their ridiculous bunny ears. Pie Evans had been the sort of woman who wouldn't have hesitated to put metal through her own daughter's chest. Lenore's overly sentimental nature made for its own share of problems, but at least she'd put her arms around Ducey's neck when she did it. Faced with the same choice, Ducey didn't know if she'd be as merciful as her daughter . . . or if she were more like her mother.

She'd given her life to protect her girls, but what in the hell could she do for them in her death—or in theirs?

Ducey took another glance at Gil and let the door flush itself shut again. Nothing less than what her own mother had done, she reckoned.

"What?" she asked when she turned into Kim's smirk.

"I didn't know you could . . ." The girl stared too hard at a tube of mascara before she set it aside to stare too hard at a pot of concealer. "Didn't know you could, you know . . ."

Ducey fingered the hot spot on her chest while the girl went on beating around the bush. "Go on," she said. "Spit it out."

"Feel interested?" Kim nodded at the stack of dog-eared romance novels along the bookshelves and spoke to the floor. "In men, I mean. In, well, *you know.*"

Ducey glanced at the book covers. She'd once spent her nights with a handsome Frenchman named Phillipe before Clyde Halloran chewed the life out of her. Now she pushed all those pesky thoughts about her dead mother out of her mind and wondered how Gil Wallace's handlebar mustache would feel on her undead skin.

"'Cause I'm old," she asked, "or 'cause I'm dead?"

"Both?" Kim said, but Ducey was still imagining the tickle of those silvery-white whiskers, and hell if she didn't know the answer to either.

"The way I see it, I promised Royce till death do we part—" Ducey couldn't feel the weight of her diamonds when she waggled her wedding finger, but she could see them sparkle. "Figure I held up my end of the bargain. Besides," she said, "I'm just lookin'."

Kim finished with the instrument tray, popped on a pair of gloves, and headed for the cooler. "Like I said, Peeping Zom."

Belle snorted in her sleep and Kim shot a smirk back at Ducey, who squinted behind her bifocals.

"Can I ask you a question?" Kim checked the name on the tag on the cooler door before pulling the slab open.

All that talk about one kind of appetite had stirred up another. Ducey pulled her trocar free of her apron. "As long as it ain't about my love life."

Pink rushed into the pale girl's cheeks, but she tried to hide the color inside the cooler door and pulled the tray out, settling it into place on the metal exam table before she thumbed box-black hair behind her ear. "Why is there a door that joins the lab to the chapel?"

An easy one, at least. Unlike the remains still zipped in its bag on the metal tray.

Ducey hid her trocar behind her back. She'd forgotten about the principal in the cooler.

"We only have one reposing room," Ducey said. "If we have two viewings or services going on and need a second space, we use the chancel." She watched as Kim wheeled the metal exam tray over the drain and set the brakes. "Easier to move a body through the doors than take it joyridin' down the hall."

Plus, best to keep an exit open when the dead came home, Ducey thought. The dead, restless or otherwise, always came home to the Evanses.

Kim smiled, but her fingers faltered when she reached for the zipper. She let the little tab drop.

Ducey stepped up to the tray, trocar behind her back. "I can take care of this one if you want to get a head start on someone else," she offered, but Kim looked at the name on the coroner's tag affixed to the next cooler door and shook her head.

"I didn't like Principal Brevard very much, but it's still hard to . . . see him turned into stew." Kim scanned the lumps concealed beneath the plastic bag, all the bits and bulges that used to form a man, and chewed her purple lips pink. "I also haven't had a lot of experience with reconstructive makeup, so . . ."

Kim raised her upper lip, exposing lipstick-stained teeth as she grimaced and shrugged at Ducey.

The wolf did him good, the dead woman almost said, but something about lying to the girl didn't sit right with her, and so she kept her mouth shut and pushed her trocar back into her apron pocket. Ducey wasn't ready to go spilling the family beans just yet, but Kim and Roger already knew more than anyone outside of the Evanses ever had about the dead that rose in their small town—and so far, no one had shown up at the parlor with pitchforks.

'Course, there's still time for all that, Ducey thought, and reminded Kim that Brevard's service would be closed casket.

"No need to bother tryin' to make him look nice," she said, gesturing to the tray of cosmetics before stepping around Belle's dog bed to open the metal cabinet against the lab's back wall. "We just need to try and make sure the body is clean, then we'll put him back in the cooler until his funeral."

Kim pulled out a bundle of emery boards, eyeing the chemicals and cleaners Ducey collected from the cabinet without commenting, and Ducey watched questions pile up behind the girl's heavy-lidded eyes.

"The last thing a person wants to see is their loved one lookin' like they've been pulled through a knothole backwards," she explained. "We can't do much to hide the mess, but we can clean Brevard up some so his folks don't get nightmares worse than they're already gonna if they want to see him before we seal the casket—"

Kim pulled a face, and Ducey shrugged at the disconnected body bits hidden under the plastic. "But I doubt they will."

She motioned the girl to the table. "Hope you've got an iron gut, because this one ain't gonna be pretty," she said and pulled the zipper.

Ducey took one look at the man's remains and got real thankful that she couldn't smell. Refrigeration kept the odor in check, but probably it wasn't the stench that made Kim put her hand over her mouth, pinch her nose.

Probably the bugs did that.

Insects in the dead weren't unusual. Bits left to swelter out in the sun just got nibbled on sooner was all.

Little white grubs wriggled in the torn spaces of Brevard's body, in his throat, his nostrils. Ducey's fingers didn't so much as twitch in the direction of her trocar. She had a pretty good idea that sipping her meals out of the newly dead paled in comparison to chomping on fresh meat, but even she didn't have an appetite for a spoiled supper.

"His family didn't want to cremate him?" Kim asked after she'd blinked that first image away, shoved her hair behind her ears again, and used an emery board to file away the skin slipping from his one wrist.

Ducey shook her head. "They're the religious sort," she said, "the kind that believe in physical resurrection. Cremation's a sort of destruction of property." A fat white wad squished itself free of one of Brevard's fingernails and Ducey stuck out her tongue as she dredged the hand with vinegar. Half her own skin tone came from spray paint, but at least she didn't have to bathe herself in bleach to keep from being feasted on.

Being undead had *some* perks.

"I know the type." Kim heaved a little when she pushed an eyelid open to insert an eye cap, and a beetle crawled out of the cavity. She flicked the bug away and popped the cap on.

A month back, when Ducey had met the girl behind Jimbo's, that day they'd found Belle bleeding out from a ghoul bite in the alley, Kim had said something about her parents, about everyone not taking her seriously, not giving her a fair shot because she wore eyeliner thick as paint and was allergic to colorful clothing.

Odd duck that she was, just yesterday morning the Cole girl had taken one look at Ducey's restless body and fixed her right up. Took a special sort to do something like that. Hell, even the Evans girls needed a little extra push now and then to look past the state of a person's breathing.

Maybe Mother was wrong, Ducey thought while the girl filed away the dead man's slippery skin. Pie had trained her daughters not to tell anyone about what they did, who they were, but Roger knew their secret, and now Kim helped them care for the dead—even helped care for Ducey. Maybe some secrets needed sharing.

Ducey'd been wrong before. Maybe Pie Evans had, too.

Maybe it don't matter one way or the other. Ducey studied the stew of dead-man bits still inside the body bag on the lab's metal table—Brevard, who'd had one limb torn free of his body, the last of his hair shorn off his head. She looked at the frayed edge of his shoulder, the bone poking loose from the socket.

Maybe some secrets forced their way into the open, whether anyone wanted them to or not.

"Your folks still giving you trouble?" Ducey asked.

Kim shrugged and muttered something about how the Coles were just like everybody else in town, all brimstone and judgment about anyone they didn't understand. "They've been better since I moved out," she said, "but my brother still lives at home, and Dillon—"

The sound of breaking news ruined the rest of her sentence.

That blonde from Channel Six flashed on the screen, a graphic wrapped in police tape floating over the reporter's shoulder. "Brett Haney, the father of one of the two teenagers allegedly killed in last month's rabid animal attacks, took matters into his own hands in the hunt for the mysterious ghost wolves prowling the small town on the Texas-Louisiana border." The scene cut away to footage of fur and bone, a blurred-out mess of dead canines stacked among pines, then cut back to the smiling woman at the anchor's desk. "More on what he found on a quiet country road . . . tonight at six."

Kim grunted. "It isn't really rabid ghost wolves, is it?" she asked, eyes darting up to the cooler, to the other body waiting there, to the bag on the table, to the file in her hand.

"What do you mean?" Ducey knew what the girl was getting at but asked anyway.

"I mean—" Kim kept her eyes trained on her work, on the crust around Brevard's empty shoulder socket, as she spoke. "You're . . . you know, a zombie, and you said Uncle Clyde was one." She set down the file and looked directly into Ducey's good eye. "Maybe there are more."

Ducey didn't care for the word *zombie* any more than she liked being called a Peeping Zom.

"I am a *ghoul,* one of the restless dead," Ducey said, but yes, there were more. So many more that she looked away. "But a ghoul ain't what did this."

Kim shrugged. "My boyfriend thinks it's a werewolf."

"Sounds like your boyfriend watches too many movies."

Kim just frowned, and waited until Ducey made eye contact again. "But he's the sheriff's deputy."

"Maybe." Kim frowned, waiting until Ducey made eye contact again, then, "But he's the sheriff deputy," she said.

The two women stared at each other until the news alert faded back into steel guitar and blue skies on the television, and the back door of the parlor swung open. Lenore's voice trickled down the hallway, followed by Roger's, the two of them going on about the "mount" of grave dirt in the funeral parlor's gardens that wouldn't bloom, the circumstances of the latest wave of attacks, and déjà vu prickled along Ducey's undead skin.

"Oh, hell." She zipped the bag over what was left of Brevard's face. "Put the principal back in the cooler," she told Kim, one bunny-eared slipper dropping off her foot as she stepped over Belle's sleeping form. "I need to go break the news to Lenore and Roger."

Kim's eyebrow stayed up as the girl looked toward the television. "About the dead wolves?" she asked.

No, Ducey thought, and headed for the breakroom. *Not about the dead ones.*

CHAPTER 21

Sheriff Roger Taylor

No matter how many times the dead woman repeated herself, Roger still couldn't make heads nor tails of the words coming out of Ducey's mouth. He couldn't stop looking between her one bright eye, one cloudy eye, either, never mind the painted-over wound on her throat, the trocar visible in her apron pocket, the bunny slippers on her feet. The oxblood-red stains on her apron might be from her last client or her last meal.

A lump lodged itself in Roger's throat. Deaths in a small town always hit close to home.

Sometimes too close, he thought as he studied the grave dirt smeared across his palms.

A month ago, things like the restless dead only existed in horror movies, clawing their way out from under teetering gravestones to chase after shrieking teenagers for a living feast. Now, one reclined in a funeral parlor breakroom, her bunny-eared feet propped up on a La-Z-Boy recliner, and told Sheriff Roger Taylor how to do his job.

"I'm sorry, but you want to do what now?" Roger asked, just in case the dead woman's words would make sense if he heard them one more time.

Ducey crossed her ankles on the footrest. She readjusted the bifocals on the bridge of her nose, squinting mismatched eyes at Roger through the lenses like he was a bug on a glass plate. "You heard me right the first time," she barked from the recliner, waggling twin sets of long pink ears. "We need to make sure that old fart stayed where you two put him."

Yep, he'd heard her right the first time, all right.

Lenore set a steaming coffee mug on the breakroom table and Roger held both hands palm up, the scar tingling under his sleeve. "Okay, now wait a damn minute," he said. "We can't just go out onto Buck Johnson's land with a couple of shovels and start digging around under the cover of night—"

"That's exactly what we're gonna do," Ducey cut in so fast that Lenore's coffee mug clanged against the tabletop when she took a seat beside Roger. "And I'm bettin' we're gonna find it empty."

Lenore jerked her head toward the hallway. "Keep your voice down, Mama," she hissed. "We don't want the girl to overhear you." She snatched up a dishrag to mop her spill. "Kim knows too much already, and she's not one of us."

"She's as good as." Ducey's eyes rolled, but her fingernails gripped the ends of the chair's arms and her shoulders lifted off its back. "Didn't run screamin' when she saw me, now did she?"

"Knowing what you are and understanding the extent of the Evans family responsibility are two very different things, Mama." Lenore spooned sugar into her coffee and kept her eyes on the swirl as she mixed in cream. "We have to be very careful about who we trust," she said, voice as neutral as the shade of brown in her mug.

Roger held his breath until he was sure Lenore wouldn't look his direction.

"*You* hired the girl, Lenore Ruth," Ducey snapped. "Don't go blamin' me for makin' friends."

Lenore tapped her spoon on the mug's rim, her lips pinched so tight Roger worried that her jaw might break.

"Like I was sayin'," Ducey said, hands unfurling to palm the recliner arms. "We need to exhume Buchanan's grave, make sure his remains are where they're s'posed to be." She tapped the chair. "I'm guessin' they're not."

Roger's eye twitched. He looked to Lenore for backup, but her eyes were busy drowning in her mug. Abruptly she thrust her chair backward, marched to the sink, and dumped the coffee down the drain. She clamped her palms on the edge of the sink and kept her back turned.

"There's a process for these kinds of things," Roger said. "A right way," he finished, weakly, the argument already lost when Ducey's one good eye sparked. Whatever progress he'd made with Lenore the past few weeks, Ducey had been dead and buried for all of it.

"I don't remember invitin' you to the party, Sheriff Big Britches," she snapped now. "This is the Evans family responsibility, our business. We'll take care of it."

Roger took a sip of too-hot coffee, then he pulled his hat from his head, twisting it until his fingers ached, like the wound on his arm.

"Okay, let me get this straight," he said. "We pinned the attacks on a rabid animal, a ghost wolf, and now you're telling me that has actually come to pass, and the mess of Buck Johnson we put into the ground last month is up and has already chewed through two people, a cow, and a whole pack of wolves?" He tossed his hat on the table and rubbed his palms down his face. "I'm sorry, but I'm gonna need a little more to go on here."

Lenore pivoted at the sink. She straitjacketed her arms over her chest, tightening until her knuckles went white. "Strigoi don't attack animals," she said.

Roger couldn't help but look down at Belle, though he thought he heard one of Lenore's ribs crack.

Ducey grunted, but she kept her mouth shut.

The two women shared a look that made Roger's skin crawl, like there was more the Evans women weren't letting on. Again. He resisted the urge to scratch at his elbows, his forearms, the backs of his hands. On his wrist, the Timex bit into flesh, into bone.

But on his hip, six bullets.

Lenore's hair swished under her jaw when she shook her head. "Roger put six rounds into Buck's heart."

That's right, Lenore, he thought. Shot Buck, then faced Grace's killer with an empty gun.

"I watched for signs," she said. "Buck's not restless, Mama. He can't be."

"Ghouls aren't the only things that come back, Len," Ducey said, and Roger saw Lenore's arms falter around her, saw her jaw slide loose and snap back into place.

His gut churned. Whatever was happening around here, Lenore was just as in the dark as he was.

They stared at Ducey, Lenore propped against the sink, Roger glued to his seat. They waited while the old woman grumbled in her chair, muttering to herself while she patted her apron pockets, hunting for the butterscotch candies she just kept spitting out.

"Mama?" Lenore prompted, when the puttering went on for a solid two minutes.

"Oh, hell." Ducey clapped her palms against her knees and sucked at her teeth. "I already told you, there are other monsters that claw their way back from the dead. Angry, vengeful things—worse than any ghoul we've ever encountered."

Roger should have held on to his hat. He reached for his mug, swallowed a gulp of coffee, and tasted nothing. Just the weight of the cup was enough to make his arm throb. "What kind of monsters?" he asked after he sucked down the rest of the mug, switching it to the good hand. "Trust goes both ways, ladies," he added when the silence stretched. "I'm here to help, but what you're asking is not only illegal, but potentially dangerous."

Ducey scoffed, muttered something about danger, and Roger lifted a palm. "Now I know I'm not telling either of you anything you don't already know," he said. "But you've seen the condition of the bodies. I need to know what we're up against."

"Pricolici." The dead woman spat the word out like one of her precious candies.

Roger didn't catch it. "Come again?" he asked.

"*Pree-co-lee-chi,*" Ducey enunciated each syllable and Roger hung his head. Some other monster, something else he didn't know how to fight, how to put behind bars.

"And what, pray tell, is a pricolici?" he asked.

Lenore detached her backside from the sink, folded herself into the chair, hands still wrapped around her arms so she could dig into the back of her ribs with her fingertips.

"Well, I reckon that depends on which myth you're followin'," Ducey started, "but—"

Roger felt his jaw come loose, felt his mouth stretch halfway to the floor before he figured out how to work his tongue again. "You're telling me," he said, speaking slowly, because he didn't trust anything he said to come out right, "that we are dealing with a shape-shifting man beast?"

"Not the silly kind you see in movies, howlin' at the moon," Ducey said and rolled her eyes, patting at her breast pocket. "A revenant, intent on destruction. Spiteful, angry men are said to become pricolici if they die before they get the chance to let all their violence out," she said, "and unlike a ghoul, which can rise male or female, angry or otherwise, when they come back, they don't eat to feed. Pricolici kill for pleasure." The dead woman shifted in her chair, sighing as she continued. "They're known to kill cattle, to be more aggressive than wolves. They tear the skin and hair off their victims, collect claws and teeth, use them as weapons."

Ducey's good eye sparked. "That sound about right to you?" she asked Roger.

He thought of the missing teeth, missing fur. From Myrtle the Cow to the principal, the kid, the slaughtered coyotes—everybody they'd found so far had pieces taken from them. Now Roger knew why.

Buck Johnson, or whatever the dead man had become, was taking them.

"What do they do with the pieces they take?" he asked.

The dead woman shrugged. "Hell if I know."

Roger's eye twitched so hard that he worried he might lose his sight. Lenore's voice, barely a whisper, saved him from having to speak too soon.

"Where did you learn about pricolici?" she asked her mother.

Ducey shrugged again, mumbling, "Mother."

"Grandmother Pie told you about pricolici, and you didn't think to tell me sooner?" Lenore's question came out in a screech. "How could you not tell me about this?"

Ducey recrossed her ankles. She shuffled the bunny-eared slippers on her feet as she looked toward the window. "Been dead," she said to the blinds.

Lenore blinked while her shoulders squared up. "*Before* then!"

"Hell, Len," Ducey snapped, her head swiveling back so fast she'd have whiplash if she were still alive. "Now ain't the time for *shoulda-woulda-coulda*," she said. "Not like I needed to fill your head with any ideas anyway. Besides," the old woman went on, "I thought Mother's jibber-jabber about other undead critters was just more of her paranoia—not that she said much of nothin' about anything. I'm just sewin' up the scraps where I can."

The two women glared at each other to let Roger know there was more to the conversation than they'd share with him in the room—and whatever it was, nothing he could do would get it out of either of them.

"Okay," he said, sighing because, Christ God Almighty, he couldn't believe he was about to uproot a dead man. "Buck's buried on his own property, out back behind the house."

"Hot damn!" Ducey clapped so loud the sound stung. "Now we're talkin'."

"First things first," Roger said. "People are suspicious. I can't have someone seeing one of your cars at Johnson's place. We'll take mine. Easier to explain a sheriff's department cruiser checking things out."

He turned to Lenore. "I'll swing by the house and pick you up this evening." Last thing he needed was nosy Penny Boudreaux getting wind of him tromping around a murdered man's house after dark. "We'll go together," he told her. "That way, anyone sees us, we can say we're making sure the grave site is secure, all the paperwork signed off."

Lenore nodded, one quick jerk that might have snapped her head right off her spine, which Roger assumed meant approval.

"Y'all can swing by here and pick me up on the way," Ducey said, and when Roger and Lenore both told her she'd be better off waiting at the parlor, that the only thing harder to explain than the sheriff and funeral director traipsing around a burial site would be a dead woman wandering around, too, Ducey came unglued from her chair.

"Now you listen to me, both of you," she said, index finger raised so sharp it might cut. "I died to protect this family. I've been lookin' for a reason to give Buchanan Johnson a piece of my mind for over sixty years. Besides," she added, still simmering, "if we have to face down a pricolici, the only one expendable is me."

Ducey fixed Roger and Lenore with a cloudy glare that dared them to disagree. "I'm already dead," she said. "Whatever we're up against, I'm the only one it *can't* hurt, and so I'm the one who should lead the charge."

No matter how much he wanted to, Roger couldn't argue with the woman's logic.

"And Luna will want to come, too," Ducey added.

Lenore reanimated. "No way," she said. "I already lost my daughter, I won't put my granddaughter in harm's way again."

"I don't like it, either, Len," Ducey clucked. "But Luna is linked to the dead, thanks to that daddy of hers, and I'm a ghoul. We might need her."

Roger didn't know near enough to argue with that logic, either. Judging by the set of Lenore's jaw, neither could she.

"It's settled then," he said. "We go at midnight."

CHAPTER 22

Luna Evans

During lunch hour, writhing student bodies filled the Forest Park High School cafeteria with industrial food scents and teenage noise. In the last hour before dismissal, the room reeked of frustration and glitter.

Dillon groaned as he shook loose another long string of glittery silver star cut-outs. He flung the glittering wad into Luna's pile, then dusted glitter from his hands and reached to the center of the table, pinching off a chunk of the giant chocolate-chip cookie centered between the three friends. "When I suggested Starry Night, it was to match my *eyes*," Dillon said, batting his baby blues as he consoled himself with a bite of chocolate. "It was *not* so I could spend the next thirty-seven years scrubbing crap off my skin."

Crystal's cheeks glittered, half from her usual glittery makeup and the rest from all Dillon's dusting. "You said you suggested Starry Night because you didn't want Michelle Bryant to get her way with Under the Sea," she said, scowling over giant bags of frosted blue and white balloon skins. "One hundred and ten cubic feet of helium, two hundred balloons," she counted, and began sorting bags.

They'd had to lock up the helium tanks in the Student Council supply closet, where seniors pulling pranks couldn't fill up on balloon juice and go full Alvin and the Chipmunks on the school PA system. Brevard had confiscated one of the closet's Master Lock keys, but Vice Principal Flores had had no idea Crane ran a lucrative side gig selling copies when she'd picked up the dead principal's mantle.

Speaking of keys, Luna thought. She needed to remind Crane to sneak into her old apartment. Probably he wouldn't find anything helpful, but at least he'd have the chance to look. She'd go herself if Nana Lenore would ever let Luna set foot near her old home.

Dillon helped himself to a second cookie chunk. "Two things can be true at the same time," he said, still talking about the dance.

He ripped into another bag of glittery stars with chocolate-stained front teeth, then peeled a sliver of plastic wrap off his tongue. Dillon dangled the strand in Luna's face and flicked the shrink-wrap skin to the floor with almost enough fairy dust glittering down to make her fly.

She accepted the glimmering string like a length of a chain—penance for skipping out of seventh period to help with dance décor.

"Besides," he said, "can you imagine what pink coral-reef monstrosity Michelle would wear if we went with Under the Sea?" His eyes turned to plates. "Remember Bianca's hideous prom dress in *10 Things I Hate About You*?"

"Sissy Spacek wore a pink dress in *Carrie*." Luna kept her voice low, but Dillon's hearing was tuned for gossip frequencies.

"Oh my god, if she's crowned Homecoming Queen, we could dump red paint on her." His round eyes scrunched over a frown like a sudden storm breaking on the horizon. "No," he said. "That'd make her too likeable."

Crystal rolled her eyes as she finished sorting balloon bags. "Don't be catty, Dillon. It's rude," she said. "You're making us wear matching glow-in-the-dark ties."

"I'm turning us into *icons*, you mean," he shot back, with an even bigger eye roll. "The dance theme is Starry Night and there will *literally* be stars in our eyes."

Dillon rounded on Luna. "What are you and Crane wearing?"

Luna chewed at the inside of her lips, squeezing her shins around the backpack stashed between her feet. She'd only agreed to help oversee the midnight sky unfurling itself across the long cafeteria tables to get out of world history. Easier to coast along until the dismissal bell while mindlessly sorting cardstock stars and crescent moons than worrying about who battled who over the right to rule Vienna.

Her ankles dug into her backpack, feeling for the loot concealed in the front pocket. Sixteenth-century throne toppling paled in comparison to last-night throat tearing.

"The dance is *tomorrow*," Dillon pressed. He stabbed one finger upward, just in case she had any delusions about how much time she had left to plan her outfit.

She checked the clock on the cafeteria's back wall. Not long now, and she'd hear the bell.

The strand Dillon had just shaken loose retangled when Luna let her hands drop to the table, but screw it. She cut her eyes at Crystal. "How are you so into the Homecoming Dance with everything that's going on around here?" Luna asked. Dillon never missed an opportunity to throw himself into party planning, but her other best friend was far too practical to be caught up in a silly school dance when more unexplained phenomena rippled through town. Crystal loved Student Council, but she loved true-crime mysteries more.

Plus, midterm season waited just around the corner, and midterms were Crystal's Academy Awards.

She finished sorting balloons and ticked off something on her checklist before shrugging at Luna. "They found the ghost wolves," she said, a smidge too matter-of-factly, even for the daughter of two lawyers. "It's over."

Luna's breath caught, her leglock on the backpack slipping, and she adjusted her feet. Just this morning, she'd found a mangled pair of headphones hanging from the tallow tree branches outside her bedroom, right before Sheriff Taylor had tried to give her a ride to school in the coroner's van. Since when had they found any ghost wolf?

Since when are rabid ghost wolves real? she wondered.

"Oh, yeah, I heard that, too." Dillon's dimples popped. "Ms. Nelson stopped class to watch the news," he said. "You'd know that, too, if you stayed in class in English instead of 'studying'"—his eyebrows danced over his finger air quotes—"in the library with Crane."

More like finding more dead ends. Third time's the charm, they'd figured, when she and Crane decided to take one more trip through the school library's lackluster shelves.

Luna waved Dillon quiet and implored Crystal with her eyes to go on.

"Alison's dad went out to try to hunt them down," Crystal said. "The ghost wolves. He drove into one on Farm Road 121, and when he tracked it into the woods, he found the whole pack already dead—they killed each other." Crystal pulled her lips flat. "The news said the pack probably turned on itself because of the rabies." Her lips stayed as level as the Texas horizon.

"You don't believe that?" Luna asked, glancing at the time on the wall again as she squeezed her bag with her legs.

Crystal took her time sorting through more bags of balloons, and Luna knew that strategy, too. Thanks to Mom and Dad Singleton for teaching their daughter how to put together a closing argument.

"I *believe*," Crystal said, still eyeballing her hoard, "that it means whatever has been going around here, it's over." She pushed aside a sack of white balloons in favor of frosted sapphire blue and did another quick round of balloon-to-helium math. "We can—all of us, I mean— begin to heal, and to move on."

Crystal looked up finally. "Don't you think so, Luna Lou?" she asked.

Luna felt the contents of her backpack press into her legs, felt them bite all the way up her shins, into her stomach, but she didn't take the bait.

Better for her friends to believe their well-intended cover-up, for them to encourage Luna to overcome her grief, than for them to figure out she had started it all when she'd turned Andy into a "ghost wolf." No matter how much she and Crane researched, they still hadn't added anything to what they already knew about strigoi or the restless dead. Tack on that no one knew what brought Ducey back, what made her different, or what "other monster" was out there now, and Luna couldn't help but feel responsible for the collection of items cached in her backpack.

Something connected her to whatever this was—but what?

"There's a rumor that Andy and Alison will be named Homecoming King and Queen in memoriam, but I bet Michelle will get it," Dillon said, voice filling the vacuum of space between them as Luna yanked another strand of stars free, saved by the loud shriek of the dismissal bell.

Crane shielded her in black leather sleeves when she raced into his arms outside.

"Come to the parlor with me?" Luna asked, jerking her head toward the buses lined in front of the school.

He gave her an eyebrow. "Not getting a ride with our favorite officer?"

Luna bit back a chuckle and wriggled the backpack strap on her shoulder. Roger Taylor had cut the new weirdest kid in town some slack, but Crane took special joy in tormenting the new sheriff.

"He tried to bring me in the coroner's van this morning," she told him as they migrated toward the bus stall. "I don't think so."

The tall boy nodded his agreement that being delivered to school in the coroner's van, while cool any other time, would suck.

"The bus ride will give us time to chat," he said, and tucked her tighter under his leather sleeve, then whispered low enough that only she could hear while they waited to board. "I dug up some useful information on vampiric resurrection on AOL," he said, then looked at her from the corner of his black-rimmed eye when she didn't go stiff in his grip.

"No immediate rebuttal?" he asked.

"I've got something I need to show you—let's sit in the back," Luna said, the truth trying to claw its way out of her as she tightened her grip on her backpack straps and stepped up into the bus, Crane behind her.

"This ain't your bus," the driver told Crane.

"Technically, it isn't yours, either," he said back.

The driver looked at Crane's too-hot-for-the-weather leather coat, at his eyeliner and dark curtain of hair, then cut his eyes to Luna's death grip on her backpack straps and stained work shirt, sleeves too long for her arms, and decided it didn't matter. He grumbled and waved them both in.

Two sulky kids sulking in the back weren't worth worrying over, Luna hoped.

They nabbed the larger seat in the heat locker of the back of the bus. No one ever sat in the half-seat.

When the rest of the seats filled and the brakes gave way, Luna pulled her backpack into her lap and unzipped the front pocket. She pulled out the rhinestone cat collar with the little bell, twisting the band so that Crane could see the pet's name.

"I found this in the tree branches outside my bedroom window the morning Ducey came back," she said, then dipped her hand in again and lifted out a pair of foam-padded headphones, the cord snapped halfway off to expose wires. "And this morning, these."

Crane reached for the collar and the headphones, and Luna passed them over before reaching into the backpack's front pocket one more time.

She dropped the ring in his hand alongside the collar and headphones.

"Read the inscription," she hissed. "Inside the band."

Crane twisted the silver class ring in his fingers, eyes widening as he read the name etched into the metal. "They said Brevard's arm was missing . . ." he whispered.

"I don't know about the arm." A chill raced up Luna's spine, despite the suffocating heat of the bus's back row. "But I found the ring under the tree." She looked around. "The morning after he was killed."

Crane wrapped his palm around the items. "You think these are connected to the attacks?" he asked.

"Don't you?" Luna stretched her eyes as wide as they could go. "There have been a ton of missing-animals signs around lately, before Ducey rose, and then I found the ring outside after—" She cut her eyes through the bus's other seats, just in case. "After Brevard got killed, I found the ring, and then the headphones this morning," she whispered. "Remember I told you Roger tried to bring me to school in the coroner's van?"

When Crane nodded, Luna told him about the kid they'd found in the dumpster with his Discman, no headphones.

"Every time someone dies, an item appears," she said.

Crane fingered the cat collar and cocked an eyebrow at her, then stared at the backpack like he had X-ray vision. "It's like an animal delivering treats to its human," he said. "My old cat used to bring me dead spiders, stuff like that."

"Cats don't eat people, Robert."

He grinned at her. "Oh, hello, Nana Lenore," he fired back, then, "Lots of different species have been known to bring treasures from their kills to their owners. Cats, yes, and primates, dolphins, penguins—"

"Who owns primates and dolphins and penguins?" she hissed, then, "But ghost wolves?" How could he forget there *were* no coyote–red wolf hybrids running around? Not rabid ones, at least. "Ducey mentioned 'other monsters.'"

But that's all she said, of course, because Nana wasn't the only one who liked to guard her secrets.

Crane shrugged. "It is possible," he said and raised one shoulder. "But whatever it is, at least we know it's not a werewolf."

"How do we know that?" Luna had not at all considered werewolves.

The boy brandished an all-knowing smirk. "Silver," he said. He flicked a nail to ding the bell on the collar. "The bell, wires in headphones, the class ring—werewolves and silver are like vampires and garlic."

Hokum, Ducey would call it. Ducey, who, according to Nana Lenore, was hokum personified. As soon as they figured out what was killing people now, they'd have to figure out what brought Ducey back—and what to do about it.

"Vampires and strigoi don't play by the same rules," Luna whispered. "If one monster could shirk the legends, can't another?"

Crane's smirk fell.

He zipped the relics back into her backpack pocket, then wrapped his fingers around hers. "There is something we *do* know, though, about what this means," he said.

"What's that?" Luna asked, but a bad feeling had taken root in the pit of her stomach and her feet suddenly swelled three sizes inside her Converses.

Crane used his free hand to tap the backpack pocket.

"Whatever this is," he said, "it's bringing its treasures to you, Moon Girl."

CHAPTER 23

Deputy Brandon Hinson

At five o'clock sharp, Brandon clocked out of his shift, climbed into the busted old Jeep he'd driven since his sixteenth birthday, and hauled ass to Kim's. Her mint-green Buick sat parked in her assigned space. Upstairs, her little brother dusted the secondhand sofa cushions in glitter and powdered sugar as his hand plunged into a Jimbo's Java Café pastry bag.

Brandon forced his mouth into a smile. He'd spent all day chewing his fingers to the bone at his desk—chasing down missing-pet goose hunts, waiting for Forensics to call about the fabric sample he'd stolen from Taylor's office, for hellfire to rain down when Taylor discovered someone tampered with the bloody hat bagged in his bottom desk drawer. Waiting for Brett Haney or Penny Boudreaux to come stomping back into the station, demanding answers.

Not that things are any better between me and Kim lately, he thought. The sheriff he needed to convince with hard evidence, but it'd be hard for Brandon to do much about fixing things with his girlfriend with her brother going full pixie in the living room.

Much to his surprise, Kim's arms wrapped around his neck the second Brandon walked in the door, her lips warm and soft when she pressed her mouth against his.

"Babe!" Brandon let out a nervous chuckle. Dillon sat silent as a throw pillow on the threadbare couch, pastry stuffed halfway into his mouth, eyes wide as donut holes. But then Kim walked two fingers up Brandon's chest and he gripped her hips and pulled her in closer. This time, he breathed so far into the kiss that his lungs hurt when her lips ripped away.

"Babe," he said again, an octave lower, and kept his hands on her hips. "What's gotten into you?"

He meant it playfully, but Kim's eyes darkened at the question, like someone blew out a candle while he was still staring at the flame.

"Just checking your breath for booze," she said with a smirk that might be a tease, might not, and wrenched free when Brandon tried for thirds.

Kim's body heat sucked all of Brandon's along with it as she moved away. The little hairs on the back of his neck stood up when Dillon howled behind him.

"Can you two, like, get a room? You're seriously grossing me out." The kid's hand plunged into the pastry sack again, and he groaned when it came back empty. "Rhonda couldn't give you more than one lousy tea cake with your last paycheck?" He pinched the top of the empty sack between two fingers and set it on the carpet, then clapped a cloud of sugar dust out of his hands. "Stingy," he said.

"She's still upset about her missing cat." Kim shrugged in the kitchen while Brandon began to disassemble his uniform onto her makeshift dining table—his radio, his belt, all in proper order as he'd learned at the academy, from his superior officer. A familiar orange logo flashed as Corinne's business card came out of his back pocket with his notebook.

Brandon glanced at the woman's name, then tossed the card on the pile beside his gun.

He wouldn't mind seeing the pretty professor's freckles again, but he didn't feel like another conversation about missing pets. Ever since they'd found Brevard's pieces in the high school parking lot, Brandon had been nose-deep in missing cats and Labradors.

And other things.

Brandon shot another look at the business card. He could call . . . but the last thing he needed was a brawl with the new sheriff for stepping out of bounds.

"A lot of people are upset, Kim," Brandon said, which may have been the dumbest thing he'd ever said.

"Like I was," she shot back, "when you didn't bother to tell me about Daniel?"

"That's police business."

"You told me about Brevard and his missing *arm*." Kim trained those black-rimmed eyes, those dark holes, on him. "But you didn't think it would be a good idea to give me a heads-up on who I was going to find on my table next?" she shot back.

Brandon squared his shoulders. "Taylor may work for the Evanses," he said, "but I don't."

"The Evanses." The black eyeliner ringed around his girlfriend's eyes deepened into tunnels. She hovered in the tiny kitchen with all the coiled energy of a hungry shark while her little brother blinked like a deer in headlights on the sofa, like that wolf hybrid in Haney's headlights.

"Excuse me?" she chewed out finally.

Brandon could do this. When he hadn't been on the football field, he was on the debate team. He could handle a fight with one angry woman. Probably.

"Oh, come on, Kim," he said. "You see how things are. What Lenore Evans wants, *Sheriff* Taylor does." An idea sparked. Maybe he could work this to his favor, find a way to earn himself off the bench and back into the game. "You work there now—have you heard anything," he asked, "seen anything, that isn't right?"

Kim sank away when he reached for her.

"Hear me out, please," Brandon tried, changing tactics. "Before he died, Johnson suspected the Evans women were, I don't know, up to something." What he suspected, Brandon didn't know, but a man like Buck Johnson carried a grudge big enough to live on without him. "C'mon, Kim, this could be big." He reached for her hand, but she drew it back. "If you know something, just tell me—we can stop this."

Kim didn't blink. "Forget it."

"Seriously?" Brandon blinked enough for both of them. "You've worked there for two days, how can you be so loyal—what do those Evans women *do* to people?"

Kim's eyes stayed open, wide and dark.

After his girlfriend threw him out, Brandon drove to the dive bar on the other side of town—the one with a decent menu, that still handed out their own matchbooks and gave the middle finger to the indoor smoking bans that had started cropping up across the state since '97.

Small towns didn't change any faster than small minds, but Brandon didn't need stimulating conversation. He needed a beer.

The bartender had just pushed a pint across the bar top when Brett Haney took a seat on the next barstool, already two sheets and a pitcher deep.

"It ain't natural, Chuck," Haney said and clawed a fistful of bar nuts from the dish, poured the clump down his throat. "Wasn't no rabies that made that pack turn on themselves."

He chugged another glass, and Brandon mouthed the word *Cab* to the bartender, nodding at Haney. Off duty or not, he was still a man of the law. It was Brandon's obligation to make sure the man got home safe—and stayed off the road. They already had rabid ghost wolves on the loose. Didn't need any more drunk drivers.

Like the one that killed Daniel's mom, Brandon thought.

"Something else got those coyotes," Haney slurred. He gulped down another handful of nuts, smacked his lips at the salt, and helped himself to Brandon's beer to wash them down.

Brandon pushed the pint away. The bartender made his hands into a steering wheel and shot over a thumbs-up. Taxi was on its way, then, and soon Brandon could drink in peace. He'd get a fresh pint once Brett Haney wasn't around anymore to steal his beer.

The drunk man started again. "Something—"

"Killed those coyotes," Brandon finished for him. "I heard you the first time, Mr. Haney." The deputy repeated the official story, just like he'd been instructed to do. Figured he could wash the taste of that lie out of his mouth, too, once he got his fresh beer.

The grieving dad's breath reeked of booze and old vomit. His fist hit the bar top. "A monster, that's what." Haney turned on his barstool and jabbed a finger at the back of the bar, where a messy strawberry ponytail poked over the back of a corner booth, fluorescents glinting off horn-rimmed glasses.

Alongside her recorder, stacks of papers and grainy photographs covered the tabletop where a half-eaten chop steak sat dissected on a plate in front of Professor Corinne Bennick in her university hoodie. Brandon's stomach churned. For a dive bar, the Green Frog had decent food—he just had no idea how the woman could stomach it after what they'd seen today.

"That bookworm wolf expert back there knows it," Haney said, "and I know it, too, and I'm gonna find it, and I'm gonna shoot it until there ain't nothin' left to shoot." Haney slurred as he leaned in close, finger still raised in the air like the fool had pissed out all his common sense.

Hinson really needed that beer. He looked for the bartender, who was busy with some other barfly. "We'll find whoever did this," Hinson said, "and we'll bring him to justice. I promise you that."

"Not a *he*." Haney's bloated finger blurred in Brandon's vision again. "A *what*. Rabid animals *bite*, Chuck," Haney said, and Brandon wouldn't need to order a new beer once Haney got done spitting his old one into his mouth. "They don't *eat*," the drunk said.

Brandon thought about that a long time after he poured Brett Haney into the backseat of a cab.

Long enough to work up the courage to walk over to Corinne's table—interrupt her reading and her dinner just minutes before last call.

"Can I join you, Professor?" he asked without paying too much attention to the meat on her plate, the thin puddle of pale red. Of course the wolf expert liked her steak rare.

The look on her face said no, but her mouth said yes, and Brandon perched on the edge of the booth, which he figured was about as close to meeting her in the middle as he could get. A prickle crawled up the inside of his thigh and he thought of Kim—first the press of her kiss and then the way she'd pulled away—and Brandon slid a little farther into the booth.

"Can I ask you something?" he said.

Corinne squinted at him through her lenses. "As long as it's off the record."

"I'm off the clock," Brandon said, then, "Do rabid wolves usually eat their kills?"

The professor shrugged. "Depends, I guess."

On the wolf, or on the kill? On the level of infection, maybe? The wolf expert didn't specify—but she didn't say no, either.

"So, a rabid wolf might kill and eat its own pack," Brandon said. "Like what we saw today."

Corinne sliced off a sliver of red meat and thought while she chewed it. "Wolves aren't known for cannibalism, even when rabid," she said, "but coyotes are." She sliced off another bite and looked directly into Brandon's eyes when she swallowed.

"Protein is protein," she said, and Brandon's gut churned when she sliced off another bite. "Everything has to eat."

CHAPTER 24

Lenore Evans

Lenore glared at the row of small petri dishes under the fluorescent shine of vanity lights in her bathroom. Her hip bones dug against the countertop, the pinch that lived in her shoulder blades working its way up through her sinuses, into her temples as she leaned into the granite. Lenore bit back against the pain as she studied the contents of each dish with her magnifying glass, then she set the tool beside the dishes, clamped both palms on the granite, nicer than the linoleum counter at the lab, and choked down the taste of failure.

Dead, every single one. Again.

Fantastic, Lenore thought, defeat still on her tongue.

Between Ducey's new dining habits and the condition of the bodies in the Evans Funeral Parlor coolers, it'd been easy to collect small tissue samples from the town's recent dead without notice. No one would miss a small piece of skin or tissue—a clip of ligament here, a swatch of muscle there. Lenore had taken samples from the natural dead and the murdered, convincing herself with each stolen sample over the years that the research was worth the indignity, that the deceased whose bodies she'd been charged to care for would not return to haunt her for robbing their graves before they ever went in.

If those dead she'd stolen from ever rose, it would be her fault.

Didn't make a difference, because in just a few days' time Lenore had used up every scrap of stolen remains and almost all the strigoi ashes that she had left, and while the ash salve she applied made the samples swell and change color, nothing appeared *restless.*

Every sample of the dead she treated with strigoi ashes stayed dead. Not so much as a jiggle of undead life.

And yet she'd rubbed ashes into the wound on her mother's throat and Ducey had risen from her grave.

"But Mama wasn't dead when I did it," Lenore muttered to herself as she washed her dusty failure down the bathroom sink drain. Ducey had still been breathing when Lenore first rubbed Ed Boone's ashes into the hole in her mother's neck—hadn't she?

Maybe not.

Maybe it was Grace, Lenore thought. Maybe that had been her daughter, not her mother, who had breathed long enough to look into Lenore's eyes before closing them forever.

Patches of gray smoked out the memory of that night, blurring the sharpest edges of her shattered heart. Lenore knew she'd used ashes to tend to the cuts and scrapes that Crane had sustained in the fight, just like she'd done for Belle, but her memory clouded like Ducey's dead eye when she tried to recount the exact details of when she'd failed to save her daughter.

Lenore soaped off the dish, then her hands, without facing the ghosts that waited in her eyes in the mirror. She twisted off the faucet, flicked off the bathroom lights, and let her fingers slide along the quilt as she walked to the head of her bed. Lenore picked up the framed wedding photo on her nightstand and gazed lovingly—longingly—at Jimmy in his Marine dress blues, at herself in auburn curls and white lace.

The pinch in Lenore's skull pressed into her teeth. She needed to know what had made her mother rise from the dead, before she could figure out what to do with the woman now. She needed to know if there was any way to bring her husband back, to see him again, if only just one more time. And the only way Lenore knew to find answers to either was to keep trying to make the ashes work.

But tonight . . . tonight she had to put her work aside to dig up another man.

Lenore traded her slacks and blouse for a pair of old sweats and pinned her ginger bob behind her ears. She secured a dagger in her waistband and then she slid past her husband's silent clocks and stood alone outside in the dark, ears tuned for the sound of wolves, while she waited for Roger's headlights to swing into her driveway.

Dirt stained the man's fingers brown around the rim of his steering wheel when Lenore folded herself into the front passenger seat of the sheriff's department Crown Victoria. Black dirt crusted in his nail beds.

"I see you've been tending that mount of dirt again," she said to the man's fingernails.

His grip tightened around the wheel, knuckles going white as Roger turned the car toward the funeral parlor and picked up speed. He'd traded his mudpie-brown uniform for a pair of old jeans and a flannel button-down, sleeves rolled up to show the bandage around his forearm.

Roger's badge winked in his shirt pocket every time the car passed under a streetlight. The handgun holstered at his hip wasn't the department-issued revolver.

Six rounds, Lenore remembered that the revolver held. The pistol might hold ten, maybe more, in its magazine.

She touched the dagger at her hip. The Evans women's blades hadn't saved them before, but then, neither had the lawman's gun.

Roger's lips pressed together behind the wheel, but his words from that fateful night echoed in Lenore's ears. *I emptied six rounds into what was left of him.* Roger had pumped every bullet from his gun into Buck Johnson, but he hadn't remembered to reload before the restless dead descended on Evans Funeral Parlor.

Lenore knew what it looked like to be eaten alive by guilt. "You can't keep blaming yourself for what happened to Grace," she told Roger.

"I don't."

Lenore tasted the lie just like she'd tasted failure over her ashes.

Roger kept his hands at ten and two, his eyes straight ahead. "Six in the cylinder at all times," he said, braking too hard as they turned into the parlor's parking lot. "It's one of the first things a deputy is taught when they join the force. If I had just reloaded—"

Lenore put her hand on the man's bandaged forearm. Sheriff's deputies were trained to protect and serve, and so were Evans women. They put their lives on the line, and sometimes they gave them over.

"It may not have changed a thing," she said. "Love isn't a cure for Evans women, it's a curse. I reckon that applies to those who love us, too."

She thought of her husband, her Jimmy, gone too soon. Of her own father, even of Buck Johnson, who'd only hated Ducey so much because he'd loved her once. Died young, too young, too early, all of them.

"You wanted to be a part of the Evans family, and this is part of it." Lenore put her other hand over her heart, remembering the weight of her dagger as it pierced her mother's chest. "We guard the balance between life and death, and that means we live somewhere between."

The cruiser came to a complete stop at the parlor's back door, headlights pointed at the white rosebush at the edge of the garden.

They both stared at the mount of dirt Roger couldn't make bloom over her daughter's grave. Lenore thought of her house full of silent clocks, the wedding portrait on her dead husband's bedside table, her weekly pilgrimage through Eternal Flame's mausoleums.

The vial of Jimmy's ashes she still kept hidden.

Her undead mother.

"It means we learn how to live with the grief," Lenore said, patting his arm as the funeral parlor's back door pushed open. Luna, Crane, and Ducey spilled out under the cover of night. Each carried a shovel tucked under an arm. Belle's snout pressed against the glass between the breakroom window blinds. The dog would hate to stay behind, but Buck had been her master before she became an Evans. They couldn't risk her sounding any alarms on the dead sheriff's land.

Lenore let her hand fall into her lap as the cruiser's back doors pulled open. The pinch burned behind her eyes as she rushed the words out under the rustle of people climbing into the car. "We learn how to keep breathing when the ones we love become ghosts."

With Ducey calling the shots and three at a time digging, they made quick work churning up the dirt of Buck Johnson's grave. Buried without ceremony—and with no vault or grave liner—Buck's remains had been left to rot in a plain pine box. Still, Lenore had insisted the casket be nailed shut, just to be sure.

Roger stood with his hands clasped in front of him, eyes turned down, while Crane used the toothy end of a hammer to wrench the nails from the box's lid, then climbed out of the grave.

All five stood together over the hole in the dirt and looked at what remained of Sheriff Buchanan "Buck" Johnson.

"I'll be damned," Ducey said, words light under her heavy scowl. "The old fart's still here."

If Lenore's pinch squeezed any harder, the spots along the edges of her vision would blind her completely. The old sheriff had been their only hope, such as it was, but the man lay rotting in his grave, which meant whatever was chewing through town this time—whatever "other monster" had sprung forth to terrorize the Evanses—it wasn't Buck Johnson.

Which meant that if they wanted any answers, there was only one more place to go.

"We have no idea how to resurrect a strigoi," Lenore said, to beat her mother to the punch.

"We do."

It took Lenore a moment to realize who'd spoken, and then she glared at Crane. The boy shared a look with Luna, and Lenore swatted phantom ants off her skin, sweeping her hand to her hip as she turned her full attention to the tall boy in the leather trench coat and black eyeliner.

"And how, pray tell, do you know that?" she said.

Crane and Luna shared another look, and Lenore liked this one even less.

"We've been researching strigoi and other undead legends," Luna said, as sheepish as Lenore had ever seen her. "Trying to learn more about what I am—" She cut her eyes to Ducey. "What *we* are."

Ducey snorted, her bright green eye rolling along behind the clouded one. "You find much about raisin' the dead down at the public library?" she said.

"Not at the library," Crane said, then smiled so wide that the edges of his long lips brushed the dark curtains of his hair. "But I have friends overseas on the internet, other ceremonial magicians, and they turned out to be quite informative."

The dead woman cut her eyes at the smug boy, then at Lenore. Mother stared at daughter, and Lenore took a deep, steadying breath. She looked into the open grave.

Like it or not, Samael might be their last hope.

Everything is fine.

Roger's hands came unclasped as the man found his voice. "Now wait just one damn minute," he said. "You can't be saying you want to raise one of those monsters?"

"No offense taken," Ducey clucked at the sheriff.

He looked at Lenore, but she kept her eyes down. "What happens when it all goes to hell," he asked, "and we have an even bigger mess on our hands?"

Ducey hissed in the dark. "You got a better idea, Sheriff Big Britches?"

Roger looked helplessly at Lenore. "I'm barely holding things together now," he said, shaking his head, feeling for the gun on his hip. "I won't be able to keep things in check if this gets worse."

"We aren't going to raise just any monster." The pinch in Lenore's head narrowed her vision until all she saw was her granddaughter, standing there in the moonlight.

Luna's hand slid into her friend's. "We're going to raise my father."

The sheriff flinched like he'd been punched. Lenore couldn't remember if they'd told Roger the truth about Grace's beau, but it didn't matter much now, did it?

"And what happens if he ain't happy to be woken up?" Roger asked.

Ducey crossed her arms over her chest.

"Reckon that's where I come in," the old woman said. "Like I said. I died once to protect this family. Got no qualms about doin' it again."

Lenore nodded at her mother. They would resurrect the monster, because with their knowledge exhausted and no answers on the horizon, the monster was the only hope they had left.

CHAPTER 25

Professor Corinne Bennick

Dive-bar dinner hadn't been Corinne's first choice, but chowing down bad food in questionable company sounded better than another night of fast food shoveled through the driver's side window of her rented Honda Civic, and so chopped steak and greasy shoestring fries it was. She sat at the back booth, listening over and over to the notes on her recorder while she parsed research papers for insights into the rabid wolves' strange behavior and mushroom gravy congealed on her plate.

When the deputy slid into her booth with low-level flirtation disguised as off-duty banter, Corinne stuffed the papers into her bag. She forced down what little bit of food she could stomach, and when the bartender rang the bell for last call and the deputy went to refill his beer, she paid her tab in cash and bolted.

Not that Deputy Brandon Hinson was bad. He had nice eyes and good manners, enough courage to stand in the middle of a parking lot scattered with body parts, and enough empathy to drop to his knees and puke on the pavement. Just . . . high school football jocks turned hotshot rookies didn't do much to get Corinne's motor running.

Not much did, aside from wildlife biology—and Sophia Diaz.

Sophia, Corinne thought as she flopped face-down onto the mattress sliver at her cheap motel. Sophia, her beautiful, brilliant girlfriend, whom she would finally introduce to her deep-fried Southern parents this weekend when she got home. Sophia, whom Corinne had promised that she'd only be gone one night, not four.

Sophia, who purred sweet words to her on the other end of the phone line, long-distance calling fees be damned. If the university wanted Corinne to stay in this horrible little town this long, they could foot the bill for her to call home.

"I miss you, too," she told Sophia, all the way back in their shared apartment in Austin. "So much."

"What is going on there?" Sophia asked. "Did you find the ghost wolf?"

Corinne tried to find a position on the motel's stiff mattress that felt like her girlfriend's arms around her, but *nada*. "We found a pack of dead ones," she said. "Including an alpha missing its head."

Sophia bit into the air on the other end of the line. "Like the principal."

The one with the missing arm. Corinne nodded into her pillow. She'd tried to stick to the facts when reporters from Houston interviewed her about the coyote–red wolf hybrids, but even rabid, the animals' behavior didn't make sense. Sure, genetic mutations could have occurred that altered the psychology of the beasts, but the impact of the rabies virus threw another wrench into the mix. Aside from hunches and flimsy correlations, Corinne couldn't find jack shit in the literature.

"Was it male or female?" Sophia asked, halting Corinne's runaway thought train. "The alpha?"

Corinne flipped over onto her back, readjusting her glasses. The water stain on the motel-room ceiling looked like a pair of wild beasts, howling at a melted moon. Corinne shut her eyes against the unwelcome Rorschach test.

"Female," she told Sophia. "There was no alpha male—at least, not that we found."

"So he killed his own pack?" Her girlfriend's breath blew back across the line. "I'm sorry."

So was Corinne. An alpha-female ghost wolf, even rabid, would have kept her research going for years. In wolf hierarchy—particularly those bred in captivity, like the red wolves in Louisiana and Texas captured to establish a captive breeding population—males tended to dominate other males and females dominated other females. To find

198 | Lindy Ryan

a pack led solely by an alpha female was rare. But for a patriarch to slaughter his own pack, unheard of.

"Come home, my love," Sophia's voice rumbled low across the line, thrummed in Corinne's chest like a command.

She'd studied wolves since grad school, but Corinne had never met an alpha female like Sophia Diaz.

They'd met at roller derby. As the team's pivot, it was Sophia's job to teach the fresh meat how to bridge, to recycle, to snowplow—all the right moves, everything Corinne needed to know to help defend the derby pack, so long as she followed Sophia's lead. By their second week of practice, something had begun to rumble in places Corinne didn't know she had, and at their first jam, Corinne's freckles burned when Sophia grabbed her from behind.

"See you later, fresh meat," Sophia had whispered against Corinne's rookie helmet, and then she whipped herself ahead of the pack off Corinne's hips, and Corinne fell in love.

After they hung up, Corinne stripped off her jeans and hoodie, waited until the motel's pipes warmed enough not to blast her with ice water, then showered the funk of cigarette smoke and dive bar out of her hair. Half a bottle of Herbal Essences gone, and she still got a whiff of death when she towel-dried the stuff.

She lay down on the cheap motel's cheap mattress. She pulled flaky sheets over herself, staring at the melting moon on the ceiling until watery smears swam in her eyes, and then she pushed herself up onto her elbows, groaned, and climbed out of bed. So much for sleep, then.

Corinne stared at the inside of the motel-room door. The last thing she wanted was to be alone outside at night, but she'd left her bag full of research papers, her recorded notes, in the rental.

Crap.

She flopped down onto the mattress. She stared at the wolves over her head.

She kicked up out of the sheets.

Corinne wasn't some dumb country bumpkin. She was a professor, a *scientist,* for crying out loud. Corinne Bennick, PhD, University of

Texas Wildlife Biology Department. She'd dissected dead canines, investigated their kills, and she could damn sure make it twenty feet to her rented Honda and get her bag.

The principal probably told himself the same thing, she thought. But this was a well-lit gravel lot with a dozen cars parked under the neon Gladys City Motel sign, not an empty expanse of high school pavement, a late-night dumpster, a patch of woods.

Besides, Corinne had a field kit in her trunk—and the kit had a gun.

The tranquilizer gun could stun an animal at thirty paces, drop it within two minutes, but hip whips weren't the only thing Sophia taught Corinne on the derby track. A rabid wolf wasn't exactly a derby girl, but worst-case scenario, Corinne knew how to protect her vital organs, and she knew how to run for her life.

She pulled her jeans over her pajama shorts, slipped into her shoes, and snatched up the car and room keys in her fist.

Humidity fogged up her glasses and midnight air lapped at Corinne's skin as she left the motel-room door propped open on its dead bolt behind her. She scanned the tree line across the two-lane road, gravel crunching under her sneakers as she marched to the little sedan parked outside the row of motel doors, stabbed the Honda key into the hatch, lifted the trunk open.

Corinne froze. Goose bumps prickled the fine hairs on the back of her neck up through her freckles.

Just leaves rustling in the slow autumn wind, skittering along concrete behind her. *Psithurism,* she thought, one of the coolest underused words in the English language.

Her bag had spilled on the drive to the motel, and Corinne stuffed the papers back inside and pulled her bag onto her shoulder. She clasped her hands on the trunk—

That's what leaves sound like, right?

—and slammed the hatch closed—

Or gravel under footsteps?

More rustling, and this time, no wind. It took Corinne longer than she liked to turn around and face the leaves. The street. The night.

Not leaves. Not psithurism after all.

She blinked through the fog of her lenses. No one stood in the gravel lot with her, but on the other side of the two-lane road just outside the streetlight's glow, hidden amongst the shrubbery and flimsy pines, a black shape crouched in the shadows. Corinne could make out the tips of pointed ears that poked up between low-hanging branches, the familiar outline of a snout, a shoulder. But its back half rumpled out behind it on the heat-brittle grass—broken, maybe.

The male's wounded, Corinne thought, and rubbed her sleeves over her horn-rims.

The ghost wolf that the drunk lunatic had hit had been wounded already. That's how he'd tracked it back to the den, to the pack.

Corinne watched the wolf writhe in the shadows, listening to the noise of its injured body scratch against foliage as it worried at something with its teeth. Wounded animals could be vicious. A wounded *rabid* alpha—well. Nobody ever said science was easy.

She let go off the trunk lid and set her bag back into the Honda, then opened the field kit. Once she got the gloves on, Corinne picked up the tranquilizer gun, loaded a dart, and undid the safety. She found her recorder and mashed the red button to get the tape rolling.

Amber eyes tracked Corinne as she inched toward the beast, tranq gun in one hand, recorder in the other, but its head stayed forward as she approached from the side.

"It's hurt," she whispered to the tape. "Larger than a typical red wolf, but the back legs look broken." Corinne couldn't see what sort of injury kept the animal still, enveloped in darkness, but by the time the toe of her sneakers hit the seam where motel parking lot met roadway pavement, she could see its misshapen limbs. "The coat is abnormal in color and patchy, maybe mange."

The wolf's head tilted at an odd angle, the jaw limp in its gape, exposing too many rows of jagged teeth stained black in the moonlight.

Corinne gulped. "Hyperdontia," she told the recorder. More like a shark than a wolf.

The wolf stirred as she drew near it, and she saw what the beast held in its maw—a long, crooked something, with one sharp point and a frayed end.

She skidded to a stop at the dashed yellow line in the center of the road when she recognized the dismembered arm.

Corinne clenched the recorder and lifted the gun.

Aim for the heart. But the beast lay on its chest, and the humid air blew her breath onto her glasses. She forced her arms steady, waited for the gun's long barrel to still, the fog to clear. A head shot could injure the animal, or worse, spray the virus out along with its brains.

Corinne drew in a deep breath as the wolf's head turned toward her. The arm—it was an arm—dropped to the grass, the jagged edge of the humerus pale where it stuck out at the end.

Aim for the heart.

The beast stirred, mangled, matted fur rippling in the moonlight. It pushed itself onto four unstable limbs.

Then up onto two.

Bipedal? Corinne squinted past the gun's barrel as the animal staggered forward. She couldn't believe what she told the recorder.

Her body flooded cold, the chill under her skin hitting the night's heat, sending more fog onto her lenses.

The thing moved like a baby giraffe, stilted and lurching, its form a hulking patchwork of mismatched fur and dangling bone. Teeth and claws strung about its body as if every inch of it could bite, could claw. Corinne recognized the mandibles of smaller creatures pushed up its arms—up its *human* arms. The beast staggering toward her wore the decapitated alpha wolf's head like a crown, but whatever this creature was, it was not a wolf.

Corinne nearly flew out of her skin. She fired the tranq gun. She reached for the open door of her cheap motel room, to her cheap mattress with its cheap sheets.

But the toes of her sneakers stayed glued to the dashed yellow line. Fight or flight, but there was a third option, wasn't there, scientifically speaking? Freeze, and every bone in her body ached to flee, not an ounce of fight in her, and yet here she stood, frozen to the asphalt.

The creature stepped onto the road.

The alpha female's decapitated head lifted as another head turned up, exposing the face beneath the wolf-head crown.

Corinne squinted through the fog, and all the color drained out of her, from her hair to her freckles to her toes. She dropped the recorder.

She-wolf, she had time to think, before the beast lunged.

CHAPTER 26

Luna Evans

The morning after they dug up the dead sheriff, Luna got up early to check beneath the tallow tree outside her bedroom window, and found a broken pair of women's eyeglasses. Black brow and arms, strawberry hair trapped in the metal wire bridging the nose, one of the lenses cracked into spiderwebs. Luna thought the frames looked familiar.

Not as familiar, though, as Kim Cole's box-black hair and heavy eyeliner in the Evans Funeral Parlor laboratory. With Ducey holed up in the breakroom and Nana guarding the lobby from her front desk, there weren't many places left for Luna to hide until the sheriff showed up to escort her to school.

I hope he doesn't, Luna thought, because riding the big yellow dog had somehow become the better option. At least if she took the bus, she could ride back with Crane.

She huffed and hugged her backpack tighter.

Kim closed the file folder she'd been reading and set it on the instrument tray beside the lab's metal exam table. She pulled the white sheet down off a dead woman's face, then tucked the sheet behind the shoulders, smoothing the edge over the chest before she plucked a foundation compact from the red cosmetics case on the table.

Kim flicked the makeup palette open. Five fingertips went into five cream trays as she compared the foundation shades to the corpse's yellow skin. One coated finger dabbed into a second tray, thumb blending the two shades together on her fingertip, and then Kim crooked the double-dipped finger away from the rest.

Winner, winner.

"Well, Mrs. Hilda Baker," she said, "looks like you're gonna get your healthy glow back." Kim smeared color from her fingertips onto a rag, swiped a sponge in the chosen palette trays, and began to stipple color onto the dead woman's yellow cheeks. "First body I saw in here, I thought she had jaundice," Kim said. "It was just cheese."

Luna's glare snagged on her mother's cosmetics case, the familiar bottles and tubes of the products Grace favored, from the corner chair across the lab. Nana Lenore never said why she'd kept Kim's interview a secret, and Luna had done her best to avoid Dillon's older sister ever since the whole spy comment thing at Monday's memorial assembly—but did that really matter anymore?

Just because she didn't go squealing to Stripper Cop about Ducey doesn't make her trustworthy. Luna slid her backpack through her knees, pinching it between her Converses when it hit the linoleum floor, and huffed again.

"Wanna talk about it?" Kim said softly. At the exam table, she kept stippling while her eyes rolled up at Luna under a fringe of dense mascara.

Talk about what—the items stashed in her bag, or the fact that she was going to dig up her dad? Luna huffed for a third time, doing her best to sound surly while the shape of the horn-rims glared at her through the bag's front pocket. She crossed her ankles over the backpack. "About what?" she asked.

"Nothing, I guess." Kim tossed the ruined sponge into the lab sink. She selected a fluffy brush next, dusted the end in pink, and began to swirl blush across the yellow corpse's cheeks—across her forehead, under her jaw. "Because I don't know what sulking looks like," she muttered under her breath.

Luna folded her arms over her chest and studied the squiggles in the lab floor linoleum. *Whatever.*

Kim set the brush down on the table and opened the dead woman's file folder.

"The pictures that the family bring in are always from, like, twenty years earlier," she said, flipping the paper so Luna could see that the woman in the photograph had cigar curls and round cheeks. "I wish they'd send something just a bit more recent . . . but her liver disease probably took its time." Kim's frown alternated between the picture and the table. She dropped the picture onto the tray, picked up a thin-tipped brush and a mascara tube, and smudged black from the wand onto a lip brush she held under the dead woman's eyelashes.

She scowled as she swept on mascara. "So, what are you hiding in your backpack?"

Luna's heart stopped when Kim made a point to stare at the bag gripped between her feet. "Weed?" Kim asked, waggling her eyebrows. "Condoms? Satanic rock 'n' roll?"

"Nothing," Luna snapped. If only.

"Cool buttons, by the way." Kim shrugged like she didn't care one way or another. She rummaged in Grace's cosmetics case, then popped the cap off a shiny gold lipstick tube and twisted up rotten berry red. Kim scrunched her nose at the color, then leaned over to compare it to Hilda Baker's photo and shrugged. "Less is more," she said as she smeared a Q-tip against the wax and then across a thin coat of red to recolor the dead woman's lips. "Act like you don't care what's in the bag," she said, "and nobody else will, either."

Luna chewed at the insides of her cheeks. "Why do you care?" she asked.

"I don't." Kim put away the lipstick and went back to her brushes, dusting final touches over the corpse's face. "Just filling the silence. Hilda doesn't say much."

Like brother, like sister, Luna guessed. Having only met Kim a few times, she'd never have pegged her for the chatterbox type.

She did get on famously with Ducey, though.

Kim dusted on more blush, then powder, then scowled and added another brush of pink. She wiped away some of her work with a tissue, then tried again, blush then powder then blush—then another swipe of the tissue and repeat. Her lips pulled under, and Luna rolled her eyes as she pushed up from her chair and took the brush from Kim's fingers.

Luna swept pink over the dead woman's yellowed ears and gave the brush back. "Helps them look more natural," she said, then when Kim quirked an eyebrow, "I used to help my mom," she explained.

And it *would* feel good to tell someone about the trinkets stashed in her backpack pocket. Someone other than Crane, who always took her side. Or her grandmothers, who still kept secrets, even from each other. Even after they'd dug up Buck Johnson, found the old sheriff still in his grave, Ducey hadn't spilled the beans on "other monsters" to any of them. She'd mostly just grumbled about Grandmother Pie.

"If I tell you," Luna started. "You promise not to tell anyone?"

"Look." Kim rolled heavy-lidded eyes at the coolers, at the dog-eared stack of smutty romance novels on the lab bookshelves. "I know enough about what goes on around here to know there's a shit ton that I *don't* know," she said. "But I'm not a snitch."

Luna sucked in a breath.

"Dillon doesn't know," she said on the exhale. "He *can't* know. I tried to tell him—I tried to tell him and Crystal both, you know, about the dead stuff, or I guess the *un*dead stuff, the night that—"

Luna choked down the rest before it spilled out. Last month she'd tried to tell her best friends that the dead were chewing their way through town, but they hadn't believed her, just thought she'd lost her mind when grief had swallowed her whole.

It had, more or less anyway—sucked her down like a biblical whale. But more than that, Luna had learned an important lesson that night.

The Evans women were made of secrets, and whatever else she was, Luna was an Evans.

She bit her lip. "It's . . . it's not a rabid wolf that's been killing all these people," she said.

"I don't know what it is," Luna continued, before Kim could ask, "but I think it's leaving things outside my bedroom window." She walked back to her chair and snatched up the backpack, then set it down on the lab countertop.

Luna unzipped the front pocket and pulled out the pink sequined cat collar with its little silver bell.

Kim made a noise like *Oh* when Sissy's name sparkled in the lab fluorescents. "That's Rhonda's cat's collar," she said. "She kept so many pictures of that stupid cat pinned up around Jimbo's." She raised a hand to touch it, but stopped short. "I'd recognize it anywhere."

Brevard's class ring next, and Kim half-jogged from the table to Luna's side.

"No shit," Kim said, then, "Daniel," when Luna pulled out the head-phones with the torn cable. "I heard Sheriff Taylor say they found his Discman, but not the headphones."

Luna set the horn-rimmed glasses on the counter last.

"I think these belong to that professor that's here to help find the ghost wolf," she told Kim. "Same glasses, and look at the hair?"

Kim started to say, "But she isn't . . ." then broke off, and they both looked to the cooler. Only one door didn't have a tag. Not every body awaiting burial in the six-door cabinet was a victim of the pretend ghost wolf—most were like old Mrs. Hilda Baker, dead of old age and liver failure—but some were.

"You should tell your grandmothers," Kim said, as Luna shoveled the items back into the backpack pocket. "Maybe they'll know what it means."

Luna shook her head. "They don't know what's going on, either." Ducey had mentioned "other monsters," but what kind of monsters brought gifts back from their kills—and why bring them to Luna? "What if . . ." she started to say.

Her words fell off, and Luna had to force them back to her lips. "What if this is my fault?" she asked. "What if I'm the 'other monster'?"

Again, she reminded herself.

"So what if you are?" Kim didn't blink, but Luna's eyelids fluttered so fast it was a good thing she didn't wear contacts. Last thing she needed, searching for a thin clear disc on the funeral lab floor.

"A smart lady once told me that it's okay to be myself," Kim said, "because that's the most precious thing I have—me. And so, if you are something supernatural or something, then maybe instead of hating yourself for it, you should embrace it." She turned back to the exam table and began to comb Mrs. Baker's hair. "I embraced my inner weirdo, and look at me now," she said, working a cloud of mousse into the dead woman's hair.

Luna's voice came out surly again. "No offense," she said, "but I'm not sure that totally applies to what we're dealing with here."

Kim jerked her head in the breakroom's direction. "Might be right, but I'm pretty sure the smart lady that told me that qualifies as a monster now, too." She shot a look over her shoulder and wagged her eyebrows. "Hey," she said brightly, "the Homecoming Dance is tonight, right?"

"I guess," Luna said, because there was also the little matter of resurrecting her undead father. "But I don't have a dress."

"I've got one you can borrow," Kim said, then, "I'll do your makeup."

Luna tried to process the offer, because reviving her undead dad was one thing, but no way was *Kim Cole* proposing to make her over.

That afternoon when the dismissal bell rang, Luna made her way toward the school's front exit.

Dillon hooked his arm through hers. "How are things going with my sister at the parlor?" he asked. "Is it super weird having her around?"

"Not any more than usual." Luna's own surprise fizzled on her tongue. "She's kinda cool."

"Almost always," Dillon agreed. They pushed through the front doors, passed between a row of teachers, and he crooked his head close to Luna's. "She kicked Stripper Cop out last night," he whispered.

In all their sharing this morning, Kim hadn't mentioned this. It wasn't like they'd been talking about *her* secrets.

"Why?" Luna said.

Dillon lifted his shoulders. "No idea, she was super secretive about it." He waved the topic away, baby blues sparkling in the afternoon sunshine. "More importantly," he said, tugging against her shoulder as Crane came into view, leaning like a lost shadow at the bus stall. "The Homecoming Dance is *tonight*—you two *are* coming, right?"

Dillon pulled her to a stop in order to force the full weight of his pout upon her. "Say you are," he begged, voice ticking into a high whine.

Luna wished she could say, *Sorry, kinda busy resurrecting my vampire dad tonight,* but her grandmothers and the sheriff said she needed to carry on with normal teenage-girl things, and there was plenty of time between sunset and when the dance doors opened.

"I promised Crane I would be his date," she said, but she didn't add that Dillon's own big sister would be playing fairy godmother and dressing her up.

The bus driver rolled his eyes when Crane stepped onto the bus behind Luna for a second day in a row.

"Are you ready?" Crane asked when they'd taken their seats in the back of the bus.

Weighted down with secrets, Luna's backpack pulled her to the floorboard. She remembered what Kim had said this morning, in the lab, about embracing what she was, even if it was a monster, and she kicked her backpack under the bus seat.

Hell yes, she was ready.

CHAPTER 27

Ducey Evans

Ducey clicked her teeth, wishing there were a butterscotch in there. If she had to repeat herself one more time, she might go ahead and dig her way right back six feet under. At least then she'd get some damn peace and quiet.

"Now, Len," she said, wriggling her bunny-eared toes, "I'm tired of sayin' the same thing over and over—"

Her daughter spun on her heels, turning away from her mother in the recliner.

Before Ducey could finish her sentence, the burn in her chest crawled up the back of her throat. "We're out of our depth," she said to the little line of sunlight peeking through the edges of the window blinds. "And we're out of choices."

Not long now, and it'd be sunset. Best time for gardening.

Lenore stepped over the hound sprawled halfway under the break-room table and pressed the brew button on the coffeepot. "I can't believe we're going to raise that, that *thing*," she said.

"No offense taken," Ducey hissed under her breath as the Cole girl leaned in to touch up the paint job on her neck. The cool brush of the little sponge helped tamp down the sizzle swirling in her chest. Scars didn't bother Ducey none, but the paint would keep her daughter from staring too hard at the scar chewing its way down the side of her throat, too.

Lenore crossed one loafer over the other as she leaned against the countertop, rigid as a polecat about to spray. "That's not what I meant, Mama," she said.

They stared each other down until Lenore looked away. Ducey smirked. One upside to being dead: she didn't have to blink.

Kim patted the little sponge around Ducey's jawline. "Okay, let's see how this looks," the girl said, already on her way to the breakroom blinds. She twisted the plastic slats open—a hint of yellow already creeping its way into indigo—then squinted through her mascara to inspect her work in natural light, nodded her approval, and twisted the blinds closed.

Belle snored under the table and Lenore rolled her eyes, then turned toward the girl she'd so recently hired. Kim pressed one more stamp under Ducey's cheekbone before her hand froze in the air, having looked up to find herself caught in Lenore's icy stare.

Kim split her words between Ducey's good eye and Lenore. "Maybe I should finish this up later," she said.

"Ignore my daughter." Ducey jerked her thumb toward the ice sculpture who hobbled over to harass the glass coffeepot. "Lenore could start an argument in a haunted house," she said and crossed her ankles. "Ain't nothin' new."

Lenore pushed air up from her toes and out through her lips as she managed to scare up a mugful of drip for herself. She sloshed the pot in Kim's direction, but the girl shook her away, and Lenore set it back into its cradle. She closed her eyes, sipped, and exhaled whatever air she had left in her lungs.

"I just wish we had more time," Lenore said.

Ducey snorted. "And I wish my butterscotches didn't taste like chitlins." The sweet caramel hard candies used to make her sweet tooth water, but every time she tried to suck one since she'd risen, another layer of nasty stained itself onto her soul. "We can wish all we want, but don't make a lick of difference," she told her daughter. "We still gotta do what we still gotta do."

Whatever Lenore mumbled into her mug, it sounded like *Godawful Mess*. The ant bed in Ducey's chest lit up, and she itched at her arms, her thighs, the jean waistband digging into her craw. For as much as she'd worried about being buried in her brassiere, having to wear britches might be worse.

"Either we ask the dead man," Ducey said, "or we may as well join him, because whatever is goin' on around here is only gonna get worse."

Under the table the hound huffed, driving Ducey's point home while the yellow began to boil under the window blinds. In the chair beside her, Kim turned to stone where the light hit her skin.

Girl's so quiet she might not be breathin', Ducey thought, while Lenore prattled on about fool things like time, and ashes, and what might happen if things went wrong, went wrong again, and they'd need to put the ghoul back in the ground, and didn't anyone understand that the white rosebush might not survive a second uprooting, so soon and—

"Oh, to hell with your rosebush, Len," Ducey cut in when she couldn't take any more of the girl's hemming and hawing. "Mine's good as new, and I ain't usin' it. Bury him under that."

Lenore glared over another sip of coffee. She stared at the blinds, but Ducey knew she was looking at the mound of dirt that refused to bloom in the garden at the edge of the old farmhouse turned funeral parlor.

"He killed my husband, Mama," she said.

Ducey squirmed in her recliner. The child's house slippers drove her crazy, but the trousers were hell. She'd rather her usual muumuus, but Lenore insisted Ducey don a disguise if she were to go outside the parlor's walls.

"Your husband got in the way," she reminded her daughter. "Jimmy had no right putting himself in Evans business."

If the man hadn't put himself between them and the ghoul that night, he might still be alive. But he'd wanted to play hero, gotten himself killed.

Nothing like a man trying to do a woman's work.

Lenore just pouted into her mug. "Jimmy was trying to protect his family."

If Ducey's blood had still been moving in her veins, her daughter's voice would have frozen it solid. But spending a few weeks dead had given the old woman a new perspective on what happened that night fifteen years ago. She forced her teeth not to chatter and said, "So was Samael."

Lenore flinched like she'd been slapped, just like Sheriff Big Britches did last night when they'd told him who they'd dig up next. Brown spilled down the side of Lenore's mug like Ducey's midmorning snack out of her trocar, and she spun around, dumping what was left of her coffee down the sink.

"Who's Samael?" Kim chirped against Ducey's ear, and the dead woman hopped so high in her chair that one of her slippers came loose and she nearly banged her head on the ceiling.

At the sink, Lenore flushed water after coffee and rinsed the mug. "The monster who put my daughter Grace under his thrall," she said, shaking water off the ceramic before she set it on the drying rack.

Kim looked over, full of questions. *Oh, hell,* Ducey thought. The girl hadn't batted an eye at Ducey's undead habits, and she didn't ask questions about the Evanses' business, but they hadn't nearly told her everything.

They hadn't told her about Luna.

Ducey clicked her teeth. By all rights, this part should be Lenore's problem. But even dead, Ducey still had to be the one to give the Evans history lesson.

"Samael is Luna's father," she said. "Whatever I am, he's worse." The girl's eyes bulged with the pressure of even more questions, and Ducey waved at her to hold on. "I'm not the first one by a long shot," she continued. "When the dead rise, we have to put them back down. We keep this town safe, you understand?"

Ducey held Kim in her gaze until she nodded.

"The dead rise and you put them back down," she said, chewing the words into more digestible pieces. Her lips twisted into a pretty purple balloon knot. "So, Luna's dad is a zom—"

"Strigoi." The only word Lenore Evans hated more than ghoul was the Z-word.

"Like an earlier version of the vampire, got it," Kim said, and Lenore twitched while the impending lecture on Old World monsters died on her tongue. "So," Kim said, "Samael was a master then, could pass for human."

Belle snuffled, dreaming in her sleep, and Ducey couldn't help but feel a little bit proud of the pair of strays she'd found in the alleyway behind Jimbo's.

Bus brakes gassed outside and Ducey's cloudy eye followed her good one to the clock on the breakroom's back wall. She itched where the pants cut into her middle.

Kids were home, and daylight burned. Soon five o'clock would stretch its shadows over the parking lot, and once the dark got a foothold, it didn't stop until the world went black.

"Speak of the devil," Ducey said when Luna and Crane entered the breakroom, all backpacks and leather coats and scowls.

The two kids draped in black sized each other up.

"You must be Kim Cole," the boy said, sweeping the arm of his long coat into a bow. "I'm known as Crane Campbell."

"*Crane* Campbell," Kim drawled. "Or *Count* Campbell?"

The boy snapped up to full height, and his smile lifted with him. Luna clutched her backpack in her arms, then shared a look with Kim and dropped it beside the door. One corner of Kim's lips twitched up, but she rolled her eyes when she looked back at the boy.

Good thing I clawed my way back from the dead to play babysitter, Ducey thought. That little pocket of dirt out in her daughter's garden sounded better and better.

"All right," she said. "Tell us how to resurrect ourselves a ghoul, Count Campbell."

The boy pecked Ducey on top of the head in her recliner, then pulled out a chair for Luna before settling into the table's only available seat.

"Technically, we want to *revive* him," Crane said. "True resurrection of one of the undead may return them to a natural state, but in doing so, may kill them completely." He tapped his rings on the metal table. "Samael may have died a young man in his prime, but resurrection may return him at his true age, in which case, his natural life would have already expired."

He paused for a round of approving blinks and went on. "What we want," he said, "is to *revive* Samael—reawaken him, so to speak."

"Crane, honey, I appreciate the detail, I do." Lenore turned at the sink, back into her polecat stance. "But let's stick with the short version for now."

Crane rolled his hand, continuing. "To revive Samael," he said, "we need to give him the gift of life—" He looked at Luna. "Undead smelling salts, so to speak."

All three of the Evans women exchanged looks, but Kim's palm slapped a snort out of Belle when it hit the tabletop. "Holy shit." She stared at Crane and pointed at Luna. "She's *Blade*."

Before, it'd looked like the Cole girl really chapped Crane's hide. This time the two gave each other the sort of look Ducey often shared with her daughter—a sharing-secrets sort of look.

"I know y'all ain't talkin' about a knife," she said. "What's a blade?"

Crane turned to Luna. "Not a what. A *who*."

Kim shook her head, smiling, like whatever a blade was, it solved everything.

Hell, maybe it did. Evans women were blades women, after all.

"A child born of a vampire and a mortal is called a *dhampir*," Kim said. "A daywalker retains some of their undead abilities—" She pulled the word out, hung on until Luna made eye contact. "But otherwise lives a more or less mortal life."

Kim shrugged when she caught Ducey's glare. "They made a movie," she said.

Luna shrank into her chair, so small she almost got swallowed by her mother's old long-sleeve work shirt. "I'm a monster."

"No way, girl." Kim's voice snapped the littlest Evans's eyes back to attention. "What you are is a badass."

"A badass who's going to use her own power to awaken her undead father," Crane added.

Lenore bristled. "How?"

"Yeah," Luna echoed, then she and Kim both asked, "How?"

Ducey sat up straight in her recliner. This oughtta be good.

"A drop of your blood." Behind his dark curtain of hair, Crane's cheeks had the decency to turn pink. "A drop of your blood . . . on his lips."

Kim huffed back in her chair. "Did you get that spell straight out of *Dungeons & Dragons?*" she said.

"What about dragons?" Ducey was just starting to catch on before she got thrown off the wagon.

"Legends say the veil between this world and the next," Crane said, talking right through Kim, through Ducey, "is thinnest when the sun slides below the horizon."

'Course they do. Like she always said, best time for gardening was sunset.

Ducey caught the glow under the window blinds when the repaired grandfather clock in the chapel struck out the hour.

"Well, that settles it, then," she said, clapping her hands against the tops of her thighs. "We'll get to diggin', and when the sun sets, Luna can prick her thumb and wake up Sleepin' Beauty." She shot a look at her daughter. "And if anythin' goes south, I'll handle it."

Lenore better know what that meant—meant she'd better stay the hell out of the way, not try to be a hero like her damn husband. The face she made, though, that look said she didn't like it one bit.

"Just because I'm sittin' here talkin' to you don't mean I'm not already dead, Len," Ducey added, just in case her little girl got any big ideas, if the occasion called for it. It'd do permanent damage to Lenore if she had to see her mother die twice, but that still beat the alternative.

"I am ready to begin." Crane flourished the long tails of his leather coat as his hands plunged into the pockets. He liberated bits and bobs from those deep folds—a half-melted candle, a nappy feather, a matchbook from a dive bar he wasn't old enough to enter.

A diner saltshaker with the logo etched into its side.

The boy's kleptomania she didn't so much mind, but Ducey rolled her eyes when the sage wand came out. Goofy kid already tried that once. Guess he hadn't learned his lesson.

"Go on and stuff all that junk right back into your pockets," she told him, waving one of her bunny-eared slippers at the flea market on her breakroom table. "We don't need none of it."

Crane eyed her from behind his dark curtain of hair. "These are the items required for the ritual," he said, like Ducey was the one who didn't know her head from a hole in the wall. "We need them to revive Samael."

He glanced at Kim for agreement, and the girl warded him off with her palms.

Ducey sucked her teeth. "Only thing we need to raise that ghoul is Luna—" She pointed at her great-granddaughter, then at sticky fingers and little miss spray paint. "And for you two to skedaddle."

Kim's lip twitched while the boy's curtains swung. "But it's my spell," Crane said.

"And it's the Evans family responsibility," Ducey snapped back. "Evans business."

Everyone stared at everyone else, but only Ducey didn't blink. Rest of them could stare all they want, but she had work to do. Ducey kicked one bunny-eared slipper loose and tugged a rubber boot over her bare foot. Socks were for the living.

"But Crane is the one who found the spell," Luna said, shrugging in her goofy boyfriend's direction when Ducey looked up. "Shouldn't he—"

"He should get out while the gettin's good." Ducey kicked off her other bunny, wriggled her foot into rubber, and stomped both boots on the tile. Barefoot would be better, but she'd take rubber-boot blisters any day over those darn child's slippers Lenore made her wear. "I know I'm dead, but I didn't stutter," she snapped when the kids still didn't budge.

The boy puffed up his shoulders. "I am a ceremonial magician," he said, like she had a damn clue what that was.

Ducey grunted. First the new sheriff in her craw, and now this boy thought his eyeliner and internet spells qualified him to fool around with the undead. All the things she had to worry about, and keeping these kids out of harm's way wasn't something she wanted to add to the list. "What you are," Ducey said, "is in my way. Now don't make me tell you again."

The boy pushed his hair behind his ears, but Luna tugged on his shoulder. He bent his head, and Luna whispered in his ear. Crane flicked his wrist toward his magical nonsense, but Luna tugged him closer, whispering until he nodded.

Kim raised a shy hand.

"I'm supposed to do Luna's makeup for the dance," she said when Ducey caught the girl in her good eye.

Lenore clicked her teeth like that settled it.

"Kim can return to help Luna get ready for the dance when the breakroom lights turn on," Lenore said to Kim, then turned that icy glare on Crane while Ducey rubbed at the burn in her chest. "And you can meet Luna at the dance," she told him.

Luna finished her whispering and Crane jerked his head in one quick nod. "I shall leave you with my tools, should they be of use," he said, pocketing the matchbook, and then Kim told him to get in her car and Luna gave him a little nod of encouragement before he headed out the back door with the Cole girl.

Ducey twitched in her trousers, pulled a straw gardening hat on top of her head to help hide her face, and dropped her wedding band in the soap dish on the sink.

"All right, girls," Ducey said. "Let's get to work."

CHAPTER 28

Sheriff Roger Taylor

The slam of the back doors on the coroner's van punched Roger square in the chest. The call came in over lunch, but it had taken all afternoon to locate the professor's body—what they found of it, anyway. Like the high school principal, they'd found the woman's abandoned Honda Civic and pieces of her field kit, her busted tape recorder—but a good number of the wolf expert's remains were still unaccounted for.

The woman's head, in particular.

Just like that damn wolf out on 121, Roger thought, twisting his hat until his knuckles and forearm sparked and caught fire. So much for the pack of slaughtered wolves being a convenient end to things. 'Course it wasn't, Roger had known that just as well as he knew the day was long, but Ducey and Lenore planned to dig up another monster at sunset, and he'd been fool enough to hope that would finish whatever this was before things got any worse.

Wrong again. So far, Roger had kept a lid on the scene at Gladys City Motel, but all hell would break loose the minute the wind picked up the story, blew it all the way to Houston—which wouldn't be long now, by the way his deputy glared at him across the two-lane road, the glimpse he'd caught of Brett Haney's Ford rumbling past the detour sign.

Roger knocked on the van's back doors, waiting as it pulled away, turned out of sight, headed for the morgue. He forearmed sweat off his brow and set his hat back on his head, squinting into the strip of light that glared through the trees along the road's edge and turned the pines to silhouettes.

Not long now at all.

Still, would have been nice to kill the rabid-wolf cover story before Roger had to face the creature that fathered Grace Evans's daughter.

He ran his fingertips over the loaded Colt 1911 on his hip.

Roger resisted the urge to pull his hat back off, but lost the battle not to finger the bandage under his sleeve. The thing still gave off phantom pains, though most of the torn flesh had knit itself back together. Roger figured he'd carry that night's scar on his arm forever, right along with the hole that the wound left in his heart. Way he saw it, the man buried under Lenore's white rosebush may be the girl's father, but Roger had come to care for Luna as his own. He'd failed to protect Grace, but Roger would do whatever it took to keep her daughter out of harm's way.

He wouldn't make the same mistake twice.

But right now, he had a rookie glaring at him over the top of his notepad from across the motel parking lot.

Roger sucked in so much air, his belt slipped under the swell in his lungs. *One problem at a time.*

He hitched his pants back into place and ducked under the police tape strung around the trees, careful to keep his boots clean as he climbed out of the muck. Enough chalk lines decorated the two-lane road, Girl Scouts could hopscotch halfway to the other side of town before they ran out of squares. Tomorrow morning when the sun came back up, they could hunt the little yellow tents like Easter eggs tucked along the roadside grass.

Roger shook his head. No wonder Jed Quigg licked on bad jokes like lollipops. Kept a man from crawling out of his own skin.

Back in the gravel parking lot, Hinson's pen raced over his notepad while the proprietor's mustache did most of the talking.

"Noticed her rental-car trunk open first thing this morning," the bristle brush over the man's upper lip said. "Figured she was loading up, but when checkout time came and went and she never dropped off her keys, I sent housekeeping over." The mustache twisted toward the open door marked 18, the gaggle of cleaning women giving the untouched room a wide berth.

Hinson tapped his pen on the page. "And what did you find there, Mr. Rhodes?" Grass stains marked the young deputy's pantlegs and brown splattered over his boots, but he scribbled on his notepad like a man out for blood.

Rhodes's mustache shrugged. "Door was propped open, but no one home," it said. "*That's* when I called down to the station."

Roger thanked the man's mustache for its time, and Hinson flipped the notepad shut with a promise to follow up as soon as they had information to share. Once Rhodes disappeared back into the motel's office to worry over quitting time, the deputy rounded on Roger.

Worse, with the coroner's van gone, Brett Haney's truck made it past the detour. Gravel flung from the rusty Ford's wheel wells when it rumbled into the motel's lot, then braked to a stop.

Haney leaned out his driver's side window like a resurrected Sheriff Buck Johnson, red and seething in his mechanic's coveralls. He slapped his hand against the side of his truck hard enough to dent the metal.

"Still think it's a rabid hybrid, Sheriff?" the man yelled, so loud that motel-room window blinds fluttered, doors cracking open against their chains. None of those occupants' eyes had seen whatever killed Professor Bennick last night, but they'd enjoyed front-row seats while Quigg's guys loaded her body into the coroner's van. Now they watched Haney fist another dimple into his driver's side door.

"How many more people you gonna let die before you boys do something about it?" he yelled.

Roger felt Hinson tense at his side, like the man had pulled the question straight out of the rookie's throat.

Roger put his good hand up, tried for peace. For order. "We're doing everything we—"

"Whatever monster killed those wolves," Haney said, "is the same one that killed my daughter, killed all the rest of those folks." He spit out words as his old rust bucket crawled closer in the motel's gravel lot, engine revving.

Matted fur still clung to the truck's guard grille. Flecks of brown on the headlight plastic, like dried blood on eyeglass lenses.

They'd searched everywhere from Corinne's car to the tree line, but whatever took the woman's head made off with her horn-rims, too.

Haney kept on yelling, pushing the truck closer and closer, until Roger felt the hot breath of the grille through his uniform pantlegs. Any other time, Roger would force the man out of his vehicle, cuff him for drunk and disorderly. But better he kept his mouth shut, didn't let any of the motel-room looky-loos hear anything they could carry to the papers. Couple more barks and Haney would wear himself out, take his grief and fury someplace else.

Home, hopefully.

Haney said, "Me and Chuck saw her last night at the bar." Roger figured he must mean Corinne, but the man's nod looked like it hit Hinson. "I told Chuck I'd find whatever this thing is, and I'm gonna kill it—and after I do, I'll make sure everybody from here to California knows the kind of hellscape you're covering up," he said. "I'll make sure you pay for what happened to my little girl."

Roger gritted his teeth as the sky seeped orange. Grief he knew his way around, but vengeance made for a scarier monster than even the Evans women could put down. The dead ate to satisfy a hunger they could never fill. The living did it just for the fun of watching someone bleed.

The truck's headlights blinded Roger when Haney peeled back out the way he came.

Roger shook the lights out of his vision. "Who in the hell is Chuck?" he muttered out the side of his mouth.

Beside him, Hinson deflated. "Me."

When in the hell had the boy started going by *Chuck*? Roger turned his gaze on the rookie.

"They used to call me that in high school," the deputy explained, grumbling. "Old football nickname."

Roger hooked an eyebrow. For all his glaring over his notepad, the boy hadn't bothered to share that he'd been out drinking with the dead professor and the grieving dad the night before. Probably because he didn't want his boss to know.

Roger sized the rookie up. "Might want to tell your pal Haney your nickname is Upchuck now, since you can't stop dumping your guts all over my crime scenes."

The words tasted as sour on his lips as the reek of Hinson's vomit cooling on the gravel, but better the deputy be angry at Roger than angry with Brett Haney. The first might get him written up. The other one could get him killed.

Hinson clenched his notepad the way Roger liked to grip his hat. "She saw something," he said. "Corinne, I mean." Hinson jerked his thumb at all the yellow tents in the grass, the leftovers of the woman's research stuffed into evidence bags on the Crown Vic's hood. On top of the pile, her busted recorder. "Whatever she saw scared the hell out of her, but she documented it. Why else would she have her kit out, the tranquilizer gun loaded?"

Roger would like to know the answer to those questions, too.

"It's not a wolf, Taylor," the deputy said, "even a rabid one. Animals hunt, but they're not smart enough to lure someone into a trap," Hinson kept on. "There's something else out there, isn't there—something that behaves like an animal, but thinks like a man."

Over the rookie's shoulder, the sun's glow reached the horizon. The boy turned his eyes to the sky while the Timex on Roger's wrist ticked in his bones.

A question stuck on Hinson's tongue, but he bit it free. "You believe in werewolves, Sheriff?"

The sweat beading along Roger's hairline turned to ice. Crazy as it sounded, the rookie was working himself too close to the truth. Roger needed to get the boy out of here, away from the scene of the crime.

"This sounds like a conversation that'll taste better over coffee." Roger kept his voice gruff as he worked to coax the boy like a dirty cat to the bathtub. "Come on, son. Let's go someplace where we can talk."

Hope lit up the boy's eyes, and Roger hated to see it.

Then the radio pinned to his shoulder crackled to life.

"Come in, Sheriff." The voice on his shoulder didn't belong to Darla. Sounded more like the boys over in Forensics.

Roger pushed the mic. "Go for Taylor."

"We got a match."

Forensics, all right, but that look lighting up the rookie's eyes now, that wasn't hope.

"What do you mean *a match*?" Roger said into his radio. "A match to *what*?"

"To the blood on the fabric Deputy Hinson brought in?" The voice on the radio came out unsure. "We ran it with the hair sample found at the first attack," said Forensics. "And we got a direct match."

To the sample Deputy Hinson brought in. Roger's pulse banged in his forearm. Putting together that the rookie had snooped around and found the blood-soaked hat in Roger's desk drawer took all of five seconds—which was exactly how long it took Forensics to drop their verdict.

"Both samples are a match for Grace Evans."

CHAPTER 29

Crane Campbell

nstead of allowing Kim to drive him home, Crane asked her to drop him off at the mall. She rolled her eyes, muttered something about not being his personal taxi service, but she turned left instead of right at the intersection and headed for Parkdale Mall. At least he and Kim could agree on music. Industrial rock blasted through the speakers, eliminating the need for dialogue. Crane tapped the half-full pack in his chest pocket, the matchbook, but when Kim kept her windows up, he left the cigarettes. Somehow everything that had happened had quenched his taste for nicotine.

That, and he couldn't stop thinking about that night at Riverfront Park, when Grace Evans gave him her Virginia Slims. He'd handed the crumpled pack over to Roger Taylor last month, never got them back. The cigs didn't matter, but the memory did. It was the only one Crane had with Luna's mother.

Kind of killed the nicotine craving, that.

"Two goths in a small town," was all he said when Kim's mint-green Buick came to a complete stop outside the Books-A-Million mall entrance. He pushed himself halfway through the passenger-side door, then leaned back in. "On paper, we should be friends."

One of Kim's cheeks dimpled when she smirked behind the steering wheel. For half a second, Crane could spot the Cole family resemblance.

"I'm more of a cinephile than a bookworm," she said—maybe referring to the bookstore, maybe to him. It'd been a good year for movies, with something new from Fincher coming any day.

A flush of cool air snaked its way up Crane's back, rushing between layers of leather and cotton as he pushed himself out of the car. He made sure Kim saw him shrug.

"Fair enough," he said.

She rolled her eyes in his direction. Sighed like a cat deflating. "I just don't hang out with a lot of my little brother's friends—no offense."

Crane put his palms up. If he could win over Nana Lenore, then surely he could peel back a layer of Kim Cole. He could try, anyway.

He tapped his rings on the hood, arching backward to drop low enough to speak into the car. "Just because our loyalties belong to different Evanses doesn't mean we don't share the same secret," he said. "Sharing such darkness for the sake of those we love makes for close bedfellows."

There, a slight loosening in Kim's shoulders, her jaw. Just a couple of words for a little bit of magic. An easy spell.

After Kim drove away, Crane hung around the bookstore long enough to decide which paperback from the occult section to slip into his trench-coat pocket, then he left the mall. He peeled a match free, lit a cigarette in his palm, and crossed the street without waiting for the pedestrian signal, watching his boots through his bangs as he made his way to the two-bedroom garage apartment Luna and her mother shared.

Used to share.

The setting sun lit the sky on fire, and Crane visored his palm across his forehead, stubbed the butt out with the toe of his boot. Rows of washing machines tumbled loads of laundry on the first floor, the windows above the laundromat staring out like two empty sockets over crooked, rectangular teeth.

He'd rather be at the funeral parlor, reviving a master strigoi, instead of breaking and entering a dead lady's apartment. But Luna had asked him, and her wish was Crane's command.

It's not breaking and entering if you have a key, he thought, and took the stairs two at a time. Disdain was easy. Real friends were harder to come by—and besides, he knew better than to argue with Ducey.

When they reconvened at the dance, Luna would fill him in on everything, and he'd give her whatever he found in her old apartment.

Assuming he found anything. Neither Crane nor Luna even knew what to look for, but looking, for anything, was why she'd sent him.

On the landing, Crane put his ear to the apartment door. Silence inside, other than the rumbling of washers and dryers downstairs, the racket of someone tossing out their trash behind the fence.

Not that Luna talked a lot about her and her mom's apartment, but she'd never mentioned the smell.

Spiderwebs collected along the front-door hinges, but didn't reach the number—a good thing, because those eight-legged freaks gave Crane the creeps. If only he had time for another smoke, but alas, already the sun had begun to disappear into a glow on the horizon and his matchbook was running thin.

He'd light one up for Grace later.

Crane fit the key into the lock and turned the knob, then cast a look over his shoulder to make sure he hadn't been seen, and slipped sideways into the dark apartment. Shut the door against the dumpster smell outside, only to suck in another lungful of putrid funk. Crane's eyes lit up like the sunset outside. The small square apartment over the laundromat had enough room for a mother and daughter, but not for that damn smell.

He kept one arm over his nose while he waited for his eyes to adjust to the dim. Maybe in her hurry to get Luna moved into her house, Lenore had left a jug of milk to rot in the fridge. Or on the counter—hell.

The living room came into view as his eyes adjusted—a couch, love seat, coffee table, a window air-conditioning unit, all washed gray by the oncoming twilight. Pillows and throw blankets lay draped across the space, and last month's issue of *Southern Living* still stood tented on the end table. But energy thrummed in a current in the space—as though at any second now Crane would blink and the room would fill with color, burst into life.

But when he blinked, it all came back gray. And he could taste it.

Crane's fingers twitched toward the Camels in his pocket.

A closed door beckoned at the other end of the room, but Crane slunk through the open archway into the kitchen. Aside from the breakfast-table chairs turned all helter-skelter, the slow drip from the tap, everything appeared in order. Empty fridge, empty trash can.

But whatever Crane came to find, whatever truths might be hidden in the apartment to help Moon Girl, they weren't in the kitchen.

The door that fed off the kitchen led to a small bedroom, where Tori Amos sang silently at her piano above a bed littered with stuffed animals.

If he were a different sort of guy, he'd snoop. Every poster tacked to the wall, every dresser drawer, every nook. He'd rifle through the closet, sniff all the clothes. Finger the spines on the bookshelf in the corner. Maybe caterpillar himself in the patchwork quilt balled at the foot of the unmade bed. Swaddle himself in the familiar energy of this space.

But Crane wasn't that type of guy.

He jumped when the window unit in the main bedroom clicked on, and the sudden movement rushed stink back into his nose.

If you smell an odor long enough, you stop noticing it, Crane reminded himself. *Eventually.*

Gray tinged the living room, kitchen, and Luna's bedroom, but the door to the Jack-and-Jill bathroom sucked Crane into black. Shapes lurked to the side—the sink, tub, toilet. In two long strides, the other door that would funnel him into Grace's bedroom.

He fumbled for a light switch but found the doorknob instead.

The apartment's energy staticked under Crane's palm when he twisted.

Heavy curtains blocked out any light that remained outside, leaving the larger bedroom as dark as the tiny bathroom. A darkness he could feel.

The Nothing. He'd been meaning to show Luna *The NeverEnding Story,* to talk to her about the power that took everything when it rolled through, absorbed it into nothing, and now he'd found that energy, in her very apartment.

More vague furniture shapes greeted Crane on the other side of the bedroom door. More stink slapped him across the face. *Something* lurked in this space, but the weight of The Nothing heaved in Crane's bones.

Vomit traveled from his toes up his throat, and Crane toppled against the open doorframe. He fanned rank, musty air away, but the stench stuck to him, crawled inside him, ate through the leather sleeve pressed against his nostrils like toxic gas. If Crane had anything inside him like a soul, it also smelled like Grace's bedroom now.

But he was already here, wasn't he? Might as well take a look around if he was going to stink for the rest of his life anyway.

Wear it like a badge of honor, he instructed himself, and swallowed.

Something cracked under Crane's boot when he stepped into the pitch-black bedroom. Another crack under the next step. The third step squelched.

Crane's boot peeled up from the carpet.

More horrible stench came with it, the distinct sound of slurping, and the fizz at the back of Crane's throat came back. He leaned on one hand against the wall, using the other to lift his leg, pulling his shoe up to see. He waited for his eyes to adjust to the dark, then Crane reminded himself he was a second-degree ceremonial magician, and looked at the squelchy, sticky mass that clung to his sole.

Fizz thickened into acid and spilled over his tongue. Filled his mouth. Crane counted to three, waited out the sting against the back of his teeth, and swallowed.

Whatever stuck to the bottom of his shoe used to have fur, probably. Probably used to have a face, too.

Still had a collar.

Crane wiped his boot on the corner of the dresser at his left without even deciding to do it—and when he looked up, he finally got a look at the rest of the room.

Found the smell, he thought.

Body parts lay strewn about Grace's bedroom like the world's grossest piñata, busted wide and still dripping. Meat clung to some of the bones, but most had been cleaned—licked clean—stacked like cairns honoring their dead.

Teeth had bitten into every fragment, every bone, like the room itself was hungry.

An arm hung over the edge of the bed, fingers stripped to the bone. A woman's head leaned on its cheek against the vanity mirror. Scalp and bone peered through where the red hair had been torn away from the wolf expert's skull, but her eyes reflected back at Crane in the glass, as black as the windowless bathroom behind him.

A deep hurt hollowed out Crane's chest.

Luna had been right. Crane had found the answer in her apartment after all. Luna wasn't the monster, not this time.

Behind the closed door to the living room, the air conditioner sparked on, suckling the air from under Crane's skin. His heart knocked in his chest.

Something else *knocked, knocked, knocked,* as it made its way across the living room, to the other side of the closed bedroom door. It knocked on the thin sheet of wood that separated Crane from The Nothing on the other side of the door—and then the knob twisted.

Crane wished he could see the moon one more time, even if just the giant disco ball in the high school cafeteria, surrounded by latex balloons and glittering strands of cardstock stars.

Save me a dance, Moon Girl, he thought, and then the door pushed open, letting in a streak of sulfur-scented fading daylight, and Crane closed his eyes.

CHAPTER 30

Luna Evans

With every push of the shovel into earth, Luna's heart beat faster. She didn't look at the barren mound of dirt over her mother's grave, the mangled mess of Ducey's abandoned burial bed, the cloddy tangle of the upturned white rosebush. She just dug and dug and dug, scooping dirt upon dirt in the funeral parlor's garden, around Ducey's and Lenore's feet, until brown stained up to her own knees and her chest burned and Luna worried wings might sprout out of her chest, carry her away.

At least it was only dusk, and not twilight. There were legends about things that flew in the dark.

Bats and owls and ravens. Death omens, all.

But omens flew at midnight, and not at sunset.

The tip of Luna's shovel clanged against the stake still impaled in her father's heart. The taste of metal rattled all the way to her teeth, and she stepped back to where his feet must be and scraped dirt away from around the stake. When the shape of a man came into view beneath a layer of crusted earth, she reached out of the grave and set her shovel aside.

Luna watched the layer of earth rise and fall with the breath of the dead man beneath. Dirt fell away from the peak of his nose to reveal the sheet that covered his face. Had she been the one to pull the burial shroud back over her father's face the month before, when they'd first dug up the grave under the white rosebush? Or had it been Grace, her mother, saying goodbye once more to the man she'd loved?

Did it matter now?

Gardening gloves, the fingers stained brown, pressed against Luna's shoulders, anchoring her to the ground as Nana Lenore's voice reached into the grave, more pinched than usual. The white rosebush hadn't come willingly from the garden soil, and its roots lay in a tangled heap. Probably it wouldn't survive the night.

Luna stood locked in place as her grandmother went on talking. If she didn't show up to the Homecoming Dance tonight, she hoped Crane would carry her spirit with him always.

"Everything okay, Luna, honey?" her grandmother asked.

Just like the question of who'd covered her father before they replanted him in his grave, or what might happen when the dead man opened his eyes, Luna had no idea how to answer Nana Lenore.

"Fine," she said, then pushed out a deep breath, wondered if monsters could love, and inhaled honey and woodsmoke as she pulled back the cloth.

Samael lay asleep in his grave, just as handsome as he'd been before.

Specks of soil crusted the space between his brow. Luna lifted her hand, summer-dried dirt like sandpaper against her skin as she traced her father's features in her own face—the bridge of his long, narrow nose, the cliffs of his cheekbones, the angle of his jaw. Their uneven earlobes. Sunset filtered orange into the hole, but the silver halo on Samael's almost-black hair matched the glow Luna saw in the tips of her own hair in the lazy evening breeze.

Her fingers paused on her cheek as she tested the word on her tongue.

"Dad?"

Luna's fingertip filled a dimple when she smiled, a warm divot in the same place where she thought her father's cheek might crease if he were to smile back.

Just like in the chapel when she'd let Tanya West get too close, energy thrummed beneath Luna's skin. If he were to reach for her, Samael might lunge for her throat, but maybe he'd embrace her.

G. E. + S. A. etched inside the bottom dresser drawer.

Movement stirred overhead, but not like bird wings. Long, rust-colored ears flapped over the edge of the hole and Ducey's face appeared. The wide brim of her straw hat cast shadows that obscured her expression, while the hound dog's snout pulled overtime near her ankles, nose scrunching the grave's scents into memory.

Ducey patted Belle, looked from Luna to the dead man, and turned up her nose. "Knew I smelled something," she said.

"Mama, please." Nana Lenore's voice, from somewhere above.

Whatever her great-grandmother grumbled in response under her breath, Luna didn't catch it.

All she heard was the sound of her father's shallow breathing. Samael's chest rose and fell under the dirty sheet in slow waves punctuated by those wings still flapping in Luna's chest. From her position, Luna couldn't see the sun touch the horizon, but the music of sunset moved under her skin.

Ducey mumbled again, and the storm in the old woman's voice broke over Luna's head.

"You're gonna need to yank that spike out first," Ducey was saying.

Luna eyed the barb protruding from Samael's chest, the one the elder Evans women had put there for good measure fifteen years back, to make sure he stayed pinned in the ground.

She wrapped her hands around the metal, braced her stance, and tugged like Arthur pulling the sword from the stone. And just as easily as Excalibur, the metal slid free of the dead man's chest.

"Hang on to the spike," Nana Lenore said. "You never know."

Over her head, Ducey grumbled again, and Luna let the spike fall as she raised her empty hand toward her grandmothers, pointed to them. A quick stab of pain, sharp and sudden, and Ducey pulled the business end of her trocar away.

Luna watched blood bead on the tip of her finger. A red streak dripped from her hand. Luna felt earth move beneath her when the blood hit the dirty shroud. Wind rushed through the grass and branches overhead, ruffled the butter-yellow rhododendron bushes planted along the edge of the funeral parlor, billowed the loose cloth over her father. She saw his nostrils pull in air, watched the corresponding rise of his chest, and when another red bead swelled on her finger, Luna looked up at the sunburned sky, crouched as low as she dared, and ran her bloodied finger across her father's lips.

Color rose in Samael's cheeks, and then he opened his eyes.

Midnight eyes. Just like hers.

Nana Lenore and Ducey spoke over her, but their words became tinnitus, buzzing against her ears while Samael's hand stroked the length of Luna's cheek.

"Grace," he said.

Luna could taste her father's voice in her soul. "It's me," she said, and shook her head. "Luna."

Samael's eyes flashed full with recognition, then with fear, and then with a light that beamed across the Evans Funeral Parlor parking lot.

Headlights, followed by the crunch of tires, the sound of brakes.

In a blink, the handsome angles of Samael's face sharpened into edges, his teeth bared, his jaw stretched. Luna watched her father become a monster—but before she could translate her grandmothers' yells, clench her fist around the spike in her hand, Samael flew out of his grave. A quick flash of white shroud and midnight eyes, and Luna's breath stopped as she moved with him, the ground rushing beneath her feet, heart in her chest.

When her feet hit grass, Samael's arms held her back behind him. Luna could hear her father's monstrous snarls as he stood between her and the sheriff's department cruiser.

Luna remembered the story her mother had told of the Godawful Mess, so shortly after Luna's birth—how the now-dead sheriff had driven up that night, intent on confronting the Evans women, and had set off a chain of events that ended with the grandfather Luna had never met in his grave and the father she'd just met in his.

The silver scar on her mother's wrist.

The last thing Samael would remember would be trying to save his family. Now, she'd woken him up just so he could be thrust back into that same moment—and after fifteen years buried under the white rosebush, Luna doubted her monstrous father would let himself die again.

Don't! she wanted to yell, but her throat clenched into silence and she had lost the spike. Inside the headlight's glare, she saw men's legs racing toward the grave. She heard her grandmothers' voices muffled and indistinct, miles away. Belle's furious bays.

"Stay behind me," Samael growled—or didn't growl. Luna couldn't be sure whether he'd spoken the words aloud or not, but they imprinted on her mind just the same.

Nana Lenore's dagger flashed in the moonlight.

Roger appeared out of the light, and Ducey's voice cut him back, every bit as sharp as Samael's teeth. In silhouette, Ducey wrenched the straw gardening hat from her head and threw it at the sheriff.

"Twist on this for a change!" she snapped at Roger. "Stay the hell out of the way!"

The high beams blinded Luna—in her father's grip, she blinked as a pair of legs blocked the light again. Roger's? No, these tottered, stilted and uneven—Ducey in her britches, trocar shining like lightning in her fist at her side.

"Get away from my girl," she told Samael.

"You forget, she's *my* daughter." Woodsmoke burned off Samael's skin, but he stopped snarling. His arms fell and his shoulders softened, all those sharp angles rounding back into handsome curves when Luna turned to study his profile. His lips twitched. Luna watched her father slag, then go stiff, as Ducey eclipsed the headlights, the hound at her side.

Samael took in Ducey's undead state—her mismatched eyes, the painted scar on her neck, her dagger-scorched chest, the trocar still tipped in red—and that sound Samael made now? Not a snarl. More like a gasp.

"Ethel?" he said, the growl in his voice replaced by a low, Southern drawl. "That you, darlin'?"

Ducey flinched at the use of her Christian name, sneering at the dead man's familiar greeting, but the trocar straightened her arm into a line to jab out ahead of her. "Don't you *darlin'* me, ghoul," she snapped back. "And nobody calls me that anymore."

Samael's dimple popped, just like Luna knew it would, when he grinned at Ducey.

"You sound just like your mother," he said.

CHAPTER 31

Lenore Evans

You don't know nothin' about my mother." Ducey bit off words faster than she could chew them as Belle howled a blue streak, but even in the blinding glow of the Crown Vic's headlights, Lenore couldn't take her eyes off the monster that had once enthralled her daughter.

The radio pinned to Roger's shoulder, over there on the other side of the garden, buzzed so loud that the collar of Lenore's blouse flicked from the static. Luna's eyes itched into her like ants, and Lenore tightened her grip on the dagger at her side.

The Godawful Mess, again and again and again.

"I knew your mother as well as my own kin," Samael told Ducey, real slow. "Ever since she was a young'un."

Lenore's hand on the blade slipped. The empty pocket where the grandfather clock key should be felt cold, while the cruiser's headlights took the sun's place as darkness crawled up the sky.

So many secrets that Pie had never shared. The Evans family matriarch had kept more than just the dead buried.

Roger's boots crept up beside her. When Belle had stopped barking, she couldn't say, but if that radio on the sheriff's shoulder scratched through the air one more time, Lenore would take the dagger to it herself.

She adjusted her grip on the dagger's hilt and focused on the dead man and Luna. Restless or upright or whatever, the dead could not be trusted. Samael may have seasoned it with a few extra words, but the restless dead only knocked and called, and no matter how human he looked, the master strigoi had called Ducey's name just the same.

"I knew Pie Evans from the time she was a little girl to the day she died," the dead man was saying. "You might say Priscilla and I learned about the restless dead together. After the Spindletop fire, it was better that I not stick around town, but Pie liked to have me check in now and then," he said, "keeping an eye on her, and you, and Lenore—"

When Samael's eyes found hers, Lenore wanted them to be bleak—big empty holes, full of nothing. But they were warm and full.

Just like her granddaughter's at his side.

"And Grace," Lenore finished for him.

The dead man dipped his head. "Most of all."

The pinch in the back of Lenore's skull cut straight down to her heart, so deep and sharp that her words sliced her throat as they formed, nicking the backs of her teeth. "You—" Her tongue burned. "You fed on my daughter."

"No, ma'am." Samael's eyes didn't let go of hers. "I fell in love with her."

Love, not *loved*. Because the last thing he'd seen before they'd put him in the ground that night, the night he'd killed Jimmy, had been Grace.

Samael stepped backward to wrap his arms around Luna, and the girl let herself be pulled inside his embrace. Lenore's heart burned when he kissed the top of Luna's head. "My moon," he whispered into her hair, and scanned the space around them until his eyebrows tangled and shadows hollowed the spaces under his eyes. "Where is my star?" he asked.

Ducey just clucked, as Lenore's throat squeezed and Luna's eyes sparkled in the night.

"Damn it, Hinson," Roger said to the voice that kept crackling across the line. *"Not now."*

He silenced the radio on his shoulder, then the one on his dash when he leaned in to cut the cruiser's ignition. Darkness covered the funeral parlor's gardens in the sudden dusk.

Luna took her father's hand. She led him to the mount of dirt that wouldn't bloom. "Last month," she said.

"We had an uprisin'," Ducey said. "Grace put herself between the ghouls and her daughter."

"She and Mama both did," Lenore added.

"I didn't stay in the ground," Ducey said. "Don't know why."

Samael didn't speak, just rubbed his palms along the ground. Dirt crumbled through his fingers, and the dead man lifted his hand to his lips.

Roger stepped beside Lenore, weapon drawn, but without the hammer cocked. They'd all lost Grace that night, hadn't they? For the past four weeks, Roger had planted roses on the grave Samael now squatted over, and no matter how much he tried, nothing bloomed.

Nothing bloomed, and the dirt didn't settle, not on Grace Evans's burial mount.

The dead man scented the earth. Tasted it. Samael brushed his hand on his pant leg and pushed himself to his feet, hand slipping back into Luna's.

"Well, Ducey, you didn't stay in your grave because you're an Evans woman," he said, and looked at the bare stems poking out of the ground. "And neither did Grace."

Lenore's fist clenched empty air. Her dagger gleamed on the ground as the sky turned black, though she would have sworn it had still been in her hand. "Lies," she said aloud. "My daughter is dead."

Samael nodded. "Yes, ma'am," he said. "But she isn't in her grave."

"Now, wait just a minute." Ducey's voice snapped across the dark, and Lenore felt her bones break. "You mean to tell me that my granddaughter crawled out of her grave, and we've been none the wiser?"

"I'm afraid so," Samael said, and all the light left in the sky had found its way into Luna's eyes. "Evans women don't die easy. It's not in your blood."

The thing that they'd tricked the town into believing was a rabid ghost wolf, the thing tearing through the town's animals, through the principal, the delivery boy, the wolf expert—it hadn't been Buck John-son, still a pile of bones in his grave.

"It's not Grace," Lenore tried to say, wanted to say, finally did say, but Roger tapped the radio on his chest, and the emptiness in Lenore swallowed her whole—broken bones and all.

"About that," Roger said, and the look on his face told her the rest.

CHAPTER 32

Ducey Evans

Samael studied Lenore as she brewed coffee, then poured too many cups. She skipped Ducey and set a mug in front of the dead man, who offered a smile in return.

Lenore's lips didn't so much as twitch.

"The place looks real nice," Samael told Ducey as she took a seat at the breakroom table between Roger and Luna. "Pie would be proud."

Ducey fidgeted in her recliner, Belle at her feet. "Before we get carried away," she said, "how exactly do you know Grace isn't in her grave?"

"I was on this farm when the dead first started to rise." Samael's lip twitched. "You'll have to trust me. I've done this before, with Pie," he added. "We were here when it all started."

Lenore closed her eyes when her mother snorted.

Ducey speared the dead man with her good eye. Whatever she wanted to say, it fought with all the questions piling up on her tongue. She pulled a handful of butterscotch out of her apron pocket, untwisting them one by one, letting the candy fall upon the ground where Belle's tongue licked them up.

"You know where Mother is?" Ducey finally asked, then, when Samael nodded, "Tell me," she said.

He shook his head, all that dark hair flopping atop his skull. "Can't."

"And why the hell not?"

Samael gave Ducey a strangled smile. "Promised her I wouldn't."

Her hands slapped against the recliner, curling around the armrests. "Oh, hell."

"There'll be time for all that, Mama," Lenore said, struggling with questions of her own, the same ones rolling around the back of Ducey's mind—what exactly was in the Evans blood that made them rise? "Right now, we need to find our girl."

Luna's eyes gleamed with questions, too, but at least Roger had enough sense to agree. "You mean to tell me that I've been tending an empty grave for the past month and that Grace is . . ." He twisted at his hat. "The one responsible for all this?"

Samael sized up the other man in that way that men do before he nodded, and Ducey set after the burn in her chest.

A noise rattled up the hallway, the back door to the old farmhouse swinging open, footsteps stomping over ceramic, and all three Evans women jumped in their seats.

"Kim," Ducey said, tipping her head toward the window to the parking lot. They'd told the girl to come back when the breakroom lights came on. She'd done as they asked, but they waited out another stomp of footsteps up the hall, and when the girl didn't tap on the breakroom door, Lenore rounded on Samael.

"Did Grace know?" she asked. "About you?" Lenore needed to know, Ducey guessed. Before this went any further, Lenore would want to know if Grace had known that she'd taken a monster into her bed. "Did she know what you were?"

Samael gave her a look. "Yes."

"And did she—" The rest fumbled off Lenore's lips, but her eyes found Luna across the table, and the girl picked up the rest.

"Did she know what I am?" Luna asked. "A dhampir."

At least she didn't say monster.

At least Ducey managed to keep her mouth shut and her good eye to herself.

The dead man only had eyes for his daughter. His lip twitched again, like Roger twisting his damn hat, and Ducey got the feeling there was a lot more the dead man wanted to share.

"I'm sorry I wasn't here for you," he said.

Luna nodded like she understood. "Is that why she named me Luna?"

"Your mama named you for the moon, because when the moon

grows full, so do all that is hers." Samael smiled, and hell if he wasn't a handsome devil. "In old times, long before mine, people believed daughters of the moon could mask reality—could pierce illusion, spark visions, even make dreams come true. You did that for Grace and me, little moon," he said, "and if you choose, you'll find that you can traverse the veil that separates the living from the dead—you can see the spirits that dance under the midnight sun."

"He sounds a lot like that boyfriend of yours," Ducey said, but Luna's attention stayed fixed to her backpack on the floor across the breakroom.

"You mean I can see ghosts?" she asked, very small.

Samael nodded. "You woke me up," he reminded her. "You can call to the dead, but only the ones who want to be seen, or those who have loved ones they've stuck around to watch over."

Now Ducey snorted, but she caught that twinge in her daughter's face. Lenore's brain was probably tying itself in knots thinking about Jimmy.

"What about Mom?" Luna asked, still eyeballing her backpack across the room. "She sacrificed herself to save me. She died for nothing."

Sacrifice for love is never for nothing. Samael shook his head. "You can still save her," he said. "We just need to find her."

Luna's face tied itself in a knot and she met his eyes. "How?"

"Tell them what's in your bag." Kim's voice shot across the room, and Ducey slapped a palm to her chest. So caught up in what Samael had been saying, she hadn't heard their new hire clomp those big clunky boots of hers down the hallway, much less push open the damn breakroom door.

By the looks of it, neither had anyone else, not even Belle, dozing soundly under Ducey's recliner.

But there the girl stood, black-rimmed eyes and purple lips, a coffin-shaped makeup case in her hand and a dress bag over her shoulder like she'd just walked in the door and hadn't been banging around in the lab.

Samael's face flooded with red and half of it turned to points. "You a Halloran?" he asked, and something in his tone said it mattered.

"My last name is Cole," the girl told the dead man. "But my uncle is—was." She shrugged and Samael kept his eyes on Kim while Luna fetched her bag, spilled its contents on the table.

A collar, a ring, a pair of headphones, horn-rimmed glasses.

"Every time there's a kill, I find something in the tallow tree outside my bedroom window," Luna explained. "Do you know what this means?"

She asked Samael, Ducey noticed. Not her. Not Lenore, who flattened a palm to her chest, stricken.

"At *my* house?" she asked, then muttered, "Grace's old bedroom," under her breath when Luna nodded.

Samael smiled. "Pricolici are hateful things, driven by rage," he said, "but despite the sort of creature Grace has become, she's still your mother. She's trying to find you, even now. Reaching out for help the only way she can." He tapped the tabletop hard enough the little bell on the cat collar tinkled. "Leaving clues."

"How do you know so much about this, anyway?" Ducey had to know. "Pricolici and dancin' with spirits in the moonlight." All that about Mother.

A dimple dug into the dead man's cheek. "Been dead almost a hundred years," he said and shrugged as he raked fingers through his shaggy brown mop. "Had a lot of time to search for answers."

"How do we find her?" Luna's voice pulled everyone's attention back to the table. "How do we find my mom?"

"Before she kills again," Roger tacked on.

Samael grinned at Belle, under Ducey's chair. "I reckon we teach an old dog how to hunt."

Ducey glared her good eye at the ghoul. "I know you ain't talking about me."

CHAPTER 33

Deputy Brandon Hinson

Deputy Brandon Hinson sat at his desk until he could barely feel his body anymore. He got up, dropped his badge on the sheriff's desk, and shoved past Dispatch. Darla shouted something over his shoulder, but Brandon slammed the station door shut against the woman's words. This world didn't make enough sense to worry about following anyone's orders. He slammed the driver's side door of his Jeep, then slammed the dashboard knob on the police radio off, too. He wouldn't listen to some dispatcher with no idea how twisted things really were. He'd slam that out, too, if he had to.

Hinson might be a rookie, but he'd been a deputy long enough to know when something wasn't right, and after all this going on around town—the rabid animal attacks, the missing and murdered and mutilated—not that any of *that* was right, but none of it was as wrong as the DNA of a woman who'd allegedly been dead four weeks turning up at a fresh crime scene.

Which Taylor already knew, Brandon thought as he cranked the four-by-four and hightailed it out of the sheriff's department parking lot. When Forensics had called, Taylor sped out of that motel parking lot with barely a backward glance, and that alone was enough to prove he'd known.

Chain of command was one thing, but Hinson sure as shit didn't need to listen to a superior officer who just covered up the truth.

The sheriff had kept a hat soaked through with Grace Evans's blood in his bottom desk drawer, and he'd had a Missing Person's form already worked up for Tanya West before anyone reported her missing.

Taylor didn't let anyone get too close to the press, to the coroner's office, to the funeral parlor. Definitely not to the professor who knew all about real wolves. Just because Brandon hadn't figured out what the hell one thing had to do with another didn't make him dumb enough to miss red flags big as the state of Texas flapping over the whole mess.

"Brett Haney had it right all along." Everything about those words burned Brandon's tongue, blisters already forming by the time he pulled the Jeep behind the laundromat halfway across town. From Boy Scouts to high school football to the academy, Brandon "Chuck" Hinson had obeyed his leader, played by the rules, and followed procedure—but tonight he knew he couldn't serve under a sheriff who didn't seem to care about the preservation of life.

Human life.

He'd left his badge at the station, but not his gun.

Brandon parked between the apartment's dumpster shed and the laundromat. He flicked off his headlights and killed the engine. Even with the Jeep's windows shut and the AC off, even over the detergent from the laundromat and the undercurrent of regular garbage from the apartment complex, the stench of rot and copper still haunted the parking lot.

The last murder—poor Daniel Garland—happened here, over the fence and through the parking lot, behind the "dead" Evans woman's apartment.

Hinson held his weapon unholstered in his lap, magazine full, and leaned his head on the headrest. Kim would've told him that the waning gibbous moon in the darkening blue overhead was already half-empty, but she'd always been a pessimist. Right now, dark edges ate into the moon's belly, but the big white ball still shone more than half-full—enough to see this "ghost wolf" with.

Leaded brass and soft steel encased the rounds in his gun, and his eye-hand coordination made him an excellent shot, but between that mostly full moon and the stuff he'd seen the past few weeks, Brandon didn't know what kind of monster he'd find in Grace Evans's apartment. It might be human or it might not, and right now he'd have traded all ten of those lead bullets for a single silver one.

Especially when he rounded the building and found the door leading up to the apartment open.

And the sets of prints traveling upstairs and back.

Scouts had taught him the tracks of coyote and bear and dog, but
none of those prints stamped a sole and five toes.

Enough daylight still clung to the sky, but Brandon untucked the
penlight from his belt to get a better look. Lighter tracks flecked with
mud and grass climbed the stairs. The tracks coming back down were
red by the time they hit the bottom and headed outside into the night,
but higher up the stairs they were darker—black.

The source of the darker stain waited somewhere upstairs.

Brandon put his back against the stairwell wall, pistol gripped muzzle down with his trigger finger along the barrel, and took one step at
a time, past red prints, to brown, to black.

His stomach lurched when he hit the landing. The puddle of fresh
blood he'd expected to find pooled at the edge of the door at the top
of the steps, but he'd hoped to climb out of the stench, not walk into
it. Not even the funk from the dumpster shed outside could reach up
here, against the tide of sulfuric fumes that poisoned any breathable
air, two stories up.

If Hell smelled of rotten eggs, Brandon thought, *then it smells better
than the Evans apartment.* He clicked the safety free and raised his
gun, crossing the other arm over at the wrist, so that the penlight cast
a spotlight. He inhaled through his mouth—God, he could *taste* the
smell, he might never *not* taste the smell—took one last look back at
blue twilight, and stepped inside.

Clear. The living room couch, love seat, coffee table. The lumps in
the sofa's arms were just throw pillows, the shapes folding over its
back, just blankets. Brandon swept his light into the shadows at the
other end of the room. Straight ahead, an open threshold led into the
kitchen, clear as far as he could see, just a small table and four empty
chairs.

To the right, a door hung open, streaked with red.

Growing up in the Bible Belt, Brandon knew the story of the first
Passover, the door that the Israelites had painted red with sacrifice—an

offering of one death to stave off another. Whatever homes around town hadn't converted to red doors still bore haint-blue awnings. But red or blue or otherwise, death was death, and the source of this apartment's awful odor waited on the other side of that open bedroom door.

Carpet squelched under Brandon's boots as he crossed the small living room one step at a time, remembering the sounds at Snow Leger's house. He held what air he had left in his lungs and kept his light on the gap in the door, swallowing down bile as his penlight punctured the room beyond, darting wall to wall, ceiling down.

When they'd found the teenage girl ripped open on the pavement behind the movie theater last month, Brandon's brain had worked like hell to convince himself the body was some gory Halloween prop, drenched with motor oil. Something not real, covered in red corn syrup, for effect.

He'd known that smear on the Israelites' doors had done jack shit to keep the Angel of Death at bay, no matter what color paint God-fearing Bible Belt folks slapped on their front doors, but he took one look into Grace Evans's bedroom, and all Brandon saw was red.

Body parts lay piled over bedroom furniture. Fur and bone and red and red and *red*—flowing over the decapitated head on the dresser, the bed, the nightstand, the—

Brandon's steel toe stubbed against something that stubbed back.

He blinked and when he rolled his eyes down and opened them again, he saw fresh red, spilling out across black leather sleeves from the body prone in the center of the room.

Brandon lost his penlight to the heaves, but muscle memory thumbed the safety on his pistol home as he held back the sulfur and acid pouring up his throat. Every machine in that swirling laundromat downstairs could bleach and soak and tumble everything he'd seen upstairs, and none of it would ever wash clean.

He scrambled down the stairs under the barely half-full moon.

Whatever killed all those animals, all those people, without one shred of a doubt, up there was its den.

No, not *it*—who. Grace Evans might have been declared dead and buried, but it was her apartment that was a house of horrors. Her blood soaked through Roger Taylor's hat, hidden in his bottom desk drawer. Her secret that the new sheriff was hiding, because Johnson always suspected the Evans women, and Taylor knew Grace was a killer.

A serial killer.

And everyone knew Roger Taylor was sweet on Grace Evans.

Brandon's boots hit the pavement, thundered around the building, and he wrenched the radio free on its dashboard console. He twisted the knob on.

"Come in, Taylor," he shouted into the mic.

Nothing.

He fiddled with the button and knobs, checked the channel. "Sheriff, this is Hinson. Do you copy?" he tried again.

Silence. Brandon mashed the mic, let it free, static crackling on the return. His thumb moved to push the mic again, and Taylor's voice snapped across the line.

"Damn it, Hinson." Even in the dark, Taylor's voice came over the line red. *"Not now."*

"Sheriff, I—" Brandon stopped. Had Taylor just turned his radio off?

A truck pulled into the laundromat parking lot and Brandon saw the dent in the Ford's guard grille. He might not have any silver bullets, but now he had more than one gun.

"Come in, Dispatch." Brandon waited until Darla picked up the call. "Tell Taylor I know who's killing people around town," he said as Brett Haney pushed the passenger door open from inside the cab. "And tell him I'm going after it."

Now he and Haney could hunt this thing down and finish it once and for all.

CHAPTER 34

Kim Cole

think you're just about done."

Kim pulled the bloodred tip of the brush across Luna's bottom lip one more time, then leaned back to inspect her work. Other than Dillon, not many living victims had braved her makeup chair so far, and so Kim's practice had been more or less limited to her little brother's face and her own.

She'd smudged a silver sheen from Luna's lash line all the way up to her brow, skipping the liner in favor of a thick black fringe. Lined in crimson, a dark plum on the girl's lips brought out the pink undertones in her cheeks. Starlight glimmered in dabs of glitter at the edges of her eyes and along her cheekbones. Liv Tyler's look at last year's Academy Awards may have guided Kim's inspiration tonight, but with her hair curled in dark waves around her face, the crystal choker sparkling around her neck, the iridescent purple satin gown, Luna Evans looked every bit her goddess namesake.

Those *Armageddon* boys could travel to space if they wanted, but in this little forgotten room at the back of the funeral parlor, the one that used to belong to the family's matriarch, Kim had done her best to transform Luna into her own galaxy.

And she'd done a damn good job, if she did say so herself. Just a few finishing touches, now.

Kim set down the lipstick brush on the metal instrument tray that she'd wheeled into the unused bedroom. "Close your eyes," she told Luna, then dabbed a touch more silver under the girl's eyebrow arch, wiped her fingers on her own jeans, and held up the looking glass she'd found on the dresser so the girl could see.

"What do you think?" Kim probably had no reason to hold her breath when she asked, but she did anyway.

Seated on the edge of the bare mattress, Luna blinked her eyes open, widening them as she reached for the glass to take in her reflection. Her pupils moved across the mirror, sweeping over her features, doubling back, then rising to meet Kim's.

Luna's plum lips bloomed like a dark red rose. "Whoa," she said.

"Thought you'd like it."

Kim let the girl keep looking while she rooted around in her bag for stray bobby pins, then signaled Luna to turn so she could pin back the hair from her eyes.

"I thought you'd go heavier on the eyeliner," Luna said, twisting to give one side of her head to Kim, then the other.

"Nah, not everyone can pull off my look." Kim slipped studs into Luna's ears, twisted them into place, then fluffed loose curls over the girl's shoulders. "You deserve your own sparkle tonight," she said and reached for the mirror. "Plus, Crane will love it—not that it matters," she tacked on, because a girl didn't need a boy to look pretty any more than she needed a silly high school dance to get dressed up.

It didn't hurt, though, to know someone would soon stare at you with stars in their eyes.

Even if it was that weirdo with the trench coat.

Luna's cheeks blushed a different shade of pink, but she grinned back at Kim's best big-sister smile. "Not that it matters," Luna agreed.

Another series of knocks sounded elsewhere in the funeral parlor, and Kim began to pack her things away. By the amount of racket funneling down the hallway, the breakroom conference must have advanced into the preparation stage.

Satin rustled as Luna pushed up from the bed. The girl made her way to the large mirror over the dresser, brushed her palms over the dress she'd borrowed, and frowned.

"Is this a good idea?" her reflection asked Kim. "Going to stupid Homecoming with—" She waved her hand around like mixing cinnamon-roll batter. "All this going on? I mean, we just revived my undead dad from the grave," Luna said, jerking a thumb at the door, "and he says my mom is alive, or—or not dead, or whatever, and I've never even been in this room before tonight, you know? Ducey says Pie was—"

"Breathe," Kim told the girl. "I mean, yeah, things are a little intense, but your grandmas and your dad are figuring out a plan right now with the sheriff. Besides—" Kim checked the time on her wrist. "You've only got a couple of hours until you turn back into a pumpkin, Cinderella," she said. "Better get your butt to the ball."

Kim shepherded Luna down the hall and back into the breakroom. Both girls jerked to a halt in the doorway. Belle must have followed Ducey when she'd relocated from the recliner to the table, and now the entire group of them—Ducey, Lenore, Samael, and Roger—sat in deep conversation around the items from Luna's backpack, calm and cool, like they hadn't been banging on the walls. When Samael saw Kim and Luna enter the room, he pushed up from the table.

"You're as beautiful as your mother," the dead guy told his daughter, and Kim's sinuses tingled. When was the last time her dad looked at her like that?

"You've got my eyes, but your mother's smile," Samael said to Luna. "My little moon is every bit as pretty as her grandma, and great-grandma." He touched Luna's cheek, thumb clipping her chin as it traced down the side of her jaw. "Reckon I even see some of Pie in there if I look hard enough."

Luna sniffed. "Thank you, Dad."

Kim pushed her fingertip against the corner of her eye. Good thing she'd sprung for waterproof mascara, even if she were the only one besides Luna with a watery eye.

Still, Lenore's eyes weren't as narrow as usual, and Ducey popped Kim a thumbs-up from the table. Roger examined the inscription on the class ring, but kept stealing glances around the room—at Luna in particular.

That liquid welling under Kim's eyes almost tipped out. The Evanses might be the weirdest family in the world, with an undead woman, a master strigoi, a moon child, and who knew what else in their strange little funeral parlor—but Kim hadn't seen a group of monsters love each other this hard since *The Munsters*.

She thought about Dillon, held captive in his parents' home. Herself, prowling the perimeter of her freedom, wanting just a few more nights in the nest.

Families like the Coles had a lot to learn.

Ducey cleared her throat, rapping her knuckles on the table. "Go on and get Luna to the school," she told Lenore. "We'll pick this up when you get back."

A wisp of cool air blew through the warm moment as Lenore's eyes thinned into their usual shape. "I think it's best if I stay here," she said, and even Samael bowed his head when the chill in her voice hit his ears.

Good luck breaking that ice. Kim's first few days at the parlor had been anything except normal, but she'd seen how Lenore cared for the town's dead, the way she worked so hard to take care of everyone around her, dead or alive.

Hate didn't make you cold, but love did. Love could burn you up or ice you down, and whatever love had hurt Lenore, it had frozen her all the way to her core.

Good luck to the dead guy to thaw it.

Kim had already played taxi for one teenager tonight. It wouldn't kill her to shuttle another. "I can give her a ride," she said.

"I don't mind," Roger jumped in, pushing up from the table. "Need to check with Hinson," he added, eyes skipping over Kim as he trained them on Luna. "If you don't mind another ride to school in a cruiser?" he asked.

Luna shook her head, and Roger looked for Samael's approval. The two men sized each other up, and then Samael bowed his head and Roger waved Luna to the door.

Damn if Kim couldn't get one dad to love her. This girl had two.

With Luna and Roger gone, just the two elder Evans women remained at the table with the dead man, and it looked like the three had a lot to talk about.

"I'm gonna go clean up my stuff," Kim said, backing out of the room.

"Be sure to tidy up the lab before you go." Lenore hitched an eyebrow in Kim's direction, hooking her back with a last word. "We like to keep that room as clean as possible."

Ducey clicked her teeth. "We got a full house in there," she reminded Kim. That many dead bodies, and things could go sour real quick if they got lax on the housekeeping.

Kim's forehead went tight as she made her way toward the lab. Considering what they had to work out over that breakroom table, it was a wonder they'd keep after her about her tasks. But she'd helped Luna get ready in the old bedroom. Had she forgotten to put things away in the lab after she'd finished up with Ducey earlier? Best she could remember, she'd put her kit back on the shelf and shut the door behind her, but as crazy as the day had been, maybe.

The door of the lab *was* open, after all. Kim could have sworn she'd shut that.

She flicked on the overhead lights.

Maybe she left the lab door open after she'd finished up with Hilda Baker, but no way she'd opened the coolers.

Not all six of them.

All six coolers in the Evans Funeral Parlor lab hung open. And all six were empty.

CHAPTER 35

Ducey Evans

One of Belle's back legs hitched when she walked, and she had cataracts in both eyes, but so far, their best bet to tracking Grace's whereabouts was to remind Buck Johnson's geriatric redbone how to hunt.

The old girl barely peeled her ears off the breakroom linoleum when Samael scooped Luna's collection of items off the table. "Come here, girl," he said as he squatted beside the table, murmuring sweet nothings as he passed each stolen trinket under the old hound's long silver snout. Belle sniffed at the cat collar and the horn-rims, and when the dead man pushed himself up and patted his thigh, the old dog heaved herself off the floor and followed him to his seat.

Samael scuffed the hound's ears while her snout got a second date with the principal's ring.

Ducey sucked in a deep breath and got a distinct whiff of honey and woodsmoke.

The ghoul was stinking up her parlor and flirting with her dog. If only she could have one of her butterscotches.

She cocked her good eye at the dead man across the breakroom table and drummed her fingers. *All the things Mother said about ghouls,* Ducey thought, *and not one word about making friends with one herself.* Not a single word in over sixty years about the ghoul Pie had known since she was a girl—who'd go on to father a new generation of Evans women. The mean old biddy didn't trust her own daughters when she'd wandered off that one night like a dying cat, but she'd trusted a dead man with her burial site. All these years later, and Samael still wouldn't tell where Pie made her bed, because the old woman had made him promise not to.

Hard to imagine Pie Evans inspiring that sort of loyalty in someone other than her daughters. Aside from the family farmhouse turned funeral parlor, the grandfather clock in the chapel, and that damn letter, all Ducey's mother had left behind was a bad taste in people's mouths about the Evans family.

"Was Mother always mean as a striped snake?" Ducey asked the dead man.

Lenore's loafers squealed as she skidded to a stop by the sink. "Mama!" she screeched, spinning around like a weathervane in a tornado.

Ducey waved her daughter quiet. "Hush, Lenore," she said. "I ain't talkin' to you."

Lenore hissed from the sink like somebody splashed water on her. Pie Evans wasn't the only Evans to turn bitter.

"You shouldn't talk about family business in front of him," she said.

Samael set the cat collar on the floor in front of Belle and leaned back in his chair, eyebrow up as he crossed his arms over his chest. He looked from Ducey to Lenore and kept his mouth shut, waiting for his cue.

Smart man, for a ghoul. Guess being a master strigoi did more than give Samael back his human looks.

Ducey snorted. Dead or otherwise, the first rule men learned around the Evans women was not to get between them.

"He's Luna's daddy," the dead woman said and shrugged. "We share blood. Figure that's about as close to family as you can get."

Under the table, Belle huffed at the cat collar, finished memorizing the scent. Ducey watched Lenore squeeze the hilt of her dagger as Samael unwound himself and leaned over to reach for the floor.

"Good girl," he said as he traded the collar for the mangled headphones, scuffed Belle behind the ears, and leaned back in his chair.

Lenore's grip didn't relax until he'd crossed his arms back over his chest. The girl got her squirrelly nature from her father and her resilience from Ducey, but every time Lenore's teeth started grinding, Ducey thought of her mother Pie.

Ducey nudged her chin at Samael. "I'm still waitin' on an answer," she told him, about the question she'd asked about her mother.

Ever since she'd found Pie's goodbye letter on this same tabletop all those years ago, Ducey had pumped a lot of energy into being mad at her mother. Not for what Pie wrote in her last words, or even what she'd done after—Evans women had to do what Evans women had to do—but because the mad old bat had taken all her damn secrets with her when she left.

Didn't leave Ducey a lot to go on, other than hokum, but hell if half of that hadn't proved true already.

A smile crawled across the dead man's face. "Priscilla Evans was sweeter than stolen honey," he said. "That's how she earned her nickname, after all. Never met a little girl as sweet as Pie." Samael shook his head and his smile dropped. "That was before the fire."

Spindletop, he meant. More than greed had come with all that liquid gold shooting up from the earth. Somehow—another secret Pie hadn't shared—the Evanses had gotten themselves right smack-dab in the middle of it, and they'd been stuck there ever since.

"A lot of people died that night," Samael said. "Some of them came back."

The dead man's eyes were dark as midnight, but Ducey saw flames still burning when they met hers. "You one of 'em?" she asked.

Samael nodded.

"And my mother?" she pressed.

"Never trust a Halloran." His gaze fell, and the flames in Samael's eyes licked along the wound in Ducey's throat, made the spray paint prickle where Kim had covered it up. Heat had flared in the dead man's cheeks when he'd pegged the girl's family name. The Hallorans went as far back in this town as the Evanses. One of them had taken a bite out of Ducey's throat, and now another worked in the parlor—but the way Samael had stared at Kim suggested there was more to that story, and now it looked like it might go further back than she could have imagined.

So many things Pie had taken to her grave. How many of those secrets could have saved them hell if they'd only known the truth?

The dead man's words came slow and careful, like they might spark against each other if he spoke too fast. "A lot of people died that night," he repeated, quirking an eyebrow. "Reckon that's why they named the cemetery what they did."

Eternal Flame Cemetery. Ducey curled her fingers around the trocar in her apron pocket and caught Lenore rolling her eyes. That part of the story they both knew, at least. When the oil boom started and the land became worth more than the crops that grew there, Conchobhar Evans had sold off a strip of the family farm to plant the dead instead.

"Connie Evans wasn't the only Evans with a green thumb," Samael said, offering a grin in Lenore's direction while Belle shifted from the headphones to the class ring he laid on the linoleum between her ears. "Can't say I enjoyed the last fifteen years, but the roses sure made for a pretty view."

The poor girl blinked so hard Ducey worried her daughter might shatter.

Pie Evans had taught her daughters how to put down the dead that tried to claw their way back to the world of the living—taught them that the restless dead were nothing but empty husks, hungry to fill up the hollow inside them. Now here Samael sat, and Ducey had been a ghoul herself long enough to see he hadn't looked at Luna with any kind of hunger tonight, nor had he looked at Grace with a ghoul's hunger the night the Evanses had put him in the ground.

Samael looked at his daughter the same way Ducey looked at hers.

Ducey reached inside her pocket and fingered the butterscotches she couldn't eat. *Ain't any monsters that hold the Evans women in thrall,* she thought, and harrumphed. *It's our own damn secrets.*

"History sure does have a way of repeating itself, doesn't it?" Samael said, but Ducey didn't have time to figure out what he meant, because Kim's footsteps thundered down the hallway like a girl trying to outrun hornets buzzing up her pants.

She burst into the room, arms behind her back, eyes big as saucers, and the burn in Ducey's chest threatened to swallow her whole.

"They're gone," Kim gasped—winded, but not from the run down the short hallway.

"Who's gone?" Lenore asked, but Ducey already knew.

"The dead," Ducey said.

Kim nodded. "All of them, even—" Her eyebrows scrunched and she bit her lip at Brevard's ring under Belle's nose. "Even the one in the bag," she said, shifting from foot to foot, arms wiggling behind her back.

Lord, what a sight that one would make, barely enough parts left to pull itself across the ground.

If Lenore hadn't started blinking again, Ducey might have thought she'd frozen solid. Six dead had awaited burial in the parlor's coolers, four from age and natural causes. Grace's monster had brought in the other two, but not one of them should've had the strength to rise.

"How?" Ducey asked. "I've checked them all, made sure. None of them were restless." Hell, half of them had been her dinner.

"Luna." Samael scratched Belle behind the ear and palmed the trinkets. "When she woke me up," he said, "the others heard her call."

"That's not possible." Lenore's mouth barely sounded out the words, but Ducey'd had a lot of practice reading her daughter's lips.

Samael set his hands on the table, spreading out the evidence. "I'm afraid it is."

"When the dead rise," Lenore said, "they come to the parlor, because this is where it all started, whatever *it* is." She stared daggers at the dead man. She gave him a beat to confirm, to disagree, and when he didn't, she said, "But if they've left the parlor—"

"Then they're looking for the one who woke them," Samael finished. "The earth pulls the dead here, but these aren't ghouls. These are risen, and Luna's power is calling them to her."

Just then Belle bayed, catching the scent on the items found outside Luna's window, and the dead man scooped up the cat's collar, jingling its little silver bell. "And if the dead are tracking Luna, then so will be Grace," he said. "She might not know what she is, but there's enough left of her in there to protect her daughter."

"The dance," Kim said, half out the doorway, eyes flicking between Ducey and the others.

Lenore's hand rose to her throat so fast she didn't have time to blink. "They're going to the school," she said. "Oh, Mama, all those kids."

Samael shoved up from his chair. He tapped his leg, clicked his teeth, and Belle pushed herself to her feet, tail ramrod straight in the air behind her.

"We need to get there before they do," he said, and all that honey in his voice hardened to amber. "All of them."

Lenore was on her feet, the dagger in her hand. "Mama, you stay here with Kim," she said.

"Like hell I'll stay here." Ducey snatched the dead principal's class ring from the table, pushed it up her finger against the pretty diamond band Royce had given her, bless his heart. She waved her hand under Belle's nose, looking first at Kim, then at her own daughter.

"We've got more problems than we can say grace over," Ducey said, and wished she'd used another expression. "You two—" She crooked the ring finger at Samael and Lenore. "You get to the school. Deal with the restless."

Samael nodded, but Lenore's eyes narrowed at the dead man. Probably she'd rather go it alone than team up with a ghoul, but now was not the time to split hairs over being undead. Lenore opened her mouth and Ducey pushed her bifocals up her nose, licked the wishful taste of butterscotch off her lips, and gnashed her teeth at her daughter.

"Don't start with me, Lenore Ruth," she snapped. "There are six ghouls headed to the high school. You can't take them all on your own." Ducey met Samael's eyes, the same midnight shade as her great-granddaughter's.

"I'll keep Luna safe," he promised. "Hell or high water."

Then Ducey rubbed the paint off her neck and looked to Kim. "You up for a hunt?" she asked.

Against the threshold, the girl stood as straight as the hound dog's tail.

"Hold on, Mama. You two are dead," Lenore said, and pointed her blade at Kim. "Don't bring her into this."

"Between Belle and me, we got a couple good knees and one pair of workin' eyes," Ducey said. She waved the dog over, and when Belle rubbed against her knee, Ducey held her ring hand down for the dog to sniff. "We can track Grace, but we need someone to drive."

"You don't have to do this," Lenore told Kim, pursing her lips when Samael nodded his agreement, all that pink heat in his cheeks again. What was that he'd said before, never trust a Halloran?

Fool. Ducey rolled her good eye. There was more at stake here than old grudges. "You in?" she asked the girl.

A smile broke over Kim's face like dawn when Ducey's good eye came back down. One arm peeled free from behind her back, and the girl raised a bone saw straight in the air like a slasher-movie villain. "I'm in," she said, nine inches of toothy steel thrumming in the air by her head.

Ducey clapped her hands before anyone could disagree. "All right, kids," she said, to the dead man, the daughter, the employee, and the dog. "We've got work to do."

CHAPTER 36

Sheriff Roger Taylor

Roger grunted as he flashed his blinker and turned the cruiser into the Forest Park High School bus-only lane. Music thumped through the night air from the school's main building, and confetti still rained down victory in the football stadium lights on one side of the lot, while over in the faculty lot orange cones and police tape marked where the cleaning crew had scraped the principal off the hot top.

Funny how far a good football win can go in small-town Texas, he thought. Far enough, apparently, to overlook the bloodshed painting the streets red. Three dead, butchered livestock, and a pack of slaughtered hybrids stacked on top of rabid reporters, a nosy rookie, and more missing pets than he could shake a stick at—and still none of that compared to Roger's biggest problem.

Somehow the rookie had figured it out. He'd get the details wrong, but he'd be right enough.

Roger cleared his throat, peeking at the girl beside him in his peripheral vision as he shifted the cruiser into park in front of the school's exterior doors. Blue and purple lights flashed inside the cafeteria's wide windows, lighting up shapes of students inside. Not a bone in Roger's body felt like dancing, Homecoming or not, but this fifteen-year-old girl probably had a different set of priorities.

A clump of teenagers brushed past the cruiser, shoved through the cafeteria doors in a burst of bass and glittering lights, and Roger stuffed his hands under his thighs before he could grab at his hat on the dashboard. He thought of those dead kids he'd helped bury last month, the smoke alarm he'd heard screaming from Katherine Brooks-Haney's mouth when he told her what happened to her baby girl, the CD in the dead kid's Discman when they'd found his face ripped off in the dumpster shed.

The cop half of Roger wanted a word with every single mom and dad who let their kid out of their sight on a night like this, in the face of everything they'd seen on the evening news. His other half was just as much a fool as all those parents—he was also sending something precious out into the dark, pretending someplace well-lit and full of life was the safest place for Grace's daughter.

He snaked a glance at the girl in the passenger seat, pretty as starlight in her dress. Which half was Roger: the badge or the fool? Hell if he knew. Not like he'd ever done any of this before.

You aren't the only one, he thought when he noticed Luna's hands curled into fists in her lap.

"We're going to find her," Roger promised Luna. "Your grandmas and your—" His eye twitched. Roger had seen the monster in Samael when he'd caught him by surprise in the cruiser's headlights—the gaunt edges, the razored fangs, the unnatural stretch of the jaw.

The man seemed like a nice fella, though. The master strigoi would just take some time to get used to.

"Your dad and me," Roger finished. "We'll find your mom."

For the first time in a long time, Luna's eyes didn't roll when she looked at him. Instead, all that light glittering out of the school sparkled across her face, across the collar around her neck, and tingles sprang up somewhere inside Roger's chest. Samael had called Luna his moon, and Roger figured that fit the girl just about right.

"I know you will," she said, but her fists stayed curled, and the little tingle in Roger's chest poked up in goose bumps down his arms. Whatever had Luna wound up, maybe it didn't have to do with her mother.

She waited in her seat while Roger pulled his hat off the dash, stuffed it over his head, then pushed out the driver's side and ran around to open the door for her. She accepted the hand he offered to help her out of the cruiser, even gave him a grin.

Roger stood with his hands clasped in front of him as Grace's daughter disappeared inside the school.

The girl really was just as beautiful as her mother.

Music poured out between double doors, lots of drums and guitar. Roger caught a glimpse of bobbing balloons and glittering stars. When the doors sealed shut behind Luna, he unclasped his hands, looked up at the moon overhead, and returned to duty.

The flapping caution tape on the other side of the parking lot caught his eye as he slid back behind the wheel of his Crown Vic. Roger pulled his hat off, gripped it over his chest, tossed it on the dash.

Time to finish this, he thought. Time to find Grace and bring her home.

Before things got any worse.

Roger shifted into drive. It took him until he'd pulled out of the school to get his heart rate under control. Around the steering wheel, color didn't come back into his knuckles until he'd made it past the funeral parlor. He kept his hands at ten and two, eyes straight ahead, and by the time he'd made it past the laundromat and halfway to Jimbo's, Roger almost felt like the sheriff again.

He twisted on his radio.

If Hinson asked, he'd say he'd switched it off to follow a lead. Or he wouldn't make up an excuse at all. *You are the sheriff, for crying out loud,* Roger told himself, and pressed the mic.

"Come in, Hinson," he said.

Static.

"Hinson, go for Taylor." This time it was an order.

Roger waited a full five seconds before he growled into the mic, "I said come in, Hinson."

"Hinson's off the deep end, Sheriff." Dispatch Darla screeched over the radio, breathless, like she'd been running laps around the station. "Stormed out of here a little over an hour ago."

An *hour* ago. Roger glanced at the clock on his dash. He hadn't checked his Timex when Hinson had buzzed him over and over, and Roger had turned his radio off—but he'd guess that had been about then.

"Where in the hell did he go?" he barked at Dispatch.

Back in the station, hoarse hysteria crackled in Darla's voice. "Hell if I know," she said, "but he left you a message before he went dark."

Something caught Roger's eye, flapping like police tape as he turned the corner half a mile out from the station. He let off the accelerator and squinted through the cruiser's front glass, scanning the pine trees up ahead.

Just trees. Whatever he'd seen coming must have been a trick of the light.

Roger kept his eyes on the tree line as he spoke into the radio clipped to his shoulder. "What message?" he asked.

That flicker again, under the streetlights. Roger squinted. Up ahead, moving toward him, a darker spot in the shadows behind the pines, a smear deeper than the rest.

Arms, he thought he saw, maybe a head, but he blinked and it slipped between pine boughs and was gone.

"Hinson said he knows who's attacking people around town," Dispatch radioed back.

The dark smear smudged itself between the trees again, now moving east, and Roger flicked on his brights.

"And that he's going to kill it," Darla said.

Roger's foot tapped the brake.

When Forensics called in the results back at the Gladys City Motel crime scene, Hinson had been right there at Roger's side. He'd heard the name that came across the radio. Knew all this had something to do with Grace.

An hour gave the rookie plenty of time to get to her apartment, if he'd been fool enough to follow a lead on his own.

Roger stomped the accelerator and flipped on his blue-and-reds when the radio on his shoulder crackled to life again.

"And Sheriff—" Darla's voice trilled along Roger's bad forearm.

There—the dark shape, blurring between the trees. His hand dropped from the radio, boot against the brake as he flicked off the high beams. The cruiser slowed to a crawl, and he stared into the dark at the edge of the road, waited to catch the shape in the shadows.

"You should know," Darla said. "He's with Brett Haney."

A streetlight caught the edge of the shape as it sped between the trees, faster now, the tips of its ears, the lumbering bulk on two legs, the long claws hanging at its side.

Grace.

Headed toward the school.

CHAPTER 37

Luna Evans

Luna pushed through the heavy cafeteria doors and stepped into the Homecoming Dance cosmos. A disco-ball moon sprinkled specks of gleaming silver through flashing purple and blue stage lights that formed galaxies with the pale moonlight filtering in through the windows. Confetti rained starlight from the ceiling sky, glittering along Luna's skin as she scanned the celestial student bodies swirling across the star-dusted floor for a pair of black leather sleeves.

A DJ spun silver in the corner, pumping radio hits into the room. Cans of soda and bake-sale goods lined the cafeteria serving stations, all set on shiny metallic trays. And centered on the stage, those wooden assembly easels with Andy's and Alison's portraits. Strung with sashes and lights, the dead kids had made Homecoming court.

Michelle Bryant swirled by in a gust of pink satin and hair spray, her stupid pink lips folded into a stupid pink pout. *Guess she didn't get to be Queen after all,* Luna thought, as the cheerleader noticed her and doubled back.

"Did your weirdo boyfriend stand you up, *Lunie?*" she whined, twirling away as the bathwater warmth Luna had walked out of the parlor with washed away, leaving her cold.

Dillon was right: a bucket of red paint *would* make the stupid cheerleader too likeable.

A chill blew across Luna's exposed shoulders as her eyes made another orbit around the room. Blue and white balloon nebulas bobbed along the room's edges, and between them, a cluster of glow-in-the-dark stars near the back wall. No Crane, but Dillon and Crystal waved her over from a table heaped with glittering cardstock stars.

"Luna Lou, where have you been!" Dillon's baby blues sparkled over the pinpricks in his tie, but he gave her borrowed dress, her careful makeup, an approving nod as a pop star sang around them. Did he recognize his sister's dress? "We've been here for *ages*," he said, bobbing and snapping his fingers as if he had pigtails like the girl *Oh, baby, baby*-ing through the PA system.

Beside him, Crystal rolled her eyes, and spoke over the music. "He means fifteen minutes." The shiny silver butterfly clips in her hair matched the sparkles on her cheeks, her blue dress the same navy shade as Dillon's suit.

Should Luna and Crane have coordinated their outfits, too? No, she decided, palming the purple satin. The surprise would be better.

Not that it matters. The thought wasn't as funny now, without Kim. Without Crane.

Dillon crooked his elbow on the table as Luna scanned the room again. "Fifteen minutes *plus* three hours of setup," he countered. Three fingers shot up, in case they didn't hear the count over the music.

Crystal rolled her eyes. "You're the one who insisted we drape every surface in glitter."

"Excuse me for making this a magical night." The boy pursed his lips, but pride lit up his eyes. Galaxies collected in pools of moonlight that shone through the cloud-frosted window glass. "Did you know there's a delivery door that goes into the kitchen?" he asked, and when Luna shook her head, he added, "I bet Crane already has a key to that door, too."

"Speaking of, where is he?" Crystal asked in the quiet between songs.

Each word sank like a stone in the pit of Luna's stomach. If Crane wasn't already at the dance, that'd meant he'd been held up at her apartment, and if her mom was the monster . . .

"We're supposed to meet at the dance," she said, and those stones, their weight stacked up in her throat, weighed down her tongue until she gagged.

The dress's bodice squeezed the bulk in her chest, pushed it right up to the choker that sparkled at her throat, and Luna moaned into her hand.

"Are you okay?" Crystal reached across the table, and Luna winced when their hands touched.

"I just didn't expect to get here before him," she said.

Crystal stared at her for a beat before she shrugged. "I'm sure he's just running behind." She nudged Dillon. "Right?"

A salsa number queued up, and starlight hit Dillon's eyes. "At least one of us gets to be fashionably late," he said.

Luna nodded. Such a simple explanation. But every time the music changed, another hair lifted on the back of her neck. The cairn in her stomach kept stacking higher, suffocating her from the inside, and one by one, every cell in Luna's body turned to ice. Her friends chattered and sang along as the tracks clicked by, but three songs later, the chill coursing under Luna's skin had grown so cold that she pulled Dillon's jacket over her shoulders.

This is what a corpse feels like, Luna thought when her friends got up to dance. *A normal corpse.* Cold and heavy, and unable to do anything about it.

A slow song crept in on acoustic guitar, and someone hit the fog machine. Gauzy light embraced Dillon and Crystal. Michelle Bryant wrapped her arms around the neck of some football jock. Under the weight of all those frozen rocks, Luna sat alone at the table, picking foil stars and tissue-paper confetti off her soles as couples paired up under the flashing disco-ball moon.

And a boy stood alone on the dance floor, caught in a shaft of pale blue light.

Luna blinked through the wet shine in her eyes. Black suit over a white vest, his collar popped like Bela Lugosi. White bow tie petals bloomed at Crane's throat. He wore his hair slicked back, and he'd taken off his leather trench coat, but when Crane smiled at Luna across the twinkling sky, she knew those wide, thin lips, the smudge of black beneath his eye line. All that cold in her bones went warm, and Luna left the jacket on the table as Crane's gravity pulled her across the moonlit floor.

Goose bumps prickled her skin as her feet slid toward him, but the disco ball spun, the light shifted, and then the handsome boy washed away, leaving some other figure standing in the shadows.

Cold rushed into Luna's eyes, fogging her vision like fake snow glistening from the corners of the Homecoming Dance windows.

Crane still stood in that spot, but now his hair fell in a curtain over his face like always, black leather wings billowing out behind him. His stomach gleamed, but not like sparkles, and then silver glittered across his suit, his long, crescent smile. Luna's steps faltered as she watched the boy change in the moonlight.

When the song's drumbeat kicked in, Luna saw the way starlight glittered over Crane's skin, the halo at his back, and she knew.

You can see the spirits that dance under the midnight sun, her father had said.

She'd sent the boy she couldn't help but love to her apartment to find secrets, and something else had found him instead.

Her words came out wet when she met him in the milky twilight. "You're late," she told him, and her first tear slipped free.

Crane's fingertip brushed cold across her cheek. "Looks like I'm right on time, Moon Girl," he said as he cupped her cheek, following along to the song's lyrics as he led her to the moonlit floor by the cafeteria windows, pulling her close under the silver moon sparkling.

Tears pushed against the backs of Luna's eyes, fireflies dancing. "My mom killed you," she said.

Crane leaned down to put his cheek to hers.

"No tears," he whispered in her ear. "You can still see me, and right now that's all that matters."

When the bridge picked up, a guitar soloed into the melody, and Crane swirled her under the celestial sky. She clung to him as they spun, orbiting their own space at the edge of the Homecoming Dance floor. His lips brushed against hers, warm in the cool silver light, and Luna wished they could stay this way forever—her in her pretty purple dress, Crane with the white bloom at his throat. She wished this moment would last. That the song wouldn't end.

The magic wouldn't die.

But when the final verse kicked in, stars began to shine through the edges of Crane's dark suit. Luna's hand reached to touch his face as that long, crescent smile paled over the swirling celestial student bodies.

"No," she said, when stage lights beamed through Crane. *Don't leave me.*

"You'll always find me in the moonlight, Moon Girl," Crane whispered in her ear as the cymbals crashed at the end of the song, and then Luna stood alone in a room filled with stardust.

She reached out into the emptiness in front of her as somewhere in the center of the room Michelle Bryant began to scream.

CHAPTER 38

Lenore Evans

Lenore had the driver's door open before the Rambler came to a complete stop at the curb in front of the high school. She left the engine running as she fingered the vial of Tanya West's ashes, and then Lenore snatched the dagger out of her lap, squinted at the dead man in the passenger seat, and pitched herself out of the car. Samael raced past her, the cool of his body sending a chill through Lenore as they shoved through the cafeteria doors.

Bass thumped under the sound of screaming.

The hammering drumbeat knocked the wind out of Lenore, rooting her loafers to the confetti floor as blue and purple lights streaked across a sea of screaming eyes and stretched mouths.

Too late. The pinch between Lenore's shoulder blades stabbed through her chest. *We're too late.*

Teenage shoulders slammed against her as bodies rushed out to the street, their satin gowns and polished shoes like rushing wind and static as confetti rained down in a hail of glitter. The music cut out completely and more screams filled the space it left while the disco ball overhead spun starlight over the faces of the dead.

They converged on the crowd of high schoolers—Daniel Garland with half his face torn away and eyeball hanging, coagulated bits of Paul Brevard sludging across the confetti-littered cafeteria floor— another dead, another, another. In the center of the room, directly under that spinning moon, Hilda Baker buried her teeth in Luna's bicep.

Blood poured over Luna's chest. Her skin split, soaking her taffeta dress red, splashing onto the tile floor. Lenore's hand went slack, the dagger clanging at her feet as the room rolled beneath her. She blinked and it was Grace falling to the ground, a dead boy's hand plunged inside her stomach, the silver scar on her wrist flashing in the real moonlight. Lenore blinked and an empty vial shattered in her hand, all gone, all empty, just like the last time, and—

"Nana!" Luna's voice—far away, not in front of her, not the bleeding girl—slammed Lenore back into herself.

Her eyes flicked to the other end of the room, found her grand-daughter with her friends.

Luna. This deer-in-headlights bleeding in the center of the room under the disco-ball moon wasn't Luna.

Lenore's fist clenched around the vial of ashes. Her loafers kicked up glittering confetti as the rush of cold air at her side flung her for-ward. Samael wrenched the yellow corpse away from the bleeding teenaged girl.

"She bit me, bit me, *bit*—!" The girl's scared doe eyes flickered from the wound in her shoulder to Lenore to Samael, and back to the red coursing down her forearm, dripping from her fingertips. "She bit me!" she bleated as blood pulsed down over her skin, voice hitching into a scream as her body crumpled to the floor. Pink lipstick smeared across her face like a sad circus clown.

Lenore dropped to her knees in front of the wounded dear, bat-ting away the teen's flailing hands as she raked back blood-soaked hair and pressed down against the wound. Overhead, a sickening crack, like twisting loose an ice cube tray, and the yellowed corpse dropped, eyes wide and unseeing, into the fog of confetti.

Hilda Baker's rotten blood spilled across the glittery confetti on the cafeteria floor. Something much more terrifying hulked over them all—over the yellowed dead woman, the bleeding, doe-eyed girl, and Lenore.

"Don't get the dead's blood in the ashes," Samael snarled over her head, then he disappeared into the screams.

Lenore searched for Luna, found her still with her friends, bathed in disco-moon shimmer at the edge of the room.

Her two friends. Where was Crane?

Thunder boomed through the air and Lenore's head jerked in time to see the cafeteria doors flung open. Belle's teeth bared as the hound burst through, Ducey and Kim on her heels, trocar and bone saw raised. Ducey's good eye flashed in Lenore's direction and relief flared in her chest as her mother pointed Kim toward the back of the room, then plunged her trocar into the dead man from cooler two—stroke victim.

"Get movin', Len!" Ducey's voice reached Lenore in the center of the room, spurring her back into movement.

They could contain this. None injured, other than the girl in her arms. One strigoi already lay dead beside her. With Samael and the rest, the Evanses might stand a chance of stopping the dead before they ate their way through Homecoming.

"She bit me!" the teen under her whimpered. Shock dulled the girl's voice and her eyelids fluttered, that pink across her jaw smeared down her chin. Lenore scanned the toothy imprint, the depth of the cut on her arm. The bitten might grow restless, but not before they bled out, and a bite from a strigoi will not stop bleeding until there is nothing left.

Lenore stabbed her dagger into the bloody hem of the girl's dress, shearing free a length of pink satin that she tied to the wounded upper arm. The tourniquet slowed the blood enough that Lenore could let go and twist open the vial.

She spit into the glass tube, then pressed her finger over the open end as she shook the mixture into paste. "Hold still." Lenore spoke directly into the girl's doe eyes as she poured the paste onto her wound. "You're going to be all right."

But the cafeteria doors flung open again, and this time Sheriff Roger Taylor barreled through. His eyes scanned the room, locking on to Lenore's. He jerked a thumb over his shoulder, at the only entrance to the cafeteria, and his mouth shaped one word.

Grace.

He pulled the doors shut behind him, forcing the horde of students back into their Homecoming Dance cosmos. He wedged a long metal rod through the handles, locking them all inside with the dead.

They had to do what they could to take care of the restless dead inside the school. If the kids rushed outside, a starving revenant hellbent with hunger would tear them to pieces in the night.

CHAPTER 39

Ducey Evans

Aim for the heart!" Ducey called as Kim raced across the Homecoming Dance, where girls in taffeta dresses hid behind a pair of easels holding the dead kids' portraits.

Luna and her friends clustered behind that damn dead boy's school picture. Ducey counted three. Easy to spot the two kids with glow-in-the-dark ties even if she couldn't quite make out their faces, but if a tall boy in black leather stood with them, then he'd managed to dodge the silver specks flickering across the walls.

Rolling blue and purple lights flashed off the business end of Ducey's trocar as it stabbed into a ghoul's chest. She spun around looking for another one, squinting through the twinkling lights to see Roger Taylor bar the cafeteria doors behind him. He pointed to the other end of the cafeteria, past the bobbing balloons, to the hallway that led into the interior of the school, and Ducey got it.

If Sheriff Big Britches saw fit to lock the kids in with the ghouls, there could only be one reason why.

Roger's voice cut through the screams as he spread his arms, trying to funnel kids away from the glittery dance decorations and into the school hallway.

Ducey spared another glance to make sure Lenore had things under control on the confetti-covered dance floor. When she saw her daughter toss away an empty vial and prop up a girl with a scrap of her taffeta dress tied around her arm, she rubbed at the burn in her chest, clicked her teeth at the hound to follow, and took off after Kim toward Luna and her friends.

They'd had six in the cooler. One was on the floor under Lenore, two more at Ducey's feet.

Leaves three, Ducey thought, and plunged her trocar into the dead young car-accident victim she'd had for lunch just that afternoon. Now two.

And Grace.

Ducey hobbled quick as she could to the other end of the cafeteria. "Get the kids into the school," she hollered at Kim, at Luna and her friends. Where in the heck was Crane? Not out waving his sage wand somewhere, she hoped.

At her side, Belle lunged at that poor dead boy the cops had found behind the dumpster shed, Quigg's new hire. The dog pulled him off a couple of high schoolers with shoulders bigger than their brains. Ducey raised her trocar. The boys fled, but Samael yanked the ghoul backward before her arm dropped.

The master strigoi's teeth tore out what remained of Daniel Garland's throat, and Ducey's mouth watered. She licked her lips. If she couldn't stomach butterscotch anymore, maybe she didn't need to sip through the dang trocar, either.

One left. Somewhere bits of high school principal dragged itself around on the floor.

When Ducey made it to the other side of the cafeteria, Kim stood like a mother hen in front of her chicks, saw blade raised in the air.

Aim for the heart, Ducey had told her, and the girl held the sharp edge of her blade facing out. Between the pale skin and the disco-ball moon, Kim was white as a ghost, but she stood between those kids and the dead just the same.

"Ducey?" said the blue-eyed boy in the blue suit and tie. The Cole boy looked just like his sister, minus the eyeliner. Beside him, a dark-skinned girl stared at Ducey. Eyes big as plates ticked off Ducey's cloudy eye, painted throat, the bloody trocar.

"You're dead," Crystal said.

Ducey rolled her good eye. "Tell me somethin' I don't know." She thrust the dull end of her trocar into Luna's fist. "Now you quit lookin' at me and get something to defend yourselves with," she told Luna's slack-jawed friends.

"Now, I said!" she yelled when they just stood there and stared. Twice in one day she'd had fool kids stare her down.

The girl with the silver hair clips and sparkling cheeks swirled around to the easels. "Sorry, Alison," Crystal said, and knocked the dead girl's portrait to the floor, then held on to the top of the easel and kicked out one of its legs. She squatted down and snatched up the jagged leg, raising the wooden stake eye level as she stood.

Ducey hadn't had a chance to meet Luna's friends proper, but she liked this girl already.

The Cole boy floundered around. He looked at the girl's spear, Ducey's trocar, his sister's saw, and then he bent down and snatched up a shoe that'd come off in the stampede.

"What?" He held the stiletto high heel out. "These things are sharp!"

Ducey swung her eyes to his sister.

Single White Female," Kim said, and shrugged while her brother tapped the heel's sharp point against his forehead.

And Ducey thought her girls were bad.

"Go!" she shouted, stabbing an arthritic finger toward the interior corridors. Kim pushed Dillon and Crystal ahead of her as the three joined Roger funneling the mass of bodies out the other side of the Homecoming Dance.

"You keep with me," Ducey told Luna, and then Belle began to howl.

CHAPTER 40

Deputy Brandon Hinson

When he'd about given up spotting whatever had tracked bloody footprints out of Grace Evans's apartment, Brandon caught the flash of red and blues over at the Forest Park High School parking lot.

"There!" he yelled, pointing at the strobing beacon. Haney jerked the steering wheel so hard, whiplash cracked Brandon's neck as the truck bounced over the median. The Ford barreled back toward the school and salt rushed up Brandon's throat. Kim's mint-green Buick sat parked along the curb between Lenore Evans's Rambler and Taylor's Crown Vic—all three with their lights on and doors hanging open.

Screams hit Brandon's ears when he and Haney grabbed their guns from the back and pushed out of the truck. Brandon searched for prints in the grass, pistol at his side while the other hand itched toward his shoulder, where it found no radio. Haney raced toward the building, less like a hunter now, rifle up like a soldier heading into battle.

From the school, stage lights flashed through the windows, illuminating silhouettes of frantic students inside. Brandon thought he saw the brim of the sheriff's hat, but he lost the shape in a blur and suddenly Haney chugged back into the field.

"Doors are locked," the man growled. "Need another way in." His eye flicked back to the windows, and his finger twitched along the trigger.

Brandon pushed the barrel of Haney's shotgun down. They needed to get in, but not bad enough to risk hurting someone inside.

He nodded toward the back field. "There's a delivery door," he told Haney, and jogged toward the far side of the building. It'd be locked, too, but Haney could blast a crater through that thing for all Brandon cared. Roger might be hiding the truth about the killer, but he wouldn't forget his duty to protect all those innocent kids. If the main doors were locked, that meant he must be pushing them farther inside the school. Something terrible must have happened in the cafeteria—or else the sheriff had trapped something there. Roger would herd the kids deep into the heart of the school, leaving room for Brandon and Haney to come in from behind.

All that salt pooling around Brandon's tongue began to trickle out the corners of his mouth when he rounded the back of the building and saw the delivery door.

Open.

And bloody mud footprints tracked from the back field right through. Into the school.

Homecoming Dance, Brandon thought, *Student Council.* Dillon Cole's face washed up in his vision. All that setup prep, and the last one in probably forgot to grab the stopper from under the door. Any kid could have done it, but he'd put odds on his girlfriend's little brother.

Maybe that's why her car was here?

Or maybe it had to do with the Evans women.

Brandon and Haney crashed through the cafeteria's kitchens, Haney tipping over a stack of plastic trays as they tracked the prints around the serving line and into the dance. A stink slapped him—copper and must, soured and old—as Brandon's steel toe tripped over some huge cut of meat, though it made a sound like the carpets in Snow Leger's.

When his eyes found what slicked under his boot, that sound, that *smell,* forced itself up his throat. Vertebrae pushed through a jelly-covered spinal column, snaking behind a pulp of ruined shoulder. Shards of bone chewing the rubber floor as the squelching mass slithered beneath Brandon's boot.

"Ppnnyy," the meat wheezed, a sight so much worse than Haney's daughter, before it tried to coil its way up his shin.

"What in the shit is that!" Haney's eyes bugged while Brandon kicked the wriggling flesh free, and when the wet lump landed on the other side of the kitchen, Haney pulled the trigger.

Didn't let go until birdshot turned the spine snake into fireworks, splattered on the stainless-steel cabinets.

The men braved up in each other's stare, and then Brandon stepped past the fog machine and into the cafeteria.

He retched as he swallowed lava and his lungs caught fire.

The stage lights still swept the floor, the disco ball still turned, but a low growl echoed through the open space.

On one side of the room, Luna Evans held a metal stake. Brandon's stomach dropped into his toes. Ducey Evans stood at her great-grand-daughter's side.

Ducey Evans, dead and buried. He'd read her obituary in the paper.

And snarling at her ankle, the dead sheriff's missing dog, Buck Johnson's hound Belle, with blood on her bared teeth.

"Hinson?" Roger's voice cuffed Brandon's ears from the other side of the room. "Get the hell out of here!" the new sheriff said, hand at his holster. At his side, Lenore Evans stood with a goddamn dagger high as a lightning bolt above her, over a girl in a bloody taffeta dress.

At Brandon's side, Brett Haney sputtered and choked up on his twelve-gauge.

Brandon swept the scene for one more person.

Dusted by spinning stars, Kim stood at the end of the hallway as students in rented outfits fled uninjured into the school behind her. The disco moonlight flashed silver in his girlfriend's hand, her face twisted in fear and fury as she kept her eyes on two kids running toward her from the other end of the cafeteria's kitchen. "Hurry up," she yelled, eyes not for Brandon, only for those kids.

A girl with sparkles in her hair and on her cheeks raised the pointed end of a wooden shaft, meat kabobbed and sludging down the stake. Maybe her dress was blue, under all that red, the same color as Dillon's suit, running beside her. Red sprinkled the boy's face, eyes bright as that stupid disco ball overhead when he lifted a—a shoe? A red stiletto, maybe not really red, with a cut of meat hanging off its heel.

"We found the principal!" Kim's little brother called, and then both kids took their places on either side of Brandon's girlfriend, with her silver hand and twisted face. All three gathered behind Roger, behind Lenore and that bleeding girl, and that's when Haney exploded.

"What the fuck is going on around here!" The man pulled out the shot, racked another slug, pitched his waist forward. He kept the gun's barrel low, but he staggered his stance and bent his knees.

The deputy made eye contact with the sheriff, whose mouth formed words Brandon couldn't hear over the sudden thud in his own chest. Taylor pointed, and dirty prints clung to the edges of Brandon's vision as he saw the beast at the other end of the cafeteria.

Not a woman. Not a wolf. Something else.

Something worse.

Haney's gun sprang up. Across the room Taylor's mouth dropped open, unholstering his revolver, thumb cocking the hammer as he drew on Haney.

"Don't shoot!" Taylor's words landed, but not before another monster tore into Brett Haney.

Hot splashed Brandon's cheek. Salty hot. Metallic hot.

Brandon's trigger finger twitched, the twelve-gauge fired, and, over in the center of the room, Grace Evans hit the floor.

CHAPTER 41

Luna Evans

I
t happened so fast.

Moments ago, Luna had been in Crane's arms, dancing beneath the false moonlit sky. Then screams and blood, Mrs. Baker sank her teeth in Michelle Bryant's shoulder, and a wolf eclipsed the light twinkling over the Homecoming Dance.

It towered over the dance floor, its fur a matted patchwork of the towns' missing pets, its mutilated livestock, its slaughtered ghost-wolf hybrids. Raw hide and matted pelt, strung together with lengths of rotting sinew over a skeleton of bones splintered and jagged. Rows of teeth, of mandibles, hung around the beast's neck, stacked up along its arms, chewed over its hands and feet. And on its shoulders the wide, snarling maw of a great red wolf, the silver tips of its pointed ears shadowed against the glimmering light of the disco-ball moon.

Terror quilled Luna's skin when the beast spoke her name with her mother's voice.

Then, gunshots. A blast, a clatter, a pop. All at once.

Before the twisted shape of her mother had hit the floor, the strigoi's teeth tore into Brett Haney's neck. Blood pouring from his throat, the man slipped lifeless from Samael's fangs. Over the master strigoi's shoulder, Nana Lenore's face like stone, nodding as Haney's gun hit the confetti cafeteria floor before his body.

And then Grace crumpled under the spinning moonlight, and sound rushed back into the room.

Roger's voice. "Hinson, don't shoot!"

Another shot, and red burst through Samael's shoulder. Luna's father turned, face sharp, his teeth bared, jaw stretched, and Hinson fired another red blast through Samael's chest. The monster faded as the man, the father, reached for Luna.

"My moon," her father called, and then Samael's midnight eyes flicked to the beast crumpled under the moonlight.

Roger shouted, and Hinson fired one more time.

"My star." Samael's voice floated across the Homecoming Dance floor, he brushed a hand along the beast's matted fur, and then he threw himself through one of the cafeteria's windows and into the night.

Moments ago, Luna had been in Crane's arms, dancing beneath the false moonlit sky. Then screams and blood, a wolf in the moonlight, and now the sound of shattering glass, the smell of gun smoke, as her father disappears.

Shadows fill Ducey's cloudy eye, the blue light sweeping the scar along her throat. Nana Lenore glitters like frost. Kim and Belle, Dillon and Crystal, Michelle Bryant still bleeding and Roger Taylor and Brandon Hinson.

Dead Brett Haney.

All of them, beneath the false moonlit sky.

Luna's knees buckle as the room surges forward in a rush of sweeping blue and purple light. She tugs at the crystal choker Kim had loaned her and throws it on the sparkling floor.

In front of her on a bed of confetti under a swirling starlight sky lies the ghost wolf.

With each breath in, blood rushes over the beast's chest from the wound in its back, staining Luna's hand as she pushes through matted fur, finds fingers, her fingers, Grace's fingers. The scar on her mother's wrist flashes silver under the glittering disco-ball moonlight.

"Mom," Luna says, and maybe the beast's breath catches in its throat, catches as if it hears her, as if *she* hears her, and all those tears, the ones Crane had tried to wipe away, spill out of Luna's eyes.

Stars sparkle along her vision from the tears on her cheeks, but even in the dark Luna sees the red on her own hands.

Layer by layer, Luna strips away her mother's monster. Away, the animal parts, the bone, the fur. The teeth. And then she touches Grace's long dark curls, her white burial gown, the silver chain with the silver ring flashing starlight around her neck. Grace, with a hole in her chest that no amount of ashes and full-moon wishes can heal.

Luna's mother lies dying at her feet.

Voices pulse around Luna, somewhere out in the dark, but her mother's voice twinkles in her ears like starlight.

"Luna?" Hoarse breath blows the sound through Grace's lips, more wind than word.

"Luna," Grace says again, and Luna holds her mother, her *mother*— not the beast, the rabid ghost wolf, the monster. A current stirs under Luna's skin, this one not the earth that she'd felt move when she stood over her father in his grave. Warm wind lifts within her, it doesn't rush through, doesn't billow, just breathes, and she bends her head over her mother's.

This will be the second time Luna holds her mother while she dies. But this time Luna knows what she is—a daughter of the moon, named for a goddess.

And this time she can say goodbye. She can save Grace the only way she can be saved.

"It's okay, Mom," Luna whispers. "You can rest now."

She kisses her mother's forehead, and then she lets all that warm wind push out of her, and there in her arms, on a bed of confetti under a swirling starlight sky, Grace Evans closes her eyes.

Moments ago, Luna had been in Crane's arms, dancing beneath the false moonlit sky. Then her father's midnight eyes reflected the moonlight, her mother's voice sang from the stars, and Luna's world went dark.

A long time later, velvet curled into Luna's legs where Belle lay at her side. Someone's hand touched one of Luna's shoulders, then someone else's touched the other. Her grandmothers spoke over her head, joined by men's voices—Roger, probably, maybe Hinson—and Luna's attention pulled up. The disco ball glared fluorescent light. The colors had all been turned off, the Homecoming Dance cosmos swallowed by a black hole.

"'Killer'?" she said, because she'd heard her father's name in all that talk.

Roger looked at her like a stranger, and Luna knew she'd take the bus from now on.

"That's what we saw here tonight," the sheriff told her. "What we *all* saw—" He looked at Hinson, face locked open like a ventriloquist's dummy. "The killer dug Grace Evans's body up out of her grave so he could use her remains to make it look like she had something to do with all those kills, while he hid out in her apartment with his collection of dead animals. He stole those other remains from the coolers, too, then he attacked the school tonight," he said.

Roger put his hand on Hinson's shoulder. "He killed Brett Haney," Roger said, staring until the younger deputy nodded. "A serial killer, like you said."

"My dad is not a serial killer." Luna flew up from the hard floor, thrusting those old women's hands off her shoulders. "He tried to stop—"

"Someone has to take the blame," Ducey cut in, low enough that only Luna could hear. "I'm sorry, Luna, honey. But that's the cold, hard truth."

Luna turned on the dead old woman. "He tried to save Mom," she said, fury flecking off her tongue like poison.

"He did," Nana Lenore said. "And now he'll shoulder the blame, save the rest of us."

Another voice, Dillon's maybe. "Where's Crane?"

Kim shushed him.

Luna settled boneless onto the glittery tile. With Samael blamed for the murders, the sheriff's department would issue a description of the lunatic responsible for those seven murdered, two missing. The principal and Daniel Garland, too. The state police would oversee a manhunt. Hand it off to the FBI at some point. Luna's father, masked as a serial killer, would share the blame with the rabid ghost wolves, with the professor's blood on his hands as well.

The professor's, and Crane's.

Everything else could be explained away with rabies, with crazy, with perfectly natural *evil*.

But they wouldn't find him. Luna knew that much.

And the town would be quiet, just like it was before.

They could all go on—the town, the restless dead, and the Evanses. At least Grace would be at peace.

No one turned the disco-ball moon off when Hinson drove Dillon and Crystal home and Roger headed into the gymnasium where a tiny lady cop spit orders and the paramedics tended to the staff, the chaperones, and the rest of the students from Homecoming. The three leftover Evans women sat in the center of the dance floor, covered in blood and stardust.

"We bury this night just like we bury the restless dead," Ducey told them all, Lenore and Luna, the Cole girl, and the old coonhound. "We let the dead lie."

"And what about the rest of us?" Luna asked only half looking up.

The dead woman smiled, her one bright green eye flashing in the dark. "We get back to business."

Dear Ducey,

By the time you read this letter, I'll be long gone. Don't you dare come looking for me. I mean it, Ethel. The dead can steal your life, even when you're still living it. I've waited a long time to rest. Let me do so in peace.

Almost a hundred years ago, when I was just a tiny little thing, Daddy brought Mama and me over from the Old Country to start a new life. Fool that Daddy was, he wanted something better for his family. He thought farming this knobby little scrap of Southeast Texas would bring prosperity to our family, and, for a while, it did. The twins came along, and the farm flourished, just like Daddy hoped— but it wasn't long, and men came for the oil buried under these hills.

The prospectors promised Daddy all the riches in the world if he invested in the derricks going up, but Daddy's superstitious roots clung to him all the way from the Scotland. He'd heard tales of the ghosts under these hills, the lights they carried out in the dark. He smelled the sulphur rising up from underground, and he told those oil men to put their offer where the sun don't shine.

When the geyser struck, even Daddy regretted not getting his hands full of that liquid gold. He sold off a parcel of land, made a deal with the devil just like the rest. Greed is a funny thing, girl, and greedy men funnier still. No matter how much oil, how much black gold they dug up, they kept digging—deeper and deeper, until they dug so far down, they struck something else.

The geyser caught fire and evil spilled up in those flames, and all those men and all that money didn't do nothing to stop the burn.

By the time they got the fire under control, the twins, my brothers, were dead. I wish like hell I'd died with them. Almost did, but one of the farmhands traded his life for mine. That young man died so I could go on. He saved me, and tonight, girl, that's exactly what I must do for you.

I've kept a lot of secrets. Maybe one day you'll learn some of them, but the rest I'm taking to my grave. I'm only telling this to you, my final secret for you to bear: I don't know if I brought it with me or if it's from the night my life was saved under that oil well, but there's something in our blood, and that's why it falls to us to deal with the restless dead. I've carried this curse for as long as I can bear, and now it's up to you all to carry on—not just for this town or for its dead, but for each other.

Don't let the dead steal your life like they did mine. Give the restless dead hell, girl, and no matter what else, what sort of secrets claw their way back from the grave, never forget who you are.

You're Evans women.

With all my heart, your mother,

Pie Evans
September 1982

Ducey Evans

Ducey stepped one bunny ear–slippered foot over Belle's sleeping form, then the other, as she settled herself into a straight-backed chair at Lenore's kitchen table, hitched one knee on top of the other, and refolded her mother's letter.

"Well, girls," Ducey said as silvery light slipped through the back-door window blinds from the full moon outside, "that's all she wrote."

A lifetime spent keeping the dead buried, and one single page was all Pie Evans had seen fit to pass on to her daughters. Ducey had read her mother's final words hundreds of times since the morning she'd walked into the funeral parlor, found the letter on the table, a bowl of banana pudding in the fridge, and her mother gone. Age had since yellowed the paper, and a fair amount of the writing was worn away from years of unfolding, but Ducey knew every word by heart. Every single word, and they'd only ever confirmed what she'd already known: Pie Evans had gone to her grave off her rocker, a bee the size of Texas in her bonnet about the dead.

Left them to deal with the rest.

Lenore wiped her palms on her slacks as she pushed up from her seat at the other end of the table. "Grandmother Pie could have told us more," she said as she pulled fresh linens from the hutch. "Given us a little bit more to go on. Might have changed a lot."

Tell me about it, Ducey thought. Her daughter wasn't the one who'd crawled out of *her* own grave, who sat breathing in fresh fumes from the painted-over wound on *her* neck while phantom heartburn scorched *her* chest.

"A lot of people died that night," the dead man had told them about the Spindletop fire—he'd said it twice, if memory served. Samael, who'd known Pie, who'd loved Grace, who'd fathered Luna, he had died that night. Pie herself had almost as well. Would have, if the farmhand hadn't traded his life for hers. Ducey and her girls didn't know the whole story yet, had more questions now than they'd ever had answers, but all those secrets Mother wanted to keep buried?

Piss on that. All those years spent furious at her mother for all the things she never told them, kept to herself, took to her grave. Only now did Ducey realize that Pie had left them everything they needed to know when she'd instructed Samael to watch over them. And they'd gone and buried him under a white rosebush in the funeral parlor's garden, while the truth ate them alive.

She might be dead, undead, restless dead, but being a ghoul gave Ducey plenty of time to spend digging up every bone in the cemetery, in the funeral parlor gardens—hell, on the Evans property, if she had to. Whatever it took to get to the bottom of the Evans family legacy, such as it was.

Lenore spread fresh linen over the table, then Ducey tossed the worn paper onto the cloth as Kim followed behind with the place settings.

If this didn't work, well, then she'd take up a shovel.

Game show chatter from the living room television set followed Luna as she wound her way around the kitchen table—the familiar clack of a spinning wheel, a murmur followed by a single sharp syllable, dings as consonants lit up the puzzle board. Someone bought a vowel, but chair legs scratched across ceramic as Luna pulled out her seat, Lenore cleared her throat, and Ducey missed which one it was.

Luna stared moony-eyed through the back-door kitchen window, squeezing a too-long sleeve of one of Grace's old work shirts in her fist and chewing her lip like it was going out of style. Dark rimmed her tired, raccoon eyes, making the rest of her paler than usual.

The littlest Evans yawned and Ducey rubbed the heat in her chest. After what she'd been through, who could blame the girl for not sleeping. Some nightmares were easier faced with your eyes open.

So far, Luna hadn't said a word about the boyfriend her mother had killed.

She's bonded with Kim, though, Ducey thought, as their new employee reached over Luna's shoulder to set a candlestick on the table, giving Luna a sisterly pat when she pulled her arm back. And Luna's school friends, the two that had helped with the surge of ghouls at the school, they'd come to the parlor to help lay Grace to rest. That counted for something.

"Never trust a Halloran," Samael had warned Ducey, and piss on that, too. Whatever old grudge the dead man held on to, no matter that it'd been a Halloran who sent Ducey to her own grave, one of his descendants had stood with the Evanses and fought. Her brother, too.

Some old hates were just that: old.

Ducey waggled one of her bunny slippers loose under the table and buried her bare foot in the hound dog's velvet fur. Blood might come thicker than water, but some Evans women could be made, not born. Hell, some, like old Buchanan's geriatric hound, weren't even human.

Then again, neither am I, Ducey considered. And neither was Luna.

But both were here, and the dog, the employee, and the breathing Evans matriarch Lenore, who'd finally taken back to winding her clocks. Just because a house was haunted didn't mean it couldn't still hold life. Here at the end of it all, it didn't make a lick of difference if family was the one that made you or the one you made. Real family, you'd die for them either way.

Twice, if you had to.

Ducey would have explained all this to the women around her, too, but the sound of a news broadcast broke through the game show noise. When she craned her neck to look into the living room, Penny Boudreaux's teased blond hair filled the television screen. Beneath her smiling face, a banner: HOMECOMING DANCE MASSACRE.

"Oh, hell," Ducey announced, "we're on the news again."

When Sheriff Roger Taylor joined Penny on-screen, Lenore used the remote to mute the set. Nothing new, nothing worth listening to. Penny would ask about the serial killer that had preyed on the small town, about the rabid coyote–red wolf hybrids that may or may not have added to the body count, but Roger would repeat his official line, that the investigation was ongoing, and that would be that.

Which, of course, it wasn't. Samael had fled and the dead stayed buried. Most of the missing-pet posters came down after the victims were interred, and the case had been closed.

"He looks good," Lenore said when Roger gripped his hat on-screen.

Every once in a while, they'd find a single flower tucked amongst the roses that had finally bloomed over Grace's grave. The man came and went without a word, and they left him to it, honoring Roger's unspoken desire for privacy.

Evans women knew what it meant to grieve their dead.

When Deputy Brandon Hinson came into view beside his commanding officer, Ducey patted Kim's hand and said, "He's a good man," and Kim folded into the chair beside her. "Pay no mind," she told the girl. "Evans women don't mix well with law enforcement." She thought of Buck. "We never have."

Truth was, they didn't seem to mix well with men in general. Maybe Grace had been right, choosing to fall in love with a ghoul. Samael had given his life to save Pie, and even after they'd put him underground, he'd traded his freedom to save them all.

"He'll come back, you know. When things have cooled down," Ducey told Luna as Lenore joined them at the table and set a framed portrait on the cloth beside Pie's letter. "Isn't that right, Len?" Ducey asked.

Lenore bristled, but then again, Lenore always bristled. "Sure he will," she agreed, and it didn't really matter if she thought he would or not. Samael had made a promise to protect the Evans women, and besides, he had his daughter to care for.

The dark circles under Luna's eyes yawned as she turned away from the window, faced the table. "I just wish he hadn't had to leave."

And Ducey wished she still had a taste for butterscotch, but she was almost as sick of secrets as she was of waiting for answers.

She winked her good eye at Kim, who removed a long paper box from the brown grocery sack waiting on the ceramic floor. She lifted the box by its top, shook until the lid separated from the rest, and then set the cardstock slab in front of Luna.

"You really think this is going to work, Mama?" Lenore asked, those bony fingers of hers clenched around the picture frame. "Talking to the dead seems . . ."

"Like hokum?" Ducey shrugged. Of course it was hokum, but so was she, and so was the Evans family business. "We've been on wild-goose chases before," she said. "At least this one is easy to clean up after."

Kim arranged the board in front of Luna, then situated the candlestick on one side, and the planchette on the other. "Okay," she said, "when you're ready, light the candle."

Luna stared at the Ouija board. "And then what?"

The corners of the Cole girl's purple lips tugged down as she looked to Ducey, to Lenore, and back to Luna. "Think of who you want to call for, I guess," Kim said. "Send your energy or power or whatever out, and call them to you."

The littlest Evans's raccoon eyes lit off Pie's folded letter, the portrait that her grandmother clung to, and the shirtsleeve clenched in her own fist.

"Okay," Luna said.

She lifted a matchbook from the breast pocket of the work shirt. Ducey could see a few sticks missing from the book, and she could make out the logo on the book's front as well. Just like the one that Crane had offered up for his vampire resurrection ritual, tucked back in his leather coat when Ducey kicked him out of the parlor.

Luna peeled another match free and struck it on the backside flint. She lit the candle and tossed the matchbook on the table alongside Pie's folded letter and the portrait Lenore brought in from her bedroom, and Ducey put the Green Frog matchbook out of her mind. Just because the girl's dead boyfriend had a matchbook from a dive bar he was too young to enter didn't mean it'd been the only one circulating around town. Luna could have gotten that little green book anywhere.

Then again, coincidences were rarely coincidences for the Evans women.

And the dead had been known to bring the littlest Evans gifts.

Ducey's chest burned, but she brushed her toes against Belle's rusty fur and resisted the urge to rub the heat out of that scar. Lenore closed her eyes on one side of the table, Kim shot Luna a thumbs-up from the other side, and at the head, Luna exhaled.

The candle flame licked the air once, twice.

Luna looked at Ducey, at the moonlight pouring in through the back-door window blinds. "It's time we got some real answers," the girl said, and then she closed her eyes and mouthed a name.

Acknowledgments

About a month after *Bless Your Heart* was released, I received an email from a beloved former writing student. "I finished *Bless Your Heart,*" she wrote, "and can only say: YOU KILLED YOUR MOTHER??? You saved the dog and killed off the character based on your own mother."

I wrote back, shamelessly: "But of course, I will always save the dog."

That student has yet to read *Another Fine Mess,* and I fear the eventual email I will receive once she realizes that I killed off the character inspired by my mother not once, but twice. (For what it's worth, my actual mother was quite pleased with Grace's arc—though she remains, as I expect many readers might, a tad furious at me for what I've done to poor Luna and Crane. For now . . .)

In my defense, though all the Evans women are inspired by my real family members—and their world inspired by the characters in my very real Southeast Texas hometown—it's Grace who binds the Evanses' two worlds together. In *Another Fine Mess,* all the Evans women begin to confront the consequences of a matriarchy built upon secrets, but it's Grace whose suffering is so great and whose fury is so strong that even death cannot contain her rage. "Hell hath no fury like a woman scorned," wrote the playwright William Congreve, and indeed, Grace Evans breaks the mold of pricolici—a male-dominated monster, even in mythology—and rises to claim her vengeance. Consider this a battle cry against a world that would rather see women buried than embrace their power, their wildness, even their monstrousness.

Consider it a warning to those wielding the shovels. Not all secrets stay buried. Not all silenced stay quiet. Some rise, roaring, to tear out your throat.

And speaking of beautiful, fierce, wonderful women, thank you, first and foremost, to my mother, Lydia, for her grace.

Thank you to my fearless agent, Italia Gandolfo, for championing my work, and to Alexandra Sehulster, Sarah Melnyk, Allison Ziegler, and the entire team at St. Martin's Publishing Group and Minotaur Books for opening their arms and hearts to the Evans women. To Amanda Rutter, Jess Lofton, and the Solaris Books team for introducing the Evans women to UK readers.

To Katrina Monroe, the first to read and blurb this book. To Rachel Harrison, George C. Romero, Josh Malerman, Nat Cassidy, Clay McLeod Chapman, Darcy Coates, Gwendolyn Kiste, Maureen Kilmer, Christopher Golden, and Kristi DeMeester for supporting this series from the very beginning, but more importantly, for being the most wonderful friends and colleagues in the horror community.

To each and every single one of the incredible librarians, booksellers, reviewers, and readers who have given the Evans women a home on their bookshelves.

To Stephanie Wytovich, my very dearest friend, who reminds me every day to be a more feral Lindy.

To Pete Vilotti, who takes such superb care of Feral Lindy.

To Phil Conserva, Louis Milito, Rob Wolken, and Emily Whitesell, for believing in the Evans women.

To Jamie Flanagan, for believing in Grace Evans.

To Christopher Brooks, for the blood, sweat, and tears he's poured into both me and this series from the very beginning (and who actively encourages my more gruesome ideas).

To my dad, John, an open-minded clock collector, for spending a full hour discussing various methods of dispatching strigoi with a grandfather-clock pendulum without so much as batting an eye.

To my sister, Lisa, for our two-member SNC.

To Wake, always and always.

And to Finn, the very best dog there has ever been.

About the Author

Pete Vilotti

Lindy Ryan is an award-winning author, anthologist, and short-film director whose books and anthologies have received starred reviews from *Publishers Weekly, Booklist,* and *Library Journal.* Several of her projects have been adapted for the screen. Ryan is the current author-in-residence at *Rue Morgue.* Declared a "champion for women's voices in horror" by *Shelf Awareness,* Ryan was named a *Publishers Weekly* Star Watch Honoree in 2020, and in 2022, was named one of horror's most masterful anthology curators. Born and raised in Southeast Texas, Ryan currently resides on the East Coast. She is a professor at Rutgers University.